# WHAT'S AN FBI AGENT DOING IN A PLACE LIKE THIS?

Rising from the plateau, nearly transparent but of obvious substance, like photographic negatives, but alive, came the monsters which had perished here within the rock of Arba'Il'Tac millennia ago, animated in all their horrific glory and power. Everywhere he looked, more of the beasts were rising from the rock, towering into the night sky, slobber dripping from enormous fanged jaws.

Suddenly, Garrison's horse tripped, the animal's off-front hoof catching on a fissured rock slab hidden beneath a ghostly thin layer of snow.

The animal began to cartwheel forward.

Garrison spilled from the saddle, forward along the horse's neck, rolling head first over the horse's head. His left hand still grasped the reins, a torn hank of mane bunched with them in his fist. The horse shrieked agony.

He rolled, still clutching his pistol. The downdraft in the wake of the monster's now frantically beating wings pummeled Garrison. The instant of slipstream, nearly cyclonic in strength, slapped him brutally to the rock floor. . . .

# THE
# GOLDEN SHIELD
# OF
# IBF

## JERRY & SHARON AHERN

THE GOLDEN SHIELD OF IBF

This is a work of fiction. All the characters and events portrayed in this book are fictional, and any resemblance to real people or incidents is purely coincidental.

A Baen Books Original

Baen Publishing Enterprises
P.O. Box 1403
Riverdale, NY 10471

ISBN: 0-671-57825-1

Cover art by Bob Eggleton

First printing, August 1999

Distributed by Simon & Schuster
1230 Avenue of the Americas
New York, NY 10020

Typeset by Windhaven Press, Auburn, NH
Printed in the United States of America

For Ahern family stalwarts Ed Kramer
and the Jerry Buergel Family,
friends of value beyond measure
in this or any other world or time;
and, for Betsy, who suggested
a home for the Virgin Enchantress.

# Chapter One

Swan was naked except for white silken ribbons binding back her hair at the nape of her neck. She swirled the blue-gray surface of the Memory Pool with the tips of her toes and her skin goosefleshed and her nipples involuntarily hardened with the water's chill.

Swan glanced over her shoulder, along the high meadow's expanse. Her horse was hobbled beneath the drooping boughs of a Ka'B'Oo, its main trunk thrusting nearly a hundred spans toward the snow-threatening clouds. The powerfully built white mare grazed peacefully, showing no sign of alarm.

Swan would be dangerously vulnerable to attack: alone, all of her clothes, her charm bag, her sword and dagger set aside. There was, however, no choice if she was to know what she should do. Her skills as an Enchantress not withstanding, she had never divined the future: the very thought of such ability was terrifying. Rather, to plan for tomorrow, it was necessary to interpret the yesterdays which had gone before. That was why she came to the Memory Pool.

Swan stepped forward, one foot instantly immersed

to the ankle, reliving a fleeting recollection of someone whom she had never been able to call "father."
He had vanished from her life when she had not yet
lived long enough to possess the power of speech.
But the enigmatic words that he would whisper to
her as he rocked her in his arms echoed now from
the roots of her soul.

"L'Ull B'Yan G'Ite!" Swan cried.

As if she were an infant again, Swan felt the warmth
of her father's breath against her cheek, the roughness
of his face as he touched his lips against that cheek.
But that was all the recollection that she had of him,
and the waters of a Memory Pool promised nothing
more, could not create memories where none existed.

Swan took another step. The pool began to engulf
her, its waters reaching toward her in great towers
of cold froth, wildly crashing over her shoulders, her
breasts, a fierce tempest assaulting her body, as waves
would surge over rocky crags along some lonely shore.
And the full power of the Memory Pool began flowing
through her, mingling with her body's life force
energy. With each step that she took deeper and
deeper into the Memory Pool's churning waters the
past gripped her more tightly, consumed her in long
ago realities . . .

Eran, Sorceress Queen of Creath, Mistress General of the Horde of Koth, galloped hard across the
plain, wind riding hair black and flowing, arrow
straight. Eran's eyes, gemstone green, deep beyond
deep, glistened like dragon's blood, were brighter than
the sun gleaming snow over which she rode.

"Mother," Swan whispered, alone on the wind-
lashed parapet overlooking the plain. It was her
second sight which allowed her to see in such detail
at such a distance.

A quirt was looped to her mother's wrist, but Eran's
black gauntleted hands alone, knotted in black leather

reins, subjugated the dapple grey stallion. The grey
would know the whip's sting and not wish to taste
it again after learning it so well when first broken
to the saddle.

The stallion was named Mul'Din. Eran, the Queen
Enchantress, never rode mares, always stallions, never
gelded until she was through with them. Each one
of them was once a man. Mul'Din was a young lieutenant of the Horde, a lover who refused to submit
to Eran's erotic demands, who wished to dominate
rather than be dominated. Eran spell-changed him,
as she had with all the others, dominated him with
the lesson of the whip, rode him wherever she went.
Inside him beat a man's heart, functioned a man's
brain; and, although Eran had taken from him the
power of speech, he could still understand as a man.

Swan cocooned herself more deeply within her fur-
ruffed greatcape, raised her skirts and started down
the narrow steps. Flakes of snow blew in clouds like
smoke. By the time Swan reached the base of the stone
steps, the gap between horsewoman and castle wall had
noticeably diminished, less than a hundred warblades.

Swan no longer needed second sight, merely
watched as any ordinary mortal might. Eran wore a
bodice, tightly cinched, greener almost than her eyes.
A tooled black baldric was suspended from her right
shoulder, buckled between her breasts over the knot
of her crocheted shawl.

The deeply engraved hilt and pommel of her sword
swashed against her left hip. The blade's scabbard
vanished beneath, then reappeared from within the
crimson folds of heavy winter skirts hitched high
above black boots, skirts and linen petticoats raised
so that Eran could ride astride like a man as she
always did.

The great horse Mul'Din skidded on its haunches
in the snow, reined back. Righting itself, it reared,
shook its head. Lips drawn back, a ray of sunlight

striking the steel bit in its mouth, the stallion's teeth gleamed white beneath blood red lips. Mul'Din flicked its tail and hurtled itself into the final charge, billows of steam issuing from wide flared nostrils.

With an all but imperceptible shrug of her left shoulder, a tug of her left hand, Eran urged Mul'Din across the lowered drawbridge and up the flagstones along the castle's ramped outer defense rampart.

Swan left the landing and walked onto the ramp, waiting. The thrumming of the stallion Mul'Din's hooves had slowed. Eran was cooling the animal as she closed the distance.

Strapped to Eran's boots were glinting silver spurs, their tips blunted so that they would neither snag the hem of her gown nor rip the hand-sewn lace beneath it. Her cheeks looked cold flushed, flawless. She sprang from the saddle, skirts falling into place, swaying round her ankles.

"You are exquisite as always, mother."

Her mother's eyes swept over her. "A woman your age should wear brighter colors, Swan. Your cloak, for example. Such a dark green! Now, if only the fur trimming the hood weren't black—"

Swan smiled, touched a fingertip to her lips—they were shaded a deep red—and then whisked the finger through the fur ruff framing her face.

"That color is much better for the fur, Swan. That was a very nice bit of magic."

"I've always trusted your eye for clothes, mother."

"And I've always trusted your good taste, in everything but companions. My spies have made it perfectly clear to me, Swan, that you totally ignore my warnings against consorting with the Company of Mir. You conspire against me with my enemies, themselves madmen who follow the teachings of the maddest madman! You have great abilities, my young Enchantress, but they are conjurer's tricks compared to the powers which I command. You well know this, Swan, yet you persist in goading me, giving me no choice but to kill you." Eran's voice, in the mid-range as women's voices went, rose and fell, musically, hypnotically. Swan had witnessed her mother kill by voice.

"And, mother, did you ride here for that? To kill me?"

"I rode fifty lancethrows here to warn you one last time. Killing you would have been vastly quicker and ridiculously easier."

Mul'Din whinnied.

"Silence, Mul'Din!" The whip swung up from the loop on Eran's wrist, settled into her hand and lashed across her one-time lover's muzzle. She returned her gaze, her attention to Swan, the horse silent, great head bowed. "I am your mother, Swan, and for that reason only you still live. I am first the Sorceress Queen of Creath, Mistress General of the Horde of Koth. Heed well where my priorities lie, child! Continue in your foolish ways and perish in agony beyond any that you can now comprehend, daughter or no."

Swan steadied her breathing before she spoke. "If my magic will not grow stronger as did yours— Your powers were once no greater than mine. You yourself told me that once. But if my magic will not grow stronger, how am I a threat to you?"

"Threat!?"

"Mother, what possible mischief might I or even all the Company of Mir cause which your powers could not overwhelm in the blink of an eye? And you command the Horde of Koth, the creatures in your armies outnumbering the Company of Mir better than a hundred to one! How am I or are they a threat?"

"You are an annoyance, girl! They are a blasphemy with their talk of freedom. Soon, they will all be dead. It is your magic alone which hides them from the Horde, shields the Company of Mir's stronghold. I have come to order you to break your spell."

Swan laughed. "You can't break my spell because

you don't know how I wove it. You might spend years and never find the right combination, or never know if you had. The only way for sure would be—"

There was the ringing of steel whisked from leather. The blade of Eran's sword arced across the grey winter sky, sliced a ray of sunlight escaping through an instant's rip in the scudding clouds of the snow shower. Razor sharp steel rested against Swan's neck, sliced through the fabric of her greatcape's hood, but drew no blood from Swan's flesh. "Kill you? Break the spell in a day and live. This blade would have continued on its path and your path would have ended here and now forever if I had not wished to give you this one last chance." As quickly as it had appeared, the sword returned to its sheath. Swan shrugged off the damaged greatcape, her shoulders bare beneath it, the flakes of snow which touched her skin no longer cold seeming, but life affirming.

Eran settled her left foot into the stirrup of her black tooled saddle and swung astride Mul'Din. "Send word to me that the spell is broken or I will send the Horde to take your life. Good-bye, my daughter."

Eran's spurs jabbed against her hapless former lover's flanks and she jerked Mul'Din's reins, wheeling the animal around. "Ride, beast!" Mul'Din leapt into a full gallop, a spray of snow in the wake of its steel-shod hooves.

Swan gathered her skirts and stooped to pick up her greatcape. With a touch of her finger, the rent in the fabric rewove itself as it was before her mother's sword had sliced it. Again, Swan touched a finger to her lips, then whisked it over the fur which trimmed the hood, the fur once again black. Swan stood up, stared after her mother.

The snow was growing more intense, the flakes larger, heavier. Swan returned the greatcape to her shoulders, nestled the hood about her head. She had survived, both her mother and the Memory Pool. Only a K'Ur Mir could dare fully to immerse herself in a Memory Pool—seven such pools were known to exist in Creath—and ever hope to retain sufficient willpower to emerge again. Her mother had done it when she began womanhood, as was always the custom for the daughter of the ruling Queen Enchantress ever since the dawn of Creath. Her mother had broken the custom, telling Swan, "Your father was not of proper birth, was not K'Ur Mir. You are not fully of the Enchantress blood. You would die."

Children would dip their hands into a Memory Pool, and a careless mother would lose her child forever if she let the child reach deeper. Some persons, whom age or sadness had weakened in spirit beyond life's redemption, willingly surrendered their lives, hoping for a last glimpse of long ago happiness. The wretches would relive life's agonies equally among life's joys. Some very few philosophers still existed in Creath, not yet hunted down, eradicated by her mother's evil. And they argued (when idle hours in some safe haven allowed) that death in the waters of a Memory Pool was not death at all, that time and the "reality" of memory became ever more compacted, hence the willing suicide or hapless accident victim was dead by objective standards in mere minutes, but those minutes were an infinity to the dying.

Swan had stood to her shoulders in the Memory Pool and let the waters do their magic, her memories swirling within her and the full knowledge of her memories filling her. She was K'Ur Mir or she would not have lived. Her mother lied. But if her father were of the blood, where had he gone? Drawing her greatcape about her, Swan ran along the ramp to find her own horse. Her mother refused to allow her any attendants at the castle which was the official residence of the Virgin Enchantress, Daughter Royal, Princess of Creath. So Swan used magic to make the castle clean, to bring food and wine, to create her clothes, to tend the watch on the parapets, to raise and lower the drawbridge, to keep her horse. Her magic already at work, the white mare—the only other living thing in the castle—would be saddled and waiting.

Swan reached the otherwise empty stables, nuzzled her horse's head for a moment, then mounted. She could ride astride as well as her mother or as well as any man. Today would not be a day to ride any other way but astride. Swan tucked up her skirts in her left hand as she clasped the pommel of the saddle with her right, then slipped into the saddle. "Ride!"

The white mare cantered from the stables, Swan ordering the doors closed behind them. The pace quickened as they crossed the drawbridge, Swan ordering it raised after them.

Erg'Ran, chief scribe within the Company of Mir, had sent a message to her to meet with him, the arrow to which it was attached shot and re-shot twenty lancethrows distance or more before impaling itself in the door of the main hall. He had information for her which would change everything, the message had said. Swan had long contemplated risking the Memory Pool, and dismissed the idea as dangerous, foolhardy. Although she had no idea what information Erg'Ran now possessed, the tone of his written words was what forced her to make the decision. And she was glad for it.

The miller's cottage that was the meeting place was half-burned, more than half-roofless, and remote in the extreme, accessible only by means of an eroded forest path well-overgrown. It was once a road, clear from being well-traveled when people still lived in this portion of the Land. But those who were not killed had fled, when the Horde of Koth swept through. Those who had neither died nor fled were impressed to slavery and taken off. Only the dark, evil, nameless things which had once hidden deep in the forests now dwelt here, free to roam about as they wished.

They would not usually see her or the horse that she rode. Swan's magic could cloud their senses. But she dared not use it this day. Magic was additive, she had learned long ago. One could always close a door, light a fire, make a broomstick or lance shaft dance. But serious magic drained away and had to be replenished. And Swan had no idea how much of her magic she had used today to survive the Memory Pool. Rather than cloaking her animal and herself in invisibility, she held tightly to the mare's reins with one hand and to the hilt of her saddle-mounted sword with the other. Despite her caution, she was still maintaining two very difficult spells. One brought confusion upon the Horde of Koth when they neared the hiding place behind the Falls of Mir where the Company of Mir took refuge. The other spell, admittedly less taxing, obscured both her and her horse from view by birds. Her mother was known to use the simple creatures as an extension of her second sight.

The ride took longer than usual, because she rode more slowly, with greater caution than ever before. But at last she dismounted before the cottage.

Erg'Ran limped out to meet her, holding the reins of the white mare while Swan dismounted, as if she were somehow less than physically capable of handling her own horse. She did not resent the gesture, however. Erg'Ran was merely an old man with a wooden peg in place of a chopped off foot, robbed of everything except his dignity, subconsciously recalling that he had been raised well in better times, doing a gentlemanly service to a lady. It was something that came naturally to him despite the life he was forced to live.

As Swan's feet touched the ground, Erg'Ran

stepped back and bowed stiffly. Swan touched a gloved hand to his shoulder. Unbidden, she entered the cottage, leaned against the small table at its center and breathed. "I had to conserve my magic. Riding openly through the forest is a very scary thing. And you do it all the time!"

"Most of us have no significant magic, are merely mortal, Enchantress."

"I wonder if I could ever get used to that."

Erg'Ran laughed softly. "That's the least of our problems, Enchantress."

"My mother has given me a single day to break the spell which protects the Company of Mir or she'll send the Horde of Koth to kill me."

"Your father lives, Enchantress," Erg'Ran told her, then lowered his still clear brown eyes to light his pipe.

Swan was content with her womanhood, except for one thing. Men's clothes—she had worn them a few times out of necessity—had pockets. Anyone could wear a pouch or haversack, but pockets patched to the outside of a jerkin or slit within the side seam of a robe were wondrous. Only men had these. And Swan wanted desperately to do something with her hands, to hide them away. But she could not. She could clasp them demurely together at her abdomen, one cupped in the other as though she were a supplicant (but they would still shake), or let her hands lie limp at her sides, supported by skirt and petticoats, the trembling still obvious. Rather than either of these, and failing having pockets, she hugged her arms close to her body, hands hidden by her elbows.

Resolution of the hand problem accomplished, the next problem was speech. What should she say to this one she trusted so, who had told her— Nausea swept over her, but she held it back. Her father, alive!

As was usual for her more and more as she gained in wisdom and maturity, Swan said nothing, only listened. "I know that Eran, curse the Queen Sorceress—forgive my unintended rudeness, Enchantress. But I know that the Queen Sorceress told you that your father was dead. He is not and I know this for the truth that it is." Erg'Ran exhaled a cloud of grey pipe smoke, sweet smelling. "He is and has been a prisoner these many years where you are forbidden to go."

"Barad'Il'Koth," Swan murmured.

Erg'Ran placed his clenched right fist to his forehead, invoking the courage of Mir to fill his heart, then spoke the name himself. "Barad'Il'Koth. He is there, your father."

Swan's momentary feeling of nausea was gone, in its stead a feeling she not often experienced and despised in her sex: faintness. Perhaps Erg'Ran noticed the blood draining from her cheeks, because he took her elbows in his hands and all but lifted her, taking her to the far side of the miller's cottage, easing her into a rough-hewn wooden chair. Swan covered her face with her hands, remembered at last to breathe.

"The secret of my mother's evil is at Barad'Il'Koth. And so is the secret of my father."

"And the Horde of Koth guards Barad'Il'Koth, thousands of men and other creatures and there are fewer than ten score of the Company of Mir. And even, somehow, if we were to defeat the Horde, there is the magic of the Queen Sorceress."

Swan nodded, almost angry with Erg'Ran for stating the obvious. "Her magic is stronger than mine. Yes, I know, I know. G'Urg!"

Horrified, obviously embarrassed by her reference to fecal material, Erg'Ran said, "It is a testament to the times in which we live, I suppose, that the Virgin Enchantress, Daughter Royal, Princess of Creath should even know such a word, let alone utter it. Forgive my boldness, Enchantress, but—"

"You feel as if you are a father toward me—I know that and find that endearing about you, old friend." Swan stood, ungloved her hand and out-stretched it to him. As if he were the most elegantly costumed courtier from the days before her mother's reign, Erg'Ran stepped back, bowed, a shock of his grey hair falling across his forehead. His lips lightly touched her hand. "I have less than a day," she told Erg'Ran, "to master what spells I can which might prove useful against my mother and her armies, then forsake my castle and join the Company of Mir behind the Falls. Good will prevail over evil. Some-how it will."

"Take Gar'Ath with you, then, Enchantress, to guard you lest the Queen Enchantress should count the time differently than you and catch you unawares. He is the greatest warrior in the Company of Mir. I can have him here in less than half a day, sword at his side."

Swan shook her head. "No, my friend. That would be half the time I have to prepare. I will know if my mother sends the Horde against me sooner than she had promised. Gar'Ath should see to the defenses of the encampment, and you should help him to find routes to safety lest—"

"Lest the Horde takes your life and your spell can no longer shield us. Yes, I know. Perhaps you should break the spell and the Company can—"

"Can what? If I surrender to my mother, you might all die, and there would be no one remaining to stand against her evil." Swan held Erg'Ran's hand. "It is foretold in the Prophecies of Mir that in the future of Creath there would come a time when a Virgin Enchantress would attempt to seek the origin of her seed in order to break the power of evil. You are the one who taught me this prophecy, old friend, taught me that perhaps my mother was that evil, and that I was the Virgin Enchantress spoken of by Mir himself. You started me along this path. Would you have me deny what I've come to believe in?"

"You discovered the prophecy in the hidden writings your mother had thought she had destroyed. I only translated it from the Old Tongue with the help of your magic," he reminded her. "You cannot win the day by yourself, or even with the Company of Mir fighting beside you. The prophecy in no way guarantees that you will be able to defeat your mother's evil, only that you will attempt to. There is more to the prophecy, too, but it is a riddle."

Swan sat down again, hands resting limply in her lap, her mind suddenly devoid of focus, certitude gone and resolve leaving her. "What riddle, Erg'Ran?"

He closed his eyes, cocked back his head, inhaled deeply and spoke haltingly, translating from the Old Tongue. "'In a place that is not but is, the Virgin Enchantress will seek a champion who is not but will be. If death does not claim one or the other, the power of one will be the power of the other. Goodness is the fruit of evil and also its seed.'"

"What does that mean?" Swan gasped.

Erg'Ran looked embarrassed, his face seaming with an odd smile. "I don't know! All of Mir's prophecies end cryptically, almost contradictorily. It must mean something, or Mir wouldn't have said it."

"How do we know Mir said it? Maybe somebody just wrote it down and said that Mir said it."

"Well, I suppose that's possible, Enchantress, but hardly likely."

"Then where do I go to find this champion person?"

"Well, that's right in the prophecy. You go to a place that is not but is."

"What if there isn't a place like that? Or, well, what if there are a thousand places like that? How do I find it, Erg'Ran?" He was searching for his tinderbox to relight his pipe. Perhaps pockets had their disadvantages, because he seemed unable to locate it. "Let me," she offered, recognizing the edge of exasperation in her voice. With a look and a flick of a finger, a tiny tongue of flame licked upward from the bowl of his pipe.

"Thank you, Enchantress."

"Where do I look?" Swan persisted.

"From my study of the Prophecies of Mir, from what I have seen happening in your life, Enchantress, I can only say that there is no answer which you can seek, only an answer that you will find."

Swan stood up, on her toes, back arched, shoulders raised. "That word? The one you don't like me to use? G'Urg! Hear it? G'Urg!!" She stomped from the miller's cottage, calling out over her shoulder, "Be careful, Erg'Ran! And I'll see you with the Company of Mir a little over a day from now." Out the door, before she lost her temper with this wonderfully sweet old man and turned him into a frog or something and then felt guilty about it for the rest of her life. And if she didn't hurry, that might not be too long.

Swan hitched up her skirts, mounted less than gracefully and wheeled the mare toward the forest path. . . .

The ride through the forest was frightening but also restored Swan's resolve. If her mother triumphed all of Creath would be like that forest, no one would be safe and everyone who somehow managed to survive would exist in constant terror.

The trouble with looking up anything—she was in her tower, her sanctum of sanctums, where all of her precious spell books and her most special charms were hidden away for her use alone—was that as one searched, other things were noticed, catching one's interest. Swan was searching for an herbal compound that would allow her to cast just one spell, then administer the resultant elixir to the Company of Mir in order to keep each member safe. She hoped to achieve the same effect with this elixir as the spell that she constantly kept reweaving by conscious and continuous force of will. But she found something else that attracted her attention. "I never heard of that," she exclaimed aloud to herself. It was an incantation which could be used to turn the force of a volcanic eruption back into itself. "About as useful as a sword made out of bread dough," Swan laughed. The last volcanic eruption on Creath near any populated area was in the time of Mir. And she was beginning to think, that was an awfully long time ago.

Swan returned to her search for the herbal compound.

She came across a spell which could change good wine into foul-tasting vinegar. The same effect could be achieved by leaving the wine too long in the bottle, no magic involved. The more she learned of magic, the more she realized that much of it was simply accelerating normal processes in an abnormal way. "Oh, well."

Water clocks were the fashion for logging the passage of time, had been since before she was born. She never liked them. When she was just a child, she found a book which explained how to assemble gears and springs and make a time-telling device that was much more accurate (and never needed water). She glanced at it now. If her mother kept her word, time enough remained to gather together some special books and scrolls and favorite articles of clothing and use a compression spell to reduce them to a size that would fit in a man's pocket, then get her horse and escape before the Horde came for her. Compression spells were long and involved to conjure, however.

Swan felt a subtle tingle along the back of her neck and in her fingertips. The guarding spell which she had set on the castle walls and gates (as she cast afresh once each day) was abruptly broken. Had her mother done it, Swan would never have felt it. Bridging spells would have been cast and the lifting of the guarding spell would have been unnoticed. Her mother, Eran, could do that sort of thing with ease. Swan had tried it, too, knew that such complicated spell casting was not beyond her capabilities.

But, whoever had lifted the spell had powers beyond those of an ordinary military spell breaker. Even those assigned to her mother's elite guards, the Sword of Koth, were not that good. Probably a group of the Handmaidens of Koth had done it. Taken from their mothers at birth, the Handmaidens were taught the old Witchcraft. Individually, they had some basic magical skills. But in a group of six, one for each of the cardinal directions—above, below, right, left, before and behind—their powers could be significant enough to be dangerous. Confirming her suspicions, Swan felt her heart beginning to race.

The Horde had come for her, and they were using magic to slow her response to their attack.

There was no time for a compression spell. Her precious things would have to be left behind, perhaps to be retrieved later. Swan slowed her breathing, reduced her heart rate to normal. Her hands moving in all directions, she ordered the books and scrolls and vials and retorts to their hiding places, ordering the notes she had taken to fly into her leather spell bag.

There was the noise of heavy footsteps coming up the winding stairs to the tower. Not much time.

Swan extended her left hand, calling, "Sword and sheath and belt, come to me!" They flew immediately from the small couch on which she'd placed them when entering the tower, coming to her hand. She cinched the double wrap belt around her waist. "Dagger!" She had used the tip of her dagger to open the stubborn cork which had sealed one of her vials. There was always the temptation to use magic for everything. That was wasteful, and led to laziness. The dagger slid across the long rough-hewn table where she'd set it, coming to her open right hand. It was the only weapon she always carried. She raised her skirts to sheath it on her left calf.

The footsteps were loud enough now that her second sight only confirmed what she already knew. Six Handmaidens on the heels of a dozen black-clad warriors from the Sword of Koth, the warriors wielding crossbows, axes and fireswords.

The window would be her only escape. If she used her Enchantress powers to fight these persons whom her mother had sent to kill her, she would be so drained that she might not have enough magic to escape if ordinary means should fail.

Summoning her cape and her spell bag as she ran, Swan reached the window, twisting the latch. Her plan was simple enough. She could summon a strong night wind in a matter of moments, then cast herself from the window and the powerful air currents would set her safely in the courtyard. There'd be time to reach the stable and escape.

Throwing open the sash, the first words of the wind summoning spell were on her tongue. Swan screamed instead, throwing her shoulder against the open window, slamming it shut, but not in time. Swan staggered back.

The warriors from the Sword of Koth, the six Handmaidens, the breaking of the guarding spell. They were all a diversion. Her mother was about to kill her, personally. Only her mother could have summoned what lay beyond the window and was inexorably creeping across the tower floor, along the tower walls.

Her mother had somehow, using magic Swan could not even begin to comprehend, summoned the Mist of Oblivion, the blackest of all magic, a fog but denser than the deepest, darkest night, damp and cold,

consuming all that it touched, rendering everything
into nothingness. In moments, the castle and all within
it would be devoured by the Mist, would utterly cease
to exist, not just as flesh and bone, stone and steel,
but even as dust. If her mother somehow lost control of the Mist of Oblivion, all of Creath and all of
the universe of sun and stars of night would be lost,
every life within it gone forever.

The stout wooden door at the far end of the tower
shattered inward. Three of the Sword of Koth, faces
swathed in black leather battle masks, ran into the
room. The six Handmaidens, black robed beneath
their cloaks, followed after them. The Handmaidens
immediately formed a circle, joining hands. And they
began their chant of power.

"Fools!" Swan screamed at them. "My mother is
murdering all of you along with me!" The other nine
warriors were coming through the doorway now. A
crossbow bolt was fired, streaking toward Swan's head.
She flicked her hand, diverting the missile from its
target.

The window, the wall where the window had been,
the floor near the wall, all were gone, enveloped in the
creeping blackness of the Mist. In a matter of eyeblinks,
the warriors would be closed off with her where she
stood and the Mist of Oblivion would devour them all.

Swan's heart beat savagely, her chest visibly pulsating, her breathing labored. It was the magic of the
Handmaidens at work against her body.

Swan started to raise her hand, to counter the
magic the six Handmaidens worked, but this was what
her mother wanted her to do, waste her magic, waste
the precious eyeblinks it would take. So there must
be an option, something that she could do in order
to survive.

And though her mother was now trying to take her
life, if Swan survived she would have her mother to
thank. Her mother had spoken once of a casting she

had made, taken from an old scroll. It drained Eran of almost all her magic for a period of several hours.

Swan let her mind drift back to the Memory Pool, to recall the incantation if she could.

Another crossbow bolt. To deflect it would not drain her. Swan waved her hand. The Mist of Oblivion rolled toward her, was only a few spans from her feet. Two warriors lunged toward Swan with their glowing hot fireswords.

Swan stretched out her arms, her hands grasping for the magic in the air around her, feeling its current surging through her body, strengthening her. She uttered the words of the incantation as she pressed her palms together between her breasts, becoming one with the energy around her.

Light, dazzlingly bright, filled her, exploded from her, magical energy beyond anything she had ever experienced or even imagined, a sound crackling like thunder from chain lightning—

A darkness that glowed like light but was neither light nor dark was all around her, then gone.

Swan looked up. There was a different light, that of the sun, but the sun was different, too. Tall castle towers, unlike anything she had ever seen, soared into the blue sky above. Her gaze trailed downward along the castle walls. They were filled with windows, larger than any she had ever seen. An army of coaches moved along smooth black stone roadways on either side of her, but no horses or other beasts drew them.

There was magic here. Of that, Swan was certain.

Someone spoke to her in a tongue which she did not understand. Swan turned toward the voice. It belonged to a girl, a girl about her own age, black coloring around her eyes, a spiked animal collar around her neck. The girl spoke again to her and smiled. Swan smiled back. The girl was attired only in a leather binding around her breasts and a skirt that was too short to be a skirt and boots which rose to her thighs, their heels too high to be practical for riding.

The girl spoke still again, and when Swan did not respond, the girl nodded, then began using her hands in some sort of gesturing symbology. Swan did not comprehend the gestures, but realized clearly their intent: the strangely dressed girl thought that she was deaf. A very large lantern swayed over the road. It had been emitting a red light, which seemed to serve no practical purpose of illumination on such a bright and sunny day. The light changed to green and the oddly dressed girl touched at Swan's elbow and propelled Swan with her into the road.

Swan was about to protest, but then she saw something on the other side of the road which gladdened her heart. Yes, there were men in odd metallic suits carrying strange weapons, a female creature that seemed to be half cat and woman, other oddities. But, she saw a girl attired similarly to herself, in long dress and hooded cloak, although the girl carried no sword, no spell bag. With her were two men, one of them a great teacher or philosopher from the look of his cowled robes, the other dressed in the finery of a courtier, like the ones whom she had seen pictured from the days before her mother's reign, in bright red hose and gleaming black knee boots, a black jerkin over his white shirt, a bonnet with a feather plume on his head. A sword—a little too flashy looking to be very good steel—hung from an elaborate frog at his hip.

Reaching the far side of the road, Swan saw others dressed in similar finery, and others attired even more oddly than the girl who had guided her across the road. What land was this? Swan had learned spells to translate writings so that she could assist Erg'Ran in his translations from the prophecies of Mir. They required little magical energy once mastered. She cast such a spell now to interpret the runic symbols on the cover of a colorful book the courtier with the flashy sword held in his hand. And Swan wondered, what was a Dragoncon? A Comics Expo? What was an Atlanta?

She would need a spoken language spell, and very quickly, because the girl who wore the animal collar and overbound her breasts with leather was talking to her again and so was the half-cat, half-woman creature.

# Chapter Two

It was stuffy in the back of the FBI field command vehicle, the Saturday afternoon sunshine defeating the air conditioning, aided by the heat inside generated from the banks of electronic equipment. A row of video monitors was running real time surveillance feeds from cameras hastily positioned to surround Dragoncon's principal venue and the other two buildings in question. Even a moment's glance at the monitors confirmed that a seemingly unending stream of people, many of them costumed after their favorite characters in science fiction and fantasy, were busily entering, hanging out in front of or leaving the convention. The camera operators and two agents did nothing but study the monitors, looking for one particular face.

So far, no one had seen that face and chances were good that the suspect they sought was still inside, mingling with the convention crowd. A third agent, monitoring the systems, could work a switcher and replay tape of the real time video feed. There had been one false alarm, but other than that not even a sign of the bomber.

Tom Criswell's fingers were a blur over his computer keyboard, hacking into Dragoncon's computer system. The BATF bomb specialist, Jim Sutton, was using a laptop—this was an FBI van and Sutton was BATF—for the purposes of getting all the background he could on William Culberton Brownwood, self-styled right-wing fanatical avenger. "Well, he's never had a moving violation," Sutton announced, "and his next door neighbor drives a Pontiac."

Alan Garrison's attention was divided between listening to Matt Wisnewski, the SAC who was running the operation, and checking his weapons. "I'll tell you right now, gentlemen," Wisnewski said, "that I'd rather we use standard procedures to evacuate the buildings and isolate the suspect. And, no offense to BATF, Sutton, but I've always felt that the Bureau can best handle situations of this nature on its own."

"What you're really ticked off about, Wisnewski, is that I called the U.S. Attorney and, for once in history, Justice listened to Treasury and decided there was a situation that couldn't be played by the Bureau's rulebook," Sutton declared. "If we tried a mass evacuation, we'd lose our bomber in the crowd. If we checked every parcel and bundle and purse, the suspect would either detonate his device as a diversion to cover his getaway or slip out some other way because it would take fucking forever."

Without looking away from his computer screen, Tom Criswell remarked, "I'm in. This Dragoncon convention? They've got over eighteen thousand registered attendees in three separate buildings that are all interconnected!"

"It's the largest science fiction and fantasy convention in the Southeast, one of the largest in the world, and Saturday is always the best attended day. I've never missed one. I was here last night, as a matter of fact, so I've already got my convention badge," Garrison informed them.

"By the time this is over, Garrison, that may be the only badge you'll have," Wisnewski cracked. "Just because you can blend in here with these science fiction people doesn't mean squat, Garrison. And getting your BATF buddy Sutton here to go around me to the U.S. Attorney so that you can grandstand and try apprehending the suspect on your own is irresponsible conduct that we'll discuss quite seriously after this is over. If the suspect uses his device and lives are lost, it'll be on your head, Garrison, and yours, too, Sutton. The same if we lose him."

Wisnewski snorted again.

The spare magazines for Garrison's brace of SIG P-220 .45s were checked, both guns already secured in their shoulder holsters. Something he hadn't been taught at the FBI Academy at Quantico but had been taught by some old friends who'd gone professionally armed all their adult lives was that the best way to disguise the presence of a gun carried in a shoulder holster was to carry two guns of identical or similar size in a double shoulder holster. This equalized the bulges.

Garrison stood up. He was as ready as he could get, armed to the teeth and a wire under his shirt. Thank God, he thought, that the wire didn't have to be taped on, because that meant shaving his chest or waiting for the inevitable pain of removing body hair along with the tape.

Criswell asked a reasonable question. "How are you going to try finding this guy out of all these people?"

Garrison answered, "I got down here for a little bit last night, like I said, and I was planning to come back this afternoon anyway and spend the rest of the day. I pretty much know where everything is, where the panels are being held, like that. If I can't locate him during the day, he'll show up where the crowds are at night. Saturday night there's always Atlanta Radio Theater doing a live production and later there's the masquerade contest."

Sarcastically, Wisnewski asked, "And do you dress up for this masquerade like all these other weirdos we've been seeing going in and out?"

"No, I don't. And, they're good people, not what you called them." Figuring he was in line for an official reprimand at any event, Garrison decided it was just as well to be hung for a sheep as a lamb. "But, now that you mention it, Matt, I did show up once in a blue suit just like the one you're wearing, with FBI cufflinks just like yours. They wanted to give me a prize for the best Washington bureaucrat costume."

Sutton laughed.

Before Wisnewski could respond, Garrison continued. "Most of the costuming you're seeing on the surveillance cameras isn't for the masquerade contest. People wear hall costumes and just live in character for a few days. It's fun. Our guy might have knocked somebody over the head and stolen a costume. At first thought, that might make finding him harder, but it could make it easier, too, if I know what costume to look for. A lot of these folks will dress as the same character year after year." What he didn't tell Wisnewski, but had told Sutton, was that he intended to take certain people within the convention into his confidence, give them a description of the bombing suspect, and let them be extra eyes and ears. Because he had attended Dragoncon ever since its inception, a lot of the people there—some of whom he didn't even know by name, only by face—were people he cared about. If Wisnewski had his way and used standard Bureau procedures, Brownwood might indeed be desperate enough to detonate his device and take thousands of lives. It was a lose-lose situation from the starting gate, but Alan Garrison had to reconfigure it so there'd be at least some slight chance of winning.

There were a few other details that Alan Garrison hadn't bothered to mention to his boss, the Special

Agent in Charge, Matt Wisnewski. Wisnewski had a personal policy against agents carrying more than two guns. Garrison had a third handgun in his right front pocket. Wisnewski strictly forbade any type of fighting knife, particularly a switchblade or push button, on the grounds that such a knife was the weapon of a street thug, not an FBI Agent. Garrison also carried two Benchmade AFO automatics.

Garrison started out of the van. Sutton waved him a thumbs up.

Criswell said, "You can do it, Alan. Be careful, huh."

Wisnewski shook Garrison's hand, then looked away.

The handshake thing from Wisnewski was spooky in the extreme . . .

Bill Brownwood's convention badge read, "Tim Castor," a one-day pass with a name to match one of his fake driver's licenses. Even though it wasn't declared as such, the FBI would be handling this as a hostage situation. He was inside, with enough explosives in his backpack to bring down half a high-rise; the law was outside, with bomb disposal equipment, snipers, SWAT Teams and enough manpower to lay siege to the gold depository at Fort Knox. Brownwood found himself grinning. The New World Order would have given the secret orders that Bill Brownwood should not be taken alive, but be terminated with extreme prejudice while resisting arrest.

He knew how the FBI and all the rest of the idiot United Nations stooge agencies worked. Manpower saturation rather than subtlety. They were waiting for him to grab a room full of hostages and make some demands. "Yo, Feds! I want pizzas up here now! And a million dollars and a helicopter and a police radio, or I see how big a crater ten pounds of homemade plastic explosives can make where this fuckin' building used to be! And no damn anchovies!"

The Feds couldn't understand that they weren't dealing with criminals, that they were dealing with freedom fighters. Would the men at Lexington and Concord have seized hostages and ordered takeout and a million big ones? This was a war. If civilians died, they died, casualties in the greater scheme of things. But a hostage situation would net him nothing at all. And even if he got a million dollars—which he would give to the cause—and got away with it, the computer strips hidden in the money could track him every mile he went.

Brownwood didn't want to stay in the building, but wanted to get out of it and on his way. There was a special place where he wanted to set his device, and a science fiction and fantasy convention wasn't it. But the FBI would have surveillance cameras all around the area, watching for his face. He needed to get past those cameras without being seen and one of these costumes would be the perfect vehicle. They weren't for sale. Books, swords, videotapes, jewelry, all of that was for sale in abundance. So were masks and clothing of all sorts—some of the clothes were disgusting, typical of the corruption liberalism had brought to America. But what he needed was a complete costume and there was only one way to get that . . .

Swan supposed that, once her magical abilities had returned to full strength, she could get back to her own universe merely by summoning the magical energy in the air—she could feel that this place had such energy in abundance—and repeating the incantation which had brought her here, only completely backwards. That was, at least, the usual way of such things. There was, of course, the problem that she might return to exactly the same spot she had left, which would now be nothingness. Then, just like a mortal, she would die.

Logic again came to her rescue, or at least she told

herself that it was logic. If she had stood a span to her right or left in the instant when she left her universe, she would probably have arrived here a span to the right or left of where she had. So, if she made certain that when she used her magic to leave here and return to her own universe she was a commensurate distance from the spot where she had arrived (as if that paralleled the castle) to be well out of range of the Mist of Oblivion, she would be all right. On the other hand, if she had stood a span to the right or left before leaving her own universe, she might have come to still a different universe than this. That would mean that unless she left this universe from the exact spot where she had arrived, she would not return to her own universe. But if this spell had to be all that exact, logic dictated that she would return to her own universe within the Mist of Oblivion, in which case she would be dead. Under her breath, Swan muttered that word that Erg'Ran didn't think proper for her to use.

"What's that mean?" It was her newfound friend with the studded animal collar and the short skirt who asked.

"Oh, just a local expression where I come from," Swan answered. The language spell had required little magical energy and was working remarkably well. She understood these people's speech perfectly, and they seemed to understand her just as easily. The girl's name was Alicia, and Alicia had been joined by her friend Gardner. Gardner was dressed even more strangely. He, too, wore an animal collar—usually worn by something called a dog, Swan had learned—and there was a leash attached to it, the end of which Alicia kept looped around her wrist. Gardner also wore something called handcuffs—they appeared to be rather flimsy seeming but nonetheless well-made manacles  on his wrists. They were linked together by a length of delicate chain. When Gardner first joined them, Swan had asked Alicia, "Is he some sort of prisoner?"

Alicia winked at her, announcing, "He's a prisoner of love, honey!"

Swan was uncertain what that meant, although she felt that she had the general idea.

For some time, Swan, Alicia, Gardner and the half-cat, half-woman had been seated on a very comfortable staircase. Many strangely dressed persons went up and down its length. Some of the women were very beautiful, some of the men very handsome. This universe seemed like a nice enough place to visit, but she hoped she wouldn't have to live in it. The future of Creath was her responsibility, as was the safety of the Company of Mir. Almost certainly, her spell which had protected the Company was dissolved when she made her escape. There was much to do.

Periodically, Alicia would say, "I wish I could smoke." At first, Swan was aghast that someone wanted to be set afire (despite Alicia's bizarre appearance, the girl didn't seem that strange). Later, Swan realized that Alicia wanted to set fire to something else, not actually smoke herself. But, it was hard to imagine Alicia with a pipe like the one which old Erg'Ran habituated.

Alicia had been consulting what was called a mini-program. After a moment, she announced, "There's a sword fighting demonstration. Sounds neat. Wanna watch?"

"Sword fighting? Yes!"

"Come on Gardner." Alicia tugged at Gardner's leash as she stood up. Gardner walked a little behind them as they wove their way through the crowded corridor. A creature covered in fur, with a horrible face and weapons of all types festooned about its body, passed by them and called out, "Hey, Alicia."

"Neat costume, Farley!"

"So, everyone here is costumed as some character out of a book or—"

"Book or movie or TV maybe," Alicia informed her.

The meanings of "movie" and "TV" were unknown
to Swan, but she would somehow divine them.

Their band wandered along many passageways, the
sounds of speech and laughter filling the air. At one
point, there was a doorway leading to the outside,
and Swan accompanied her companions, Alicia proclaiming, "I gotta grab a smoke."

In fact, Alicia's "smoke" was nothing like that of
Erg'Ran, but a white paper cylinder, the ground leaves
encased within it as they would be in the bowl of a
pipe.

"Drag?" Alicia asked her.

"Drag what?" Swan answered.

"You're cool, Swan!" Alicia laughed.

Swan remarked, "No, it is a little warm with this
dress, actually. Where I come from, it is cold now,
and snow is falling."

"The weather has really been crazy bad lately," the
half-cat, half-woman named Brenda announced.

"Has it?" Swan asked. "Crazy" seemed to be a word
describing mental aberration. Was the "weather" here,
rather than a combination of natural forces occasionally tampered with by magical means, regularly
controlled by some sorceress with evil intent? If that
were so, did evil like that of her mother, Eran, the
Queen Sorceress, exist throughout the universe?

Swan and her friends re-entered the structure and
wove their way along many more passageways until,
at last, they reached a hall of some considerable size.
From within, she could hear the clanking of swords
beaten against shields, and Swan reached to the hilt
of her own sword. At the entrance to the edifice, right
after she had magically changed pieces of paper from
her spell bag into looking like the thing called
"money" so that she could pay for her membership,

her sword was "peace-bonded." A fibrous material, like a length of semitransparent vine or small intestine, was wound round the hilt of her sword and to a strap in the frog, to lock the blade in its scabbard. She was ready to magically break this peace bond should the swordplay from within the hall demand . . .

Alan Garrison leaned deeper into his chosen corner near the doors, scanning the faces of everyone who entered, looking for William Brownwood.

If Brownwood had a package with him of any kind, it would be the bomb. What if he saw Brownwood and there were no package, meaning that the device was hidden somewhere? At the very moment that he would see Brownwood, a chain of decisions would have to be made. Should he take Brownwood down, attempt to follow Brownwood until reaching a less peopled area, what? Should he call in backup on the tiny radio that he wore? Should he attempt to arrest Brownwood—there were charges aplenty from which to choose—or should he go for an instant kill?

Alan Garrison had never killed anyone. He'd come close to doing so on three occasions, once having to shoot a suspect twice in the chest in order to prevent the suspect's killing of another agent. But the suspect lived, stood trial, was convicted. In the close confines of the convention, there could be no chances taken, especially considering the bomb.

Wisnewski was right, perhaps, that this was a foolish move, going after Brownwood alone. But the other way, an evacuation and a siege, would either let William Brownwood slip through their fingers and use his explosive device, create a hostage situation of ridiculous proportions or force Brownwood to prematurely detonate his device out of desperation.

"Hello, Alan! Good to see you. I hope you're having a good time. I'm late for a meeting." The dark-haired, bearded man who ran Dragoncon greeted him with a smile, then began talking into a cell phone. As he continued past, he looked back over his shoulder at Garrison and added, "Gotta run. Let's get together for a drink later." And Ed Kramer was there and gone.

"Hello, Ed! Good-bye, Ed!" Alan Garrison resumed his watch. He was finally rewarded, not with the face of a mad bomber, but with the face of an angel, the loveliest face he had ever seen. She was dressed as some sort of medieval fantasy character, so authentically attired in long midnight blue gown, grey hooded fur-ruffed cape and elaborately hilted sword that she must have spent either a ton of money or a ton of time creating the costume. Soft waves of impossibly beautiful auburn hair cascaded to her waist. Her features were at once delicate, yet strong, her cheekbones the kind that a high-fashion model would kill for. Her eyes were the softest, most strikingly beautiful grey-green color that he had ever seen. The convention badge that she wore read, "Swan Creath."

Alan Garrison wondered what nationality "Creath" might be . . .

Upon entering the hall, Swan's attention was immediately drawn to several handsome warriors engaged in furious battle on a raised platform. They wore armor and emblazoned on their battle-worn shields were symbols of dragons and other beasts. One of the fighters was brought down with a two-handed blow from his opponent, his shield beaten aside. The victorious warrior was chivalrous. Rather than taking the fallen man's life, he let his vanquished foeman yield.

At this point, an oddly handsome fellow with no hair at all on his head but a neatly trimmed beard at his chin stepped onto the platform. "That's Hank Reinhardt," the half-cat, half-woman Brenda informed Swan.

"Is he the leader of these warriors?" Swan asked.

"He runs Museum Replicas and those guys are the Museum Replicas fight team."

"Then they always fight beside one another and this is a practice bout only?"

"It's a demonstration, Swan," Alicia said.

"With swords so mighty, one of these warriors could cleave the chains which bind you, Gardner," Swan suggested to her new friend who wore the manacles and leash.

"These are good handcuffs! Why would I want somebody to screw 'em up?" Gardner declared.

Swan merely shrugged her shoulders. Whoever this warrior Reinhardt was, he knew the language of steel, and the use of steel as well. He demonstrated a draw cut, executed as deftly as she had ever seen. Were these people who watched him from their seats wishing to train under him as warriors, Swan wondered? If so, some of them looked as if they would do well. Others, sadly, looked nearly beyond hope.

"This Reinhardt raises an army against whom?"

"He isn't raising an army, Swan," Alicia told her. "He's just telling people about swords and stuff."

"Oh." Swan looked around the hall.

And she saw the handsomest man she had seen in all of her life. He was tall and well set in the shoulders and chest. His hair was the same red-brown color as her own. His eyes—she needed her second sight to be sure—were a deep brown. They were clear, somehow strong and good. He wore a short brown leather jerkin of some sort, with a leather collar, long sleeves of leather and what appeared to be knit trim at the cuffs and at the bottom. If he wore hose, she could not see them, each leg covered instead with a medium blue material, the tops of his boots disappearing beneath. He seemed to wear no weapon, but that he was a warrior was beyond doubt. Using her second sight, she read the runes emblazoned on his badge, "Alan Garrison."

"Who is Al'An Garrison, Alicia?" Swan asked.

"Al-on? Oh! Alan. He's cool, even if he is a Fed."

"Is Fed his ancestry, or the name of his village?" Swan inquired further.

"You are cool with the way you talk, Swan! Alan's one of these guys who keeps telling himself he's gonna be a writer someday. See him here every year and at some of the other cons, too," Alicia informed her.

"He has never learned to write!"

Brenda told her, "He wants to write stories and books and like that."

"Be a teller of tales! Yes! There were such people once where I come from. Perhaps, someday, there will be again."

"Anyway," Brenda continued, "if he was illiterate, I don't think he could be a Fed."

"A Fed," Swan repeated.

Gardner finally spoke. "He's got a shield, right? You know, like Dan Akroyd in that old *Dragnet* movie? He's got a shield with writing on it, says he's a Fed."

Swan still did not understand, but decided that she should change the subject before her ignorance of this world became too much more obvious than it already was. When she looked back toward the corner, Al'An Garrison, the Fed, was gone.

The warrior leader Reinhardt was wielding a different sword now and cleaving through a large white object. Swan refrained from asking her companions if the white object was an enchanted block of snow. . . .

The liberal regulation-mongering idiots with their no-smoking regulations were his unconscious allies this time, Bill Brownwood mused. Whether the doors leading out onto the segment of roof were supposed to be opened or not, they were, and for the last hour, while Brownwood sweltered in the afternoon heat, a parade of people in small groups had exited the doorway and stood around smoking.

Bill Brownwood did not smoke, but wished that he did. Allergic to cigarette smoke ever since childhood, he had nonetheless tried smoking on several occasions and only become terribly ill. Lighting up was a way of saying, "Fuck the establishment," and he liked that. At last, with no one else in sight, a solitary smoker of appropriate size emerged onto the roof, the man dressed in some sort of movie swordsman get-up with a big, ugly mask clutched under his arm.

Brownwood walked from behind the air conditioning unit and toward the railing, looking out over the downtown area. "Would you look at that!" Brownwood said as loudly as he could without sounding fake. "What the fuck next, huh!"

"What do you see, man?" The voice from behind Brownwood sounded interested.

Without looking back, Brownwood said, "Topless right out there for everybody to see! Wow, what a pair, too!"

In the next moment, the costumed man was beside him, peering down into the street. "I don't see anything at all."

Brownwood glanced over his shoulder. No one had come out onto the roof. Brownwood started saying, "She must have ducked inside. Knockers like you've never seen."

The man Bill Brownwood was about to kill leaned out further over the railing.

Brownwood looped the piano wire garrote over his victim's head in one motion while hammering his right knee into the small of the man's back. There'd be a little blood, but that couldn't be avoided. . . .

Alan Garrison had mentioned to certain of his friends as he encountered them, "I'm looking for someone who might be extremely dangerous. Take a look at this photo. If you see him, call this telephone number immediately and get patched through to me on my radio. Try to keep an eye on the guy, but don't be obvious. And under no circumstances should you attempt to apprehend the guy or even approach him. Got it? Also, if you see something odd—yeah, I know—but I mean like somebody in a costume that just doesn't look right on him, or a costume you're familiar with but the wrong person seems to be wearing it. We think the guy might have tried to disguise himself so that he can get out of the con without being recognized."

Several different variations on the same general speech secured promises of cooperation and caution.

Alan Garrison kept plying his way through the corridors of the con, going through the hucksters' room—too enormous to be covered by one man, he realized—and going through the art exhibit.

By late in the afternoon, Wisnewski's voice buzzing in his earphone like some sort of fly, Garrison stepped outside, lit a cigarette (he smoked very rarely, less than a pack a week) and got on his cell phone. "Yeah, maybe it was a bad idea. Got a better one?"

Wisnewski's voice paused for a moment, then said, "I'm giving you until six P.M. You've got almost an hour and forty minutes to find this guy your way, or we seal the convention and send in the HRU and bomb disposal."

In the middle of eighteen thousand people, a Hostage Rescue Unit looking for a man who might be in costume would make a Three Stooges routine look like something out of *Henry V*. Garrison almost said that, but realized there was no use in arguing. And, in the final analysis, Wisnewski's idea might be the only chance they had. "Fine. I'll call you at six, but don't send anyone in until I call. We could get a lot of people hurt for no reason. And start telling HRU now that guys with swords or axes or rayguns or empty tubes from LAW rockets aren't bad guys, they're just in costume, okay?"

"Six. By five after, we're going in." Wisnewski clicked off.

Garrison closed his cell phone and put it away. "Shit," he murmured.

"What is shit?"

Garrison was so startled, he almost reached for a gun. It was the girl named Swan, the exquisite girl he'd seen at Hank's demonstration, the loveliest woman he had ever seen in his life. Her voice was like music, a lilting alto. And she had just asked him what was shit.

"You're kidding."

"I'm Swan."

"I'm Alan."

"Al-An, yes."

"Whatever."

"Whatever? Whatever is shit?"

Her syntax had lost him totally. His mouth was very dry. He thought, "My God, is this love at first sight?" Instead of saying that aloud, he asked, "Want to have a drink with me?"

"Yes. I am thirsty."

Brenda the cat-girl, standing beside Alicia and her idiot boyfriend, Gardner, gave them a wave. Alicia grinned and called, "See ya at the masquerade, Swan!"

If Alan Garrison had just been set up, he was happy.

Garrison touched at Swan's shoulder, starting back inside with her. He ground out his cigarette under his boot heel.

Swan asked him, "What is a Fed? Oh! And don't forget to tell me what is shit!"

Soberly, Alan Garrison reflected upon the fact that he was still chasing a lunatic bomber and that the woman who might be destined to be the great love of his life was a complete ditz. "I'm having a great day. Let's start with what a Fed is," Garrison began.

# Chapter Three

Bill Brownwood rose from behind the air conditioning cowling, adjusting his mask. He was some sort of burly creature who walked and dressed like a man, but had the face and short tusks of a wild boar. There was a sword belted at his side, which was probably dull as a butter knife, and a pistol on his other hip. The pistol was an elaborate toy, about the same size as his Beretta 92F 9mm. Brownwood took the raygun from the flap holster and slipped his own real pistol in its place. The flap covered the gun completely, not good for a rapid draw but great for hiding a real gun where a fake should have been. He dropped the raygun beside the body of the man he'd taken it and the costume from, someone named "Wilton Hyde" according to the convention badge.

Wilton Hyde wouldn't be needing his cap pistol anymore, nor anything else ever again.

Brownwood bent over, finished stuffing Hyde's corpse into the housing, then lowered the cover. The air conditioning on this side of the building might be a little screwed up, but it would be several hours at least before anyone thought to look for a body in the ductwork.

Brownwood was already warm under the mask, and going inside into the air conditioning wouldn't help that much. He started inside, anyway. . . .

"This tickles my nose," Swan announced happily.

"It's Coca-Cola. You've never had a Coke before?" Garrison asked.

"No. It tastes very good," she told him. They'd found a table in a small snack shop and sat huddled around it, Garrison's eyes dividing their attention between the face of this funny, gorgeous girl named Swan and the faces passing by in the corridor. "Then you don't like being a Fed? Alicia said that you wanted to write stories and be a teller of tales."

"Alicia's got a big mouth, sometimes," Garrison observed.

"She is able to change the size of her mouth? Is that common here?"

"That's just a figure of speech. Where are you from?"

"Creath."

"Creath?"

"I was fated to come here and find a champion who will fight beside me with the Company of Mir against my mother, the Queen Sorceress."

"I don't think I've read that book. Who's the author?"

"I wasn't talking about a book, Al-An."

"All right. Sure. Swan. That's a lovely name."

"Thank you. Al-An is a strange name, but I like it," she told him. This girl had the most wonderful smile Garrison had ever seen. Her eyes lit her entire face with a radiance unlike anything he'd ever imagined in a woman.

"So, you know I'm an FBI Agent, now. What do you do?"

"I make magical spells, potions and incantations."

"Oh. So, are you a witch?"

"No, I'm not a practitioner of the old ways. These were taken over by my mother, Eran, and are used now only for evil by the Handmaidens of Koth."

"Now, I don't understand," Garrison told Swan.

"I am the Virgin Enchantress, Daughter Royal, Princess of Creath. And, as I said, I have been fated to come here in search of a champion who will go with me to Barad'Il'Koth and fight with me against the Horde of Koth, in order to free the people of the Land from my mother, Eran, Sorceress Queen of Creath, Mistress General of the Horde of Koth. It's very simple, really. Will you come with me when my magic is fully restored? That shouldn't be very long."

"Come with you where?"

Swan shook her head, for all the world looking as though he were the one saying goofy things. "To Creath, to fight beside me with the Company of Mir, as I've told you."

"Okay—wait a minute. How come you speak English, or is Creath like one of these sci-fi movies where everybody has a British accent?"

She smiled patiently again. "I merely used a spell so that I could read the runes of your world, then another so that I could speak and understand your tongue."

"Sure. So, where is Creath, exactly? How many light-years away in space?"

"What are light-years? What sort of space?"

"What? Did you beam down or come here in a UFO?" He was being sarcastic and the last thing in the world that he wanted to do was be offensive, turn her off to him. But time was running out and he was terribly on edge. "Look, Swan. I think you're the most incredible girl I've ever met. I want to see you again, and again, and probably again and again. But I've got something I've gotta do. Can I meet you at the

masquerade, or send word to you if I can't get there?
What's your phone number?"

"So many questions. I want to see you, Al'An, very
much again and again. I don't have a phone number, at least I don't think so. Why can't I go with
you?"

Telling her what he felt compelled to tell her was
sheer stupidity. "Look."

"At what?"

"No, I mean listen to me. You know I'm an FBI
Agent, a Fed. A cop. I go after bad guys and I'm after
one right here and now. He's a very bad guy." Garrison lowered his voice. "He's a bomber. He thinks
the government is plotting to kill him and he's fighting
back. He's killed three people at least and he's ready
to kill a whole bunch more people. You can't go with
me."

Swan smiled benevolently. "Oh, Al'An, you are a
champion! It is only right that if I expect you to fight
beside me with the Company of Mir against the
Queen Sorceress, that I should fight beside you
against this evil person. I pledge to your cause my
magic," and she stood, grasping the hilt of her sword
with her tiny right hand, "and my sword, Al'An."

Alan Garrison didn't know what to say. But she was
still standing there, waiting for him to say something.
He couldn't hurt her feelings. So, he stood up and
said something, something wholly in character with
his actions as he interpreted them so far this day—
stupid. Garrison told Swan, "All right, but you do
exactly as I say, and when I tell you to run for it,
run for it."

"What is it that I am to run for?"

"Never mind. Just come with me." And, under his
breath, although he wasn't Jewish, Alan Garrison
murmured the familiar Yiddish expression, "Oy veh."

Stopping in her tracks, Swan enthused, "I know
these words well from my own tongue! But, Al'An,

what does what we are doing have to do with the poison bladder of an ice dragon?"

Garrison just kept walking, his hand at Swan's elbow.

Al'An told Swan, "It's almost half-past five." From the worried look in Al'An's beautiful brown eyes, this "half-past five" must have something to do with "six" which was a designation of the passage of time here. And at six, something bad was to happen unless Al'An located this evil person before then.

"It is time that I use my second sight, Al'An."

"What?"

They had been walking rapidly along the passageways, looking inside every room that they passed, persons who were writers such as Al'An wished to be sitting at tables at the far ends of these rooms, facing a host of other persons who were listening attentively or asking questions. But the face for which Al'An searched was not among these faces.

Al'An had shown her what was called a photograph, a very accurate seeming picture of a face, this face very unfriendly looking, as she imagined the faces of her mother's masked killers, the Sword of Koth, had been when they had come to take her life.

"What are you talking about with second sight?" Al'An asked again.

"If it is that important that this evil man be found before this six happens, perhaps my second sight will help. I have never used it with a picture of any kind, but I can try. I will need a spell which is usually quite difficult if I am to look other than in a straight line."

"You mean remote viewing, or clairvoyance?"

The trouble with a language spell of any sort was that, like much of magic, it was only the acceleration of natural processes. So, despite the spell, less commonly used words or expressions were more difficult to understand. But the concept of viewing something remotely became apparent to her in the next instant. "Yes, Al'An. Remote viewing."

"The Navy did it to track Soviet submarines. Fine. Try it, Swan." Al'An took the picture from the pocket of the jerkin he called a "bomber jacket." She supposed that he wore a bomber jacket because it might magically aid him in pursuit of this bomber. She began reciting the spell.

Al'An handed her the picture.

Swan appraised every feature of the man's face. His hair was dark and even shorter than that of Al'An, his forehead high, but combined with very deepset wrinkles, the effect being that of a forehead that was very low. His eyes were deepset as well, and furtive seeming, as if trying to avoid the gaze of the device or entity which replicated his features on this piece of paper. His chin was remarkable, extremely broad but pushed-in seeming, as if it were withdrawing into his throat. His lips were thin, drawn out very long from side to side, ending in deepset creases in his cheeks.

In the next eyeblink, Swan announced, "He is a creature with the face of, of—" She searched for the word. "A pig! But he has great teeth protruding from his face like horns."

"Tusks?"

Swan thought for a moment. "Tusks, yes. Curved teeth made of horn. He is returning the mask to his face. He is dressed in black cape and grey doublet and grey hose. He wears no baldric, but a belt, his sword and another weapon at his sides. He carries a leather bag slung to his shoulder. Is this the man you seek?" Swan saw him clearly in a distant passageway within the structure. And she did not like what she saw.

"Can you see where he is?"

This would be hard to describe to Al'An. "He moves toward the stairway where earlier today I sat and talked with Alicia and Gardner and Brenda, half-cat, half-woman."

"Take me there," Al'An commanded.

Swan was not used to being commanded. But, somehow, under the circumstances she did not mind it. Al'An broke into a run, Swan flinging back her greatcape, gathering up her skirts and running with him. Al'An let her pass him, so that she could lead him, she realized, to the stairway, to his quarry. She could still see the evil man with her second sight. As she and Al'An ran, she told Al'An, "He carries something that looks like a rock. It is in his right hand. There are many square shaped ridges on it and there is a small handle and a ring through which his middle finger is passed, Al'An."

"That's a fragmentation grenade!"

Al'An took something from beneath his bomber jacket. A weapon? He folded it open, pushed a button, then began to speak to it as if it were alive. Perhaps it was a magical advisor. She had seen many people speak with such objects since she had arrived here. "This is Garrison. Gimme Wisnewski, quick." Al'An paused. Then, "Wisnewski, I think we've got him. And he may have a grenade. Be ready. I'm on the south end of the main building, proceeding west along a corridor. I'm keeping the line open."

"This way, Al'An!" Swan turned the corner of the passageway through which they had run, raising her skirts higher now as she started down the stairs.

"Is this the stairway that you saw?"

"He is two levels below us, moving toward the entranceway to the great hall through which all who come here must pass."

"He's heading for registration on the main floor. Don't move on him yet, but be ready. He's wearing a pig mask with tusks, got a sword, a bag that's probably got the device in it. And he may have a gun on his sword belt. Black cape, grey thing like a sportcoat Christopher Columbus could have worn, grey tights," Al'An told his magical advisor.

"Your enemy quickens his pace, Al'An."

"If he detonates a fragmentation grenade in the main lobby, Brownwood could kill dozens of people. You stay back well behind me by the stairs. Don't get anywhere near me. I mean it, Swan!"

When they reached the level one above where the evil one trod, Swan fell back, letting Al'An stride past her. But she would not let him battle his evil foeman alone. Magically breaking the peace bond which secured her sword, she ran down the stairs, in Al'An's footsteps.

Al'An was a fast runner, and a good jumper, Swan observed. He was bounding down the stairs three at a time, then leapt the final five treads, breaking into a long-strided run. She could hear him still as, once more, he spoke with his magical advisor. "I see Brownwood heading for the doors. It's a grenade. Wait for him outside. Move! Move. Move now, Wisnewski! I'll be right behind him coming fast!"

As she ran, Swan tried picturing in her mind what a bomb must be like. This "grenade" thing must be some sort of bomb, as well. It would be an explosion, an eruption of great force and energy, like—

Reaching the bottom of the stairs, Swan could see both Al'An and his black-caped foeman. The evil one was walking determinedly past a small group of people. Brenda, the half-cat, half-female, stood among them.

Brenda called to the evil one. "Hey, Wilton! Where you been?" Brenda reached out to him. He shrugged away. She stepped toward him. He pushed her to the floor.

The young man Swan had earlier seen—the one dressed as a courtier—jumped toward the evil one, fists clenched and ready.

Al'An shouted, "No! Don't touch him!"

Al'An's magical advisor fell from his hand. In its stead was an object such as she had seen earlier worn by a passerby on the stairs. Gardner had told her that it was a laser pistol, and explained its use. But Alicia had told her that a laser pistol was not a real weapon, only a toy. Al'An needed a real weapon, a sword, and Swan was about to make hers appear magically in his hand, but things began to happen too quickly.

The courtier threw a punch and missed, then smashed his body against the evil one. The evil one stumbled back, raised the hand which held the grenade and cried aloud, "I'll blow up everybody!"

Al'An did not use his laser pistol weapon, but instead hurtled himself against his foeman, Al'An's upper body colliding with the evil one's chest, both Al'An and the evil one falling to the floor. Al'An grappled with the evil one, Al'An's knee hammering against the evil one's face and chest, Al'An's hands struggling to pry the grenade thing from his foeman's grasp.

Swan ran forward to join the fray, brandishing her blade in the air above her head. "Give way! Give way!" Swan commanded, the crowd of people in the great hall splitting asunder before her.

Swan stopped, a few spans from where Al'An and his foeman writhed in combat, her sword clasped in both hands beside her right shoulder, its blade readied to arc downward and cut the life from Al'An's foeman.

Something happened.

Swan had experienced the phenomenon only once before, when she was but a girl. Powerless to act because there was no time, her mother refusing to act a moment earlier, Swan witnessed a horse and its rider attempting to outrun an avalanche on the far side of a valley in the high mountain snows. The feeling was as if time itself slowed, moving only imperceptibly forward, allowing the incident which

was occurring to be viewed in the most minute
detail.

The grenade rolled from the evil one's grasp. The
flat thing attached to it like a handle, which she had
seen earlier with her second sight, sprang away from
the grenade.

Swan saw Al'An's eyes, wide with horror. She heard a
solitary scream. It was Alicia's voice, Swan thought.
Around the evil one's finger was the ring which had been
attached to the grenade as she'd second-sighted him.

Somehow, Swan knew that this combination of
circumstances was very bad.

Al'An shouted, "Get to cover! Everybody!" Al'An
pushed to his feet. His foeman grasped Al'An's right
foot. Al'An shook free, kicking his foeman in the side
of the face.

Al'An lunged toward the grenade, looking toward
Swan for an eyeblink. And their gazes met. In Al'An's
beautiful brown eyes, Swan saw two things revealed,
that somehow Al'An cared for her more deeply than
anyone had ever cared for her, and that he knew that
he was about to die.

The grenade thing was a bomb.

The spell that she had happened upon before the
attack by her mother's forces, a spell to be used
against the power of a volcano, to turn it back against
itself—Swan recalled it now, shrieking the words as
she cast it. It was untried by her. What if it did not
work?

She sheathed her sword.

In the same breath as the first spell, Swan began
to recite the incantation which had brought her here,
but totally backwards, sound for sound, rune for rune.

Swan's arms stretched out, hands grasping for the
powerful magic she had felt in the air around her here
since she first arrived. The magical energy pulsed
through her limbs, spiraling into the very core of her
body.

Swan walked the few spans separating her from Al'An, her palms pressed together between her breasts, the magical energy filling her, one with her.

Swan dropped to her knees beside Al'An, his body tented over the grenade, shielding all from its deadliness at the sacrifice of his own life. In truth, Al'An was a brave and noble champion, the Champion foretold in the Prophecies of Mir. The deadly little bomb was about to make its evil felt, unless her untried spell succeeded. She could not risk Al'An's life if it failed.

Magical energy flowed from Swan's hands as she turned them open, her arms folding around Al'An's upper body, drawing his head to her breast.

The energy crackled and arced, coursed wildly through their bodies. Her very being shuddered with its force.

There was a roar, not from the bomb, but a roar of thunder, cracking, tearing through the magical fabric of the universe.

In the same eyeblink that the grenade exploded, so did the energy which flowed from within Swan and Al'An, a light glowing whiter than the brightest sunlight, enveloping them. The liquid darkness came again, then was gone. A snowflake touched Swan's cheek, another settled in Al'An's eyelashes. He stared up at her in silence, his head still clutched to her bosom. Another snowflake landed on the tip of her nose and Al'An brushed it away with his hand. . . .

Eran, Sorceress Queen of Creath, Mistress General of the Horde of Koth, shrieked with a pain she had not known since childbirth. She stood. The gem-encrusted goblet from which an instant earlier she'd sipped red wine flew from her ring festooned fingers, hurtling across the banquet table, skipping over the flagstones of the Great Hall of Koth.

Her lover for the night, obedient enough to retain

human form if he kept his manners, dragged himself stuporously to his feet, reaching for the sword at his hip. "My Queen? What is . . ." Eran wondered fleetingly if he were at a loss for words or merely too intoxicated to complete a thought.

"The Virgin Enchantress lives, and she's brought someone with her. Curse her! Curse them both!"

Eran knotted her fingers into her lover's hair, pulling his face down to hers, kissing him violently on the mouth. Blood trickled from his lips. Eran tossed back her hair, howling with rage and delight, knowing that for her both feelings always were and always would be one in the same.

# Chapter Four

Erg'Ran gave heed to the advice proffered him in the miller's cottage by the Virgin Enchantress, that he must look to options other than Swan's magic for the survival of the Company of Mir. Pursuant to the dire warnings that Swan's spell would no longer confound the Horde of Koth in their search should the Queen Sorceress make good her death threat, Erg'Ran threw himself into directing the building of additional fortifications behind the Falls of Mir, consulting maps to preplan escape routes and rendezvous points in the event their encampment had to be abandoned. In the midst of these endeavors, and sooner than the time allotted by Swan's mother's ultimatum, an arrow was brought to Erg'Ran in his tent. The message wrapped to the arrow shaft detailed an eyewitness account of the Mist of Oblivion appearing near the castle residence of the Virgin Enchantress, how the Mist of Oblivion was seen to consume the castle and all within and vanish. Erg'Ran collapsed to his knees and wept. He felt the hand of Gar'Ath, mightiest warrior in the Company, clasp his shoulder.

Erg'Ran raised himself to his foot and peg, the tears still flowing from his eyes. Through the open tent flap, he felt the cold wind blowing from the precipice over which the falls cascaded for the last several hours. Somehow, it was colder to him now.

Struggling against the emotion engulfing him, Erg'Ran blurted out his words in staccato phrases. "The Virgin Enchant—Enchantress may not be—be dead, may have esca—escaped, may have escaped and—and if she did we need to find her immediately before her mother's—her mother's minions find her. To horse, Gar'Ath, with five—five others and I will go—go, also." Snorting back his tears, or at least attempting to do so, Erg'Ran's eyes scanned across the assembled Captains of the Company. "We must assume—" Erg'Ran cleared his throat. "We must abandon the encampment at once except for a small, highly—highly mobile unit which can escape—escape at an instant's notice when, if the Horde arrives. We will meet—meet by the old summer palace, within three days. We must assume—assume—that—Swan is—that Swan is dead."

Erg'Ran sank forward over his maps, head aching, his throat so tight that he could barely breathe, heart hammering within his chest. He wanted to say that he would somehow, no matter the cost, avenge himself on Eran, the Queen Enchantress, kill her and obliterate her hideous evil from Creath. And, if Swan were dead, whatever price he must pay, he would exact revenge. Erg'Ran wished to say all of that, but could not utter even a solitary word. He could only weep and touch his fist to his forehead, invoking the courage of Mir. . . .

Alan Garrison stood up, brushing the snow from his Levi jeans. "We're dead, right?" Maybe Swan was an angel; if looks were the benchmark for angelic nature, she was that benchmark personified.

On two sides of the barren expanse on which Garrison stood were high, snow-splotched walls of granite, mountains coursing upward to vanish within the low, heavy overcast. Behind him, the plain stretched for what seemed an interminable distance, disappearing past the horizon. Ahead of him lay a deep wood, snow accumulating heavily at its boundary, within the wood an assortment of trees both famil-iar and strange, unlike anything he had ever seen.

"We are not dead, Al'An."

"Where are we, Swan?"

"Creath."

"Where is Creath?"

Swan did not answer him, merely stood there, wrapped within her cape, its hood so obscuring her face that he could not read her expression.

The snow felt like snow, the air smelled like air. Garrison rationalized a scenario. Somehow, when the explosion came, he was knocked out, near death (unless he was really dead). The bright light had been the same light people talked about in near-death experiences. If he wasn't dead, then they had been kidnapped while unconscious, drugged perhaps, aban-doned here for some obscure reason. One of his .45s was still in its shoulder holster, the other in the waistband of his pants, where he'd placed it when he tackled William Brownwood. From their heft, the pistols were still loaded. He could check them in greater detail in a little while. His third pistol and his knives were where they belonged.

Garrison reached for his cell phone. "Where's my cell phone?"

"Cell phone?"

"The thing I was talking into," Garrison rephrased.

"Your magical advisor? You flung your magical advisor to the floor as you joined battle with your foeman there in the great hall through which all who entered passed."

"No matter. In the mountains like this, we're probably nowhere near a cell, anyway. So, tell me what's up."

Swan's right arm emerged from beneath her cape and she gestured toward the cloudy sky. "That is up. Are you well, Al'An? Was your head injured?"

"No, I knew which way up was, Swan. That's not what I meant."

"Then, you were testing me?"

"No, that's not it. What I meant to say was that I wanted you to tell me where we are and what's happened, if you know."

"Of course I know," Swan answered defensively, moving closer beside him. He could see her face quite clearly now beneath the folds of her hood. There was nothing but honesty there, honesty and loveliness. "You were about to be killed by the grenade bomb." Garrison let her English usage slide. "I summoned all of the magical energy that I could, while reciting backwards the incantation which brought me to your world from mine originally. At the same time that the grenade bomb was about to release its energy, and perhaps kill you, I brought us here. And there is probably no reason to be afraid for Alicia and Gardner and Brenda the half-cat, half-female. Before my mother's minions attacked and the Mist of Oblivion was summoned to devour my castle and all life within it, I chanced upon a spell useful in combating the energy force of a volcano. I thought that it was a clever spell and committed it to memory. I cast that spell over the grenade bomb. In the moment that my magic took us from the great hall through which all who entered passed, the grenade bomb exploded. I am certain that the spell worked. But, I could not be sure beforehand, which is why I brought us here at that moment."

Garrison frisked his pockets, found his cigarettes and his lighter. This was nuts. He placed a cigarette between his lips. His hands shook with the cold and the lighter didn't work the first time. As he made to roll the striking wheel again, his cigarette lit itself and he heard Swan laugh. "That is the easiest kind of magic. The energy is all around us; I merely direct it."

Slowly, Garrison said, "This is Creath."

"Of course it is!"

"And this magic of yours can bring us back to Atlanta?"

"Not now," Swan responded, shaking her head. "You see, Al'An, magic is measured by quality and quantity. It is something which can be temporarily exhausted and then must renew itself."

"You just lit my cigarette with magic," Garrison insisted, amazed that he said such a thing.

Swan smiled indulgently. "If you run for only a short distance, do you have trouble breathing afterward?"

"No. Even though I'm smoking, I don't do it very often and I take health and fitness very— What's running have to do with magic?"

"If you run very rapidly over a great distance, your breathing does not immediately return to the way that it was before you began to run."

"Obviously. So what?"

Swan smiled, triumphantly this time, as if she'd just taught him the meaning behind Einstein's theory of relativity. "That's how magic works, Al'An. The harder the magic, the longer it takes for the magic to return to the way it was before it was used. Just like running long and fast. But even after running long and fast, it is usually possible to take a few steps, and sometimes it is better to walk while breathing becomes normal again. Giving fire to the end of your cigarette, or anything like that is just a tiny step and simple to do, requiring virtually no energy at all."

"So, we can't go back."

"It will be a day or longer for my magical energy to be sufficiently renewed. Bringing the two of us to Creath consumed more magic than when I alone left Creath to go to your world. And, anyway, I need you to be my Champion, to fight beside me with the Company of Mir against the Horde of Koth and my mother's evil magic. That will take some time."

"Look," Garrison began. "I have—" Before saying another word to Swan, it dawned on him to question himself concerning what he really did have in his world, assuming again that he really wasn't dead or dreaming and actually had been brought to Creath. He had a job, one that he was good at (usually, at least), an important job that gave him a great deal of satisfaction, but not the job he wanted. Ever since high school, he'd been aching to get fantasy or science fiction published and he had never gotten anything finished to the point where he could even hope for a form rejection letter. Garrison had boxes of unwritten stories and novels, always jumping from one idea to the next.

The rest of his life wasn't that much more goal oriented, so far. At the insistence of his parents, after college he got a law degree. But Alan Garrison had no interest at all in being an attorney. The FBI was head-hunting healthy guys with law degrees and the next thing Garrison knew, he was a recruit under the hot sun at Quantico.

He could have used some of that hot sun in this place; Garrison's entire body was shaking now, shivering in his unlined bomber jacket with nothing but a shoulder holster, a T-shirt and his body armor underneath. Instead of asking Swan to find some way to take him back to his world, Alan Garrison bit the bullet and asked, "Is all of Creath cold like this?"

"In the winter season, yes, this part of Creath, all of the inhabited part, is cold. But it is hot in the summer, hot like Atlanta."

"Is there someplace we can go, something we could do to escape the cold?"

Swan's brow knitted with thought for a moment. "I don't have sufficient magical energy yet to cast a place-shifting spell. And my castle has ceased to exist because of the Mist of Oblivion. But—"

Swan's hands appeared from beneath her cape. She stepped toward him, so close now that their bodies almost touched, her cape falling fully open. She raised her hands to the cowl of her hood, then swept them back and down along her sides to her cape's hem, crouching so low that she was almost kneeling.

Swan rose to her full height. Her fingers seemed to vibrate slightly as she tented them together. Swan raised her clasped hands toward him, over him. He felt her hands touch at the crown of his head, move back and down along the sides of his head, his neck, along his shoulders, starting down along his arms, mimicking how she had swept her hands over her own body.

A cape began to enshroud Alan Garrison, from a deeply cowled hood over his head to the hem at his ankles. And warmth spread through him. "Thank you," Garrison told her.

"It is a very manly greatcape, not trimmed with fur like mine, Al'An. It looks well on you. Would you like a different color other than brown?"

"Brown's fine," Alan Garrison reassured her. He decided that he could try to help Swan with this champion thing that she wanted him to do, for a day or so at least, until her magic was strong enough to send him back. Or he could think of an excuse to stay for a while longer. . . .

It was nearly full darkness. The light from the twin moons would not penetrate the low, dense overcast this night. But the whiteness of the fresh snow helped to diffuse the light from the magical globe which the

Enchantress had given to him. Erg'Ran could see quite well enough to keep to the trail. In daylight, the globe seemed like an ordinary ball of heavy glass, but as night fell, it began to glow, stronger the darker the night became.

Erg'Ran slowed his dark brown mare's pace along the once well-used road leading toward the Castle of the Virgin Enchantress, reined back so that Gar'Ath's mount would come abreast of him.

Erg'Ran had to see the devastation for himself. He had to know for certain that the Mist of Oblivion had totally consumed the massive structure where Swan had lived alone for so long, in willing exile from her mother's residence at Barad'Il'Koth.

As he drew guidance from the globe's light, so did Erg'Ran draw faith from it, faith that somehow the Virgin Enchantress still lived. If she did not, how could her magic still power the globe which lit their way?

Gar'Ath drew up beside him. "Is there something wrong, old friend?" Gar'Ath tossed back the hood of his cloak, his dark hair falling free of the hood and across his shoulders. In the globe's light through the more heavily falling snow, Erg'Ran could see the younger man's face quite clearly. The smile seemed forced, but genuine; considering the circumstances this night, it was the only sort of smile that could be possible.

"We are near to leaving the wood, and from the boundary we should be able to confirm whether or not the Mist of Oblivion accomplished the Queen Sorceress's foul work. If I know the workings of her evil heart, there will be a scouting party of the Horde—at the very least—lying in wait lest we should hear of the castle's destruction and go in search of the Virgin Enchantress."

"Then we fall right into their plan, old friend. Yet, there's no choice, I think. I am with you that we must know the Virgin Enchantress's fate. And, if the castle is, indeed, vanished from the universe, she may still live."

"We cannot give up hope, Gar'Ath."

"My soul and my sword are with you, as always, old friend, however we end."

"I know that, lad. I rely on them both."

"Should I scout ahead, do you think then, Erg'Ran? One man will be less noticed than seven, I'd wager. If I come up from the far side of the plateau and stay near the rock walls, I'll have a better chance of seeing any of the Horde before they should see me. They are predictable, these bastard foemen we fight. They will expect us to come from the wood."

"Take no chances, if you do go ahead, Gar'Ath. Your plan seems a good one. But we cannot afford to lose you, tonight or ever if we are to take the fight to Barad'Il'Koth." And Erg'Ran touched his clenched fist to his forehead, invoking the courage of Mir at the thought of the evil stronghold of the Queen Sorceress.

"If I ride around to the far side, you and the others should be only a short while behind me when I get there."

"We will be there, lad."

"I'll be waiting then!" Gar'Ath's eyes were younger, stronger. He would not need the globe's light to guide him through the wood.

Gar'Ath's mount veered off the path and into the darkness.

Erg'Ran called after him hoarsely, "Not through the wood, lad! Not at night!"

But, Gar'Ath was gone, either out of earshot or choosing to ignore the warning. Since the Horde of Koth swept through the wood, all living things that remained were creatures of darkness. They might not have the courage to attack a company of seven men, or even six; but one man who strayed from the path might be too tempting for the foul beasts to resist.

Erg'Ran touched his clenched fist to his forehead once again, asking the courage of Mir to be with Gar'Ath. . . .

Swan made light appear from her left hand, to guide them through the swirling gloom: her right hand lay in the crook of Al'An's elbow. His right hand grasped one of his weapons. The wind blew more strongly and the snow fell more rapidly than before. The snow piled up in ever deeper drifts the nearer they approached to the boundary with the wood.

Once there, she would search for the track that had been the road, the track over which she had lately ridden to the miller's hut on her strongly built little white horse. The gentle creature was devoured, of course, when the Mist of Oblivion enveloped the castle and all within it.

Upon reaching the wood, Al'An and she could spend the rest of the night with some protection from the cold and wind and snow. By morning, her magic would be stronger, adequate at least to cast a place-shifting spell that would bring them to the encampment behind the Falls of Mir. And adequate to get them out of there quickly if need be. There was a strong chance that the encampment had already been attacked, or that Erg'Ran, learning of Swan's mother's use of the Mist of Oblivion, had wisely decided to break camp and go deeper into hiding. She would gamble on finding her compatriots in the Company of Mir, but only when she was strong enough should her worst fears prove out.

It was probable that her magical energy was sufficiently restored to place-shift them at this very moment. Yet if she did so, her magic would be too depleted to whisk them away again to safety should the encampment have been overrun, occupied by the Horde of Koth. That she could not risk.

She would wait.

Al'An, ready for danger as best he could be and telling her, "I have a very good reading knowledge of swords, but have never used one. You keep the sword," held one of his pistols ready still. When she had asked if it were a laser pistol, he told her, "Hardly. Aren't any laser pistols for real yet. This is the next best thing, a SIG P-220 .45 loaded with Federal Hydra-Shoks. Rest easy." He had winked his eye; it was most charming. Swan hoped that he would do so again.

Swan did not wish to dishearten him, but a mechanical device could be bewitched much more easily than a sword, which was all but impossible to be cast upon, even by means of magic as powerful as her mother's. Swan mentioned nothing at all of that to Al'An for the moment.

"Once we're in the forest, what next, Swan?"

"I must locate the track which leads to the miller's hut, Al'An."

"We're going to stay at this miller's hut place, then?"

"It is too far to travel on foot, and too dangerous a journey at night," she informed him. "I have more than enough magic to make a warm fire for us, and you needn't know how to fight with a sword to use my sword to get us more wood that might be lying about."

"Sounds like a good plan, except for one thing." Al'An laughed. Swan liked the sound. "I don't eat breakfast."

"Neither do I. What is breakfast?"

"The first meal of the day."

"Oh."

"And, I didn't eat any lunch. And, on my body at least, if my wristwatch isn't screwed up, it's after nine. I'm hungry. Can your magic make us anything to eat?"

Now, Swan laughed. Men were always hungry, at least as far as she was able to discern. She would ask him about the "wristwatch" word later, unless her language spell provided her with its meaning. As to food, she told him, "I make food appear for myself whenever I am hungry. I have the magical energy to make enough for two."

"Considering how long it's been since I've eaten, any chance that magic of yours can rustle up seconds?"

Swan had no idea what he was talking about specifically, but assumed that he was concerned with the quantity of the food that she could provide. "There will be plenty, Al'An."

As they'd walked, she'd been thinking, trying to fathom what to do after the immediate needs of shelter and reuniting with the Company of Mir were attended to. Despite her mother's vastly stronger magical abilities, magic was still magic. To summon, then direct, then dispel the Mist of Oblivion, her mother had used an inconceivable amount of magical energy. And, because of this, her mother's power would be drastically depleted for at least a day, likely longer. Much of this potentially valuable time was already lost. More would be lost while they rested for the night—and she produced food to fill Al'An's empty stomach.

But there would still be some space of time left in which she might be able to do something which would later prove useful against her mother.

The question was, what?

They were as near to the boundary as she needed to be to find the track, and the nearer they approached the deeper were the drifts of snow. Swan told Al'An that and they began searching for the track . . .

Lurking on the crest of a knoll in the darkness of the wood, the blackness of his cloak obscured by the whiteness of the snow fallen over it—he had remained all but motionless for a considerable time—Moc'Dar at last spied not only one item to capture his attention, but two.

There was movement in the deep snowdrifts along the boundary of the wood, two figures, one so tall that it had to be male, and the other, considerably less broad at the shoulder and a head shorter, almost certainly a tall female.

There was a development of interest along the track, as well.

From the hand of the figure which Moc'Dar presumed to be a woman, there emanated a light, blue-white, illuminating the couple's steps. A similar light shone from the rutted, drifted track, approaching nearer and nearer.

Moc'Dar rasped to his Yeoman Spellbreaker, "Use your pitiful magic to second-sight me what is behind the light moving along the track."

"I am not good at the second sight, my Captain. I have had very little training in its use."

Moc'Dar wished his face could have been visible to the Yeoman Spellbreaker huddled in the snow beside him. But, Moc'Dar was fully uniformed, his features hidden beneath the skintight leather battle mask of the Sword of Koth. "Try very hard, boy, as if your life were to depend upon the outcome," Moc'Dar urged him, laughing grimly.

"I, uh—I see riders ahorse. Five, my Captain."

"Very good, Yeoman. And, how are they armed?"

There was a pause, a long one, then, "Each has sword and dagger. One has a ball-headed mace. There is a great sword lashed to the saddle of one of the men. I see a poleaxe. There is a crossbow and there is a longbow with two quivers of arrows."

"And how are the horses?"

"Strong seeming, fresh enough."

Moc'Dar was fairly pleased. "Now, to the couple there moving along the boundary. See the face of the shorter one for me and tell me what manner of object is ahand to the taller figure. A weapon or what?"

"Yes, my Captain. I will try."

To try was never good enough, because in trying
one accepted the potential for failure as being on a
par with the potential for success. Moc'Dar would kill
this Yeoman Spellbreaker, perhaps. For the moment,
there were more pressing matters and he would
reserve his judgment.

"The Queen Sorceress protect me!"

"What makes you take the name of the Mistress
General of the Horde in vain, boy!?"

The Yeoman Spellbreaker's voice trembled as he
replied, "I saw her once, once only, but I could take
my oath that when the wind shifted the cowl of her
hood for a moment that I second-sighted the Virgin
Enchantress, Daughter Royal, my Captain!"

Moc'Dar said nothing. If the boy was right, the boy
would live. If not, the boy would die. So far, the boy
seemed to be doing well enough that he might,
indeed, survive the moment.

"The man with her, Yeoman. Second-sight me what
you can tell of him. Before, I asked if a weapon is
in his hand."

Moc'Dar waited.

The young Yeoman Spellbreaker began to speak,
his hushed tones barely audible over the keening of
the wind. "If it is a weapon, my Captain, it is unlike
any that I have seen. It is some strange device. I know
not what."

"What do you see of the man holding it?"

"He is tall, like you, my Captain. Beneath his great
cape, I thought that I glimpsed odd raiment covering
his legs. He moves powerfully through the snowdrifts.
The woman with him holds tightly to his elbow."

If the Virgin Enchantress had not been consumed
by the Mist of Oblivion, what was she doing so long
afterward—a full day—tramping about near the
boundary of the wood with a strange man beside her?
This man, Moc'Dar mused, might prove very interesting to question.

With Moc'Dar, not counting the Yeoman Spell-breaker who was borrowed from an ordinary unit within the Horde, were twelve from the Sword of Koth, more than enough men to handle five from the Company of Mir (doubtlessly the origin of the five riders approaching along the track). But the presence of the Virgin Enchantress, with her very powerful magic, altered the equation considerably.

Did he dare attack, or should he follow his orders to the rune and only observe?

The Queen Sorceress, when personally charging him with this foray, had not said to avoid engagement, only that his purpose was to closely watch the plain where lately the castle of the Virgin Enchantress had been.

If he could strike quickly, Moc'Dar reasoned, he could capture alive at least one, likely two from the Company of Mir. Should his own methods of persuasion fail somehow to loosen the captives' tongues, the Queen Sorceress's ministrations would not fail. Success here could lead to the speedy and permanent obliteration of the Company of Mir. If he did not act, it was inevitable that the Virgin Enchantress and her enigmatic companion would join with the five riders—perhaps this was a planned rendezvous—and all hope of seizing a prisoner for interrogation would be gone.

Moc'Dar's decision was made.

In a future time, Moc'Dar mused, there would be some magical spell much like the second sight, but one which would enable a commander to talk with those who served under him while they were positioned for battle, a way in which whispered words might travel through the very air.

For now, however, there was the Action Cord. Carefully, disturbing as little as possible the snow camouflaging him, Moc'Dar unwound the black cord from the spike he'd driven into the snowy ground when he'd first taken his position.

Moc'Dar tugged on the Action Cord, a series of long and short pulses, the Action Cord Code that each new recruit to the Queen's Sword of Koth had to commit to memory within a single night or suffer a hideous death the next morning. Moc'Dar applauded the skillful use of subtle incentives to bring out the best in a man.

The message he sent read, "This is Moc'Dar. Every second Sword of Koth joins me beneath the Ka'B'Oo tree at the edge of the boundary near the track. Move with silence and stealth. No fireswords. Enemy forces nearby. Ends." Moc'Dar relashed the Action Cord to its stake.

Moc'Dar's lieutenant, Bog'Luc, would hold to his operational orders and hold this position, continuing to observe. "Go to Bog'Luc, Yeoman," Moc'Dar ordered. "With stealth. Inform the lieutenant of the details you have reported with the second sight. Serve Bog'Luc well. Go!"

"Yes, my Captain."

The Yeoman Spellbreaker was up and moving with surprising rapidity. Moc'Dar would have laughed at him had there been the time. Instead, he too was up and moving through the wood, battleaxe in hand. A firesword's red gleaming steel would alert the Company of Mir.

Moc'Dar reached the small bower overhung by the enormous branches of the Ka'B'Oo, the track lying only a few warblades beyond it. Soundlessly, first one, then another, then soon all six of the Sword of Koth he had summoned were with him there.

His voice low, Moc'Dar rapidly issued his orders. "You three will cross the track. Five men from the Company of Mir, all ahorse, well armed. They move along the track beyond the glow of light. They are perhaps five lancethrows back. Move with speed and stealth. Standard ambush pattern at contact after confirmation. Be wary, lest the Virgin Enchantress, who is about some distance from here along the boundary with the wood, should hear and alert them with her magic. I want prisoners who can be made to talk. Questions?"

There were none.

"Remember, axes only and silence at all cost. Be about it then, Sword of Koth!"

The three he had designated to cross the track moved first, disappearing soundlessly among the trees. Moc'Dar gauged the time that it would take them, then summoned the three who remained with him to follow him, paralleling the track, deeper into the wood, toward the light from the five riders. . . .

Erg'Ran cautioned his four companions, "Weapons close and ready, lads. We near the boundary."

There was no way to exactly judge the distance, one stretch of the track looking so very much like another, but he had a good feel for the time which had so far passed along the track. Based on that Erg'Ran gauged them to be under four lancethrows from the boundary of the wood and plain.

Gar'Ath was somewhere out there in the snowy darkness, perhaps overseeing their progress, perhaps observing a Sword of Koth scouting party. If there were such a force lying in wait for them, Gar'Ath would warn his companions, or surely die in the trying.

When Erg'Ran chopped off his foot, his balance in the wielding of a weapon had somehow been altered for the worse. In his youth, he was a fair hand with a sword, although his skills approached not at all those of Gar'Ath. No one's did. Since the loss of his foot, Erg'Ran (although he still wore a sword) had taken to using the very implement by means of which he'd lost his foot. He carried an axe. Its shaft, carved from the trunk of a stout Ka'B'Oo, was just less than five spans in length. Its head, of the finest hand-wrought steel, measured two spans from the tip of the dorsal spike to the outermost arc of the curved blade.

Many men would name their weapons, but Erg'Ran did not. It was his axe, and that was all. He longed for the day when its only purpose would be that of a decoration over the hearth of some pleasantly remote cottage.

They continued along the track, Erg'Ran riding at the little column's head, periodically craning his neck to reassure himself that the rearmost man—young Bin'Ah—had not been taken by surprise.

So far, there was no cause for concern, and this concerned Erg'Ran quite a bit. It would be impossible to imagine the Queen Sorceress not sending out a scouting party. So, where were her minions?

As Erg'Ran looked back once more, the answer came to him: Bin'Ah was swept from his stout red mare and into the shadows, the gleam of an axe blade caught for an instant in the light from the globe.

"They attack!" Erg'Ran shouted to the remaining three of the company, wheeling his horse about so suddenly that the ordinarily sure-footed creature nearly went down under him.

Sword of Koth swept at them from the shadows, four of them, axes only. Why did they not use their fireswords? There would have to be a reason, but there was no time to worry it. A giant of a man, black cowled hood over black battle mask, charged toward Erg'Ran, axe swinging for the legs of Erg'Ran's mare.

This was a captive hunt, not a murder raid!

Erg'Ran's axe was just as quick, and stronger, its long downstroke hesitating only an instant as it severed the other axe's shaft, the axe head flying. Its flat struck hard against Erg'Ran's right thigh and he winced with pain. The giant Sword of Koth who'd wielded the axe threw his body weight against the mare. The horse fell, Erg'Ran spilling from his saddle, nearly pinned.

Unhorsed, his axe flown from his fist, Erg'Ran drew back, reaching in desperation for his sword.

The giant Sword of Koth had the greatsword carried by Fo'Len only an instant earlier. How he had gotten it was no mystery. Another Sword of Koth stood over the fallen Fo'Len, axe dripping blood, readying for a second, killing strike.

The greatsword swung and stopped, a span only from Erg'Ran's throat. "Yield, old man!"

There was the whooshing sound of steel against air, then the crack of bone. The head of the Sword of Koth who had been about to finish Fo'Len separated from its body, flew into the darkness. "I don't think he's wanting to do what you suggest, you evil black-masked bastard!" In the same breath as his words, Gar'Ath's sword swung into the light, interposed itself between the greatsword and Erg'Ran's throat, arced upward along the greatsword's blade flat and forced the greatsword up and away. "Why don't you try me, hmm? Maybe you'll have better luck than your headless friend did."

"I am Moc'Dar, Captain Leader of the Third Company Sword of Koth, Elite Guard to the Mistress General of the Horde. You should know the name of the man who kills you!"

"That's an awful lot you're asking a simple country lad like myself to remember, Captain. But, if it's proper manners to know the name of the man who kills you, then I'd better tell you my name, and rather quickly, too!" As Gar'Ath spoke, he lunged, Moc'Dar's stolen greatsword making to parry the thrust, but Gar'Ath's sword was not where Moc'Dar had thought it would be.

Gar'Ath, gleaming bastard sword flying in his fingers, was the embodiment of grace and strength, the perfect coordination of every aspect of body and nature, death incarnate, magnificent to behold. And, Gar'Ath knew it and laughed about it. He was that way.

Gar'Ath had sidestepped, forcing Moc'Dar to move off balance in the attempt to recover. Gar'Ath's sword was still in motion, never stopping, with elegant fluidity executing a drawcut across Moc'Dar's right forearm and wrist. The greatsword spilled from Moc'Dar's hands as blood spilled from Moc'Dar's arm. Gar'Ath wheeled, his blade arcing hungrily for Moc'Dar's throat.

But there were suddenly two more Sword of Koth springing from the darkness.

"Beware!" Erg'Ran shouted, the time for being an enrapt spectator ended.

Moc'Dar fell back into shadow as Gar'Ath changed the vector of his blade, for an instant only parrying one enemy's axe. Gar'Ath dropped to one knee, disengaged from the first of the two Sword of Koth; on the back swing, Gar'Ath's sword opened the second man from crotch to chest. Gar'Ath threw himself to the side, the already dead man's axe cleaving downward into the ground. Gar'Ath thrust the heavy pommel of his sword forward, into the abdomen of his remaining foeman. As Gar'Ath rose to his full height, his fist then hammered upward into the Sword of Koth's face. Gar'Ath backstepped, both hands gripping the sword's hilt as Gar'Ath arced the blade downward from and through his foeman's shoulder, slicing deeply through chest and belly.

There was not a pause in the blade's motion, steel arcing through night air, searching for engagement. There was none.

Erg'Ran, axe in hand again, shouted, "Bin'Ah—we must find him if he lives!"

"Oh, he lives all right, but there's a bump on Bin'Ah's hard skull big enough to remind us all of this night's misadventure for a quite a goodly time to come."

"Usually," Erg'Ran began, collecting his wits and calming his breathing, "the smallest Sword of Koth scouting party is comprised of ten line warriors, a master warrior, a lieutenant and a captain, not to mention a spellbreaker. I know you don't like my asking, but—"

"These two, the one who was about to finish Fo'Len, the one who unhorsed Bin'Ah. Add in that big bastard of a captain who ran off, and there's another dead one over there. That's six accounted for."

"There are eight left, nine if the captain survives his wound well enough to fight."

Erg'Ran turned away from Gar'Ath, getting down awkwardly to his knees beside Fo'Len. Another of the company already attended the man, but he would not live through the night. "The castle is gone, vanished, every stone of it," Gar'Ath supplied, unbidden. "But at the same time that I spied these Sword of Koth moving against you, I saw a man and a woman trudging through the drifts along the boundary of the wood. Perhaps the Virgin Enchantress lives. Who the man could be, I cannot say. Under the circumstances, old friend, I think we should take horse and ride to intercept this couple before the Sword of Koth chooses to do so."

Erg'Ran nodded his agreement, then shouted his orders. "Bin'Ah—you help watching over our good lad here. We'll not abandon Fo'Len until his spirit has gone from him. And then we'll not leave his body here for the creatures to sport with." Erg'Ran looked at his men in the light from the globe. Exhausted, frightened half out of their wits they looked. "Gar'Ath and I will ride on alone. If we are not back by sunrise, go to the rendezvous point." Erg'Ran was not about to mention where that was, since one of the Sword of Koth could be hidden, listening somewhere out in the darkness of the wood.

Erg'Ran intended to leave the light sphere with those who waited behind, but before doing so he swept its beam over Gar'Ath. There was a darkening bruise near his left temple, and a redness leading down to his cheek. The left sleeve of Gar'Ath's black shirt clung to Gar'Ath's arm by blood alone, a long but not terribly deep gash leading from his shoulder halfway to his elbow. Gar'Ath swung his cloak round his body. "None of those wounds are from the fighting here, are they lad?"

Gar'Ath smiled wickedly. "The creatures of the wood had a mind to eat me, it appeared. I didn't let them." He laughed.

Erg'Ran told him in a fatherly way, "We'll get a healer to look at that gash, lest it become fouled with sickness. Now," and he looked around to the others of the company, "would somebody please help a peg-legged old man to get mounted?"

Bin'Ah, of the great bump on the head, accomplished that, and as Erg'Ran eased up into the saddle, he told the fellow, "You and the others keep a watchful guard. There are at least eight of the many abroad in the darkness. Be vigilant!"

Gar'Ath swung effortlessly into the saddle, and Erg'Ran and his brash young swordsman friend were off along the rutted track. They held their animals to a tight rein, lest one of the horses should move too quickly and break a leg. . . .

"I felt it when one of them used the second sight. Looking at us." Swan whispered, her lips close to Alan Garrison's ear. "It was probably a new Yeoman Spellbreaker, because normally the second sight isn't felt. The only time it is felt is when whoever's using it isn't very good at it. Yet."

Without warning, Swan had jerked at his elbow. "Remain perfectly still while I cast a shadow spell. Then come with me quickly."

Since he'd had no idea what she was talking about, there had been no sense arguing.

The shadow spell turned out to be a remarkable thing. And Swan's magic seemed so essentially effortless. Alan Garrison had grown up watching reruns of Barbara Eden folding her arms and doing shoulder shimmies, Elizabeth Montgomery crinkling her nose, but Swan's magic was nothing like that. And, so far, the results hadn't proven humorous. They were, however, effective. Her shadow spell, however Swan did it, created two vaporous-looking replicas of his shape and hers, black and featureless but perfectly formed.

Swan evidently held the shadow beings in perfect synchronization with their bodies as they began again to labor their way through the snowdrifts. Then, as they passed a singularly heavily trunked tree, Swan whispered to him, "Hide here with me quickly, Al'An."

Garrison did as he was told, looking back, was amazed to see the shadow shapes continuing onward, as if they had somehow taken over in the search for the road leading through the wood.

When Garrison asked, "How are you controlling those things?" Swan responded only with a smile. He could barely see that, because the light which had lit their way had ceased to emanate from Swan's left palm. Instead, a literally disembodied light was visible from the hand of her shadow counterpart. "We've been spotted," Garrison said, stating the obvious. "Where and how many?"

She told him she had no idea how many persons watched them, but she was certain that they would be warriors in the Sword of Koth, her mother's elite guard. The "where" would be a knoll, itself barely visible through the swirling snow, perhaps two hundred yards distant as Garrison judged the range. Too great a distance for a pistol, at least in his hands.

"We can't stay behind this tree forever," Garrison told her. "Can't you make us invisible or something, so that we can move without them seeing us?"

"Invisibility is not part of nature, and such magic as that requires spell-casting of the most difficult type—it would consume virtually all of the magical energy remaining to me. The same would be true if I were to spell-cast those who watch us, so that they alone could not see us. Anyway, I don't quite know where they are or how many of them there might be. But whoever second sights us will likely continue to observe the shadows which I summoned. Before it is realized that these are shadows only, we can hatch a plan."

This wasn't an opportune time for Theory of Magic 101, but Garrison had to ask her, "What do you mean when you say that you summoned the shadows?"

"They are our shadows. Now, the light is so dim that we cast no shadows. But our shadows are a reality, only unseen because of circumstance. I merely summoned the shadows from the darkness by means of light. The summoning wasn't hard, but separating them from ourselves takes some continuing effort. I cannot maintain the magic for more than a short while longer, Al'An."

Guessing from Swan's remarks that they had been spotted some twenty minutes earlier, that allowed plenty of time for her enemies—his enemies, for the moment at least—to have done any number of things. Garrison had no military background, but was well familiar with the concept of an envelopment, in this case the bad guys circling around behind the good guys in order to get the good guys caught in a crossfire. Anybody who had ever watched a western movie knew that much of small unit tactics. Garrison loved Westerns.

The key element to surviving an envelopment was to be someplace else besides where the bad guys thought their prey would be when they struck. Evidently, there was some equivalent to the western movie on Creath, because what Swan whispered in Garrison's ear perfectly echoed his own thoughts. "We need to betake ourselves from here, into the wood, so that if there is an attempt to trap us, we will be out of the trap before it closes."

The snowdrifts were no deeper where they were than anywhere else. Garrison suggested, "How about entering the forest right here? Shall we?"

Helping her to manage the highest of the drifts while still attempting to stay crouched and low, Garrison started forward, Swan beside him.

Once beyond the boundary where the vast, empty plain behind them met the forested area ahead of them, the drifts were considerably lower and the going was easier. "There are evil creatures which dwell here, the further from the track, the greater their strength. Be cautious, Al'An."

"Are you any good with that sword?" Garrison asked Swan, mainly to get her mind off boogie-creatures and monsters and stuff.

"For a woman, yes."

"That's a sexist attitude toward your own gender, isn't it? What I've read about sword fighting—unless you're talking the really big two-handers—always made me think it was more a matter of skill than strength alone."

"Yes, but a woman ordinarily has other skills that she must learn to ply beyond combat, and there is less opportunity to practice for combat. I acquit myself well enough, Al'An."

It dawned on Garrison that she must be getting a much better handle on English, because she hadn't been asking as many of her weird questions, such as, "What is shit?" That was a really good one. He'd have to get Swan to do a language spell on him so that he could become fluent in something like Japanese or Chinese. Either language would be a real plus for his career with the Bureau—if he stayed with the Justice Department.

They were several yards within the treeline, visibility poor. Garrison thought he heard something. He ceased all movement but placing a finger to his lips in what he hoped was a universal symbol for silence. Very slowly, he edged down from a crouch to his knees, Swan did the same.

He had heard something. Hearing it again, he recognized the sound as a voice. Waiting, listening, barely breathing, Garrison realized that there were two voices, speaking to one another in hushed tones. They grew almost imperceptibly louder, nearer. Garrison's right fist balled tightly around the butt of his pistol.

There was something odd, odder still than anything he had so far endured. He could understand these voices, about every third or fourth word. That should have been impossible, however he did, as clearly as if—

Garrison turned abruptly on his knees in the snow beside Swan, almost shouting aloud. His hands went to her shoulders. Her eyes glanced toward the pistol, then back into his. Swan's eyes were the most beautiful eyes he had ever seen.

Evidently, Swan heard the voices as well. There was an impish look in her eyes, then she shrugged her eyebrows and her lower lip looked pouty. He'd never noticed her lower lip looking that way before. She shrugged her shoulders under his hands, then smiled broadly.

Garrison heard one of the voices almost perfectly clearly now, however subdued. ". . . says that the only way to take the life of the Enchantress is for all of us to rush her. I will do as my Captain orders me; but, by the Queen Sorceress, I hope Moc'Dar is right."

"Some of us may perish, Gol'Hoc, but she cannot magic us all at once. And whoever is the man accompanying her, he is likely not a sorcerer, merely mortal."

"She is powerful, this Enchantress, or otherwise

how did she survive the Mist of . . ." The last word faded off.

The sounds of boots softly crunching snow faded as well.

There were two questions Alan Garrison had to ask Swan, and immediately. His left hand pushed back her hood far enough that his lips almost touched her ear. "Did you use a language spell on me without asking me?" Garrison whispered emphatically.

"Yes. It seemed the best thing to do under the circumstances. I can lift it in an eyeblink, should you prefer, Al'An."

Garrison was tempted to tell Swan just that, but being able to use the language here would be an asset while he was here, wherever here was. Garrison asked his second question. "Why do they talk about me as just mortal? Are you not mortal?"

"I would only die after the course of many human lifetimes. I am as human as you, but it is the magic which prolongs my life. I have never been truly sick, though I've had aches in my head or my belly. I feel other pain, hope someday to know the pain of child-bearing. I broke a toe once, but it healed within a day. Had I used my magic, the bone would have grown together instantly. The magic lets me cure myself—and others, too—for the reason that I told you. Most magic is only the acceleration of what would happen naturally. And I heal myself even if I am unaware of being ill. In that way, I am not mortal at all. Were someone or something to take my life— then I am as mortal as you, Al'An," Swan whispered back, her lips beside his cheek.

Garrison was tempted to try the old movie routine, and ask her to pinch him so that he would wake up. Logical fallacies inherent to the idea aside, it never worked in the movies. And, if he were to awake and she were gone— The thought made him momentarily as cold as he had been before she magically wove the warm hooded cloak which he wore. Garrison started to speak, but Swan held a finger to her lips now, her eyes staring off in the direction the men belonging to the voices had taken. She turned to Garrison quickly. "I used the second sight. They are Sword of Koth, those two. There should be thirteen or more of them. We must leave this place."

Garrison started to agree with her, but stopped as he heard the soft beating of horse's hooves. Swan heard it, too.

Swan stared toward the new sounds. A smile lit her face with a radiance beyond any he had seen there since coming to Creath.

Little girl-like, Swan whispered, "It is Erg'Ran, and Gar'Ath! Erg'Ran is the smartest man who ever lived, I think. And Gar'Ath the finest and bravest swordsman who ever lived. They have come to aid us, Al'An, to follow you, my Champion!" And she kissed Garrison on the cheek.

The smartest guy ever. The best swordsman ever. Under his breath, Garrison posed the rhetorical question he hoped no one would hear. "And these guys are gonna follow me?"

Swan crept past him, toward the sounds of hoofbeats. Garrison crept after her, to meet his troops. . . .

Surrounded by trees and on the far side of the track from where the Sword of Koth were apparently positioned, the snow falling much more heavily now and muffling sound, Swan, Al'An, Erg'Ran and Gar'Ath were able to stand and talk freely for a few moments, with little fear of detection. Al'An offered his open right hand to Erg'Ran. The gesture was slightly different here, but Al'An's meaning was unmistakable. "Alan Garrison, Special Agent, Federal Bureau of Investigation, United States Department of Justice, USA, Earth."

Erg'Ran took Al'An's hand and held it. "I am

Erg'Ran, Counselor to the Virgin Enchantress, Daughter Royal, Princess of Creath; Chief Scribe, the Company of Mir; acting Commander of the Host since the death of Ir'Ba, Commander General. You are the one, then, the Champion."

Gar'Ath mimicked Al'An's hand gesture. Erg'Ran released Al'An's hand and Gar'Ath clasped it. "I am Gar'Ath, Champion! You can count my sword as yours, and my life."

Al'An laughed, saying, "Look, guys. Just call me Alan, okay? Otherwise, I'm gonna start thinking you're confusing me with Gene Autry's horse."

"I do not understand the reference, Champion. Forgive my ignorance," Erg'Ran said.

Gar'Ath interjected, "I'd be more of a mind to debate this name over that after we take care of the bastards—forgive my slip of the tongue, Enchantress—the lads lying in wait for us."

"Gar'Ath is right, Champion," and Erg'Ran turned to face Swan. "Enchantress, although I do not wish to further jeopardize you, especially after almost losing you to the Mist of Oblivion, I must agree with our swordsman friend. If you are of a mind to use magic to aid us, we could fight them a few at a time."

"My magical energy is sorely depleted, Erg'Ran, so I can do but little, hopefully enough. My sword arm is unaffected, however. What is the plan?"

"Champion will need a stout blade, Enchantress," Gar'Ath suggested. Unsheathing his sword and turning toward Al'An, he offered, "Take mine. There's no other like it in the Land, Champion!"

Swan was proud of Al'An as he answered. "I am not a swordsman, and I would not risk dishonoring such a blade, despite my best intentions. I have weapons in which I, also, hold great store. You've honored me, Gar'Ath."

Gar'Ath resheathed, shrugged his shoulders, then

asked, "So? How do we go about killing those nasty—
uh—men?"

"We arrest them, then let a jury decide their fate,"
Al'An informed them, as if such procedures were
commonplace here.

"You propose, Champion," Erg'Ran inquired, "that
we should attempt to take captive Sword of Koth,
alive?"

Al'An answered, "If they resist to the point where
deadly force is justified, then that will be their choice,
not ours."

Gar'Ath seemed about to speak, but Swan noticed
that he held his tongue. Such restraint was uncharacteristic of Gar'Ath, and extraordinarily wise at the
moment.

They formed their plan, such as it was, that she
would create a diversion, once the main body of the
Sword of Koth was located. With eight or nine the
most likely number to be dealt with, the Sword of
Koth would send three of their number to hold the
track more deeply in the wood, keeping the horses,
as well. Meanwhile, the rest of their force would lie
in wait to make an assault on what they should still
assume were herself and her companion.

Maintaining the shadow spell was wearisome,
depleting Swan's magical energy to the point of
physical exhaustion. She judged that, after releasing
the spell, she should be able to cast something which
would divert attention long enough to give herself and
the others the element of surprise. After that, there
would be nothing left of her magical energy.

Moving cautiously, without light, as soundlessly as
they could, they set out. Horses tethered well away
from the track (and hopefully out of harm's way from
the evil creatures of the wood), they clambered over
the steadily heightening drifts at the boundary between
wood and plain. At one point, where the mounds of
snow were nearly to the height of her waist, Al'An

gallantly swept her up into his powerful arms, carrying her. Al'An's touch stirred things within her which
she had never experienced, making her feel at once
embarrassed yet wonderfully happy, despite the grim
purpose for their travel.

They exited the wood well over a hundred warblades distant from the track, moving slowly, stealthily.

The second sight—that was a skill, not magic—
allowed her to see the positions taken by the Sword
of Koth. There were five in all at the point where
the track left the wood and met the plain. Erg'Ran
had mentioned that Gar'Ath grievously wounded the
Sword of Koth captain, one named Moc'Dar. One of
the five held a battleaxe in his left hand, right arm
heavily bandaged. This would be Moc'Dar.

There were horses for none of the Sword of Koth
save Moc'Dar, the beast perfectly still, lying beside
Moc'Dar in the snow. The animal, to be so quiet
and unmoving, would have to be a Rac'Ar'Kar, spell-
changed by the Queen Sorceress to be perfectly
obedient to the will of its master. There were few
such animals, and that Moc'Dar had been given such
a great gift by the Queen Sorceress spoke well of
his success in battle and the esteem in which he
was held.

Swan signaled halt, huddled with the three men
who were her companions and whispered to them
what she had seen with the second sight.

Erg'Ran nodded. Gar'Ath rubbed his hands along
his stockinged thighs, flexed his long fingers, then
soundlessly drew his sword.

Erg'Ran, who had been using his axe as a staff to
assist him in walking, set the weapon down and began
to cock the prod of a crossbow.

Al'An nodded his understanding, drawing from
beneath his cloak and the bomber jacket under it a
small book covered in leather. But as he opened it,
it proved to be no book at all. Pinned within it was

a golden object emblazoned with the runes of his world, and other symbols as well. Al'An opened the pin clasp, removed the object from its cover, then pinned the object to his cloak, over his heart.

If this were some magical talisman to protect him in battle, Swan could not feel its energy. Attributing this to her temporarily weakened powers, she promised herself to ask Al'An about it later.

Al'An took first one, then another pistol from within his clothes.

Gar'Ath stared at these in amazement, as did Erg'Ran. Al'An smiled, raising his thumbs from the pistols and gesturing skyward. A battle ritual of Al'An's world, perhaps.

They started moving again, closer and closer to the track. Ahead, Swan could make out the shadows she had spell summoned. Soon, Moc'Dar and his Sword of Koth would see the shadows for what they were, and Swan could release the spell, create her diversion. And, if her magical energy were sufficient, she had just the perfect distraction in mind. . . .

Erg'Ran, crouched as low to the snow cover as he could while yet retaining hope of being able to stand unaided, waited. And, he wondered. The Champion was not what he had expected. To be sure, he'd had no definite idea in mind, but still. The Champion Al'An was tall, broad of shoulder, yes, but not particularly formidable seeming. The strange attire visible beneath his cloak when he'd unsheathed his weapons was unlike anything Erg'Ran had ever seen. What were those things covering the Champion's legs, a type of heavy stocking?

And the weapons! Objects little over a span in length, with no visible blade. They were not magical, but technological. Such technology was unknown to him, so he tried to resist being critical out of ignorance. But what could these objects do?

Erg'Ran had the feeling that he would find out, and very soon. His crossbow ready, it was the Champion who would signal the attack.

Erg'Ran waited.

The shadows that Swan had spell-summoned vanished. There was movement from the hiding positions of the Sword of Koth. Where the shadows had seemed to walk an instant earlier the air pulsed, a vortex forming a few spans above the ground, rising higher and higher. From within the vortex a tongue of flame appeared, licking into the wood, vanishing with a crack like thunder. Swan's diversion was spectacular to behold, however brief its duration. And it served its purpose. The five Sword of Koth, their Captain included, appeared momentarily hypnotized by the image.

A strange battle cry now echoed through the wood. The Champion rose from behind a snow-blanketed dead fallen Ka'B'Oo, shouting, "FBI! Federal Officer! Freeze! You are all under arrest!"

The mysterious objects called pistols were clenched in the Champion's hands, pointed toward the Sword of Koth.

No one moved, neither Erg'Ran with his crossbow, Gar'Ath with longbow or sword, nor Swan.

The villainous Sword of Koth, including their Captain, Moc'Dar, remained motionless as well. Somehow, despite their features being wholly masked save for eyeslits, mouth and nostril holes, the enemy gave the appearance of being weirdly perplexed.

The Champion took a solitary step forward.

Moc'Dar bellowed the order, "Kill him!"

The enemy nearest the Champion, red glowing firesword in hand, lunged. The Champion Al'An spun toward his attacker, shouted, "Halt! Drop that weapon or I'll fire!" The Champion backstepped as his attacker charged.

A tongue of flame, like that Erg'Ran witnessed in

Swan's diversion, spat from the front of the pistol. In the same instant, the Champion's foeman was hurtled backward, sprawling to the ground, lifeblood spilling into the snow.

Erg'Ran touched his clenched fist to his forehead, invoking the courage of Mir.

Moc'Dar shouted, "Withdraw! Withdraw!" His great black mount rose from the snow beside him, and Moc'Dar, despite his injury, sprang into the saddle. The Roc'Ar'Kar leapt into stride, a hail of snow and dirt and rock thrown up in its hooves' wake.

The three remaining Sword of Koth sprinted from their positions, making for the track. An arrow whistled from Gar'Ath's longbow, piercing the throat of one of them. Erg'Ran brought the crossbow to his shoulder and fired, his bolt burrowing deep into the chest of still another. Swan, not to be outdone, stepped into the third enemy's path, sword raised in challenge. "Hold villain, or show steel!" Swan cried.

The Sword of Koth unsheathed firesword from scabbard to test her steel.

The Champion, his cloak gone from his shoulders, angled toward the firesword-armed enemy. Would one of his pistols spit the deathflame again, Erg'Ran wondered?

But the Champion's pistols were nowhere to be seen.

In the blinking of an eye, the Champion fell upon his enemy, the Champion's body lunging toward its target in a manner strange, yet very impressive to behold. Both feet vaulted from the ground, then hammered against his foeman's upper body. Firesword tumbling from black gauntleted hand, the Sword of Koth collapsed into the snow, but only for an instant. As he jumped to his feet, the Champion wheeled about in a half circle, one foot kicking the Sword of Koth in the ribs, then the other raising, kicking his opponent in the stomach, then in the chest, then the groin, each alternating blow hammering the Sword of Koth back and back. Springing fully into the air again, the Champion kicked his foeman square in the chest with both feet, simultaneously. The stunned Sword of Koth reeled, dropping like a felled tree beneath a final axe blow as the Champion's left fist, then his right punched his foeman's face.

As if in the same motion, the Champion Al'An fell to one knee beside the vanquished foeman, rolled him over onto his chest, then wrestled his hands behind him. Strange manacles emerged from beneath the Champion's even stranger garb, a leather doublet but unlike any Erg'Ran had seen. Clamping the manacles to the wrists of his fallen adversary, the Champion Al'An began reciting a litany, perhaps an invocation of thanks for triumph in battle, but strange to hear. "You have the right to remain silent," it began.

# Chapter Five

"Speak to me of this weapon which kills with the kiss of fire, Moc'Dar."

On one knee before the Sorceress Queen, Mistress General of the Horde, his eyes lowered in her presence, Moc'Dar began, "It is terrible and wondrous, Mistress General. It is small, not much over a span in length. There is a magical summoning, perhaps to invoke the fire, Mistress General."

"What words does my daughter's new friend use, Moc'Dar?"

"Clearly, the word which was alone was the magical summoning, the other words a warning that the Sword of Koth who was about to attack should lay down his firesword, Mistress General."

"The word, Moc'Dar," Eran insisted, keeping her voice low and level and even, almost soothingly compassionate, patient.

"It sounded like he said 'Halt,' but that cannot be, Mistress General."

"Perhaps, Moc'Dar, it was not magic at all, but an implement of technology. Kneel there while I explore the concept," Eran commanded. "The stone is cold and hard and rough, good for discipline."

"Yes, Mistress General."

Eran turned abruptly on her heel, skirts swirling round her ankles, leaving Moc'Dar to wait in discomfort. The place-shifting spell which Eran had used to travel from Barad'Il'Koth to Moc'Dar's command post had wearied her, her magical energy not yet fully restored from summoning, then controlling the Mist of Oblivion. "Little over a span in length, a tongue of flame. Hmm," she cooed. From her spell bag, placed on Moc'Dar's map table when she arrived, Eran withdrew something little longer than a span's length. It was hard to the touch as her fingers stroked across it. She raised it to view and turned to face Moc'Dar again.

"Was the wondrous and terrible weapon anything like this, Moc'Dar?"

He raised his gaze to hers, his eyes widening beneath his black leather mask. And he almost fell back as she pointed it at him. "Very—very much like that, Mistress General."

"This is called a 1911A1, Moc'Dar. Do you want to see it spit fire, or do you wish to go on living in some lesser capacity than a human man? You have served me well, so I give you that choice. Choose carefully and wisely, Moc'Dar. But quickly."

He paused, his body visibly trembling. At last, his voice subdued, he spoke. "Whatever is your will, Mistress General. That is my choice, only to serve your will."

Eran pursed her lips. She could not decide this so easily. "As you know, Moc'Dar, I have plenty of horses, although I'm certain that you'd be an excellent mount. I must think. Stay on your knee. In fact, prostrate yourself there on the flagstones in obeisance to me while I ponder your fate."

"Yes, Mistress General," Moc'Dar responded, laying

his body facedown on the stone, arms outstretched
to either side, not daring to look up. He looked quite
ridiculous, and she liked that.

Still holding the item which she had taken from
her spell bag, Eran slowly began to pace about the
room, stopping after a time, beside Moc'Dar, raising
one booted foot and letting it rest on his neck. "The
object which spits fire, as you described it Moc'Dar,
is called a pistol. The flame that you witnessed is not
magic, but merely the flash from the burning of a
mixture of natural elements. The loud noise which
you doubtless heard, but failed to mention, is also
a natural result of these elements interacting. What
killed your Sword of Koth was not magic, either. It
was something that is called a bullet. This is, to help
you understand it, a very much advanced version of
a crossbow, but rather than the tension of the released
prod propelling the missile forward to its target with
killing force, it is the pressure from the burning of
these natural elements which I mentioned. If you
understand what I have said, kiss my boot."

Moc'Dar turned his head—the motion was visibly
awkward for him, because her other foot still rested
on his neck—and he kissed her right boot.

"So, you see, Moc'Dar, you ran away from something quite natural, not magical. What to do with you!
My boots are soiled, Moc'Dar. You may rise to your
knees and lick them clean for me while I continue
to ponder your fate. But do not speak." Eran removed
her foot from his neck.

Silently, Moc'Dar rose to his knees, his tongue
flicking against the sparkling leather of her boots.

"Keep cleaning until I tell you that you may stop,
Moc'Dar." Resting her elbow in the palm of her hand,
Eran cocked her head back and contemplated
Moc'Dar's punishment. He had always been the most
ruthless of the Sword of Koth. That was something
in his favor. But, of course, his punishment had to

be spectacular, a lesson to others of the Sword of Koth, and of the Horde of which the Sword of Koth was the elite. So it had to be an enduring punishment.

An idea came to her in the very moment that she looked down on him and took notice of the diligence with which he licked her boots.

"You may stop licking my boots, Moc'Dar. Raise your eyes to look at me, but do not speak."

Moc'Dar obeyed.

Eran had never had a male body servant before. Of course, when he took up those duties, he wouldn't be quite as male as he was now. Yet, the idea had a sort of appeal to it.

"I have determined your fate, Moc'Dar," Eran began. . . .

Alan Garrison sat in the snow under what he had learned was a Ka'B'Oo tree. The things were enormous.

Force of habit had made him act like he was taught to act when he went through Special Agent training. What did these people in another world, or maybe another universe, care if someone flashed a badge and shouted, "Freeze!" Alan Garrison had never killed a man before, in any universe. And, he could not help but think that his ineptitude in handling a unique situation had brought about that man's death.

Swan approached, her boots packed with snow. Garrison looked up, saw her face smiling down at him from within the folds of her hood. She dropped to her knees in the snow beside him. "How are you feeling, Al'An?"

"I'm angry with myself."

"No Sword of Koth has ever been taken alive, captured. You have done the impossible."

"All I did was deck somebody and bust him. That wasn't much. I'm an idiot."

Swan's pretty eyes widened in amazement. "How could you speak so cruelly about yourself, Al'An? You are—"

"All the time I've been with the Bureau," he began, interrupting her, "I've always figured that guys like my boss, Matt Wisnewski, were airheads, idiots because they went by the book when circumstances dictated that they be a little creative."

"The book?"

"You know, having a fixed set of responses for every situation and sticking to them—like rules that can't be broken—regardless of the reality of the thing. Do you know what I mean?"

"Yes," Swan nodded, "I think that I do. And you blame yourself for doing what you tell others not to do."

"Exactly!" My God, Alan Garrison thought, a woman who understood him! Really understood him. It was just his luck, he thought, to meet the perfect woman, but she just happened to be from another world or universe, she was more or less immortal and she was in the middle of a war. With every moment that passed with Swan, Alan Garrison was becoming more and more certain that he loved her like he had never, ever loved anyone before or would again.

"We need to be on our way, Al'An. We have the extra horses from the Sword of Koth who were killed. We must ride to join with the Company of Mir near the old summer palace by the shores of Woroc'Il'Lod."

"Is that an ocean?"

"Yes," she told him, "an icy sea. At its center," and she brushed a smooth spot in the snow, then sketched an outline with her gloved fingertip, "is the Edge Land, shaped like this. At its very tip, in the high coastal mountains, is Barad'Il'Koth, my mother's stronghold, where we must go."

Garrison studied Swan's drawing in the snow. "So where we are now is known as the Land, and where we must travel over the sea is the Edge Land, which we could get to overland, but would mean traveling a greater distance. The Land is the principal continent here."

Swan seemed to contemplate his meaning. Half the time, Garrison didn't even know if he was using English, nor was he conscious of slipping back and forth between his language and hers. Everyone—the kind of neat old guy, Erg'Ran, and Gar'Ath—seemed to understand him, and he understood them.

"I see the meaning," Swan went on. "There is but one continent here, connected by many wide expanses of land. The ocean flows around us, and it is made of many seas."

"How many people are there in Creath, in your world?"

"People? There are—" Swan paused. "I am trying to calculate, and determine a reference that you will understand." She shut her eyes, not making magic, he guessed, just thinking. She nodded her head, opened her eyes, said, "At one time, before the reign of my mother, Eran, there were many great cities, like Atlanta, but different, but with many, many people living and working in them.

"In those days, before I was born, the magical energy was used by all. Some used it better, more wisely, while others eschewed its use except for extraordinary purposes. Still others lived by its power."

"So, your mother destroyed everything?" Garrison asked her.

Swan's look visibly saddened. "Yes. She did that."

"Why?" Garrison asked her.

"She was K'Ur'Mir—of the royal line, the royal blood. My ancestors and hers have ruled Creath since the time of Mir."

Garrison wanted to ask who "Mir" was, but saved that for later. He was more concerned, at the moment, with learning why her world was as it was.

"My mother," Swan went on, "was gifted beyond even the most extraordinary of our ancestors, gifted with the ability to use the magical energy. I don't know why she did what she did, because she never told me. Erg'Ran, who, of course, knew her then, before and after, has told me that my mother devoted her every moment to study of the magical energy. She became obsessed with mastering all of the magic of the universe. That is impossible, even for her now, and she is the most powerful sorceress that there has ever been. No mortal, or immortals such as we, can master all magic.

"But in the pursuit of her obsession," Swan continued, "she discovered spells and summonings which had been unused since the dark days before the coming of Mir. She used these, and with one such spell was able to draw into herself more magic energy than any K'Ur'Mir before her. And used this spell and this magical energy to transport herself to another realm."

"Like you did," Garrison said soberly.

Swan nodded, closing her eyes, continuing. "I used the spell to save my life, to keep from being consumed by the Mist of Oblivion. My mother used it in the quest for more magical power. Evidently," Swan told him, looking at Garrison again, "she found it. When she returned, Erg'Ran recounted to me, her power had increased manyfold. She learned to transmute living things from one to another. I know how, but have never done it. I learned it from her without her knowing it."

"What do you mean when you say she could transmute living things?"

Swan drew a deep breath, exhaled, saying, "Do you remember the difference in types of magic, Al'An? For example, when I used a very little bit of magical energy to heal the wounds Gar'Ath sustained in the wood, all that I did was to accelerate a natural process. To

transmute is wholly unnatural. The horse which my
mother, the Queen Sorceress, rides? Mul'Din? Mul'Din
is a man's name. There is good reason for that. The
horse was once a man, her lover. Every horse that she
has ever ridden since I was a child was once a man.
They retain a man's mind and emotions, but no power
of speech. After she has run them into the ground, or
tired of them, they are gelded and left for age and
madness to destroy."

"Holy shit," Garrison murmured.

"Is this a special kind of g'urg?"

Alan Garrison rose to his knees, swept Swan into
his arms and kissed her harder than he had ever
kissed anyone, the sweetness of tasting her beyond
anything he could have imagined. In the stillness of
the falling snow, he could hear Swan's heart beating. . . .

Virtually every officer of the Horde was assembled
in the Great Hall of Barad'Il'Koth, crowded shoulder to shoulder on both sides of the narrow aisle
within which Eran walked. General, captain, lieutenant alike, each man bowed deeply as she approached,
not daring to raise head or eyes until she had passed.
The smell of fresh leather, of the copper metal which
trimmed a jerkin here, a sword scabbard there, the
very scent of their male bodies, all blended in an
intoxicatingly heady mixture. Eran, Sorceress Queen,
Mistress General, inhaled it, tasted it, consumed the
adulation as deeply as her body would hold.

Eran ascended to the dais on which her throne was
set. Great torches burst into flame on either side of
her as she moved past them, lighting in series, their
fires rising at the slightest beckoning of her mind.
Arrayed prostrate along the low steps, the sleeves of
their robes arranged to carpet the stone beneath her
feet, were the Handmaidens of Koth. Their voices
chanted of her power.

A tossed glance over her shoulder toward the long train of her heavily brocaded gown and the hands which bore it made everything perfect.

Moc'Dar, once strongest of the strong, carried her train as a woman would.

The onetime great captain of the Sword of Koth was heavily shackled about the neck and wrists and ankles, attired in a shift of sacking cloth and a short, hooded cloak. And he was no longer the man he once was. Although her magical energy was still depleted from managing the Mist of Oblivion, what remained had been more than adequate to alter Moc'Dar.

The rather ruggedly handsome face which she'd seen so rarely because it was covered by his black mask when he was uniformed was attractive no longer. In its place was a mask that he would wear forever. She had left his features recognizable, merely turned his skin into layers of scales, red and orange and green and black, with no pattern to them, the sight of them sickening. The effect was so disgusting, she transformed all the skin which covered his body to match. Where once a flowing mane of black hair had crowned his head, jellied lumps of flesh floated, their shapes altering as he moved. His once broad shoulders were diminished to sloping blobs of quivering skin. His legs were twisted and bent, his feet as well. His walk was torturous to watch, and she hoped even moreso to endure.

And the obvious symbol of his manhood was gone from between his legs. Eran had altered his demeanor, as well. No longer was he the courageous warrior, fearing no man. He now feared everyone, everything, shivering in terror at the slightest glance, cowering even from his own image.

Moc'Dar's punishment was delicious, and obvious to all who might be tempted to transgress or shirk.

Eran reached the height of the dais, standing before her throne, glancing down, watching as Moc'Dar, crawling about on hands and knees, fumbled her train. "Cover yourself and be still, Moc'Dar!" He obeyed instantly, or tried to. The moment that she had finished his transformation, then created for him what he wore, she had taught him—with the lash—how to comport himself. Moc'Dar had learned well. He was curled up into a ball near her feet, struggling to mask every part of his body beneath a too-short cloak and enormous hood. To do so, he had to draw his knees up to his chest, fold his arms tightly about him, bend his neck and back to an all but impossible degree. And, of course, he was in a constant state of terror, terror that he would displease her. On the contrary, he pleased her greatly this way.

Eran looked up, surveying the sea of frightened manly faces as she addressed her assembled officer corps. "Behold the great Captain Moc'Dar, his very name striking fear in the hearts of all who opposed him! Behold the officer who failed to obey me, who ran in cowardice. Behold what will happen to each or all of you should I be disobeyed or betrayed or merely feel the whim to see you forever undone! In pleasing my slightest wish is your only hope!"

Shifting her train, Eran lowered herself into her throne chair, her fingernails tapping against the armrests. The only other sound in the vast hall was the labored breathing she had given Moc'Dar in order to make his slightest effort even more painful, so that even in rest he could never rest.

Her voice low, even, Eran began again. "The Virgin Enchantress, Daughter Royal, Princess of Greath has defied me for the last time. Rather than lift the spell under which she masked the accursed Company of Mir from the Horde, she chose to transport herself to another realm and return again with a supposed champion from that world.

"This creature she has taken in thrall is not of you, but will appear like you. He relies on a magical weapon which kills with tiny tongues of fire. Without it, he is the equal of no man here. Soon, my magical power will render his weapon useless against you.

"My daughter and the unnatural creature which accompanies her as a familiar even now march on Barad'Il'Koth. With the bastard followers of Mir fighting beside her, the Virgin Enchantress naively hopes to unseat the ruling blood of the K'Ur'Mir, for she is not fully of the blood and she knows it and envies me."

Eran stood.

Moc'Dar must be peeking at her feet, she thought, amused, because his pitiful excuse for a body shuddered.

"I charge all officers to go forth to seek out and destroy the Company of Mir, destroy them utterly. I charge you further that you should go forth and seek out my daughter, the Virgin Enchantress, and assault her by all means of force and guile to bring about her death and doom. And the foul creature with her— kill him if you must, but better reward to the officer who brings me this creature alive that I may make another toy with which to amuse myself, as I have done with Captain Moc'Dar. All this I charge you do, under pain of incurring my terrible wrath!"

Sweeping her train behind her, Eran started down from the dais, with a snap of her fingers bringing the cowering once-man Moc'Dar to heel.

"Almost there, lad," Erg'Ran remarked to Gar'Ath, who rode beside him. They were riding a track and just passing the miller's hut, and soon their small band would be at the Falls of Mir.

"If the fighters left behind have not themselves been forced to flee, behind the Falls there could be welcome rest, old friend."

They rode side-by-side at the rear of the column, the Virgin Enchantress and her champion at the column's head. The other survivors from the previous night's fight on the track in the wood, the shackled and bound prisoner, and the body of their fallen comrade were all at the column's center.

It was just after dawning, the sky more grey than black. The large flakes of snow were falling steadily and softly.

"It's a long way yet to Barad'Il'Koth, Erg'Ran. If I don't make it—" Gar'Ath started to say.

Erg'Ran stopped him in midphrase. "You'll make it if any of us do, lad. It's the Virgin Enchantress I'm worried over. She is the one they most wish to kill, Gar'Ath. Her champion strikes me as a good lad, and he'd give his life for her, as would you or I or any of the Company of Mir. But there are dangers of which Swan is unaware and must remain so for a time, at least."

"What sort of dangers, old friend?"

"I can say nothing of it now, lad, except to tell you this. Her mother—curse the Queen Sorceress—was once, like Swan, an innocent girl."

"Are you saying the Virgin Enchantress is in danger of becoming like her cursed mother! That's madness, Erg'Ran," Gar'Ath charged.

"Madness there is, lad, but not in my words, but in power." And Erg'Ran struck his heel and the stump of his peg to his mount, urging the animal forward. . . .

"When I was little, sometimes my mother was very good, loving. I remember that, and I try to believe they are two separate people," Swan told him, her horse close beside his. She was a better rider, Garrison knew. By the same token, if he did stick with her, doing this Champion thing, all the way to Barad'Il'Whatchya-macallit, his horsemanship would have plenty of opportunity to improve. "I want to believe that I can still love my mother who was while I fight against the evil of my mother who is. Do you understand what I mean, Al'An?"

He considered her words, thought about them very hard, then said, "I think that I can understand what you mean, but only to a point. We've all had people we liked or loved who had traits that we disliked, or maybe despised. For that to be the case with a parent would be very tough, Swan. How about your dad?"

"Dad? Oh, my father," Swan said. "I never really knew him. I have a few memories of his voice, his touch, the way his beard felt rough. But then he was gone."

"I'm sorry that I asked, Swan."

"No," she told Garrison, "it's all right, Al'An, because I wish for you to know these things."

"Did your dad, uh—"

"I was told that he died, but now I know that he did not. It is very possible that he lives still, at Barad'Il'Koth."

"Then, your mom and dad are still together?"

"I don't think so," Swan responded. "Tell me about your, your mom and dad, Al'An."

Garrison shrugged his shoulders. "Not much to tell, really, except they're nice folks. Always pushed me to be practical, which I resented a lot more then than I do now, but I still resent. They loved me a lot, and still do. They were pretty young when I was born. They were in college. Usual thing for those days. Met, fell in love, got married, she dropped out to help pay his way through school, then got pregnant with me. They always told me that they intended to have a baby then. Kinda hard to imagine a pair of twenty-two-year-olds, wife working a full-time job, husband working a full-time job and going to school full time, going into his senior year, deciding suddenly to have a baby. She had to quit work and he got a part-time job to try and make up for the money they lost with her income gone. You know how it is."

"No," Swan said, the expression on her face totally honest. "My mother was born Princess Royal, as was

I. I don't know about my father, but my mother never wanted for anything that she desired, except more power of magic. I never wanted for anything, except to have my father with me and for my mother to cease to be evil. College is a learning place?" Swan asked.

"For some people, anyway."

"We learn from our elders, and then from books and scrolls and by trying things."

"Kind of the same thing for us, but it's a little more formalized, more structured."

"Within a day, my magic will be fully restored, Al'An. Will you stay to fight beside me?"

"Dropping the other shoe, huh?" Garrison replied.

Swan smiled, then glanced down at her feet. "I wear boots, not slippers, and I have dropped neither boot."

Garrison glanced at his wristwatch, a black-faced Rolex that he was given when he'd graduated law school. "I've noticed something, Swan. Time here, it moves differently than it does where I'm from. I caught it that when that Mist of Oblivion thing ate up your castle and nearly got you with it, it was nighttime, and more or less a full day had passed between then and the time you and I arrived here.

"But," Garrison continued, laying his argument, "when I met you at Dragoncon, I got the impression that you'd arrived only a little while before I got there myself. That seems to make me feel that what was a day for your world was only less than half a day for mine. And my watch." Garrison shot the cuff of his bomber jacket and raised his arm from beneath his cloak so that she could see what he meant by a watch. "Sometimes, I can look at it and the sweep second hand doesn't move, and sometimes the minute hand seems to be spinning. My body's telling me that it's been a day and a half at least since I've eaten anything—remember you promised me a meal?—but here it's been less than a day. That doesn't make any sense at all, unless I'm nuts and my watch is broken. It's like time moves whenever it damn well pleases here, or stops for the same reason."

"It is different, I'm sure. I'll try to formulate an explanation, if I can."

"Don't worry about it, Swan. The point I was so belaboring is an answer to your question. If I stay and help you fight, I might be gone from my world for an eternity, or I might have been gone for a couple of minutes. Heck, I mean, a hundred years could've gone by where I'm from and I wouldn't know it. So, I'll make you a deal."

"A deal, Al'An?"

Garrison nodded. "Yeah. I'll help. You know I can't refuse you. If that kiss in the snow under the Ka'B'Oo this morning meant half as much to you as it did to me, then you know why, too." My God, Garrison thought. She was actually blushing! Garrison cleared his throat. "But, if I go back, when I go back, when, if, I don't know. But you've got to try to get me back to DragonCon just when I left it, because I could never explain what happened here and I'd wind up getting put away in the laughing academy."

Swan seemed to consider his words, but before she could speak, Garrison blurted out, "And, no, that's not a school where they teach you to laugh. It's a place for people who've lost a grip on reality, maybe gone nutso."

"Like 'nuts' that you said a moment ago. People would think that you were sick in your mind."

"Yes, exactly," Garrison said.

"I can try, and that is all that I can honestly promise, Al'An, but I hope that you choose not to go." She leaned out of her saddle, reached across and held his hand.

"I hope I don't, either. And, under the circumstances, an honest promise is all I can ask for."

Swan smiled at him, withdrawing her hand. Garrison reached across to her, taking it back. . . .

In one of the stories Alan Garrison had read or seen in his youth about Butch Cassidy and the Wild Bunch, the outlaws were sometimes known as the "Hole-in-the-Wall Gang." This was because their hideout was behind a waterfall, in the hidden box canyon beyond. As a kid, he'd always wanted to go there, ride in behind that waterfall. When, as an adult, he learned that there really was such a place, between being a good FBI agent and being a good son and being a good boyfriend to various and sundry girls he'd never had a steady relationship with, there wasn't the time to go there.

As their horses mounted the steep, narrow rock ledge and started to pass behind the cascade, Garrison found himself humming Elmer Bernstein's theme from *The Magnificent Seven*. It was the wrong movie, but it was the only appropriate-sounding Western movie music that he could think of.

Gar'Ath rode beside him now. Erg'Ran had told them as they approached the Falls of Mir—who was this Mir guy?—that, "It is best that the Champion and one other go ahead in the event that danger or carnage lies beyond. Gar'Ath has volunteered to accompany you, Champion."

"It's Alan, all right? Yeah, I'll go."

So they went ahead, a quarter mile or so, Swan, Erg'Ran and the others well back with the prisoner. There would have to be time to interrogate this Sword of Koth badass, and pretty soon, Garrison reminded himself.

"The style of fighting that you used with your feet, Champion. I liked it. I'll make an offer I've never made before to any man."

"What's that, Gar'Ath?"

Gar'Ath shot him a broad smile. "I will teach you every secret that I know as concerns the use of the blade, if you will teach me your fighting style."

Garrison considered the offer for what it was, at once a great compliment and a great opportunity. He'd read about swords all of his life, examined them, but never learned how to fight with one. On the other side of the coin, Garrison had just seven rounds left in one of his SIG .45s, eight in the other and only two spare magazines, for a total of thirty-one rounds. The little Seecamp .32 in his right front pocket was another seven rounds with no spare magazine. "You're on, compadre."

"Compadre?"

"A great man of action in my world used to use that word a lot, and he said other things like, 'Listen up, pilgrim.' Like that."

"So, we're agreed then. Here's my handclasp on it!" Gar'Ath extended his hand, and Garrison his, but Gar'Ath's fingers closed on Garrison's forearm with a powerful grip. Garrison did the same.

They started their horses behind the Falls of Mir, the murmur that had been the sound from the rushing water building rapidly to a roar.

Gar'Ath freed a shield—round, much like a Scottish targe, with a center spike emerging from a center boss—from lashing thongs which bound it to his saddle. The shield slipped onto his left forearm, his left hand holding the reins of his mount. Gar'Ath then drew his sword. It was plain looking, in the sense that it was devoid of ornamentation, but beautiful nonetheless. Its tip came to a spear point, the almost three feet of blade with multiple fullers starting only a few inches back from the point and running the blade's length to the fist-long ricasso just forward of the guard. The guard itself was wide and spanned a little under a foot from end to end, the quillons drooping slightly, terminating in circular lobes large enough to have been a man's finger ring. What Garrison could see of the hilt beneath Gar'Ath's fist was brown leather covered. The ribbed pommel was about the size and shape of a plum, designed as a skull crusher.

"You may care to borrow my dagger. Your fire-spitter might be noisy for what work may lay beyond the falls, Champion."

"I've got edged weapons if I need them, thanks." Gar'Ath nodded.

The environment behind the falls was extremely cold. The air was filled with a heavy, frigid mist. Ice, thick and slick, covered the pathway and the rock wall beside them. Garrison hoped that his horse felt more confident of the footing than he did.

Garrison slipped his left hand under his cloak and bomber jacket, his fingers touching against the butt of one of the SIG .45s. He had no intention of giving the pistol a soaking in the icy spray unless he had to.

Gar'Ath slowed his mount, Garrison doing the same. Swan had second sighted beyond the Falls, seeing nothing of alarm, but warned them, too, that her mother might be back to full magical power. If that were true, and her mother's soldiers had taken the hidden camp, her mother could have cast a spell to block Swan's second sight.

Garrison was amazed at his own thinking. He was beginning to accept things like second sight, spells, summonings. He'd started to light a cigarette about a mile or two before they came in sight of the Falls of Mir and hadn't even given it a second thought when Swan lit it for him with her magic. She seemed to get a kick out of doing it, anyway.

Gar'Ath didn't seem to have anything to do with magic, a "what you see is what you get" kind of guy. He leaned over from his saddle, his voice a loud whisper and still barely audible over the noise of the

Falls. "If you'd hold the reins of my horse, I'm of a mind that it might be best to reconnoiter on foot, Champion."

Garrison liked him, despite the fact that he persisted in calling him "Champion" and despite his haircut. Gar'Ath's dark brown hair, wavy and full like a woman's, was grown almost halfway to his waist, the sides bound back by a leather thong knotted at the nape of his neck. Garrison could just see some guy with the Bureau showing up for duty sporting a haircut like Gar'Ath's. The look on Matt Wisnewski's face would be worth a few weeks' suspension without pay and a reprimand in the personnel file.

As Garrison took the reins of Gar'Ath's mount, the swordsman flicked his cloak out of the way of sword and shield, shooting Alan a grin, and started forward along the icy pathway.

Garrison's hand tightened on the butt of the pistol he held.

After a moment, Gar'Ath came running back, leaned up toward Garrison in the saddle, his voice barely audible. "There's a small band of Ra'U'Ba roaming about in there, looking for information they can sell to the Horde. Our lads that we left behind may still be up in the rocks. We must act, and quickly too, Champion."

Garrison bent low in the saddle in order to hear better. "I'm missing something, here. Who are the, the, the whatever you called them?"

"The Ra'U'Ba are not like us. You'll see, but we must be very silent, lest they hear us. They communicate with one another over great distances by using their minds alone. And, they can use their minds to block themselves from the second sight. That is why the Queen Sorceress suffers them to live, because they are the best spies, almost undetectable.

"When one of them discovers a bit of valuable information," Gar'Ath went on, "he tells it to another by mind alone, even if that other is an incredible number of lancethrows away. Distance matters not at all to their minds, Champion. If one of them should see one of our Company, the Horde would be informed almost instantly, and troops dispatched at once. That is why they must be dealt with one at a time and quickly. This is not work for your firespitter, Champion. Trust me there. Ready the edged weapons of which you spoke. The Ra'U'Ba are tremendous fighters, heavily armed and hard to kill unless you know their one weakness."

"Let me guess. You don't know what that one weakness is, right? Shit."

"What?"

"G'Urg."

"Aha! G'Urg. I *do* know the weakness, but it'll be easier to show you than tell you, Champion. We'd best leave the horses here."

Alan Garrison dismounted. His hands began fishing in his pockets for his knives. "Telepathic mercenary spies who are terrific fighters. Wonderful," Garrison groused. . . .

At the end of the pathway behind the Falls of Mir was a steeply sloping downgrade. There was less snow here, as the canyon beyond the Falls was sheltered from much of the wind. Angling along the downgrade was a road of sorts, snow covered but still discernible.

Prowling about on the canyon floor were creatures looking for all the world like heavily armed mutant humanoid monsters from some cheap horror movie, but with better makeup and weirder costuming. Either that, or they were a cross between a gargoyle and a Tyrannosaurus Rex.

The Ra'U'Ba stood at least two heads taller than the average professional basketball player.

Unless the one closest to them, which Garrison

could see in the best detail, just happened to be particularly ugly, calling the Ra'U'Ba "grotesque" would have been a compliment. Spiked horns grew from the sides of their otherwise humanlike heads, the horns curled forward like those of a bull, but not quite that distended. Their ears were more pointed than the ones Leonard Nimoy used to wear. From Garrison's vantage point, Garrison would have sworn that they had three eyes, two dark and one yellow, the yellow eye between and slightly above the other two near the center of the forehead.

Their hands—six long fingers each—were easily large enough to palm a basketball while still holding a hotdog and a drink cup. The Ra'U'Ba were obviously jointed oppositely from humans at both the elbows and knees; merely watching them motion with an arm or walk a pace or two was nightmarish.

Their bodies rippled with muscles superimposed upon muscles; not even Arnold Schwarzenegger had calves like they did. With long tails balancing enormously powerful-looking torsos, the Ra'U'Ba gave the appearance of walking on three tree-trunk-sized legs.

If the Ra'U'Ba appeared physically formidable, they also looked sartorially ludicrous. Naked from the waist up, barefoot, the only garment any of them wore was a skirt. These were nearly knee-length and of a color most reminiscent of vomit. The skirts obscured their thighs and the roots of their tails.

Their skin was reptilian, covered with grey-green scales, but since they were nearly naked they had to be warm-blooded creatures, considering the ambient temperature. Admittedly basing his observations on limited experience, Ra'U'Ba armament seemed to Garrison as bizarre as their physiology. Great shields, the size and general rectangular shape of those used by the armies of Ancient Rome, all but covered their backs like the shell of a tortoise. Helmets hung from each shield, the helmets peaked in the style of feudal

Japan, but hinged in order, he assumed, to accommodate the horns on their heads. Built into the helmets were metallic face masks, these almost as terrifying looking as their real faces.

Baldrics, overly wide, were crisscrossed from each shoulder to the opposing hip and blades the size of broadswords were carried high in the frogs. A belt of similar width girded each Ra'U'Ba's midsection, suspended from or attached to it various other weapons—short-shafted axes with wickedly broad heads, daggers and shuriken-like throwing stars, only much larger than any Garrison had ever seen.

Gar'Ath leaned toward Garrison, his whispering more easily audible beyond the roar of the Falls. "We must lie in wait and take them quickly lest their minds tell the other Ra'U'Ba what we are about." Gar'Ath returned his sword to its sheath and drew his dagger.

An automatic folder in each hand, Garrison was as ready as he would ever be. That wasn't very ready at all. He'd never sneaked up on somebody with the intent to kill, nor certainly had he ever used a knife to do harm to anyone. Like any cop who took his survival seriously, he carried knives not only for ordinary and extraordinary chores, but for last ditch self-defense. He had practiced with the knives, developing a kata or technique for use of one on its own or both together. Rehearsed as a series of martial arts moves in front of a full-length mirror, the routine looked confident, intimidating. Holding the knives, preparing to confront a heavily armed living adversary, Garrison felt no confidence at all, and intimidated rather than intimidating.

Some Champion, he almost verbalized.

Gar'Ath was on the move, creeping forward through the snow, weaving his way along the boulder-strewn downslope. Alan Garrison caught up and stayed beside him.

Garrison had counted three of the Ra'U'Ba, and three horses, too. He wondered how something with a tail that long and large could ride a horse? Maybe the tail was jointed at its root and could sling to one side or the other, or rooted high enough to hang out behind, over the saddle's cantle. If he kept concentrating on something else, he might be able to slow down his breathing, control his heart rate.

Garrison and Gar'Ath stopped behind a pile of broad, flat rock slabs, snow accumulated several inches high. He and the swordsman were only a few yards from the nearest of the Ra'U'Ba.

This would be a waiting game, like marking time in the predawn over too many cups of coffee, the word yet to be given that it was a go to serve arrest warrants on a heavily armed group of suspects. But the word always came, no matter how long it took. The biggest problem was always nerves, because there was so much time to think about what could go wrong, like getting killed or crippled, or doing something stupid and causing someone else to be hurt or killed.

Swan hadn't magically made him any heavy winter gloves. Garrison only had the thin shooting gloves that he always carried in the pocket of his bomber jacket, kept there for emergencies. Despite the cold and the thinness of his gloves, Garrison's hands perspired.

He stripped away the gloves, to better handle the knives.

Beside him, Gar'Ath whispered, "The way to kill one of the Ra'U'Ba is simple, Champion. Creep up behind the Ra'U'Ba with your blade at the ready for the death strike. When you have a close look at a Ra'U'Ba's face, you'll see that what appears to be a third eye at the center of the forehead is not. It is an unprotected portion of the brain. When a Ra'U'Ba is helmeted, he is virtually invincible because of his

strength and skill with weapons. The helmets they
wear are reinforced over the forehead. Only the most
powerful sword or axe blow, accurately delivered, can
reach this spot beneath a Ra'U'Ba helmet. Failing
that, to kill a Ra'U'Ba is difficult, even for me."

"So, I sneak up behind this guy, jump on his back
and stab him smack in that third eye that really isn't,
right?"

"Exactly."

"Have you done this before, Gar'Ath?"

Gar'Ath grinned, shrugging his eyebrows as he said,
"I was never so fortunate as we are now. When I've
fought Ra'U'Ba before, they were always helmeted."

"So this is a real break. Great," Garrison said. "I
guess we just must live right to be this lucky."

"Your words are true, Champion. Wait until I get
close to the two on the far side of the canyon. I think
that I can kill two of them quickly enough, unless
you want the honor. I see that you have two weapons ready. Do the blades unfold from within?"

"Yeah. That's what they do. But, uh, you go ahead
and take the two on the far side there, and I'll get
in there with you as soon as my guy's down for the
long count."

Gar'Ath nodded soberly, then was off, moving with
the grace and speed that was second nature to someone who lived for combat, had lived for it all of his life.

Alan Garrison's eyes flickered from Gar'Ath to the
Ra'U'Ba nearest him, and when Garrison looked back,
he could no longer spot Gar'Ath. "This guy's good,"
Garrison murmured under his breath. He'd noticed
that he'd begun talking to himself since coming to
Creath; and some contended that talking to oneself
was symptomatic of early-stage mental illness. "All I
need. Go nuts here where I've got no health insur-
ance. That'd be just great."

If there'd been an encampment here, the Company of Mir had to be great at cleaning up evidence

after themselves. "Lucky this isn't a crime scene."
There were no signs of old campfires, litter, anything
beneath the snow cover. And the Ra'U'Ba really were
looking.

Garrison forced himself to look at his own particular Ra'U'Ba. He judged the height difference
between himself and the Ra'U'Ba as roughly equivalent to that between Herve Villechaize and Andre the
Giant.

Garrison knew that he would have only one chance
at this.

Gar'Ath had to be in position near the two Ra'U'Ba
who seemed to be conferring about something near
where their horses were tethered.

This was the moment.

Alan Garrison broke into a dead run down the
snow covered slope; his leather-soled cowboy boots
were not ideal for reliable traction and his balance
almost went once. But he kept running, one unopened
automatic knife in each hand.

"Oh, my God!" Garrison lamented under his breath.
What if the scaly skin of the Ra'U'Ba was puncture
proof? He was about to find out.

The Ra'U'Ba's body shifted just slightly, the massive shoulders sloping to one side, as if the creature
was about to turn or look over its shoulder.

Garrison put on all the steam that he had, sprinting
the last few yards faster than he had ever covered
ground before.

Garrison's left index finger hit the automatic knife's
opening button, as the blade snapped out, Garrison's
fingers twirling the handle into a dagger position. He
leaped along the Ra'U'Ba's tail and onto the Ra'U'Ba's
back, his left hand stabbing the knife blade to the
handle into the flesh and muscle above the shoulder
blade. Garrison held on, hauling himself upward along
the Ra'U'Ba's back. It was moving, a vicious sounding low roar starting from deep inside it.

Garrison's right arm snaked over the Ra'U'Ba's right shoulder, his right thumb tapping the second knife's opening button. Garrison's left hand let go of the first knife, clawed for a handhold around the Ra'U'Ba's powerful neck. The blade in Garrison's right hand stabbed toward where he hoped the exposed portion of brain would be.

The knife stopped dead.

Garrison felt sick inside himself. He'd missed. He was going to die; but, worse yet, Swan and Erg'Ran and Gar'Ath and the others and all the Company of Mir would be wiped out because this living abomination would telepathically communicate what had happened and the evil Queen Sorceress would know just where to send her armies.

The Ra'U'Ba was flexing his shoulders. Garrison tried moving the knife, but it wouldn't budge. The Ra'U'Ba raised up, balancing on its tail. Garrison lost his grip and fell to the snow, rolled, looked up. The Ra'U'Ba was lunging toward him. Even if he could risk a shot, Garrison knew that there wasn't time. He rolled to his right.

The Ra'U'Ba crashed against the ground, not onto Garrison, its body bouncing, then rolling onto its side, still. Garrison saw the handle of the knife that had been in his hand, rising out of a pool of yellow ooze.

Garrison got to his knees. "Gar'Ath!" Garrison reached for the nearest of his knives, twisted it from the Ra'U'Ba's brain, then clambered to his feet.

Garrison looked around for Gar'Ath.

Gar'Ath was on the ground, one of the Ra'U'Ba dead beside him, Gar'Ath's dagger buried to the hilt in the creature's brain hole. Garrison broke into a dead run, to aid Gar'Ath in fighting the second Ra'U'Ba, which was turning around, toward Gar'Ath.

Garrison didn't know what he'd do when he got there, but he had to do something.

Garrison stopped in his tracks, almost in mid-stride. He didn't have to do a thing to help Gar'Ath. The sword that appeared in Gar'Ath's hand in one instant flew from his hand in the next, vibrating as its point penetrated the brain hole. The Ra'U'Ba swayed on feet and tail for about a full second, then toppled backwards into the snow, dead before it hit.

Garrison stood about twenty-five yards away, remembering to breathe.

Gar'Ath turned toward Garrison, doubling over as he howled with laughter.

"What's so funny, Gar'Ath?"

"You pretending to know nothing of how to kill the Ra'U'Ba! And then using the classic method spoken of in the writings of Mir himself! Confess! There are Ra'U'Ba where you come from, Champion! Are there not? And you've slain more than your share of them, I'd wager! Am I right?"

"No Ra'U'Ba where I come from, or writings of Mir, either, Gar'Ath. Only dumb luck."

Garrison's shoulder slumped a little. Hungry, cold, tired, he started back across the snow to go get his other knife. Gar'Ath was still laughing. Garrison couldn't have laughed at anything. He had this image in his mind of how disgusting it was going to be cleaning the Ra'U'Ba glop out of two automatic knives.

# Chapter Six

A half-dozen fighters from the Company of Mir trickled down from positions of concealment along the canyon rim, calling to Gar'Ath, waving to him in greeting. Within a matter of minutes after they reached the canyon floor behind the Falls of Mir (and after Garrison's quick introduction as "Champion"), Gar'Ath dispatched them on various duties. One of them—using a mount that the fallen Ra'U'Ba would no longer need—was commissioned to ride back for Swan, Erg'Ran and the others. Gar'Ath sent out a man to get Gar'Ath's horse and Garrison's. The others Gar'Ath assigned to various sentry posts, lest more of the Ra'U'Ba or any other enemy should be near.

Everything attended to, Gar'Ath laid down the enormous sword he'd snatched up from one of the Ra'U'Ba, then proceeded to retrieve his own sword. Extracting it from the brain hole in the skull of the Ra'U'Ba looked for all the world—to Garrison, at least—like a long-haired young Arthur drawing the sword Excalibur from the stone. The scene was so reminiscent of this that Garrison called across the canyon floor to Gar'Ath, "You are rightwise King of England!"

Gar'Ath turned his head and called back to Garrison. "What was that which you called me?"

"King of England." And, Garrison started to explain what England was, the word coming out in his own tongue, despite Swan's spell, because there was no equivalent to it in the language of Creath. But, the word "King" was in English, too. "England is a place, where years ago, in our legends, perhaps in fact, a young man rose to lead his people toward a dream. And a king, of course, is the male counterpart of a queen."

"Your home must be very strange, Champion, strange indeed, to have such a thing."

Garrison was wrenching his other knife from the shoulder and neck of the Ra'U'Ba. Gar'Ath, dagger in one hand, sword in the other, both dripping blood and yellow brain matter, approached. "Let me get this straight, Gar'Ath. There's no concept of a male ruler here?"

"Warrior leaders are mostly men, Champion, although there have been a few women who've distinguished themselves greatly in battle. You really know nothing of Creath beyond what you have learned since your arrival, or what the Enchantress might have recounted before you returned with her, do you?"

"Not a thing," Garrison admitted.

"Let's see to our steel, and while we do, perhaps I can provide—"

"Bring me up to speed?"

"If you say, Champion. I can do that."

It would be nearly an hour before Swan and the others reached the canyon behind the Falls, the way Garrison figured it. Picking up on some of the local lore while he cleaned his knives might keep his mind off the fact that he'd just taken another life, and that killing wasn't really bothering him as he thought that it should be.

"Where to start, now," Gar'Ath mused aloud.

"I know the perfect place," Garrison supplied. "Who was this Mir that I'm always hearing about?"

"Ahh, you can't go starting with Mir, Champion. It's before that, the kind of place that Creath was before the coming of Mir. That's the only way to be understanding then or now."

Garrison took out one of his cigarettes, offered one to Gar'Ath. The swordsman declined. Garrison lit up the old-fashioned way, which involved a cigarette lighter instead of magic.

"Magic is a way of life here, even if you don't practice magic. I don't. But the magic is all around me. The Enchantress healed my wounds with magic. When I was being born, so they tell me, I was turned around the wrong way in my mother's womb. My mother was no user of magic, never had the way of it. My father was a swordmaker, so he knew a little magic, but not what would be needed. There was still something of a civilization left in those days, before the Horde had destroyed everything. In the village, there was a woman who was a midwife, and she was attending my mother. She knew enough magic to make most pain go away, to cure warts, things like that, but not to turn a child in the womb.

"There was a K'Ur'Mir family—" Gar'Ath continued, Garrison interrupting him.

"I've heard that term, Gar'Ath. What does it mean? The royal blood? Nobility?"

"The nobility, as you say. They fled one of the larger towns when the Horde came killing and destroying. Every K'Ur'Mir has the ability with magical energy. My father had made a sword for their son, who was named Gar'Ath. I was named after him, because of what his mother did. When my father told them that I had to be turned and the midwife didn't have the magic, Gar'Ath's mother came and turned me with her magic, then eased the birth for my mother. If I'd been born a girl, they would have named me after the woman who saved my mother and me. As it was, they named me after her son. He died less than a full cycle of the seasons later, his father and mother, too, when the Horde swept through our village. She used her magic to hold them off as long as she could, but her magic was nothing compared to the magic of the Queen Sorceress.

"But," Gar'Ath continued, "her courage, and the courage of her husband and son and village men like my father made it so that almost a hundred lives were saved. In the end, the two best swordsmen from the village—my father one of them, of course—were chosen to lead those who could be saved to safety. The village was already in flames. The Queen Sorceress sent an ice dragon to take care of that."

"An ice dragon," Garrison repeated aloud.

Gar'Ath looked at Garrison oddly. "They slept within the ice since before anyone can know, and she freed them to serve her."

"Oh. Those ice dragons." Now that he thought of it, he remembered Swan mentioning something about an ice dragon's poison bladder or whatever.

"Ra'U'Ba roamed the roads, killing, finding persons to be tortured and made to reveal where there were hiding places, where other survivors could be found. The beasts within the deep wood were summoned by the Queen Sorceress, commanded by her magic to go into the villages and devour the dead and the dying.

"Those of us from our village who survived were able to hide in the mountains, occasionally establish long-term camps. Some went on to other villages, and died when the Horde swept through. I grew up, learning to read and make runes, cipher numbers, survive in the wild, fight. My father taught me everything he knew of the blade. This sword, which I made, is a copy of the one that he left in the belly of the ice dragon that swooped down from the skies to burn our village."

"And all of this, I gather, was brought about because of the will of Swan's mother," Garrison said. He'd nursed the cigarette as long as he could, put it out and looked about to find something with which to clean the blood and gore from his knives. He followed Gar'Ath's lead and cut a large swatch from the nearest dead Ra'U'Ba's skirt. He promised himself that he'd wash his hands afterward.

Gar'Ath continued his story. "I told you about the destruction of my village so that you would understand, Champion, how it was before the coming of Mir. What the Queen Sorceress did was destroy all that had been built in the generations since Mir's coming, returning Creath to the blood-soaked land that it once was."

His sword and dagger clean, Gar'Ath took a vial of oil and various sharpening stones from a pouch hung on his belt. "Before the coming of Mir, the dark magic ruled Creath. You asked why we have no men who would rule as a queen rules. I'd never questioned the way of things before you asked me, but the answer is obvious. Magic. Men can be taught to perform specific magical processes, can teach these skills to other men. But only a woman can create magic, can take a spell beyond this to that and back again. The magic comes from within them."

Alan Garrison had always liked the word "epiphany." It rarely saw any use, however. But the point which Gar'Ath had just made brought Garrison to an epiphany—he understood Creath at last. "That's why there's so little technology in a society that must be thousands and thousands of years old, Gar'Ath, why everything sort of stopped! And why women run the whole thing!"

"What do you mean, Champion?"

"Where I come from, when we wanted to travel faster, we built sleeker ships that were better rigged, trains that ran with steam, then diesel power, and planes to fly in the air and take us from one point to another at greater speeds than were possible on the land. All you guys did was work up a new magical spell or summoning or whatever. Who needs an airplane if you can travel from one place to another with magic? And you don't even need to worry about luggage. Just make new clothes with more magic once you arrive! Magic took all the initiative out of any quest for technology here. And since women are the ones with the real magic, they run the show!" Garrison glanced at Gar'Ath's sword. "As far as craftsmanship goes, something like your sword is a real high point here, right?"

"Of course."

"Don't get me wrong now, Gar'Ath. Your sword is magnificent. But have you ever tried making wheels with little teeth on them? They're called gears. With your metal working skills, you could build machines."

Gar'Ath smiled. "You've seen an instrument like the one by means of which the Enchantress counted the passage of time?"

"She made a clock?"

"As you say, but the time-telling device was inside her castle, which is no more."

"How'd she get the idea to make it?" Garrison queried Gar'Ath.

Gar'Ath reflected for a moment, then responded, "She spoke once of reading about the device in an old book or scroll."

Garrison took off his wristwatch and passed it over to Gar'Ath. "This is such a device, Gar'Ath. These are common in my world. This one is an old-style, which uses weights and gears. We have time-telling devices which are totally different, more technologically advanced."

"It's very small compared to the one built by the Enchantress." Gar'Ath put it beside his ear. "And the noise it makes is much less."

"A clock! She built a damn clock! And someone else built one before her! Do you realize what all of that means?" Garrison felt like shouting it from the canyon rim. He didn't wait for Gar'Ath to reply. "Swan is reintroducing technology to Creath without even knowing it!"

Gar'Ath returned Garrison's watch. "Is this a good thing?"

"It could be, really could be, yes. With the magic and the technology, you guys could be—"

"What could we be, Champion?"

Alan Garrison sat down again on the rock he'd been warming. "Anything you wanted, Gar'Ath. Creath could be anything that anyone here ever wanted it to be, a paradise."

"I don't know that last word that you said, Champion."

Alan Garrison nodded his head soberly, saying, "I didn't think that you would, Gar'Ath."

Alan Garrison still had to learn about this Mir and what Mir did and why.

More importantly, he had to discover why Swan's mother was obsessed with undoing all that Mir had done, was committed to perpetuating a dark age of evil magic and death for Creath. One way or the other, the secret to understanding what motivated Swan's mother would only be found beyond the ice sea Woroc'Il'Lod, in Edge Land at evil's stronghold, Barad'Il'Koth. . . .

"You'll learn to sleep in the saddle when you must, Champion," Erg'Ran volunteered, glancing over at the newcomer as he swayed a little bit atop his mount.

"I could fall asleep in a heartbeat. Trust me. Trouble is, I'd fall off the horse."

Erg'Ran laughed, saying, "That is how you learn, Champion!"

Erg'Ran urged his mount forward, coming up beside Gar'Ath. "We can rest when we reach the old summer palace, lad. You look as tired as the Champion."

"I am that, old friend," Gar'Ath confided.

"He acquitted himself well, I understand, our Enchantress's Champion did."

Gar'Ath turned a little bit in his saddle. "He fought bravely, Erg'Ran. He has a good intuitive ability for battle, just not very much practice. All the practice in the world won't make up for a lack of that ability. The Champion's a good man, but he has very strange ideas and comes from a very strange place."

"In the old days," Erg'Ran told Gar'Ath, "you would have met a great many people with a great many ideas, Gar'Ath, in the old days before life was a day-to-day battle against the Queen Sorceress. Perhaps, someday, there will be time for strange ideas once again. Perhaps you'll live to see it. We'll see."

The trail, such as it was, wound steeply upward, toward the plateau of Arba'Il'Tac, where some said that all life on Creath once began, long before the coming of Mir or the dark magic before that, before anything. It was, some philosophers believed, the place where time began.

Erg'Ran was less worried over philosophy than tactics. Arba'Il'Tac was all but barren. The plateau sloped gradually downward, stretching on for lancethrow after lancethrow, before at last touching the cliffs which overlooked the icy waters of Woroc'Il'Lod. If the forces of the Queen Sorceress should catch them in the open on the plateau, there would be nowhere to hide, no position from which to fight. It would, almost certainly, be a massacre.

There was no alternative, however, to openly crossing Arba'Il'Tac. The snows in the mountain passes through which he had dispatched the Company of Mir toward the sea had piled too deep in the intervening day. If the Enchantress were to use her magic to clear a path through the snow, the results—avalanche, ice floe—might prove catastrophic. To use the broad track around the mountains, which led directly to the sea, would be tantamount to suicide. That track was the main turnpike to Woroc'Il'Lod, traveled regularly by the Horde, continuing on to eventually come to Edge Land and Barad'Il'Koth itself.

They would rest the latter portion of the day, and early night. Everyone needed sleep, himself included. Then, with their mounts rested, they would ride the last short distance to the summit and Arba'Il'Tac, crossing the plateau as rapidly as possible.

There was much to which they might look forward at the old summer palace. By the time that they reached it, the Enchantress's magical energy should be fully restored. Little things like being able to bathe, eat their fill without looking over their shoulders (too much, at least), even having the time to interrogate the captive Sword of Koth awaited them there. If he could get everyone to focus on the goal of reaching the summer palace, perhaps their minds, too, could find rest from the immediate peril before them and the perils which lay beyond the summer palace.

Woroc'Il'Lod had to be crossed, with its treacherous floating mountains of ice which could gut a ship or crush it, cyclonic winds and wind-driven waves of incredible height and force, torrential sleet storms with such ferocity that they could all but skin a man. And then there were the ice dragons to be reckoned with.

If the Company of Mir survived all of this, it would be only to march hopelessly outnumbered against the Horde of Koth at Barad'Il'Koth, succeeding in that only to confront the darkest of black magic, wielded by the evil Queen Sorceress herself. All of them needed the summer palace, a short rest there, renewal, a moment of happiness.

Erg'Ran tried to focus his thoughts on the summer palace, yet in his mind's eye he could see nothing but the barren plateau of Arba'Il'Tac. . . .

Swan brought a plate of food and a cup of tea to Al'An, dropping to her knees beside him beneath the windbreak Gar'Ath had shown him how to construct. The snow still fell heavily, but the wind had decreased. Using very little of her magic—she dared not use too much, lest she regret it when they crossed Arba'Il'Tac— she heated food for the men and herself; they couldn't risk a fire.

At her insistence, the prisoner Sword of Koth was bidden to take food, but he refused. Unless he hoped to die of starvation—which would take a very long time—he was quite foolish. If he planned to escape, as she assumed he must, the prisoner would need his energy, his strength. Upon further consideration, Swan wondered if, indeed, the prisoner entertained any hope at all to escape and return to his command?

Her mother dealt severely with anyone whom she considered to have shirked a duty to her, and clearly the duty of every Sword of Koth was victory. Failing that, the only acceptable excuse was death.

Despite what he was, Swan felt genuine sadness over the man's plight. Perhaps he really did intend to starve to death.

Al'An took the offered plate of food from her hand. It was a stew made from dried meat and dried vegetables. He took the metal cup of tea, sipped from it. "Thank you," he told her.

"I'm afraid it's not much. My magical energy is nearly restored, but I must save what I have in the event that we are attacked as we cross Arba'Il'Tac. But when we reach the summer palace, it will be different." Swan laughed, saying, "Then, Al'An, at long last, you may eat your fill, as I have promised."

"That'll be nice," Al'An responded. She could just make out his features by the bluish white light from the globe which she had made for Erg'Ran to use. The globe was set beneath a rock overhang and would not be visible for any great distance, nor from the air, should her mother use the birds as an instrument for finding them. Al'An was smiling at her.

"I'll be right back," Swan told Al'An, getting up, brushing the snow from her dress and cloak. She fetched her own plate of stew and mug of tea and brought them back so that she could eat with Al'An. He slid over, spreading his cloak open so that she could fit within its folds as she sat beside him. "Thank you, Al'An."

"So, tell me about Arba'Il'Tac. Erg'Ran said it's thought to be the place where all life here began. Sounds interesting, a kind of Garden of Eden."

Swan laughed softly. "It is no garden, Al'An. It is barren rock, as if there were once a great mountain where it stands now. Then some mighty sword or axe was wielded against it, sheared away its peak, left it dying."

Al'An laughed, then, "You make Arba'Il'Tac sound so inviting. If it's that barren there, why do people think it's where life began?"

Swan thought that Al'An had to be very hungry, indeed. Even with magic, the stew did not taste that good when she'd sampled it. Yet Al'An ate ravenously. Swan finished sipping at her tea, still trying to construct an answer for his question, something that he would understand without knowing the entire history of Creath. At last, she said, "There are many kinds of living things in our world, as I imagine there must be in yours. There were some types of creatures which no longer exist."

"You guys amaze me!" Al'An enthused. "A fossil record has been discovered here?"

She considered his words, their meaning, then answered, "Yes, a fossil record, as you put it. Within the rock floor of Arba'Il'Tac are the etchings of bones from many creatures which no longer live, and these markings have been found nowhere else, nor have the bones ever been found which match these markings."

"Sort of prehistoric elephant graveyard."

Swan gave up at understanding that, but agreed with him anyway by just nodding her head as she ate from her plate of stew.

"You know," Al'An said, swallowing food as he spoke, "it's really interesting—fascinating's a better word—the way that societies parallel one another."

"I don't know what you imply, Al'An."

Al'An gestured with his spoon. "We have spoons, plates, cups. Women in my world once dressed as you do, and men once carried swords. Horses? We've got horses. Have you got dogs? If I live a million years, I'll never understand this. And, those are only superficial examples. There's so much more profound stuff to consider."

"Profound stuff indeed, Al'An. What profound stuff?"

"Well, like good and evil, right and wrong, like that. It's universal, maybe, a commonality to life. But, on the other hand, we have nothing like Ra'U'Ba, and if there ever were ice dragons in my world, there aren't any now. I know you'll probably think that I'm crazy, but in one way, I'm almost looking forward to seeing one."

"Al'An!"

"Yeah, I know. Well, almost, I said. I just wish I had a camera with me, so if I do go back I can—"

Al'An fell silent.

"If?" Swan repeated.

Al'An set down his plate of stew, nearly finished with it. She was about to inquire if he wanted to eat her food, but he asked, "When I kissed you earlier, how did it feel to you?"

Swan felt her cheeks become hot as he looked at her. "I liked it very much," Swan answered honestly. Perhaps that was a custom where he came from, to make inquiries concerning things like that. To be polite, she asked him, "And how did it feel to you, Al'An?"

"I liked it very much. So much so, in fact, that I'd like to do it again, and again, and maybe—"

"Maybe what, Al'An?"

"Maybe, uh," and Al'An fell silent. But he folded his arm around her shoulders and they sat like that, sheltered by the windbreak, for some time. Swan slept beside Al'An in the little time allotted for rest, his cloak wrapped about them both. But before Swan closed her eyes in sleep, Swan closed her eyes as Al'An kissed her.

# Chapter Seven

Alan Garrison stretched in his saddle, scanning the plain of Arba'Il'Tac stretched out before them. He said to Swan, mounted on a black mare beside him, "This is like a lunar landscape, like nothing I've ever experienced."

Swan took a moment before responding, and he realized that it was probably the word "lunar" which she was working back and forth between the two languages, perhaps because of its Latin root. But, as he looked skyward, he understood another problem. The snow had stopped and the sky above them was clear. Visible along a horizon so vast that the very curvature of the planet was apparent were two yellow moons, one half-full, the other three-quarters.

Despite the glow of moonlight, there was a vast array of stars, as abundant and diverse in size and luminescence as a depiction in a planetarium, more brilliant than he had ever seen on any other night of his life. Alan Garrison had no astronomical training, but he was convinced that none of the constellations were in the slightest way familiar. Yet, wherever he was, wherever Creath was, the stellar display was beyond magnificent.

"My world is somewhere out there," Garrison told Swan, taking her gloved hand in his, holding it tightly. "At least, I think so. But don't ask me where." He turned around in his saddle to look at Swan's face. The words he wanted to say were the kind of thing that any red-blooded American ten-year-old boy hearing it in a movie would have retched at the thought of. Garrison said them anyway. "The stars, the sky, they don't compare with the beauty of your face, the brilliance in your eyes." Garrison swallowed hard. "Mushy" stuff was always hard for him to say.

Swan squeezed his hand and "Al'An," was all she said in reply.

Erg'Ran rode up beside them. "We'd best be moving, Enchantress, Champion. Second-sight for us when you can, Enchantress, if you will."

"I will," she promised.

Erg'Ran thumped his fingers against the head of the Ra'U'Ba battleaxe which was lashed to Garrison's saddle. "Don't overextend on the swing, Champion, if use it you must. Balance is the name of the game."

"I'll remember," Garrison vowed.

Erg'Ran raised up in his saddle, calling back along their column. "Remember to keep a good pace, but don't wind your horses. If we're attacked, we'll be needing everything they've got. Gar'Ath, pick another man, then the two of you ride a few lancethrows out along our flanks."

"Right!" Gar'Ath called back. Then, "Bin'Ah? Your bump on the head better now, you can ride the watch."

"That I'll do, Gar'Ath!" Bin'Ah responded, thwacking his heels against the flanks of his chestnut mare.

"We ride, then!" Erg'Ran announced, taking the point.

Garrison gave Swan's hand a final squeeze, then released it.

Although the snow had ceased to fall, there was a wind, bitingly cold beneath the clearness of the star-filled sky. Garrison huddled deeper into his cloak, tugged the cowl of his hood more closely about his face.

The combination of moons and stars illuminated the plateau so brightly that Garrison could almost make out the small print below the words "Sea-Dweller" on the black face of his Rolex wristwatch. Why he'd bothered to look at it was a mystery to him. Time in the conventional sense he had come to know since his first awareness of such things as a child was meaningless here.

Judging from the positions of the moons on the horizon—and he had no backlog of experience on which to base an opinion of any sort—he thought that the time here was more or less the equivalent of two in the morning. That disagreed totally with his wrist-watch.

Garrison's watch did, however, remind him that he needed to ask Swan about the clock which she had built. Or did she whisk it together with magic? Even so, that the concept of a gear-driven mechanical clock was not alien to her was heartening.

Gar'Ath and Bin'Ah were clearly visible as they took up their outrider positions. Garrison twisted round in the saddle, the leather creaking comfortingly. The others of their company rode in a column of twos, the prisoner Sword of Koth at the approximate center, his still-masked face held high, a blanket tied around his upper body for added warmth. The shackles of Garrison's Model 100s had been taken from the Sword of Koth's wrists exactly three times so that, under close guard, the fellow could urinate. Not a word had left the prisoner's lips, however, no request for water, not even an insult to his captors.

Despite the fact that their prisoner had provided them with no willing intelligence, Garrison and the others had learned some things from the few personal items carried on the man's person and from items found in his saddlebags and the saddlebags of the other mounts they'd seized. What data Garrison and the others accumulated largely consisted of various Sword of Koth tactical maps, many of these maps' duplicates, and items akin to notebooks, with various points concerning past battle plans written in them. Interestingly, these included the most recent entries, which called for the death of Swan by whatever means necessary. Found among the belongings of the Ra'U'Ba were maps, more crudely drawn and less informative. There was also a diary kept by one of the Ra'U'Ba. Erg'Ran could read their language, as he perused it (Swan out of earshot) informing Garrison, Gar'Ath and some of the others that it seemed like the diary's author was obsessed with rather bizarre fantasies concerning human, rather than Ra'U'Ba, females.

Putting the horses once belonging to the Sword of Koth together with the animals ridden by the three dead Ra'U'Ba, plus the extra horses the men who'd remained as a rear guard behind the Falls of Mir had kept, their column included quite a decent-sized small herd. Garrison had solved the problem of how to keep the animals in check, based on something he'd seen in a western movie. Using lengths of rope, loops were tied about the necks of each animal, the horses then teamed in fours, tethered to a single, stout lead.

Besides the maps, tactical notebooks and horses, their so-far minor military victories netted their company an abundance of saddles, spare swords, battleaxes and the like.

When Garrison had inquired about what field rations the Sword of Koth or Ra'U'Ba might have stashed in their saddlebags, on the first occasion Erg'Ran told him, "What the Sword of Koth carry is edible, but only if you are desperate." As concerned the Ra'U'Ba's food supply, Gar'Ath simply said, "No man or woman would eat their vile slop, usually dried and salted human flesh."

So far, Garrison reflected, the stew he'd consumed so quickly that it was more like inhaling than eating was his only taste of Creath cuisine. If that stew were at all typical, to say that the population of Creath's tastes were—gastronomically speaking—a bit Spartan was putting it mildly. He'd wait to be impressed at the summer palace, as promised.

Ahead of the column, the plateau called Arba'I'Tac seemed to stretch on to infinity. If anything grew here at all, it was too microscopic to be seen by the human eye. There was some snow, but it was rapidly being blown clear, just sticking in the deeper cracks and crevices of the rock floor. Few actual large rocks, even fewer which might qualify for boulder classification, dotted the landscape. Garrison's immediate impression that Arba'Il'Tac appeared almost lunar was premature; the plateau was most unmoonlike due to its total lack of craters or any major surface impressions. It was, as Swan had told him, as if something had lopped off the top of a mountain and the plateau remaining was merely the stump.

Garrison's meager mastery of equestrian-related parlance was easily strained, but if memory served he thought that the gait at which their horses moved over the plateau would best be described as a canter. It was somewhere between a slow lope and a fast gallop.

So far, nothing had arisen out of the ordinary and they were making good time. His horse, fresh from several hours of rest, seemed eager still and straining to run. "Easy, girl," Garrison murmured to her.

Moc'Dar cowered beneath the chart table, near the Queen's feet, feebly attempting once again to hide his disgusting body beneath his meager cloak, just as she had decreed him to do. He was amusing, but Eran felt that she would soon tire of him this way, perhaps spellchange him to something even more repulsive, more torturous for him to endure.

But there was no time for that now.

Eran focused her attention, instead, on the maps spread before her. The Horde was scattered to the six winds, searching for Swan and her vile companions.

The snows had changed everything, and very rapidly. Had her attentions not been elsewhere, or had she anticipated that her daughter's magic would be strong enough to escape the Mist of Oblivion, she could have altered the weather, prevented the snows from blocking the mountain passes giving access to the sea.

The sea, Woroc'Il'Lod, was beyond doubt her daughter's destination, the route by which her daughter would come to Edge Land and Barad'Il'Koth.

With the passes heavily snow covered, Swan would have no choice but to cross Arba'Il'Tac. Eran focused her second sight as she stared at the map. She'd have to be quick, because her daughter's magical abilities might have reached a level where the girl could feel that she was being second-sighted.

Eran concentrated, saw them, many men with horses, one of the men at the center of the column garbed as Sword of Koth; but he was a prisoner. The riders made good speed across the plateau, at the head of them the oldest of her enemies, Erg'Ran—curse him! Riding in his wake, Eran saw her daughter. Riding beside Swan, there was a man. His face was hidden deep within the cowl of a hood and she could not see it. But, that this man was the one, the one whom Swan brought back with her from the other realm, Eran was certain.

It was certain, too, that Swan could not have him,

each instant that Swan and he were together was incredibly dangerous.

Eran's own magic not yet fully restored from controlling the Mist of Oblivion, she had not the power to magically transport an army of any adequate size to the plateau, nor could she create some great cataclysm which would rent the plateau and destroy the riders coursing Arba'Il'Tac.

Once they crossed Arba'Il'Tac, they would go to the old summer palace, and because of Eran's own spellworking, Eran could not harm them there, nor could the Horde of Koth molest them.

Eran blinked and the second sight vision was gone. "Think!" Eran urged herself, screaming the admonition. She heard Moc'Dar groveling beneath the chart table, thinking perhaps that her wrath was directed against him rather than herself.

There were so many spells to keep in work that, if she used too much magical energy before she were fully restored, some of the crucial spells which she maintained might become broken. Except the one that she wished that she could break. Eran controlled it not.

Eran had forced the renewal twice already since learning of Swan's survival. Time was her enemy, time having to elapse before she could take the renewal unto herself again, and time that Swan and her man from the other realm would be together.

"Think!" Eran shrieked again. Moc'Dar whimpered little frightened animal sounds from the flagstones near her feet.

"Animals," Eran murmured. "Moc'Dar, you still aid me!" Eran gathered her skirts and raced across the chamber, toward the shelves where she kept her books and scrolls, only faintly aware of the sounds of Moc'Dar scurrying along at her heels.

Eran second-sighted the shelves, skimming over each item there, at last locating what she sought.

Raising her skirts still higher, Eran stepped up onto the three-legged stool which allowed her to reach the upper shelves, her fingers reaching unerringly to the one scroll she required. Stepping down, Eran dropped to her knees on the flagstones, skirts billowing around her. Unrolling the scroll, her eyes flickered down over the Old Tongue runes. "Yes," Eran purred, smiling.

Erg'Ran called in the outriders, dispatching two other riders to take up sentry positions while the company stopped so that the horses could be rested. The portion of the plateau which they chose was no different than any other, topographically identical to what lay behind and what lay ahead. It would have been terribly easy to become lost here, to wander the same ground over and over again unendingly. With the enormity of the sky and the vast expanse of Arba'Il'Tac seeming to continue infinitely in all directions, the mere act of standing still was dizzyingly disorienting.

Garrison focused on his horse, rubbing down his own mount, telling Swan, "I'll take care of yours in just a minute."

But Swan was already seeing to her animal and told him so. "Al'An. I am perfectly capable of caring for my mount all by myself. Before the Mist devoured my home, after all, I alone cared for my wonderful white horse."

"Not magically?"

"She was a fine and wonderful creature, my white horse, and she liked to be touched. The magic cannot do that, Al'An."

He started to speak, but said nothing. In perfect silence, Garrison and Swan stood almost back to back, tending their horses.

Gar'Ath was changing his saddle to a fresh mount. His animal and Bin'Ah's were getting the greatest workouts. "Enchantress, a question if I may?"

"Of course," Swan replied.

"I know that the Champion speaks always of food, but I'll confess that I'm more than a bit hungry myself. At the old summer palace, what will we eat?"

Garrison chuckled under his breath. It was the classic male to female question: "What's for dinner?"

"Well, what would you like, Gar'Ath?"

"Meat and fowl—we'll have plenty of fish to choose from when we take ship on Woroc'Il'Lod—and breads and vegetables and—"

Swan laughed, telling him, "I will produce whatever you and the other men wish, but it will be unprepared. The taste is better when food is cooked rather than magic worked. Do you agree?"

"Nothing like home cooking, Enchantress!"

Garrison laughed again.

Swan continued, saying, "The other women and I will see to it that the finest meal ever eaten is prepared, just the way you and Al'An and Erg'Ran and all the others would like it. There will be such abundance that you, Gar'Ath, will be too exhausted from lifting a spoon or knife to lift your sword, too full, too uncaring to raise yourself into your saddle, even if the most beautiful girl of Creath beckoned to you!"

Gar'Ath tightened his cinch and swung up into the saddle, winking as he told Swan, "I doubt, Enchantress, that I could ever be that satisfied by food alone." He glanced at Garrison, nodding as he said, "Champion," then heeled his horse's flanks and was off.

"So, you actually cook?"

"If I eat because I must eat, the magic will do. If I eat because I truly wish to eat for the taste, then I cook."

Garrison understood the difference better than Swan probably supposed, he guessed. He supposed the magic kind of cooking was like heating something up in a microwave, the good kind of cooking like the good kind of cooking anywhere, slow and patient.

Swan was finished with her horse, started to come over to stand beside him when she stopped, said, "Here is what I meant when we spoke about Arba'Il'Tac, Al'An. Look!"

She drew off her left glove, flicked her wrist, closed, then opened the palm of her hand and, from within her hand, the same light that had guided them toward the boundary with the wood now shone, bluish white. Swan passed the light over the rock near their feet. Garrison blinked, then realized what it was that she was illuminating for him.

Etched in the stone like lines finely drawn by an exacting artist was the outline of a fully articulated bird wing, only vastly larger than any which Garrison had ever seen. From root to tip, as his eyes followed the light, it seemed to extend thirty feet or better in length. "Holy—"

"Shit?"

"Yes, holy shit," Garrison agreed. "What do you call this thing, the creature that left these markings in the stone?"

"They bear no names of which I am aware. Here! Here is part of another one, Al'An."

Garrison's eyes followed the light, Swan casting it over the outline of a gargantuan spinal column. Its width at the narrowest part appeared to be almost six inches, appreciably wider where the vertebrae emerged. The light from Swan's hand wasn't strong enough to reveal where the skeletal outline ended or began. He was about ask if she could increase the light's intensity—go to high beam—when Swan's light went out. "Mother has found us," she whispered, her voice trembling when she spoke.

"Erg'Ran!" Garrison called out, letting his cloak fall open, to grasp the butt of one of his pistols, ready to draw. The old man came toward them in a limping run. Garrison's left arm curled around Swan's shoulders, drawing her close against him, to shield her. "What do you see, Swan?"

"What is it, Enchantress? Tell us if you can," Erg'Ran urged.

"I have never felt a spellworking like this. I thought that—that I felt my mother second-sighting us before, before we dismounted, but I was uncertain."

"Then, she's second-sighting us?" Erg'Ran prodded.

"More than that, different than that." Garrison felt Swan's body shudder against him, the paroxysm rolling through her like a wave, as if a seizure. Her knees seemed to buckle and Garrison held her more tightly. Swan's voice was soft, low, fighting for control, but building in intensity. "I feel my mother's power rising from the rock beneath us, coming. Coming for us!" Swan finally shrieked. "What magic is this?"

In the next instant, they all knew.

The rock beneath their feet began to tremble, tiny fissures spiderwebbing along the length and breadth of Arba'Il'Tac. "Earthquake!" Garrison called out over the cracking and smashing of the rock. Would they understand the word?

"It is not what you say, Al'An!" Swan shouted back to him. "It is far worse. Look!"

Garrison looked at Swan, then turned to gaze toward whatever it was which her eyes seemed to be riveted upon. As Garrison saw what she saw, one part of his brain began telling another part of his brain that this was impossible, and then ordering his mind to reject what was clearly recognizable as immediate, impending doom. He was seized with the idea that he should be laughing, his mind death-gripped onto the thought that this would be the perfect time for him to verbalize a reference to that very special kind of shit which Swan always asked him about. Somewhere, somehow, it crossed Garrison's mind that he was crazy just to be seeing this, wildly, egregiously funny farm nuts.

Rising from the plateau, nearly transparent but of obvious substance, like photographic negatives, but alive, rose the monsters which had perished here within the rock of Arba'Il'Tac millennia ago, animated in all their horrific glory and power.

The creatures snarled, they snapped at each other, they reeled with life. They discovered prey, waiting to be devoured, consumed into stomachs which no longer had flesh and substance.

Garrison started laughing, laughing so hard that tears rolled from his eyes and down his cheeks. But he grabbed Swan closer to him still, half lifting her off her feet, spinning around. Letting go of her for an instant, Garrison snugged tight the cinch strap of her saddle. He swept Swan up into his arms, the horse already going wild-eyed with terror. One fist locked on the animal's bridle. The laughter gone, the tears still filling his eyes, Garrison commanded girl and horse, "Ride! That way! Now!" Garrison smacked Swan's horse across the rump and the animal leaped away.

Alan Garrison didn't know what direction "that way" was, but none of the nightmare beasts were in that direction—yet.

Erg'Ran was shouting orders.

Garrison snugged the cinch for his own saddle, vaulting up, wrenching the animal around bodily by its reins, then digging in his heels, his feet not yet in the stirrups.

Swan's mount was already a hundred yards ahead of him. Garrison found the stirrups and leaned low over his horse's neck, its mane lashing so mercilessly against his face that the tears began anew. He glanced back. "Mistake, lamebrain!" Garrison chided himself. Everywhere he looked, more of the beasts were rising from the rock, towering into the night sky, slobber dripping from enormous fanged jaws. These things didn't just look alive, Garrison realized; they were alive. "That's good," he tried convincing himself, talking to himself again. "If they aren't alive, you can't kill 'em!"

The test of that theory was upon him Garrison realized with his next breath. There was either a shadow obscuring both moons, or—

It was the thing with the thirty-foot-long wing. With both wings spread wide to swoop down upon him and a body the length and girth of a Cadillac in between them, airborne it spanned more than seventy feet. The head, blunt faced and at least a yard wide, terminated in jaws which nearly obscured the rest of the skull. Set within the jaws were row after row of pointed, shark-like teeth, each as large as Garrison's hand.

Garrison knotted his left fist into the reins and his animal's mane. He drew one of the SIG .45s from its shoulder holster. "230-grain Hydra-Shok don't fail me now!" His target was so big, Garrison rationalized, that it would be impossible to miss, even from the wildly careening back of a moving horse.

Garrison fired. He fired again.

A clammy feeling like nausea rose from the depths of Alan Garrison's stomach, swept over him, but he knew that it was fear. He couldn't have missed the creature, but there was no effect on this thing which was about to snatch him up into its jaws and kill him.

In high school, Alan Garrison had a friend named Morry, who, like Garrison, had always wanted to be a writer, taught himself to type at age ten, wrote novella-length short stories for English class assignments. Morry even had a continuing character whom he wrote about, a secret agent. Once, Morry had his fictional creation trapped inside a burning building, clinging from one arm to a cable in an elevator shaft filling with smoke, a lusciously beautiful girl unconscious in the other. The last time that Alan Garrison saw Morry, Morry still hadn't figured out how to get the secret agent out of the elevator shaft.

This was an elevator shaft, Garrison realized, and he was the secret agent. He wasn't getting out. . . .

❖ ❖ ❖

Swan heard the sound of the firespitter, twice. She twisted round to look back from her saddle, saw what was about to happen to Al'An. Pain gripped her soul so tightly that she felt that her heart would surely die. "Sweet fool, Al'An!" Swan cried out to her Champion. How could a man of Al'An's world know that only a magical weapon could be used to combat a magical beast? She should have thought of it, used some of the magic she'd so stupidly hoarded, saved as a weapon against the unthinkable.

The unthinkable was upon them.

Al'An was about to die.

Swan reined back her animal almost too quickly, drawing the magical energy into her. Her horse reared and bucked beneath her, energy more violent than she had ever before experienced crackling around her in the night air.

There was no time . . .

Erg'Ran got his peg leg into the cup that was used in place of a stirrup on the off side of his saddle. He looked about him, his panicked horse difficult to control beneath him. A host of nightmarish creatures advanced along the plateau, the nearest of the beasts only warblades from the ragged line of horses and men forming the remounting column. A few of the extra horses had bolted.

Erg'Ran felt his face twist into a grimace. A lizard-headed monster the height of a Ka'B'Oo flicked its forked tongue, snaked its neck downward, and snapped one of the horses into its slathering jaws. A hideous cry issued from the doomed animal. The cry was silenced in the next instant, the horse's blood drooling from the monster's incisors.

Erg'Ran looked for the Enchantress. Was she in immediate peril? He saw the Champion, instead.

A horrible winged beast of awesome proportion swooped down out of the night toward the Champion,

jaws open, ranks of huge, spear-shaped teeth glinting wickedly in the starlight.

A sick feeling seized Erg'Ran. Aside from the fact
that he genuinely liked this lad from the other realm,
if the Champion were to perish so too would vanish all hope of fulfilling the prophecy made by Mir,
and so too would the future of Creath fade into an
eternity of dark magic and death.

The Champion was going to die. . . .

The winged beast's breath was a searing, fetid wind,
washing over Alan Garrison, the monster's jaws poised
to clamp closed around him.

Alan Garrison's horse tripped, the animal's off front
hoof catching on a fissured rock slab hidden beneath
a ghostly thin layer of snow.

The animal began to cartwheel forward.

Alan Garrison spilled from the saddle, forward
along the horse's neck, rolling head first over the
horse's head. His left hand still grasped the reins, a
torn hank of mane bunched with them in his fist. The
horse shrieked agony. Garrison rolled, still clutching
his pistol. The downdraft in the wake of the monster's
now frantically beating wings pummeled Garrison. The
instant of slipstream, nearly cyclonic in strength,
slapped him brutally to the rock floor. As Garrison's
horse careened forward. Garrison clambered to his
feet. The horse crashed against the plateau's unremitting stone, a cracking sound as its neck broke. Its
body bounced, and there was a thud as flesh struck
rock, the horse unmoving, dead.

Every bone in Garrison's body ached. His head
pounded almost as hard as the knot of pumping
muscle in his chest.

Garrison still clutched the pistol. Clearly, against
this supernatural winged beast a firearm was useless.
Stabbing the handgun into his trouser band, Garrison dragged himself to his feet. The axe that was still

thong-strung to his saddle was the focus of his attention.

Garrison jumped toward it, tearing it free.

He recalled Erg'Ran's admonition, not to over-extend the swing, not to lose balance.

The monster banked on its left wing, soared through a perfect, almost sensually beautiful arc, flapped both wings once, then once again, then started into its dive.

Garrison's fists throttled the axe shaft, trembling as he focused every ounce of strength through his arms.

Perhaps Creath was the place for epiphanies, because Alan Garrison had the sudden realization that the axe would do no better than his pistol had done. A bullet or two from his pistol should have had noticeable effect on a living enemy of reasonable size, at least should have been noticed, if as nothing more than a flea bite, by something this large.

The winged monster was magical, summoned out of the fossil record in stone. The one, single thing which Alan Garrison had which had been created from magic was the hooded greatcape which still clung to his shoulders.

The beast tore down for him from the sky. Garrison flung the axe aside at the last possible moment, in the same motion grasping his cloak, swirling it before him. He waited the eternal microsecond, poised, cape in hand, like a matador refusing to give ground before the charge of a raging arena bull.

The disgusting, hot breath of doom enveloped Garrison once again.

Garrison snapped the greatcape up, interposing its magical fabric between his life and the monster's gaping jaws. If magic could not work to combat magic, Alan Garrison was about to find out. Garrison flung his body onto Arba'Il'Tac's frigid grey stone and rolled.

There was a hideous shriek and the rock pulsed beneath him.

Garrison remembered to open his eyes. The monster skittered along over the plateau, like an out-of-control aircraft crash landing, the greatcape which clung to its head blinding it. As the monster struck at last with full impact, the intermittent pulsing of the rock floor transformed into a single, violent shudder. The monster skidded, stopped suddenly, shrieked again, then gave a mighty shake of its terrible head. The cape fell from the beast's eyes.

The monster stood, swayed on ridiculously skinny legs. Its talons scraped at the stone, sparks flying in their wake. It flexed its wings, then soared skyward.

Garrison didn't lie to himself. He was fresh out of magical greatcapes. On its next pass, the beast would kill him. . . .

Swan's heart skipped a beat when Al'An, braver than brave, blinded the winged monster and sent it crashing into the plateau. But her heart sank when the creature shrugged the greatcape from its eyes and once again took flight.

Swan still didn't know if there would be time enough.

The other beasts magically resurrected by her mother, none of them so far displaying any evidence that they could fly, were advancing across Arba'Il'Tac. In the space of time that it would take to draw but a few breaths, they would close with Erg'Ran, Gar'Ath and the others.

The magical energy filled Swan, but she did not yet know how she could use it in order to defeat this terrible enemy.

Dismounting less than gracefully from her terrified horse, she glanced at the animal, magically commanding it, "You will stay beside me. Do not be afraid." Her mount immediately quieted, lowered its head.

Commanding what was natural was always easier than commanding the unnatural.

Swan knew in that instant what she must do.

These gargantuan beasts, mere moments away from their unspeakable triumph, were vicious, creatures formidable beyond her imagining. But Al'An's fire-spitters and axe, the swords and axes and spears and crossbows of the others, would kill living beasts. The monsters could be slaughtered only if they lived, were of flesh which could be rent, blood which could be spilled, bone which could be crushed.

Swan had joked with herself when she was briefly angry with Erg'Ran, that she had to quit their interview lest she lose her temper and turn him into a frog. She knew the transmuting spells, but had never commanded them—until she raised her voice in a scream which echoed like thunder over the plateau that was Arba'Il'Tac.

Swan felt the power. Everything stopped, men and horses and nightmare beasts focusing their eyes upon her.

Swan's arms extended toward the night, her hands grasping at the starlight. Magical energy flowed in lightning bolts from her fingertips as the ancient words spilled forth from her lips into the fabric of the sky.

The Old Tongue words wove one with the other, the spell casting chain begun. The power of the lightning magnified beyond that of any magical energy she had ever known. Swan turned her open hands to the stars, great luminescent balls of magical energy—gold and crimson and brilliant white—born from her outstretched palms, floating, pulsating, alive.

Her voice throaty, guttural sounding to her, primal, frightening, Swan cried out the final incantation, commanding the balls of light to her bidding. "The undead beast which flies and those which stalk the plateau, all to devour both man and horse their sole reason to exist!—transmute them so that they will be living beings of flesh as once they were! Obey me, force of magic! Transmute them into living creatures so that they can be returned to the dead!"

There was a rumble, louder than any thunder, her command louder still. "Heed me, force of magic! Heed well the Enchantress's desire! Obey me now!" Swan tossed her head, energy swirling round her in a wind that was not a wind, her hair, her skirts caught up in it. Her back arched, hands and arms stretched to their greatest reach. The magic flowed. . . .

As if they were alive, the balls of energy flew from Swan's hands, sailed through the night with effortless ease, engulfing first one, then another and another and another of the translucent beasts. At the very instant in which the light touched them, the nightmare creatures began to transform.

Awestruck, Alan Garrison could do nothing but watch.

Solid bone emerged from magic shadow, cells growing, dividing, growing, dividing again, multiplying into matter in the blink of an eye. Where there had been only magical illusion, there was life. Garrison watched nerve endings fire, tissue grow, blood vessels and capillaries fill, the blood flowing through them visible in the brief instant during which they remained partially transparent. Garrison witnessed oxygenation in the space of a heartbeat. Flesh and muscle took shape. Masking the circulation beneath, skin—wet and raw and slick and new—formed, encasing all within.

The mesmerizing effect Swan's incantation held over all life on Arba'Il'Tac faded as did the light.

Garrison scanned the ground for his lost axe, took it up. Real, magical no longer, the creatures were as dangerous as before. But now they could be killed.

Swan's voice rang out to him across the plateau. "Raise your axe, Al'An! Raise it high!"

Garrison did as bidden.

A bolt of lightning flew from Swan's fingertips, struck the blade of his axe, blue-white electricity arcing along its edge. "Now, brave Al'An! Now wield your axe in triumph!"

Evidently, the winged creature did not like him. The beast flapped its enormous wings and took flight, circling above Garrison. He was tempted to shout to Swan, "Slip some magic to my .45s!" There was no time for that. The axe or nothing stood between him and the monster as it banked its wings and started to dive.

At the back of his mind, he decided that he would just as soon forego the opportunity to encounter a fire-breathing ice dragon once—if—they reached Woroc'Il'Lod.

This was a logic problem, Garrison convinced himself. All he had to do was figure out exactly where to strike the beast. The obvious target would be the reeking hole of its mouth, but was that the best choice?

In the last second, Garrison thought not and tried something else. The beast nearly upon him—Garrison remembered that it couldn't change direction all that rapidly—he ran forward with all his speed, dropping into a crouch and swinging the axe against the creature's underbelly as it overflew him. Blood and gore and intestines rained down on Garrison, as his axe twisted in the creature's guts.

Before Garrison could think or act, the beast's wings thrummed harder, and it was climbing. There was no time to let go, Garrison still grasping the imbedded shaft, tightening his grip as the monster strained for all the altitude it could attain.

Definitely the proper moment for a reference to g'urg, Garrison thought desperately as he looked at the ground racing below. To what he mentally ascribed as the "North," the plateau dropped abruptly toward a vast sea; Woroc'Il'Lod, great icesheets and towering icebergs stood well out from the shore.

The blood and gore washed from the winged beast's insides, covering Garrison in slime, and oozed down along the axe shaft. Despite his gloves, Garrison's hands were slipping. Even had the axe handle's surface remained clean, Garrison's grip would not hold out much longer.

The creature shuddered, let out a cry, and Garrison realized that it died in the same instant.

Garrison trembled. Fear, of course, but much more than fear, he shook with rage. He was going to die for sure this time, die and abandon the most wonderful, craziest, most perfect woman he'd ever known or ever dreamed of knowing. Had he been at all uncertain before this moment, now Garrison realized how much he loved her, that he loved Swan more than the life that he was about to lose.

It seemed there was to be a pause between the winged beast's death and Garrison's own. The creature's body floated along peacefully through the night sky, drifting on and supported by the wind currents. These precious few seconds passed. The wings, still outstretched but no longer flapping at the monster's volition, were beaten instead, an assault begun by the very air which had kept the beast aloft.

There had been a perfect stillness, during which Garrison heard nothing but the soft keening of the wind. But, that whispering began to increase, subtly at first, then became a roar, louder and louder, the monster's body starting to plummet.

Death was inevitable for him, but that was no reason just to take it, accept it. That he would die, he was sure, but that he would fight death to the last, of that he was also certain. He let go of the axe shaft with one hand and grasped for the stem of the nearest wing. . . .

Erg'Ran's axe blade bit deep into the throat of the

beast. One mighty claw lashed downward, but Erg'Ran, despite his peg leg, was able to dodge aside.

Erg'Ran's horse reared, whinnied, and the beast was distracted and wheeled round to silence it. Erg'Ran shifted the axe to his left hand, drew his sword, charged the monster, hacking and slashing along its flank.

The creature shrank back for an instant, as if pausing before its next attack, then flicked its massive tail and swatted Erg'Ran's horse to the rock floor. Recoiling again for a moment, it sprang toward Erg'Ran, gargantuan head reared, fangs bared.

Erg'Ran half-swung, half-flung his axe, into the juncture of head and throat. The monster screamed torment and bloodlust: the axe head was buried to half its depth, blood spewing from the gaping wound.

Erg'Ran nearly lost his balance, moving too fast for his peg leg. Lunging, Erg'Ran pierced the creature's abdomen with the point of his sword. He drew out the blade with both hands. Erg'Ran swung the sword as he would an axe, opening a ragged gash a warblade's length at least along the monster's midsection.

The beast, blood pouring from its wounds, staggered, fell.

Erg'Ran wrestled his axe from its body, his eyes scanning the plateau. Well out from the column, still mounted, sword in hand, Gar'Ath did battle with another of the beasts. Riding his horse between the creature's hind legs, Gar'Ath reined back, sprang from his mount and neutered the monster with one mighty swing.

Gar'Ath, smeared with blood and gore from head to foot, raised his sword in triumph, the body of his kill collapsing before him.

As Erg'Ran made to see how the others fared, he heard the Enchantress scream. Sword in one hand, axe in the other, Erg'Ran craned his neck, searching for her, ready to charge toward the sound. No

monster molested her. She stared, instead, into the
night sky. Was there another of the winged beasts like
the one which the Champion— "The Champion,
Enchantress! The Champion?"

Her voice was a lament, ringing out over Arba'Il'Tac
and across the sky to the stars overhead. "Al'An plunges
to his death!" the Enchantress cried. The fabric of the
air around her contorted, vibrated. There was a burst
of light. The Enchantress vanished within it. . . .

Garrison clambered up from the wing and onto the
dead creature's back. With each time that his blood-
slicked gloved hands shifted, Garrison risked losing
his balance, that he would lose his grip, fall away.
The slipstream viciously tore at him. He felt his
face contorting with its force.

The ground was getting closer and closer, faster
and faster.

So far, the dead monster's wings had not yet collapsed. Rather than dropping like a stone, its body
followed an erratic glide path, accelerating by the
microsecond. Blood pounded in Garrison's temples
and the rush of air was so great that his lungs ached.
He was losing consciousness, he knew.

"Gotta hold on!" Garrison formed the words, said
them he knew, heard nothing but the roaring of the
air around him. His eyes were squinted so tightly
against the wind's pressure that he could not make
out whether their bodies were about to crash against
the unremitting rock of Arba'Il'Tac or into the icy
waters of Woroc'Il'Lod beyond.

Garrison's arms were not long enough to go around
the creature's neck; no human's arms would have
been. But he gripped it as best he could.

"Special Agent Alan Garrison killed in the line of
duty," Garrison thought or may have said aloud. He
could no longer be sure. His ears ached and the
sound of the wind was becoming progressively duller,

like something far away, becoming fainter and fainter. "Cause of death: splattered while clinging to the dead body of a winged monster in some alternate universe place called Creath."

Garrison thought that he laughed, but he couldn't be certain. If, somehow, word concerning the manner of and circumstances surrounding Special Agent Alan Garrison's bizarre death could be gotten to Matt Wisnewski, Special Agent in Charge Wisnewski would be stuck writing paperwork on this until mandatory retirement sneaked up and bit him in the ass!

It was definite now. Alan Garrison was laughing, even though he couldn't hear it.

Garrison was instantly certain of one thing, however. He could hear Swan telling him that he would be all right. Talk about denial! "Nuts!" Garrison said, describing his own mental condition.

And then he saw this bird, kind of pretty really, about the size of a crow, but brown with a red breast like a robin. Its wingspan was pretty substantial. Garrison felt something shudder within him, blinked his eyes the rest of the way shut, then opened them. He tried to say "Crazy!" but Garrison realized that he could no longer talk. Everything had slowed down around him. Even though he still felt the rush of wind, it was somehow more normal seeming, almost pleasant.

That was it, he realized. He was dead already.

There was a light, but it looked more like one of the two moons this place had than some glow of eternal peace. Definitely dead, though, Garrison realized. Because, when he looked below, he could see the great winged creature spiraling downward in the last few seconds before it would go splat all over Arba'Il'Tac. And he could see himself still clinging to the dead monster's back.

Good-bye, body! He definitely could not make words anymore. This death thing, however, wasn't as bad as he'd thought it would be, at least not yet. He was actually enjoying this soaring around in the air routine.

And he wasn't alone. There was something with him, but he couldn't communicate with whatever it was.

Oh, well, Garrison tried to say. He would definitely miss Swan; he loved her so much. He just hoped that she'd be able to defeat her mother's evil forces, and that good old Erg'Ran and Gar'Ath the hotshot would protect her, take care of her.

All the happiness was suddenly gone from him. To make matters worse, Garrison looked below him again and saw the monster strike the stone floor of Arba'Il'Tac. He witnessed his own body being flung from its back, bouncing on the rock a few times—Whoa, that would've hurt!—and rolling over twice.

Garrison was coming down, very gently. He could see in much greater detail. The monster's wings were torn from its body during impact.

Garrison was trying to see his own body, but afraid to see it. Evidently, he had no choice in the matter. He kept going down and down, but easily, controlled, gently.

He crossed over a broad expanse of Arba'Il'Tac, then came to rest on his own chest. There was a lot of blood. His eyes were staring up at the stars, wide open in death.

He thought he saw Swan, but he couldn't change the direction in which he looked, as if something else controlled his eyes. What eyes?

Yeah, it was Swan. She was looking at him, tears flowing from her big, gorgeous eyes. Everything about her seemed big, tall, very tall, but just as beautiful. Somehow, he felt as if he sat in the palm of her hand. This was interesting. Was this a fantasy, he wondered, that Swan was with him?

Garrison tried forming words again, but could not.

He was looking at her eyes, at her tears, simultaneously wanting to tell her not to cry but that he felt like crying, too.

Swan's right hand passed over his field of vision. After that, Alan Garrison felt nothing at all but a warm, pleasant darkness.

# Chapter Eight

The rhythm of Erg'Ran's horse's gait, the creaking of leather, and the clinking of spurs and armaments composed a march more triumphal than circumstances dictated. Yet they had made it this far. Children, chickens, pigs, gar'de'thus, chased by or chasing a yelping dog, scurried from the path of the column, Erg'Ran at its head, Gar'Ath beside him.

The land surrounding the old summer palace was as Erg'Ran remembered it, except for its current inhabitants.

All those who remained alive of the Company of Mir were encamped within the magical boundaries surrounding the castle walls. There were the tents of men at arms, shared with their women and children. Each ridge pole flew the colors of clan or tribe. There were a small number of female warriors, fewer of them still clad fetchingly. One female warrior, auburn hair to her waist, barefoot, wearing a loose-fitting ankle length green dress, a hand-and-a-half sword suspended from her baldric, waved to Erg'Ran and sang out to him. "Ho! Erg'Ran!"

Her name was Liran and they jokingly flirted with

each other whenever time and circumstances would permit. She hitched her dress up well above her knees and made a deep, mock courtsey as Erg'Ran rode past. Without trying hard, Erg'Ran viewed what Liran had intended for him to see, the neckline of her dress quite conveniently cut for a spectacular view. "What say you, old friend who can't keep his eyes off me?"

"I say that it is good to be alive, my pretty friend, and I wish that you were as yet unmarried and my vision were keener still!"

"What a thing to say, Erg'Ran!" Gar'Ath protested. For all his brashness in battle, his swordedge-keen tongue in the face of his enemies, the young swordsman embarrassed easily when it came to women.

Some few of the female warriors, Liran one of them, had brought along children and a husband to care for them.

There were a handful of lusty, large-bosomed camp followers ensconced here along with the Company. Most of the horses from the encampment behind the Falls of Mir had made the trip, but a few had been lost along the treacherous mountain passes. All of the weapons and the tools with which to fabricate more had survived, along with the bulk of the supplies.

The Company of Mir was at its best and greatest strength; and, discounting willing hearts, strong swordarms and glorious truth of purpose, miserably suited to do battle with the Horde of Koth.

They turned their horses up along a gentle rise leading to the first of the terraced gardens. Bounding out of her tent to greet them—Gar'Ath in particular—was one of the most beautiful women Erg'Ran knew. Her name was Mitan, and Mitan was K'Ur'Mir. Rightwise, the long-haired girl had the magic, but she was a warrior to the bone. Mitan was clad in brown leather the color of her hair, jerkin and a skirt, the skirt barely long enough to be called one.

Her arms were bare, legs bare above turned-down knee boots. The cured pelt of a bar'de'gri was draped from one shoulder over her back, cinched between her breasts with a length of slender chain.

Erg'Ran took his old eyes from Mitan and cast a glance toward Gar'Ath. Gar'Ath's face was flushed, his eyes nervously flickering from side to side, trying to avoid contact with the liquid blue eyes staring up at him.

"Gar'Ath! Erg'Ran! Was there, indeed, a great and memorable battle?"

"We could have used your swordarm with us, fair one, and your smile!" Erg'Ran told her honestly. He felt a grin cross his lips as he looked over at Gar'Ath riding beside him. "Isn't that true, Gar'Ath?"

"Yes." And Gar'Ath's mount sprang ahead at his urging.

Erg'Ran looked down at Mitan. Hands on her waist, magnificent mane of hair tossed back, she was laughing. Erg'Ran shrugged his eyebrows. "Persist, girl!"

"That I will, old friend!"

"To be young again," Erg'Ran murmured, riding on. Beside Gar'Ath once again, their horses climbed to the first terrace. Behind them they heard the crowd call out epithets to the Sword of Koth prisoner who rode at the column's center.

Ahead of them lay the old summer palace, visible in its full glory at last.

It was, in fact, a castle of considerable size and, in the old days, great glory.

In its construction, the castle followed the contours of the rolling hill on which it was set, the series of outer walls deceptively low by comparison to the overall height of the keep within.

Each wall rose some seventy spans high, surmounted by defensive positions at the very top, below these well-designed arrow slits on a suspended walkway. The walkway was cut from the same stone as the walls and the upper defensive positions, thus reinforcing the wall's strength.

Each wall was constructed in the same manner and there were three successive walls ringing the keep.

In the days before the coming of Mir, and long before the old summer palace was enchanted, many a deadly battle was fought on the beaches leading up from Woroc'Il'Lod's frigid surf, or taken before the walls. Yet, never had the walls been breached.

The walls stood as they always had, but their presence was unnecessary to the summer palace's defense.

Flowers, in as profusive extravagance and diversity of passionate color as one could wish, lay in unconstrained beds everywhere along the first terrace, abutting the pathway along which they rode and mounting toward the second terrace onto which they'd shortly climb their horses.

Erg'Ran shrugged his shoulders out of his heavy cloak, draping it across the pommel of his saddle. The air was pleasantly warm, perfect, just as it always was.

The thinnest wisps of cloud floated within an otherwise flawless blue sky. Birds soared effortlessly overhead.

Erg'Ran and Gar'Ath led the dwindling column onto the second terrace. The cascade of flowers flowed past widely spaced trees, towering Ka'B'Oos, slender pines and graceful willows, their perfect order overwhelming in its simplicity. A few pavilions were erected on the second terrace green, the command tent among them. Bin'Ah would bring the Sword of Koth prisoner there. Despite the interrogation in store for him, the villain would be unharmed. Had Erg'Ran or any of the others wished otherwise, such would have been impossible on these grounds.

They ascended to the third terrace, the outermost of the three walls on one side, the lower terraces and the encampment on the other. The terrace terminated abruptly. Gar'Ath slowed his mount and Erg'Ran rode ahead, guiding his horse with a gentle tug of the off rein, turning the animal into the narrow throat which was the only means by which to enter the keep.

Erg'Ran passed the first wall. Had guards been needed here, they would have commanded the narrow passageway easily. It was said that a handful of determined warriors could fend off an army from these walls, and in antiquity such might well have been the case.

The tattoo of steel shod hooves against flagstone would last but briefly, as Erg'Ran and Gar'Ath were all who remained of the column.

Past the third wall, they reined in at the entrance to the courtyard. Gar'Ath swung a leg over his pommel and hopped down. Erg'Ran dismounted, but with considerably less grace and greater effort. He began to walk, carefully, leading his mount behind him. The flagstones, as with any uneven surface, played havoc with his peg leg, making it easy to trip.

Gar'Ath volunteered, "Let me take your animal's reins, old friend."

"That I'll let you do, lad." Surrendering them to the younger man, Erg'Ran continued across the courtyard, toward the three broad, low steps leading to the great iron studded wooden doors. "Leave the horses; they cannot stray." The stones were well worn at the center where Erg'Ran climbed the steps, their surface polished by uncounted generations of heavily booted men at arms and fair ladies in graceful slippers.

The doors opened as Erg'Ran reached them, just as he'd known that they would. "See! I told you the Enchantress'd be here, lad."

Erg'Ran passed through the doorway, Gar'Ath beside and a little behind him. Once through, the doors closed again.

Quickly, Erg'Ran and Gar'Ath crossed the length

of the wide entrance corridor and toward the great
hall beyond. Torches suspended in brackets along the
flanking walls lit their way.

To the side, there rose a great flight of stairs which,
if followed, would lead to the very highest chamber,
the keep's tower. "I hope she's not up there. That's
a long way to climb with a peg instead of a foot."

They would know in a moment, of course. If the
doors at the end of the corridor—identical to those
which had just opened and closed for them—were
to open, the Enchantress would be beyond them.

The doors to the great hall opened outward, like
arms outstretching to bid them enter. Torches burned
from the walls, and great chandeliers fitted with lit
candles were pendent from the vault above. The fires
were magical, and there was no smell of smoke.

Outstretched on a bier of sorts at the center of the
great hall lay the Champion and, beside him on the
flagstones, asleep, Erg'Ran imagined, knelt the
Enchantress.

Gar'Ath touched his balled fist to his forehead,
invoking the courage of Mir.

Erg'Ran merely stood and stared.

The hair brush moved to her will and Eran was
mildly surprised that she possessed the magical energy with which to command it. Even her second sight
was less than it should be. "Too much, too soon," she
chided herself, staring at her image in the magnificently framed mirror before which she sat. It was
something she used from time to time in her magic,
but more often solely for its more mundane purpose,
to see herself.

Not yet fully recovered from controlling the Mist
of Oblivion, it was vain stupidity to do what she had
done on Arba'Il'Tac. The magical energy required to
transmute images graven by time into stone into
animated specters moving at her will sapped her

magic to the lowest level it had ever been since her own return from the other realm. And, that was a very long time ago, in one way, a mere instant in another.

There was, in her present, weakened state, no way for Eran to determine whether her use of the beasts against her daughter and the Company of Mir had met with any degree of success. Experience had taught Eran that she should anticipate otherwise, plan accordingly. If she found herself happily surprised with the deaths of Swan and the others, well and good. If her pessimism proved warranted, however, she would be ready.

"Brush. Cease!" The hairbrush returned to its tray on the dressing table before her mirror and Eran stood, the gold-and-black brocade robe she wore falling open, her body naked beneath it. There was a chill in the air of her apartment at the very highest part of the very highest tower of Barad'Il'Koth. "Fire. Warm me!" The flames which flickered in the great hearth burned brighter, hotter.

Eran was tempted to go, to renew herself. She was tempted, but she resisted. That there might be some other power greater than herself, one on which she was dependent, the taking of which she craved utterly, posed a danger more grave even than Swan, Virgin Enchantress, Daughter Royal, Princess of Creath.

And, yet, the one peril was inexorably bound to the other.

Eran shrugged her robe from her body, her hair cascading veil-like over her shoulders, her breasts. She slipped beneath the quilt, willed the candles to extinguish themselves into darkness. She was very tired, and there was much to do on the morrow.

There was light. It had been the blink of an eye, yet simultaneously longer than that. Alan Garrison saw light. He wanted to see Swan.

In the next instant, there was darkness and a familiar voice howled with pain.

It was his own voice, and the darkness became darker. . . .

Gar'Ath touched his clenched fist to his forehead so rapidly, so vigorously that Erg'Ran could have mistaken the motion for a punch had he not known better. "Easy, lad."

"But, Erg'Ran, sure you saw that, heard that!?"

"I heard it, lad, heard what you heard. And I saw what you saw."

"It's a dead body and it moved!"

"Then, consider this lad. Since dead bodies don't move and we just saw the Champion's body move, the Champion cannot be dead. It's only logic, lad, isn't it now?" But, indeed, although he wouldn't say this to his young swordsman friend, for all that Erg'Ran knew of death and life, the body lying atop the bier was dead. If there was life somehow returning to that body, the young girl who knelt beside it, hands touching it at head and heart, strange words issuing from her lips, was the instrument.

Erg'Ran shook his head. There was magic that should not be done, and not because it was intrinsically evil. Such magic should not be employed because of what might happen to the one who used it, whether used for good or ill. He knew such evil first hand, knew how innocently it might begin.

He would not disturb the Enchantress; it was enough that she knew that they were here. If she required their services, she would inform them. If she wished them to leave, she would notify them of that desire as well.

Hence, there was nothing to do but sit and wait until something happened.

There was a beautifully carved wooden bench running the length of the near wall, perhaps originally placed there as a convenience for those who had come to the castle in generations past seeking an audience with the reigning Queen Sorceress.

Erg'Ran caught Gar'Ath's eye. With a jerk of the head, Erg'Ran started toward the bench.

"The Enchantress is doing it again, Erg'Ran!"

Indeed, the Enchantress had once more begun to move her hands over the Champion's body, once more begun to utter strange words in the Old Tongue, the rhythm of her speech almost that of a chant.

Perhaps the Enchantress did not realize the danger to herself; more likely, she was well aware of the hazards intrinsic to such magic and chose to ignore them because she cared more for the Champion than for herself. "She's a brave lass, the Enchantress."

"What do you mean, old friend?" Gar'Ath whispered back.

A story was a good way in which to while away some time, and Gar'Ath had never asked him concerning the trading of a flesh-and-blood foot for a wooden peg. All the young swordsman knew of it was that Erg'Ran had chopped the foot away himself.

"There's danger to the Enchantress, lad, danger in the magic that she uses. Before you were born, Gar'Ath, before the Queen Sorceress was what she is, when she was a beautiful young woman, she was very much like our Enchantress in many ways, in other ways not like her at all. But Eran was not evil."

"Hrmph! I believe that as much as—"

"That you're watching a man you thought was dead being reanimated?"

Gar'Ath smiled, laughed softly, perhaps at himself. "Fine then, Erg'Ran, what changed the Queen Sorceress to the foul thing she is today?"

"The magic, lad, in the way that she no longer used her magical energy as you might use a sword or a smith's forge or I might use a book or scroll, but instead became enslaved by the power, possessed by the magic rather than possessing it," Erg'Ran said. This was neither the time nor the place for any more elaborate an answer than that. So Erg'Ran hastily picked up the tale he'd intended to tell. "It was after Eran had changed, become the woman that she is today, using her magical energy for evil rather than good, it was after she gave birth to our Enchantress.

"We came into conflict, Eran and I, when it became quite apparent that Eran wished to wipe from the face of Creath the K'Ur'Mir, essentially all the K'Ur'Mir save herself and her daughter. I realized that if she were so determined, there would be no way to fight her because of the power she could wield. But I realized that there might be a way in which her magical powers could be rendered ineffective to sufficient degree that many of the K'Ur'Mir would survive, despite her efforts.

"It was her plan, you see," Erg'Ran continued, "that the blood line should be exterminated except as it served her purpose, that the only surviving women to possess genuine magical abilities in Creath would be herself and a daughter whom Eran would raise to be little more than an exceptionally gifted Handmaiden of Koth, but never a threat to Eran's power."

"What was this plan of yours, then?"

Erg'Ran gestured about them. "You're sitting in it, lad, breathing the very air of it."

"The summer palace? It was you who—"

Erg'Ran nodded, "And, as a result, incurred the terrible and considerable wrath of the Queen Sorceress. You see, lad," Erg'Ran told him, "I realized what Eran realized, only a half-step behind her. If all of the K'Ur'Mir were to concentrate their magical energies as one, not even Eran's magic could have been more powerful. With each one of them that she destroyed, the potential for that to happen became less and less. And that's how the summer palace came to be the one haven in all of Creath where Eran's evil has no power, and we are safe.

"As you know," Erg'Ran continued, his hands searching about in his robe for flint and steel, "what happened was that as each of the K'Ur'Mir died, the last of their magical energy was used to cast the self-same spell. The summer palace was picked because of its defenses, its command of the terrain, its access to Woroc'Il'Lod. We had no way of knowing how truly effective that combined magic would be, that defenses would not be needed. As the magical energy intensified here, Eran realized what was happening and dispatched the Horde.

"It was decided that the K'Ur'Mir should concentrate their presence in one location, here, where already the magic was building. That seemed the sensible choice. Only a very few of the K'Ur'Mir—Mitan's mother and father among them—stayed back to fight with magic and sword alongside those who had no magic. They were brave, as Mitan has come to be, but those who set out for the summer palace were brave, as well. I was asked to lead them here." Erg'Ran gazed at the ceiling, at the walls, shook his head, sighed. He struck a spark, began to light his pipe. "We never made it, as you know.

"The superior numbers of Eran's Horde engaged the K'Ur'Mir while our company was still too many lancethrows distant from the summer palace to be within its magic. Had we made it that far, there might have been a chance. We did not. There was not."

"I've heard many a tale of the killing," Gar'Ath murmured soberly.

"Yes, lad, killing. It was not a battle. That's why, since those bloody days, the chalk cliffs overlooking Woroc'Il'Lod have been called Dinad'Il'Rad. The magic of the K'Ur'Mir stood for a time against Eran's magical powers, but despite the magic the women used, with each one who died, the magical energy here increased, and the magical energy to combat Eran and the Horde on Dinad'Il'Rad decreased. It ebbed until there was no longer any possibility of holding out. Still, no one gave up. Eran's magical powers finally overcame the surviving K'Ur'Mir and the Horde swept over all. We'd set up improvised redoubts, dug trenches with both magical energy and sweat and muscle. Cavalry rolled over our position, then infantry followed. Swords flashed, bows were fired, spears were hurled. Male, female, young or old, there was no difference to the Horde's steel. Blood flowed in rivulets that morning, puddled round our feet.

"Those K'Ur'Mir who were not killed in the rush were put to death, cruelly," Erg'Ran told his young swordsman friend. His own voice sounding odd to him, Erg'Ran went on anyway. "I'd taken a spear in the shoulder and a mace split my helmet and didn't do very much good for the thick skull underneath it. When I awoke, madness ruled. I saw more use of the disemboweling hook that day than I ever want to see again, lad. The smoke from the burning flesh on the pyres where the bodies of the K'Ur'Mir were being burned was thick enough to make you choke, and if you hadn't been crying already because of the carnage, the smoke alone would have brought tears to the eyes.

"And I thought that was what Eran had planned for me, the hook for a long, slow time, then skinning me until unconsciousness ended her pleasure, then the flames. But I was mistaken. I had never seen Eran so exhausted, her magic so depleted. But apparently she'd saved enough of it to deal with me. In those days, you see, she'd already begun transmuting men into lesser animals, beasts that could do nothing but dumbly serve her will. This was the fate that she chose for me. That's how I came to chop off my own foot, lad."

Gar'Ath's eyes hardened and he swallowed several times, his J'Lag bobbing up and down visibly in his throat.

Erg'Ran told him the rest. "Eran told me that I'd be sickened by my fate when the change began, and she wanted that, for me to see what I would become. So, she started the transmutation with my left foot. If there'd been guards holding me, they might have been changed, too. So I was just supposed to stand there. In the same instant that her guards released my arms and she started to transmute me, I jumped for the nearest weapon. I was pretty agile in those days, a young lad like yourself, Gar'Ath.

"I was well fast enough to grab the axe that I carry to this day. Took it right speedily from a Sword of Koth captain. Had to kill him with it." Erg'Ran shrugged. "That's what took the time. You see, lad, I was a wee bit too slow for Eran's foul magic. It had already begun to transmute me. My left foot was drawing up into the cloven hoof of a gar'de'thu, the big kind."

"So, you hacked it off with the axe?"

Erg'Ran nodded. "Only thing I could think of, but there was the little problem of bleeding to death. I let swing with the axe, severing my foot with a single blow. I knew, from my studies, that I'd be dead within a few blinks of the eye from the loss of blood. Unless, that is, I could seal the wound. There was only one way for that. With all the speed I could muster, I jumped for the nearest of the pyres.

"Until the moment that I thrust my stump into the flames, there wasn't even any pain," Erg'Ran confided. "When the flames touched what was left of me down there, I nearly fell into a faint with it. To this day, lad, I don't know how I got myself away from the fire and to the edge of the chalk cliff. But I did. The courage of Mir was with me for sure! I flung myself over the edge, believing that if I died on the rocks below, it would be a far better fate than I'd suffer at the hands of Eran. And, as my being here happily demonstrates, Gar'Ath, there was at least a slight chance that I'd survive."

"So, you hit the water, not the rocks. But, still, old friend—"

"I know. I know. At any event, the icy waters of Woroc'Il'Lod extinguished the flame where I'd sealed my wound. I was incredibly weak, but I held onto that axe, let me tell you. I congratulated myself that I might not have a left foot anymore, but at least I wasn't a blasted gar'de'thu for Eran to sport with.

"The tide was coming in and I washed ashore, more dead than alive. What little magic I knew, I used to hold back the pain and the fever and to separate the salts from the water so that I could drink, make up for the blood that I'd lost. I lived along the shore for many days, dragging myself about as need be when I had to, living off whatever edibles I could find. Gradually, I got back enough strength to fashion myself a crutch from driftwood, then a crude peg. The first time I stood on it, I almost wished I had died. The only things that kept me going were the courage of Mir and the thought of her." And Erg'Ran nodded toward the Virgin Enchantress. "I knew that she could grow up to be the only hope for Creath, the only hope to defeat her mother. And, I'd be damned before I'd let Eran make the young Enchantress a servant to her evil."

"You're a brave man, Erg'Ran," Gar'Ath told him.

"You missed the point of the story, lad. I wasn't brave. I just did what I had to do to stay alive, and with the courage of Mir and my belief in that young girl giving me strength, I lived. The point is that there's a boundary that can be crossed with the magic, and once it's crossed there's no returning. If the Champion lives, and the Enchantress goes on to Barad'Il'Koth in fulfillment of the prophecies of Mir,

the only way still that Eran can be defeated is if the
Enchantress has magic stronger than hers. If we win
the day over Eran and the Horde, but lose the
Enchantress to the evil magic as a result, all is lost
in Creath, lost forever."

The chanting in the Old Tongue had stopped.

Erg'Ran's pipe had gone out. He sucked on it once
to be sure, and that sound was the only sound.

Swan's magic did not give her the ability to read
the thoughts of men as if they were runes inscribed
upon a scroll, but to know what Erg'Ran and Gar'Ath
had to be thinking required no such power. They
thought that she was reanimating the dead, but she
was not.

Perhaps her mother could do that—not the elaborate spellworking with the simplistically brutish
monsters on Arba'Il'Tac, but truly bring back to life
a complex, sentient being as if death had never taken
place. Perhaps she could do that, too, Swan realized,
shuddering at the thought.

What Swan spellworked with the spirit and the
body of Al'An was not that dark a magic; yet she knew
that if such were required, she would do it to save
him. And that frightened her even more.

Her magical energy was as it should be, despite
what she had expended on Arba'Il'Tac, despite going
after Al'An when he was about to die. By the time
she reached him, there was just enough left to her
to do what needed to be done, then transport them
to the summer palace. That accomplished, although
she would have had it otherwise, she had rested.

There was such great magical energy which was
one with the summer palace that within a brief time,
all that which she had expended was restored. And
Swan was able to draw upon more energy as required
for the healing spells to be employed.

At last, Al'An opened his eyes.

"I love you, Al'An," Swan whispered.

He closed his eyes, and she merely knelt beside him, watching his chest rise and fall, then rise again.

Gar'Ath had fallen asleep. Erg'Ran had not. Erg'Ran jostled the young swordsman's shoulder.

"What is it?"

"He lives, lad. The Champion lives! And so do our hopes!"

# Chapter Nine

Alan Garrison awoke to the sounds of music and laughter, opened his eyes and turned his head, a window—as large as a good-sized door—fully open to his right, near the foot of the bed, sunlight streaming in through it.

There was a very faint smell of flowers on the gentle breeze which flowed over him.

From the chest down, he was covered in a light blanket.

Without thinking, he sat up abruptly.

The blanket fell away, and he realized that he was naked beneath it. His body seemed to be without harm, moved at his will, showed no evidence of scarring, neither were there bruises nor abrasions apparent.

He was hungry without feeling malnourished.

Garrison looked down to his left. The bed was of extremely generous proportions, larger than king-size. Swinging his feet over the side, they barely touched the stone floor. The bed was so high that a single-step ladder was beside it. A ruffled canopy was stretched over it.

Garrison stood up, the stone cool but not cold beneath his bare feet. He snatched the blanket from the bed and wrapped it about himself at the waist. He felt a little unsteady, but he had no idea how long he'd been—what, he wondered? How long had he been unconscious? Or— Garrison shivered when he considered the alternative.

Garrison walked toward the window. The blanket— it dragged around his feet—nearly caused him to trip. As he approached the window, the sounds of music and laughter grew louder. When he looked out the window, Garrison blinked.

"This is it," Garrison told himself. "I died and wound up inside *A Connecticut Yankee in King Arthur's Court*." Half-expecting to see either Bing Crosby or William Bendix if he studied the faces below him, Garrison turned his back and leaned hard against the window opening.

He'd been riding on the back of the flying monster thing and about to crash when he saw a bird. Then there was this blinding light. And he was floating. And he saw Swan. After that, he was in darkness. Garrison remembered seeing Swan again, after that, and— Had she actually told him, "I love you," or— "I'm really fantasizing," Garrison half-whispered, shaking his head.

He looked outside again. If he had to wake up inside a movie, he supposed this one was as good as any. More or less, anyway. Bendix had really been good as Sir What's-his-name, one of the few actors who could play a comedic role just as brilliantly as he played a psychopathic killer, as he had opposite Alan Ladd. The spelling of Garrison's first name was due to Alan Ladd; his mother had always been a great fan of the actor.

"More stuff to think about besides this," Garrison murmured. He looked out the window again.

There were no suits of armor on the men, but some of the women wore those weirdo pointed

duncecap hats with goofy scarves flowing from them.
And the music—it sounded kind of nice, contra-
dance-like with flutes and everything—fit in perfectly.
Garrison's eyes tracked toward the origin of the music.
"Yeah, I'm dead or nuts or something!" Flutes, little
drums, mandolins, tinkling bells, all of them floating
in the air totally unsupported and playing themselves.

Garrison rubbed his hands over his eyes, realizing as he did so that he had dropped the blanket and
was standing stark naked in the open window.

He stepped back, and as he picked up the blanket, he began to look about the room. There was a
small, round table. "Round table! Oh, boy. Betcha all
the tables are round here." On the table were his
personal belongings, except for his clothes: his three
pistols, spare magazines, his knives, his wallet, money
clip, badge case, keys, cigarettes and lighter.

Garrison went over to the table, holding the blanket around his waist with one hand, shaking a cigarette from the pack with the other. He lit up. His
hand shook, and not from a craving for nicotine. The
pack was full, but it hadn't been. They didn't sell
cigarettes in Creath, nor, for that matter, in old movie
musicals set in Camelot.

There was a big wooden cabinet at the far end of
the room, the kind called an armoire. Garrison walked
over to it, opened its double doors. His clothes were
inside it, totally devoid of bloodstains. Garrison shivered again. When he'd seen his body—he remembered seeing it—there was blood on his clothing. A
lot of it. He closed his eyes. He remembered seeing his eyes open, staring. He'd seen dead bodies on
the street and in morgues; when he'd seen his body,
it was dead.

"Oh, shit," Garrison rasped.

He wondered if there was such a thing as a shower
around here? At the foot of the bed there was a chamber pot. "I'm doomed to primitive plumbing. Great."

Alan Garrison had never urinated into a chamber pot before, but he figured that there was a first time for almost everything. . . .

Neither of his SIG-Sauer P-220 .45s showed the slightest sign of being damaged from impact against the rock surface of Arba'Il'Tac. He would have figured that the one he'd had only stuffed into his belt would have gotten scratched or something. In fact, a small crack he'd had in one of the pistols' grip panels wasn't even there anymore. Short of shooting them to be sure, they seemed mechanically perfect.

All of his belongings were perfect.

There'd been a couple of scratches on his bomber jacket, and there were worn smooth places around its elbows. Not anymore.

The Pocket Natural which he used with the little Seecamp .32 had been with him for several years. As a result of constant contact with the oils from his hands, the natural finish leather had developed "the patina of use," as advertising people called it; the leather had darkened quite a bit. As Garrison snugged the holster and the little pistol which it carried into his right front pocket, he noticed that the leather looked as fresh and clean as the day he'd gotten it. All wear marks were also absent from the little pistol's surface.

Not the tiniest scratch was in evidence on the crystal of his Rolex, nor did the bar-shaped scar on his left wrist remain. The soles and heels of his cowboy boots looked brand new and the leather uppers gleamed as if spit-shined. A crown on the lower left side of his mouth wasn't there anymore; a natural-seeming tooth was where it had been.

Rubbing the back of his hand along his jawline, Garrison felt no stubble, as if he'd shaved less than an hour ago; but he hadn't shaved since Saturday morning, the day he'd met Swan.

"Okay. Sure."

The music and laughter persisted from the court-yard below his window. Alan Garrison set out to investigate.

By the time he'd descended the stairs, Garrison was used to torches in sconces along the walls flick-ering to life as he neared them, extinguishing them-selves after he passed.

He wasn't surprised when the metal-studded double doors leading from what was apparently an entry hall opened without his touching them. Beyond the door-way lay a flagstoned courtyard. If he had his bear-ings correctly, the music and laughter, which he could hear only very faintly at the moment, would be off to his left, in what he mentally labeled "the backyard," which was a perfectly logical place to hold a party. Nothing odd about that.

Garrison started off in what he hoped was the right direction, the steadily increasing sounds of music and laughter reassuring him. Leaving the courtyard, he passed beneath an elaborately latticed rose arbor, blossoms trellised above him and on both sides, the colors ranging from bright yellow to warm pink to brilliant shades of red, their smell heady on the warm air. He was, in fact, just slightly uncomfortable with his bomber jacket, but kept it on to cover the double shoulder holsters.

There was a natural stone pathway leading upward, wide enough for several men to walk abreast. Gar-rison followed it. He realized that the building seemed to grow out of a hillside, the contours of structure and grounds in perfect harmony.

The path was interrupted by a bridge, the kind of bridge one usually saw in ornamental gardens, gen-tly arched, but here crossing over a fast moving little stream. Garrison stood at the center of the bridge, looking down. There were fish swimming rapidly beneath him, patches of white foam where the tumbling waters broke around higher rocks to form miniature rapids.

The sun was strong, warm, the air so fresh that merely breathing it was nearly dizzying.

Garrison didn't keep track of how long he stood there on the bridge, but after a time he continued on, leaving the bridge and rejoining the stone path, climbing gently upward.

Trees were everywhere flanking the path, the huge ones that were called Ka'B'Oos, and ordinary seeming pines and willows.

A waist-high stone wall was coming into view as he walked on. It extended outward and back from both sides of the path, at its center a tall archway. The sounds which he had been following—partially masked by the muted roar of fast rushing water—were considerably louder. The music fell so pleasantly on the ear that it had Garrison himself wondering—stupidly—if it were available on CD.

A few yards after passing beneath the archway, the path took an abrupt left. There was another bridge; but, a moment after first spotting this, his eyes were drawn to the waterfall cascading out of the living rock perhaps a quarter mile upstream. The water still frothed, flowing along beneath the span.

Garrison paused on this bridge as well, the waterfall's beauty compelling him to do so. And the air, which rushed toward him, cooled by the water, invigorated him.

Exhaling so deeply that the act became a sigh, Garrison quit the bridge, taking up the path once more. It wound through a grove of heavy-boughed willows, the music and laughter nearly at full volume. As it passed out of the timber, the stone path ended and an expanse of lush green lawn, stretching as far and wide as a dozen football fields, lay before him. To his immediate left lay the wall in which, several stories up, the window from which he'd first looked out was set. Near the wall were well over a hundred people in groups small and large, some seated on the grass, some standing, children running about madly playing.

The majority of men were clad in leather jerkins over billowing-sleeved shirts, their legs in tights of red or green or black. Each, of course, was armed with sword and dagger. The women wore long dresses of every description and color, some quite elaborate, others simple. Although many were bareheaded, just as many wore the silly duncecap headgear or simple veils or crowns of flowers wound into elaborately arranged hair.

There were pits, what looked to be pigs—or something similar—roasting in them, small groups of the men, like men everywhere, overseeing the barbecue. Tables—these attended by some of the women—were being set with bowls of fruit and vegetables and trays of bread.

The instruments—no musicians—kept playing, floating in midair, roving, from group to group, like strolling players. He wondered, absently, if they got tipped?

Garrison took a deep breath and started walking in the direction of the throng. A freight train of frantically running children stormed past him so rapidly that he nearly stumbled into them. He heard a woman's voice chiding them to watch where they were going. He kept going, looking for a familiar face, hoping he'd find one in particular.

And he did. She was part of a group of a half dozen women, laying out food on one of the tables. Buffet-style, he supposed. Garrison quickened his pace, approaching her.

"Swan?"

She looked up from her task and smiled. "Al'An."

"We have to talk."

"Do you want to eat first? Remember? I promised you a feast. And the meat is nearly ready."

"I'm hungry, yeah, but that can wait. Okay?"

She smiled again. "Okay." Swan turned to her companions, two of the women—one of them particularly pretty—glancing furtively at him as she said something Garrison could not hear. Several of them laughed brightly as Swan pinched her skirts between her fingertips and walked toward him.

"Where can we talk?"

"Wherever you wish, Al'An."

"Over by the trees, there."

"As you wish, Al'An." Swan eased her right hand into the crook of Garrison's left elbow. "You seem rested."

"I am rested."

"And you feel well?"

"I feel great, perfect, never better. That's what's worrying me." They hadn't reached the trees yet, but Garrison stopped, turned to face her, his hands grasping her upper arms near the shoulders. "Tell me the truth. I mean it, Swan."

"What truth do you wish to know, Al'An?" She was tall for a girl, but a head shorter than he was, and her eyes were doing that thing that a woman could always somehow do even if she were taller than the man she was looking at: her eyes looked up at him, while at the same time appearing to be downcast in anticipation.

Garrison realized that he was probably hurting her arms. He let go of her. They just started walking, past the trees he'd picked as their destination, following instead along the boundary of the vast expanse of lawn. The sun was warmer here, or maybe it was Garrison's blood pressure. All the other guys back by the party were visibly armed, so Garrison determined for himself that it wouldn't be that socially taboo for his guns to be seen. He took off his bomber jacket, hooked it on his thumb over his left shoulder. Swan grasped his right hand in both of hers. They walked on, neither speaking.

The sun was warm on Garrison's face and neck, on his skin below the sleeves of his dark blue T-shirt, but he wasn't perspiring. The grass seemed to go on forever. Maybe it did, here. Garrison licked his lips, sniffed. "Uh, was I dead?"

"Was that the most important question you wanted to ask me, Al'An?"

Garrison shook his head. "No. Did you tell me that you loved me?"

"Yes."

"Was I dead?"

"No, but you were very close to death."

"Let's eat, but after we do this." Alan Garrison dropped his jacket and folded Swan into his arms. She tilted up her chin. Alan Garrison kissed her. Even if he had been dead, this alone would have brought him back.

Swan's head close against his chest, Garrison heard her whisper, "I love you, Al'An."

Garrison's lips touched her ear. "And I love you, Swan."

Alan Garrison had never meant anything more than he meant that. . . .

She straddled the body beneath her, hands twisting at his nipples, her mouth devouring, penetrating his mouth.

Her fingernails raked along his neck and shoulders and across his upper arms, drawing blood as they gouged into his chest and her finger tips squeezed at him again.

He cried in pain.

She laughed and bit his lower lip hard, the salty taste of his blood washing over her tongue. Her hands twisted his delicate flesh harder than before. He almost lifted her as he swelled within her. He shrieked with the pain she caused him. She screamed with delight. He exploded within her.

Eran sank back onto her haunches, her hair heavy and wet with sweat, her breathing hard.

The young lieutenant was not enough, not nearly enough at all. She dismounted him, caught up her robe from the flagstones and walked away from the bed. He moaned for more. Eran despised his tears and blood.

"That was great. I could do it again."

"Really?"

Alan Garrison gestured toward the far end of the longest table. "I could start eating on that end and still be hungry by the time I reached this end."

Swan's face lit with laughter. "You will be fat!"

"No, just happy."

She flung her arms about his neck and kissed his cheek. "I will bring you all that you desire, Al'An."

Swan took his plate from the grass beside them, Garrison reaching for her. She laughed, almost a schoolgirl giggle, scrambling away from his grasp. He started to his feet, but sank back to the grass, calling after her rather than running after her. "I already have all that I desire, Swan!"

She was still running, long legged and beautiful, laughing as she looked back at him over her shoulder, skirts and petticoats hitched high, flowing auburn hair bouncing Marsha-Brady perfect.

Perfect. Everything was perfect.

Garrison knitted his fingers behind his head and stretched back in the grass, looking at the perfect blue sky. This was paradise. He'd been wrong. The term was not unknown here. But in this world called Creath, paradise was not a lost gift, but made by magic.

He took a cigarette from his pack, lit it. He was

almost sorry for once in his life that he wasn't a
heavier smoker. Almost.

Here, cocooned within this perfect magical energy,
he could have smoked ten cartons a day with no risk
to his health. "Yuck," Garrison murmured. The
thought of even a pack a day held no appeal.

But a cigarette every once in a while tasted good.

Maybe magic was like that. Using a little magic
here and there didn't really hurt, was pleasant, enjoy-
able. And maybe this Queen Sorceress who was
Swan's mother had too heavy a habit.

On a rational level, Garrison knew that, sooner or
later, they'd have to leave this place, set out across
Woroc'Il'Lod for Edge Land and Barad'Il'Koth. He
accepted that as his destiny now, and so long as Swan
was an intrinsic part of that destiny, he could live with
it. He could live with it quite nicely. He still didn't
know how he'd managed—how Swan had managed
it, actually—to survive the crash, why he'd been able
to see his own body and it had looked dead. Swan
would explain it, and he'd believe it, no matter how
bizarre it sounded. She wouldn't lie to him. That he
knew he could depend upon.

The music was still playing. There was laughter.
Some of the men, who might have been drinking a
bit too much of the hearty red wine which Garrison
had more than sampled himself, were singing. They'd
be wise not to give up the day job.

Swan returned, dropped to her knees beside him
in the grass. Her hands offered him a plate heaped
with meat—it tasted like barbecue—and vegetables,
and a large cup of wine.

Garrison sat up. "I'm happy."

Swan laughed. "I know you are." She held the cup
for him and Garrison sipped wine from it, then took
his plate. He started to eat. Swan's face darkened
slightly, a blush and a hint of sadness in her eyes.
"I don't want to make you unhappy."

"How could you possibly do that?"

"Well, I have never been with a man."

Garrison touched her cheek, kissed her forehead. "Telling me that doesn't make me unhappy at all, darling."

She smiled sweetly, not responding for a moment. He knew what she was doing, trying to understand a word for which there was no perfect equivalent in her language. After another second or so, Swan's smile broadened. "I like that word. Is it correct for a woman to call a man so?"

"If you want, yes."

"Darling. Darling Al'An. Al'An darling."

Garrison laughed, careful not to choke. But that probably couldn't happen here in paradise, anyway.

Swan began again. "I know that the next thing which we should do is to make love."

Yes, it was possible to choke here, at least almost. Garrison coughed, cleared his throat, looked at her. "I'd like that, very much." More food wasn't all that important, really. He started to set down his plate.

Swan spoke again, quickly. "The prophecies of Mir say that a Virgin Enchantress must seek out the origin of her seed, if we are to have any hope for victory and freedom. And, darling, I can be nothing but a virgin in order to do so." Her eyes lowered, staring into his cup of wine as she said those last words.

"And after that?" Garrison asked her.

Swan raised her eyes. "If we survive, Al'An, I will be yours as much in my body as I am in my heart, forever if you so desire."

Garrison took a deep breath. Looking at Swan, listening to her, understanding her, what else could he say but, "Then, let's get on with whatever it is that we have to do here, and let's go to Barad'Il'Koth and do what needs to be done there. And, if we live, or if we die, the forever part will still be forever. Nothing your mother or her damned army can do will ever change that."

Just breathing the air which Swan breathed was erotic beyond imagining.

Garrison set down his plate, closed his hands around hers which still held the wine. Swan tilted the cup toward him and he sipped from it. Turning the cup in her hands, so her lips touched where his had touched, Swan drank the wine as well. . . .

"Okay, now come at me. And don't be afraid that you're gonna hurt me or anything, because you won't," Garrison told Gar'Ath.

Gar'Ath, grace personified with a sword in his hands, just lowered his head like a bull, balled his fists and charged.

Garrison sidestepped into a roundhouse kick, catching Gar'Ath's right side as gently as he could, sending him flying to the grass.

"Just like you tell me with a sword, Gar'Ath, keep your balance, and keep your wits."

Gar'Ath nodded soberly. "All right, you come at me, then, Champion."

Garrison grinned and assumed a T-stance. It was late in the afternoon, the sun warm across the grassy expanse which Garrison mentally labeled "the backyard" of the castle. Like Gar'Ath, he was naked from the waist up.

Garrison started moving in a slow, semicircle, feigned a punch and let Gar'Ath come at him. He blocked Gar'Ath's right, his left, got inside Gar'Ath's block, deflected a poorly launched knee smash, then delivered a soft heel of the hand to Gar'Ath's chin. Gar'Ath stumbled back, but kept his footing. "You're doing better, Gar'Ath!"

Garrison moved in, but Gar'Ath no longer staggered, instead pivoted left, snapping a series of beautifully executed soft kicks to Garrison's abdomen.

Garrison doubled over, Gar'Ath's foot snapping up and stopping just inches from Garrison's face.

"You sandbagged me," Garrison announced, breathing hard.

Gar'Ath lowered his foot, perfectly in balance. He stepped back. The idiomatic expression evidently deciphered, Gar'Ath smiled broadly. "Yes, I did, didn't I?"

"Been practicing?"

"More than a little, but hardly a lot, Champion."

"My ass," Garrison laughed.

This expression gave Gar'Ath not a moment's pause. "And it was your ass, indeed!"

"Well," Garrison suggested, "let's see if I've been practicing with a sword, then." This was, of course, ridiculous, Garrison knew. His hopes of winning against Gar'Ath blade to blade were as likely to succeed as either one of them separately or even both of them together taking on Chuck Norris hand to hand and winning.

"Now, remember, don't be afraid that you'll hurt me, because you won't," Gar'Ath advised.

"Ha, ha!"

Garrison retreated to his "corner" where, among other things, he'd left his borrowed sword. Its blade was about the same length as Gar'Ath's, and it had a double quillon crossguard and skull crusher pommel, but there the similarity ended. Gar'Ath's sword, made with his own hands, was sharp as a razor and gleamed like the sun. Garrison's loaner was sharp enough to hurt somebody and it wasn't rusty.

"Now, remember, if you parry with your blade, parry with the flat whenever possible. Parrying with the edge just nicks the edge. Bad for the sword, Champion."

"Right."

What little Alan Garrison had known about the various forms of classical European swordfighting (the style of Creath embodying various elements from several of these) prior to Gar'Ath's tutelage derived from novels written by Rafael Sabbatini and fine old movie fights between Errol Flynn and Basil Rathbone. In more recent times, Garrison enjoyed the resurgence of swordfighting in films and television, most of this, however, predicated on the Japanese katana used in the discipline of kenjitsu. In neither case, although he was fairly conversant with sword types as a consequence of his writing interests, had he any practical experience.

After his first session with Gar'Ath, Garrison's right forearm had been stiff and sore from manipulating the sword. Because they were at the summer palace and all was magical, the considerable discomfort vanished within minutes of onset.

After his next session, Garrison walked away realizing that much of what he'd seen in movies, old or new, had some validity, while other material was totally useless and silly.

In their third session, Gar'Ath had Garrison handle several different types of swords. Garrison learned that hand, wrist, arm, upper body and legs had to function together fluidly. Making a slender-bladed sword sing through the air with that wonderful old movie whooshing sound (which scared the crap out of an opponent just prior to cutting a candle in half) required use of the shoulder, the arm as a whole, elbow and wrist motion and hand manipulation. Simultaneously. By the end of that session, Garrison could carve a "Z" in the air, reliably whooshing three times in a row.

"Let's just fight," Gar'Ath suggested.

"Oh, you wanna hurt me, huh?"

Gar'Ath laughed, raised his sword to a guard position and waited.

Garrison had been practicing.

Garrison charged clumsily, thrashing through an

awkward, downward hacking motion, Gar'Ath waiting to intercept with a casual flick of the wrist and possibly disarm him. Garrison drew his blade rearward at the last second, Gar'Ath parrying nothing but air. Garrison's blade was already in motion again, its flat striking Gar'Ath's, deflecting Gar'Ath's parry.

Garrison wheeled right, a full circle, his blade angled downward, blocking Gar'Ath's recovering blade from inside his guard. Garrison's left fist snapped upward, lightly tapping Gar'Ath on the tip of the chin. At the same time, Garrison shoved against Gar'Ath, knocking him slightly off balance.

As Gar'Ath dodged rearward, Garrison wheeled once more, his sword arcing toward a dead stop (he hoped) inches from Gar'Ath's throat. Gar'Ath wheeled, Gar'Ath's sword in both hands, blocking Garrison's blade, circling round it, flicking upward.

Garrison was disarmed.

Gar'Ath stayed the tip of his blade, poised an inch away from Garrison's forehead.

"I was getting a little carried away," Garrison admitted sheepishly.

"You're getting considerably better, Champion. You have the makings of a fine hand with the blade." Gar'Ath lowered his sword. "Unfortunately, we may not have the time that we'll require in order to teach you all that you'll need to know."

It was a sobering thought, and Garrison nodded his agreement to it. Gar'Ath's blade snatched up Garrison's loaner, the sword sailing easily through the air and Garrison caught it at the hilt. "What if I hadn't been able to catch it?"

"You would have cut yourself quite badly, you would, Champion. And, more importantly, I'd have felt terribly embarrassed."

Garrison shook his sword at Gar'Ath as if he were going to attack again, laughed instead and said, "Gosh, we wouldn't have wanted you to be embarrassed because I cut myself!" Garrison shook his arms to loosen his muscles. "Let's call it a day, huh." It wasn't that he was tired, but he saw Swan approaching, crossing the grassy expanse toward them.

Gar'Ath glanced in Swan's direction as well, looked at Garrison and winked. "It's a bit tired I am, too, Champion. On the morrow, then?"

"Same time, same channel, buddy."

Gar'Ath nodded, walking over to his corner and donning his shirt almost a little too quickly. Gar'Ath seemed easily embarrassed around women, one drop-dead gorgeous woman in particular. Her name was Mitan and it was obvious that Gar'Ath was nuts about her, and she about him, obvious to everyone except Gar'Ath.

Or maybe it was too obvious to him. Garrison had seen guys run scared when they realized there was something serious going on with a woman. Mitan was K'Ur'Mir, Garrison had learned, meaning that a union between Gar'Ath and Mitan would be comparable to a commoner marrying into the British Royal Family.

"Be seeing you," Gar'Ath called out, buckling on his sword as he went.

Garrison shot him a wave.

As Gar'Ath made his way toward the trees, Swan and Gar'Ath crossed paths, stopped to talk for a moment. Gar'Ath's body language graphically revealed his shyness, his desire to walk on and escape the conversation. Garrison found himself smiling.

Gar'Ath escaped.

Swan continued on her way, Garrison's eyes on her. Her hair was loosely arranged in soft waves, the sides drawn back from her face, caught up at the crown of her head. She wore an ankle-length dress of pale blue satin or a similar material. White petticoats were visible beneath its hem as her fingertips clutched to her skirt, raised it to run to him. At its rounded neckline and the cuffs of its three-quarter sleeves were narrow ribbons of white lace trim.

Garrison saw no weapon, but knew that her dagger would be bound to her leg beneath her skirts.

She came into his arms in a rush. Garrison picked her up, cradling her against his chest, and kissed her hard on the mouth. "Put me down, please." But her smile said otherwise. He held her. "Please?"

"And what will you do for me if I do?"

"What would you like?"

"Well, we can't do that just yet. Make an alternate suggestion, Swan."

Swan seemed to consider this for several seconds, then told him, "I could stay in your arms like this until your muscles become numb. I know that I don't weigh much, but I'm heavier than a feather. You would tire eventually."

"Never! Anyway, I was more interested in a bribe than a threat. So think of something interesting." He bounced her in his arms like a child, and she laughed like one, her hands clutching his shoulders. "Come on! Let's hear it!"

"I'll kiss you and kiss you and kiss you until—"

"Sounds like a deal to me, darling." Garrison set her down, drew her into his arms and kissed her hard.

After a long time which wasn't time enough, they walked together hand in hand toward the summit from beneath which the waterfall spilled. When they looked toward what Garrison mentally labeled the west—the sun set in that part of Creath—before them stretched higher and higher foothills, and snow-covered mountains beyond. A segment of the vast Arba'Il'Tac was also visible, vanishing within the peaks. The sight of the plateau's unremitting stone sent a shiver of memory along Garrison's spine.

To what Garrison instinctively considered the north and east lay the sea. Woroc'Il'Lod's enormity was, at first, hard for him to comprehend. Erg'Ran had shown

him a map which looked familiarly like a standard
projection for a flat surface map of the Earth, except
for the sizes, shapes and positions of the continents
and the almost total absence of islands. As he'd
already known, there was but one continent here, but
that one more like a series of continents interconnected by vast land bridges. There was only one
true island chain, located what seemed to be a quarter
of the planet's circumference from the Land to the
north, off Edge Land.

Men of science and letters such as Erg'Ran had long
known that Creath was round, although the planet had
never been circumnavigated. It was just as the thinkers
of Classical Greece had known the true shape of the
Earth two millennia before Columbus or Magellan
embarked upon their historic voyages. There had never
been, however, nor likely would be a circumnaviga-
tion of Creath for two reasons: the planet's land masses
were all known, through the use of magic and the
second sight; and although there was no fear of "falling
off" the edge of the world, in actuality sea creatures
did wait to destroy ships and devour those foolish
enough to be aboard them.

The only race of seafarers anywhere in Creath,
according to Erg'Ran, was to be found on the island
chain, its inhabitants the Gle'Ur'Gya. The Gle'Ur'Gya
rarely interacted with the folk of the Land. From
Erg'Ran's description of them, if they shared a common evolutionary heritage at all, the Gle'Ur'Gya were
as genetically dissimilar to the inhabitants of the Land
as were the more esoteric forms of Australian fauna
to the general run of terrestrial species.

Garrison could fault no one for avoiding the vast
global ocean of which he was able to glimpse only
the most frigid part.

Woroc'Il'Lod's tidal surges were beyond anything
Garrison had ever considered possible. Once, as a
child, his family unwittingly found itself in the path

of a hurricane. Despite the intervening years, Garrison's recollection of the awesome height and force with which the Atlantic pounded against the Florida coast had not dimmed. Along the coasts of Creath, such was normal. He'd seen this with his own eyes over the last several days, from this very vantage point he shared with Swan. Erg'Ran had told him that, at certain periods of the year, there were waves of incredible proportions which moved in cyclonic rotation, floating hurricane-like, as Garrison referenced it, over the surface of the ocean. This occurred when Creath's two moons crossed orbital paths and was a result of their combined gravitational effect, Garrison presumed.

"We'll be out there soon," Garrison observed.

Swan held to him more tightly. "I wish that my magic could carry us all across it. But in order to accomplish that, I would have virtually none remaining when we reached shore. And I'll need magic there."

"Let me ask you something," Garrison began. The breeze was stiffening a little as the sun declined. He folded her more closely in his arms. "This place. How does it work?"

Swan seemed to consider his words for several seconds, then responded, "You are wondering why we are safe here."

"I can accept the fact that the magic from the dead K'Ur'Mir protects this spot. Erg'Ran told me about it the other evening. He'd told Gar'Ath how that came to be, how he lost his foot. Spooky. And the other night he told me, said I had a right to know. But how come there isn't an army of your mother's goons waiting just outside the gates for us, laying siege?"

"It wouldn't do my mother any good, Al'An. It's not just the keep and the courtyard and the walls which enjoy the protection of the spells cast by the dying K'Ur'Mir, it's the surrounding area, for many, many lancethrows in all directions, including the sea."

"Fine, then why isn't there an armada waiting

offshore to intercept us?" Garrison didn't know, for fact, that there wouldn't be.

Evidently, Swan was having difficulty with the word "armada" and Garrison explained. "It's a fleet of ships for war." Telling her about the Spanish Armada in 1588 wouldn't have done much good, he supposed.

"My mother has few ships, Al'An, only those which ply the coastal waters. There is no such thing here as an armada."

"So all we have to worry about between this coast and the far coast is ice dragons."

"And the other sea monsters, yes."

Garrison blinked. "Other sea monsters?"

"I told you, Al'An, that my mother brought the ice dragons out of their great sleep? But there were always other creatures inhabiting the great ocean, some of them in Woroc'Il'Lod."

"So, monsters, but no bad guys."

Swan paused before responding. "The Gle'Ur'Gya? Some of their number are—" Garrison realized that she was searching for a word. Then, as if the lightbulb suddenly went on in a cartoon, she said, "Pirates! Some of the Gle'Ur'Gya attack coastal ships, my mother's these days. Before my mother's rule, when there was coastal trade, the Gle'Ur'Gya were more active."

Garrison shrugged his eyebrows. "At least these guys the Gle'Ur'Gya—aren't on your mom's side. That's something, I guess. If we meet up with any, maybe we can get them on our side."

"That would be wonderful, because they are very great fighters, especially the pirates."

"Okay, so all we have to worry about between here and Edge Land is pirates and sea monsters and ice dragons. And, on the plus side, we might be able to get the pirates to help us in the battle." Garrison surmised that he really was going nuts. . . .

❖          ❖          ❖

The days at the summer palace were always warm and bright, nary a cloud in the sky. The weather was magically "programmed" for rain every day just before dawn, in order that the plants and flowers would get the moisture they required. There'd be no need to have The Weather Channel in a basic cable package here. He told that to Swan, then had to explain about basic cable which led to a short dissertation on Marconi and the invention of the wireless.

At night, the skies above the summer palace and its environs were always clear and the stars were always sparkling and beautiful. He sat beneath them with Swan, on the keep steps, a good dinner in his stomach, a cup of wine beside him, a cigarette lit in his left hand from a continuously full pack.

It was magic responsible for that full pack, magic responsible for the perfection of the summer palace. And magic, he knew, was the reason that he was here, alive.

"Tell me," Garrison almost whispered, "how you saved my life."

Swan leaned her head against his chest, her voice low. "I saw what was about to happen, with the second sight."

"And you intervened. How?"

Swan turned her face up toward him. "I couldn't let you die, Al'An. You would not have been here if it were not for me, nor would you have fought the winged beast were it not for me. That was the most formidable of the creatures my mother raised up to destroy us, which meant that she knew that you were the Champion, and had to destroy you."

"Are those the only reasons?" Garrison asked her, his eyes leaving hers, focusing on the glowing tip of his cigarette, its pinpoint of light like a star held in the hand.

"I couldn't lose you, Al'An. I knew from the first moment that I saw you that . . ."

Garrison kissed the tip of her nose. It was a very pretty nose. "When we were sitting in that little snack shop at the con, I was realizing that I loved you. Does that help with saying it?"

"Yes."

"So," he said, clearing his throat, "you just did what then?"

"I wasn't certain how to bring the winged beast softly to the ground so that you would not die. I had never done something like that, had never read a spell for that. But I did know a spell for shifting the life energy—"

"The soul? The mind?"

Swan seemed to ponder his words, then answered, "We think of things in different ways, but they're the same. I knew that I could take the life that was in you, the essence of you, and transfer it to something else, another living creature. And I could return it to your body. Healing your body was merely the acceleration of natural processes, ordinary magic. We've spoken of this."

"Yes," he nodded.

"But if your life energy left your body at the moment of death, it would be irretrievable. You never died, Al'An. I know this has worried you. Your body was grievously injured, moreso than you would ever want to know. But the body can be made to heal itself. I kept your life energy in the bird until I was certain that I could restore your body and had restored it enough that it would hold your life energy and not surrender you to death. That took very little time. The bones in your chest were crushed, and had penetrated your heart and your lungs. I commanded the bones to return to their original position and shape. They still had to heal, of course. I ordered your lungs to seal, so that air could enter and leave. Your heart would heal, but it had ceased to beat."

"And?"

She seemed oddly embarrassed. "I, uh, I ordered that your flesh and muscle should part over your heart, and I touched it with my hand."

Garrison was suddenly very cold, his body shaking. He snapped away the cigarette, rubbed his hand over his jaw. "You touched my heart," he said slowly. "Silly girl for being embarrassed." he whispered. "You touch my heart every time I think of you." And he kissed her. . . .

Because of the tidal surges, Garrison supposed, the concept of a dock or wharf to which a ship could be tied was unheard of. Any such structure, if built high enough to be left unassailed by the pounding water, would leave whatever vessel secured to it accessible only by climbing down a ladder. Meanwhile, the boat would be battered to pieces by the tides.

Garrison thought that the solution to Creath's maritime dilemma was, considering the general lack of technology, ingenious. Ships were kept to a size reminiscent to him of those used by the Norsemen. Their overall canoe-like shape, high prows and simple mast structure were similar to Viking craft as well. When put in to shore at what passed for a naval facility, the ships were brought from and back to the water on parallel skids, not dissimilar to railroad tracks in gauge. Since the coastlines were constantly eroding, as the sea claimed more of the land, the rails were merely extended to a still higher elevation. Using ropes and primitive pulleys (magic substituting for muscle when available), the craft were drawn to their dry dock or eased into the surf. They were light enough, because of their modest size, that the crew which oared them could carry them if needed.

Garrison and Erg'Ran stood at the mouth of an enormous cavern, some five hundred yards from the water's edge and a good hundred feet higher in elevation. There were five ships within the cave being outfitted and rigged.

"They'll be ready by the morrow, Champion."

"I can hardly wait," Garrison cracked. Yet he was anxious to be underway for a variety of reasons, his hopes for consummating the love he felt for Swan chief among them. On another level, he wanted to see Swan's mother get what was coming to her. If he were somehow able to marry Swan—and the mere thought of how that could be done was mind-boggling—Eran would truly be the mother-in-law of all mothers-in-law.

When the Company of Mir set sail for Edge Land across Woroc'Il'Lod, the only noncombatant would be Swan herself. The spouses of the male and female warriors, the children, the camp followers, all non-fighters would remain within the safety of the summer palace. A handful of warriors only would stay back with them, and merely as a precaution against the unforeseen.

Only three out of the Company of Mir would be K'Ur'Mir: Swan, Erg'Ran and Mitan. Although more warrior than magic user, as a female K'Ur'Mir Mitan had some considerable capabilities. Erg'Ran freely admitted that what magic he, as a male, could employ would be of precious little use for anything serious.

The five vessels were constructed using a combination of magic and (to Garrison) more conventional techniques. Since the Company of Mir was, effectively, a random cross section of Creathan society, most trades and professions were represented. Cooper-smiths saw to precision fitting of planking, stone-masons saw to the pitch caulking, while blacksmiths and even Gar'Ath, a swordsmith by trade as was his father before him, saw to the making of grommets, cleats, oarlocks and other necessary metal items.

Gar'Ath, as did many of the others, performed double duty, his principal task in what time remained before they set sail was the completion of spearheads. In preparation to combat the creatures which lay in wait within Woroc'Il'Lod's waters, everyone was agreed that a large number of extra spears would be needed. Mitan, to Gar'Ath's discomfort because of her necessary proximity to him, used her magic to apply the final edges to the spearheads, using her muscle power to mate them to the shafts. Garrison doubted that the symbology of the shafts being inserted into the orifices within the spearheads was lost on Gar'Ath, and from the mischievous look in Mitan's pretty eyes, Garrison knew that she very much appreciated what it suggested.

"It should prove a constant source of amusement, shouldn't it?" Erg'Ran commented.

"What?" Garrison inquired.

They were walking along a scaffolding set between two of the ships toward the rear of the cave.

"I mean having our young swordsman friend and the fair warrior maid taking passage on the same small ship. I wonder if Gar'Ath will survive it."

"I could lend Gar'Ath my vest—"

"Your fabric armor, yes! Why?"

"It's not only good protection against bullets—the things my firespitters spit?"

"Ah, yes. Bullets, indeed."

"But although it also provides a fair degree of protection against penetration—" Garrison didn't mean that word the way it came out in the context of their conversation, so he quickly rephrased. "I meant to say that I don't think it would provide much protection against Cupid's arrows."

"Who is Cu'Pid?"

"Cupid is a character from mythology—" Garrison realized that he was digging a hole and about to bury himself beneath a ton of inane verbiage before he could climb out of it. "What I mean is that there's no armor against love, Erg'Ran."

"How right you are, Champion. How right you are!"

At the end of the scaffolding, Garrison looked down. There was a high stack of canvas bags on something very much like a pallet. The bags were about the length and girth of a man in size, grommeted at the top, cord running through the holes, enabling the openings to be drawn tight.

They were a sobering sight: body bags for burial at sea.

A boy of about twelve, by the way that Garrison reckoned age, came as a messenger. Swan requested that Garrison join her in the keep's highest tower. She had taken this over for her new— Garrison didn't quite know what to call it. Was it a magical workshop, a laboratory? An office?

After ascending the endlessly winding stairs, Garrison crossed a small outer room and entered the chamber through a doorless archway. Quill pens wrote furiously, filling empty scrolls and pages within books floating in the air, controlled only by Swan's magical energy. Merely watching them was unnerving.

"Al'An!" The pens kept writing as Swan came across the room and into his arms.

Garrison kissed her, held her. "How do you do that?"

"What?"

"The pens writing without anyone touching them."

"I can show you the spell."

"No. That's okay. Why are you doing it?"

"When my castle was consumed by the Mist of Oblivion, all of my things were lost with it. I memorize anything that I read, so I'm rewriting all of my spells and incantations and recipes."

"Recipes? Like in a cookbook?"

Swan evaluated the term, then answered, "Some of the recipes are for the cooking of food, yes."

Garrison wasn't going to ask what other kinds of recipes she was transcribing.

"I thought that it was time that we saw to your armament, Al'An, as we will be leaving on the morrow. I will spellwork for you a sword the equal to any in the Land! See?" Out of thin air, floating among the books, scrolls and the quill pens still writing upon them, appeared a magnificent hand-and-a-half sword, double fullered along the blade's entire length, with bronze ricasso, lobed quillon guard, hilt bound in polished wire, a skull-crusher pommel in the shape of some sort of animal head, gemstones set for its eyes.

"That's lovely, Swan, but—"

"Gar'Ath tells me that you are becoming quite proficient with a sword. I am very proud."

"You're sweet to say that, and even sweeter to make such a wonderful weapon for me. And Gar'Ath's a heck of a fine teacher, but he's being overly generous with his praise. If I had a lot more practice time, I'd be mediocre, darling. Such a fine sword should be in the scabbard of someone who really knows how to use it. No, I'll make do. I wish I had more ammo, though."

"Ammo? Oh! Ammo! Please, give me one ammo."

"Cartridge. Sure." Garrison reached under his bomber jacket, not bothering to withdraw one of the pistols from its holster, merely pressing the magazine release catch button. He thumbed a cartridge free and handed it to Swan.

"Are these runes which are inscribed here of magical importance to your firespitters?"

She was referring to the Federal Cartridge Company headstamp. "No, it's how they're made that counts. That's why I use this brand—kind of ammunition for my firespitters, pistols."

Swan tossed the cartridge into the air, simultaneously speaking words which were totally unintelligible to him—had to be from the Old Tongue. The cartridge floated, weightless seeming, and a vortex formed around it. Light appeared to emanate from the cartridge, filling the vortex. From deep within it, a single cartridge fell, then another and another. The succession of cartridges became a stream, flowing out of the vortex, heaping onto the flagstones below. The pile of cartridges grew and grew, to the height of Garrison's knee, to the height of his hip. Still, the stream continued to flow from the vortex.

"Tell me when you think you will have enough, Al'An."

"Oh, anytime now really would be just fine, actually." Garrison knew that he should be used to magic by now, but realized that he was shaking his head in disbelief.

The flow slowed to a trickle, then a handful more spilled from the vortex and the vortex began to close.

The original cartridge Garrison had placed in Swan's hand, which she had flung into the air, arced back into her waiting palm. Swan returned it to Garrison. "Thank you," he told her, his eyes on neither Swan nor the thousands of rounds of ammunition, but on the original cartridge.

He heard her telling him, "I've never made ammo before. It's easy."

"You've brought a whole new meaning to hand-loading, darling."

"And," Swan continued, ignoring his quip, "your ammo is magical, now. If you must use it against a magical enemy, it will be much more effective."

Still looking at the original cartridge, seeing nothing odd or different about it, he asked, "So I should use the new stuff and put my old ammunition away?"

"Yes."

"Okay."

"If you do not see yourself using a sword, Al'An," and the sword which Swan had made and which had hung in thin air since she'd shown it to him instantly vanished, "then you will at least need protection from

the swords wielded by your enemies." This seemed
to be quite serious to her, judging from the look on
her face as he finally stopped staring at the cartridge.
"I know!"

Garrison felt movement in the left side of his
bomber jacket. As he looked down, his badge and
Bureau ID had already floated from his pocket, the
gold badge floating on into Swan's hand, the ID
returning to his pocket. "I heard this object called
a shield, didn't I?"

"Yeah, but—no, Swan!"

Garrison was too late. She'd flung his badge into
the air. For a split second, nothing happened, except
his badge still floated, and he wondered if he was
going to wind up with another vortex and another pile
beneath it, only this time— But, his badge began to
glow, differently than the cartridge had. There was
a burst of light and Garrison blinked.

When Garrison looked again, his badge was almost
two feet wide and nearly three feet long. The gleaming shield returned to Swan's hands and she presented
it to him. "It is magical and will help to protect you,
Al'An."

All of the embossing on the surface of his badge
was present, just as it had been, the letters perfectly
reproduced, but perfectly reversed. "IBF," Garrison
commented.

"IBF? What does that mean?"

"On my shield, darling. IBF."

"Oh!" She smiled sweetly. "The Golden Shield of
IBF. The Golden Shield of IBF. It sounds nice."

Garrison nodded, walked to the pile of ammunition and picked up one of the cartridges. It felt
perfectly normal, looked perfectly normal to him as
he glanced at the headstamp. The letters were not
reversed, but their order was, perfectly.

"IBF. That is a good name for your shield, Al'An."

Garrison smiled, nodded. "Yes, I think so! There's

not another one like it anywhere, I'll bet. Thank you, darling, very much."

Swan lowered her eyes, embarrassed by his gratitude he presumed. . . .

Alan Garrison wondered if all shields felt this heavy to begin with, but supposed he'd get used to the weight. The Golden Shield of IBF was slung over his left shoulder, and in his right hand he carried a wooden bucket brimming over with cartridges. "I could carry your shield, Al'An."

"No, darling, it'd be a little heavy for you."

"Don't worry!" The Golden Shield of IBF left his shoulder and fell in beside them, floating surfboard-like in the air.

Between the two bridges leading to the keep's backyard, Garrison had remembered a spot where the trees were widely spaced and there was an embankment rising into the hill on which the summer palace was built. It was the perfect spot to shoot, and he was not about to stake his life or Swan's or anyone's on magic ammunition which was never tested.

The Golden Shield of IBF was alternately at their heels or beside them, like a puppy. When they reached the spot which Garrison had remembered, he asked Swan, "Would you like to put down my shield now?"

The Golden Shield of IBF made a perfect landing to lean against the trunk of a willow tree. "Is there anything which I can do to help, Al'An?"

"Yes, actually. Would you find some pinecones?"

Half expecting a pile of pine cones to appear out of thin air, Garrison was mildly but pleasantly surprised that Swan ran off to find some in the ordinary way. While she was gone, Garrison set to unloading his magazines, then reloading them with the ammunition Swan had made for him with her magic.

Swan soon returned, carrying a woven basket which

she hadn't had when she left, the basket stuffed with pinecones.

Garrison thanked her, took the basket and set out the pinecones as targets. The maximum range he could get without the trees interfering was about fifty feet. He wasn't after all, testing his marksmanship skills, Garrison reminded himself. Swan stood beside him, but Garrison waved her back, in case magical ammo exploded when fired from nonmagical guns. "Cover your ears. Tight!"

There were a few emergency items which Garrison carried along with him whenever possible, among them a Leatherman Supertool, a folding magnifying glass and a small case containing a pair of earplugs. Unfortunately, when Swan magically whisked him into her world, none of those things—except for the magnifying glass—were on his person. On the plus side, any ringing in his ears or damage done to his hearing would be gone in no time because of the magical energy at the summer palace.

Keeping the pistol well away from his face, and partially averting his eyes as he began to squeeze the trigger, he fired. The sound was just as loud as ever, but no louder. Looking at the weapon, nothing seemed out of the ordinary. He'd seen the bullet impact the general area of the target. Keeping the muzzle pointed downrange, he spied the spent cartridge case in the grass and picked it up. Nothing unusual. "So far, so good." Garrison repeated the procedure with the same results. Confident that firing the magically made ammunition wasn't especially dangerous, Garrison fired through his two primary and two spare magazines, wiping out a considerable number of defenseless pinecones in the process. By the time he was through, his hearing was suffering. Under normal conditions, the hollow sound which some people called ringing would have gone away in an hour or two.

By the time he turned to face Swan and signaled that she could lower her hands from her ears, Garrison's hearing was already returning to normal.

"Was the ammo okay?" Swan asked.

"The ammo was better than okay," he told Swan. "It was perfect." He wondered if she'd want to use her magic to pick up the fired brass. . . .

Swan stood between Al'An and Erg'Ran, in the passageway leading to the chamber in which the Sword of Koth prisoner had been placed.

"Which of us is going to be the good cop and who's gonna be the bad cop?"

"I don't understand, Champion," Erg'Ran told Al'An. Swan was glad Erg'Ran had said it. "We are fighting for good," Erg'Ran continued, "and our Sword of Koth prisoner fought for evil. And you're the only cop who is here."

Al'An shook his head and smiled good-naturedly. "No, see, Erg'Ran, we gotta get this Sword of Koth guy feeling that he can trust one of us to protect him from the other guy. I'll give you an example. Say, you're the bad cop, right?"

"I'm the bad cop, right."

Al'An shook his head again. "No, I don't mean say it, but just pretend."

"Erg'Ran should pretend that he said it, Al'An?"

"Start over. Okay. Now, Erg'Ran, you pretend that we've got the Sword of Koth trooper there in a chair all alone in a room. Okay? So in you go, and you're the bad cop. I mean, you're not really bad, but just pretending to be. You tell this little bad ass you're puttin' him away in the house of many doors for the long count, how you're gonna make sure he's buyin' so much hard time he'll be too old to qualify for Social Security if he ever gets out. Like that.

"Then," Al'An went on, "you make like you lose your temper when he doesn't answer you, see? You get your face up right in front of his and shout at him, tell him that if he doesn't come clean and spill his guts you're gonna put the word on the street that he ratted on his homies, sang the whole opera, huh! Then, either way, whether it's the big house or some liberal judge lets him walk on a technicality, his ass is grass with his posse and, if they don't whittle on him with a chain saw first, he'll be cryin' for Witness Protection. And we won't give it to him. That's the bad cop routine, Erg'Ran."

"I see, Champion."

"You do? Good. Now, see, pretend you're the good cop. You walk in, see that the bad cop's giving the prisoner a hard time. You tell the bad cop to go grab himself a cup of coffee and a danish or somethin'. As soon as he's outta the room, you offer this Sword of Koth guy a cigarette, light it up for him. Tell him how the bad cop can really make a lot of trouble, da-da-da-da-da. You win over his confidence, telling him that you'll put in the good word with the judge, like that. Tell him you'll keep the bad cop from getting anywhere near him.

"Then, the bad cop comes in again," Al'An continued, "and he snatches the cigarette away from the Sword of Koth guy, starts pitchin' a fit. You calm him down, shag him outta there and tell the Sword of Koth there's not much you can do unless he throws somethin' your way and starts to talk."

"You have found such a charade efficacious in the interrogation of a prisoner?" Erg'Ran queried, sounding incredulous.

"On a lotta guys, yeah. See, he's lookin' at a Federal rap. Same thing here, really. When we defeat Eran, Swan's going to be in charge and you guys helping her, so you'll be the government. Same idea."

Swan cleared her throat. "I was considering using magic in order to secure his cooperation, Al'An. Is the good and bad cop technique to be preferred, you think?"

Al'An said nothing for a moment, took a cigarette from its package—Swan lit it magically—and said, "Well, we can try the magic thing first, I guess. If it doesn't work, then we go into good cop–bad cop."

"Oh, that is a fine approach," Swan assured him.

The three resumed walking along the passageway. "We're going to want to get the dope on troop strength, their overall defensive posture. Remember," Al'An advised, "if he starts telling us about which Horde of Koth units are where, we want to push him to know if the units are at full strength, like that."

"Very good suggestions, Champion," Erg'Ran noted.

"We are looking for weaknesses in their defenses," Swan observed. "Those are very good things to find out."

"How will you do this, with magic, I mean?" Al'An asked.

"It is cruel, which was why I had wished that he would speak before now. I will make him believe that he is with his comrades among the Sword of Koth, merely conversing about the topics over which we are concerned. He will be temporarily unaware that he was ever captured."

"What's cruel about that, Swan?"

Erg'Ran answered for her. "When the spell is lifted, he will remember that he has betrayed his oath and his honor, if indeed the Sword of Koth have honor."

Swan watched Al'An, who nodded his understanding.

No one stood guard, the chamber door was secured by magic. Swan caused the door to open. She looked away, burying her face against Al'An's chest.

Erg'Ran spoke. "He had some little magic, perhaps."

Al'An asked, "That how he got the knife, you think? Or maybe we missed it in the search?"

"We may never know."

"Nobody could have murdered anybody here, right?"

"Such cannot happen at the summer palace; the magical energy prevents evil from having any power here. He is dead at his own hand. No magic can prevent that, I fear, when despair seizes the mind."

"So much for getting information. G'Urg!"

"Yes," Erg'Ran responded. "As you say."

The Sword of Koth had opened his wrist and bled to death. His skin was a ghastly shade of grey, and there was blood congealed in the fissures between the flagstone beneath him.

Swan had seen worse, but the realization that this Sword of Koth had taken his own life somehow made her think of what might happen when their current endeavor had run its course and was ended. If she defeated her mother's forces, and her mother, too, then what? Swan could not bring herself to cause her mother's death.

And if her mother defeated her? That her mother would almost certainly find a worse fate than any death however horrible was the likely scenario. In that case, her magic spent, her cause lost, would she—

"I'm getting Swan out of here," Al'An said to Erg'Ran.

"Agreed. Send Gar'Ath and some others."

"Right."

Swan felt herself being moved along the passageway, almost lifted from her feet, Al'An's arms tight about her. If she failed, all that she loved was doomed to horror beyond imagining. If she succeeded, there would be horror enough as well. Tears fell from her eyes; there was no hope of stopping them other than by magical means; she would not do that.

# Chapter Ten

The children, the noncombatant women and men, the few warriors who would remain behind, all were ranked on either side of the path leading down from the castle walls to the icy sea, Woroc'Il'Lod.

The sun shone brightly. The Golden Shield of IBF, polished, was slung to Alan Garrison's left side as he walked. Swan had talked him into the magically enhanced axe carried in his right hand. He'd convinced her that this plus his two knives were sufficient edged weaponry. She asked to be allowed to give the knives magic, too. Relenting, he was now the only man in existence with magically endowed push-button opening knives.

All of the warriors, men and the few women, were afoot, no room for their horses aboard the ships. Only Swan was on horseback. Befitting her nobility as the Virgin Enchantress, Daughter Royal, Princess of Creath, this was expected. She rode sidesaddle aboard the finest horse from the Company of Mir, a great palomino stallion with a darkly flowing bronze mane and long swishing tail. Its saddle and bridle were gold mounted.

Swan, too, was regally dressed for the part.

Her hair was pinned up beneath a crown of yellow flowers trailing golden ribbons. She wore a dress of deep maroon color, gold thread woven into its neckline, elbow-length sleeves and hem. Tiny gold spurs adorned shining black boots visible below the lace trimmed petticoats. Buckled round her little waist was a sword, its burnished hilt gleaming in the sun's rays. Garrison knew Swan well enough to know that she had no intention of traveling over Woroc'Il'Lod to Edge Land so attired.

As Champion, Garrison had been told, he was to walk before her horse and lead its reins as they processed. Flanking him and a little behind him were Gar'Ath and Mitan. Erg'Ran limped along several paces ahead, wearing his finest scholarly robes, axe in hand.

The path led down past the cavern, beside the rails along which, earlier, Garrison had assisted in the launch of their five ships, now at anchor along the shore. Because of their structure—wide abeam and without a keel—and the manner in which the vessels were launched, they had shallow drafts and could be anchored close in along the surf.

The members and families of the Company of Mir who stayed behind followed in the procession's train, down the path and onto the rocky coast itself. Cold spray blew off shallow pools on an otherwise warm breeze. It was slower going along the shore, and Garrison was careful to guide Swan's mount around the deeper pools lest the animal break a leg. But the practicality of the royal personage riding horseback became abundantly clear as they turned out toward the vessels themselves. Everyone else, Garrison included, was forced to wade through the low breakers, getting drenched to the waist, while Swan, mounted, never got her dainty boots wet.

Erg'Ran was using his axe shaft as a staff to steady himself. The first to reach the vessel on which Swan would travel, he called out something Garrison could not hear. In a moment, a ladder was let down to him astern on the portside. Erg'Ran stood in the water, steadying the ladder.

Garrison had been rehearsed in this as well. As Champion, he was to take Swan from her saddle and set her feet upon the ladder. When he guessed that he was close enough to the centermost of the five ships, Garrison reined in Swan's horse. On cue, Gar'Ath took the reins from Garrison and Mitan took Garrison's axe and shield.

Garrison turned to face Swan. She smiled at him, then slipped one arm around his neck as he slid her from the saddle. Carrying her the few steps to the ladder, he was nearly seized with laughter, holding it back by sheer force of willpower. Swan's face was close to his and she whispered to his ear, "What is it, Al'An?"

"Realize how stupid we'd look if I tripped?"

Swan's laugh was almost a giggle. He held her more tightly, not from fear of dropping her, but because he liked to hold her. Erg'Ran steadying the ladder, Garrison positioned Swan so that her feet were on the ladder above the water.

In the next moment, Swan ascended the ladder. Two young teenagers, boys, came up from the crowd to lead Swan's mount up from the waves. Garrison was handed his shield and axe, then clambered up the ladder (he felt rude leaving the much older Erg'Ran standing in the water, but this was the drill). Erg'Ran was next, then Gar'Ath, then Mitan. All of the ships began loading rapidly then, everyone eager, Garrison presumed, to get out of the numbing cold of the surf. Soaked to the skin below the waist, standing beside Swan in the little ship's stern, the warm breeze felt nowhere near as warm as it had.

The ones staying behind waited along the shore. As soon as all who were coming aboard were to their ships, Swan raised her voice over the pounding of the surf—it had to be magic for her to be heard—and proclaimed, "My friends aship and ashore! With the courage of Mir as our inspiration and his wisdom as our guide, we go forth from this magical place to right the wrongs which have been done, to defeat the power of evil . . ." Garrison listened, the words different but the message very familiar.

Remember the Alamo!

Remember the *Maine*!

The war to end all wars!

Make the world safe for democracy!

Good versus evil. Alan Garrison pondered, as he supposed men and women had always pondered in his world and this world and whatever other worlds there might be, if the other guy, the enemy, actually saw himself as incarnate evil? We're going off to do great good, while you're going off to do great evil. Had Ghengis Khan encouraged his troops with pep talks about being better looters and pillagers? Probably not. Had the men of King Phillip of Spain's Armada seen themselves as ruthlessly despicable wannabe invaders while Elizabeth I's English privateers had viewed themselves as heroes reluctantly taking up the sword in defense of hearth and home? Probably not and probably so, the Spanish seeing the building of Spain's empire and the destruction of England's pirate fleet as intrinsic goods, while the British viewed both as intrinsic evils.

From what Alan Garrison had learned of Swan's mother, the Queen Sorceress Eran, she might indeed start off each morning by asking herself, "What new rotten nasty thing can I do to some unsuspecting innocent person today?" She might feel deeply depressed when the occasional day passed without some great evil being perpetrated. From all that Garrison had heard concerning Eran, she was the small-dog-kicker type in spades.

*We are good*, Garrison told himself, *and we fight for truth. They are bad, and they fight because they enjoy inflicting harm and pain and destruction. If we win, Creath will be a happy place (at least until the next lunatic dictator). If they win, darkness will cover the land (like it does).* Had Alan Garrison not already appreciated the differences between warriors and philosophers, and why the two rarely mixed, he would have understood it here, beside Swan as she concluded her address to the faithful. ". . . must steel ourselves for what is to come, be it victory or defeat. And, if it is the latter, you who remain behind will rise up again, fight again, and the victory will someday come. Good will triumph always, no matter how long or bloody the battle. Good will triumph!" Those who really appreciated the difference between warriors and philosophers knew that the warriors were the ones who were dreamers. . . .

With the second sight, Eran saw them as if in a dream, the vision of five ships blurred and unreal. She gave the orders for the ceremony to be prepared, her mount saddled, then set about dressing. Her second sight could not penetrate the magic surrounding the summer palace, but she had regularly used it to view Woroc'Il'Lod at the boundary where the aura surrounding the summer palace began to fade.

The Company of Mir was approaching, and Swan would be of its number, as would her Champion. And, so too would be Eran's old nemesis, Erg'Ran. This time, when they met, nothing would stand in the way of her revenge—if Erg'Ran lived that long.

Eran rode her newest horse, a better mount than he had been a lieutenant. He was still in training, and she used the whip and an oversized bit to regulate his gait, but he showed promise of speed and endurance under her hand. A lack of speed had never been his problem, and the endurance he'd learn.

She cantered him across the Great Plain of Koth, his rich black mane stiff on brisk wind which swept Edge Land, the only sound other than the beating of his hooves the creak of the leather and the jingle of the steel which constrained him to her convenience. Eran gave him a little spur and he quickened his pace.

Eran's troops were formed before her, encircling the craggy stones of the facelike rock formation at the very center of the plain which since time began had been known as the Great Visage of Koth.

Six companies of the Horde of Koth formed the outer ring through which she passed, the circle closing behind her. There was an inner ring, this consisting of six units of the black masked Sword of Koth, fireswords raised in salute. As Eran passed, their swords lowered and the ring closed. Within the concentric circles of her military power were six circles of magical power. Six Handmaidens of Koth, wind tossing their black headveils and black dresses, comprised each individual ring, each of the women hand-linked to the others on either side of her. The rings were interlocked, the clasped hands of two of the women passed round those of two others, so that six rings formed one.

Eran stayed her mount, stroking the side of his great head with the lash of her whip. She liked the way his eyes widened and his nostrils quivered. He was already coming to know the whip's promise.

Eran dismounted, her black cape, her voluminous black skirts, her hair caught up in the wind. Already, Eran could feel the power building. Her own magic, almost fully restored, would be too precious to squander should the Company of Mir reach Edge Land. Using the witchery of the Handmaidens would be enough for her purpose.

Two of the Handmaidens, heads bowed and eyes lowered behind opaque black veils, raised their arms and formed an arch beneath which Eran passed. She paused for a moment within this small circle of six, feeling their energy. Swan could have been one of them, the most powerful of them.

Eran reached the far side of the small circle and two Handmaidens again raised their arms to form an archway.

Eran passed through, into the circle which was six by six.

There was a Handmaiden for each of the six directions in each circle, and a circle of six for each of the six.

Six by six.

Power.

"I command the wind!" Eran began, and a single Handmaiden from each of the six circles repeated the words after her. "I command the sea!

"I command the elements!"

The fast-moving clouds above paused.

Eran raised her voice, arms limp at her sides. "I command the wind!" Two voices from each circle uttered the words. "I command the sea.

"I command the elements!"

The wind ceased and there was calm.

Eighteen voices.

The horizon began to glow in all directions and the rock beneath their feet and the clouds above turned black.

Twenty-four voices.

From within the clouds, there emanated a glow like the light of the two moons.

Thirty voices.

Thunder rumbled and lightning bolts streaked from the clouds to the ground surrounding the six circles of six and the troops beyond, forming a curtain of power and light.

Thirty-six voices spoke as one.

Balls of light soared over them, danced within their midst over the blackened rock.

Eran raised her arms high above her head, palms opened.

Thirty-seven voices spoke as one, crying out toward the sky, "I command the elements!"

Thunder roared and lightning crackled. A wind, pregnant with power, cold as death, shrieked across the plain. Eran's cape was torn from her shoulders, a whirlwind swirling round her, grasping at her hair.

Eran screamed her command. "Rise up, Woroc'Il'Lod! Rise up as when the moons cross your face and they draw you to them and your icy waters are pillars soaring into the sky! Rise up and seek the five ships and those lives aboard them which defy me! Rise up! Obey me! Bring forth destruction and sorrow! Rise up and bring forth death, Woroc'Il'Lod! Rise up, I command thee!"

All around them was night, illuminated only by the lightning and the balls of light. Magnified, louder and louder, the wind shrieked beyond endurance. "I command thee!"

Where there had been an eye's blink earlier the cacophony of the elements, there was quiet; where there had been black night, there was grey day.

Exhausted by the magical power which had flowed through her, Eran lowered her arms to her sides.

The Handmaidens, still circled six by six, knelt, heads bowed, black veils tented round them, trailing over the ground toward which they gazed.

Her young lieutenant's steel-shod hooves clicked anxiously against the stone beneath them.

Eran willed her cape to her shoulders, willed her hair into place as it had been. The magic was at work.

As their five ships were still not quite out of the magical aura of the summer palace, the clothes and boots and scabbards of the warriors dried quickly enough that Swan did not need to employ any of her own magic to assist.

There was a small tent erected on deck for her to use when she changed. The bodice of the elaborate dress she'd worn for the procession was laced closed beneath her breasts.

She untied the knot and began to loosen the cords. Out of necessity, Swan fabricated her clothes through the use of magic, but refused to use magic to dress herself (except with the style of dress which was laced up the back from waist to neckline and required magic or an attendant because it was otherwise impossible to close). She stepped out of the dress and the comparatively fragile lace petticoats beneath its skirt.

Quickly, using magic to help her, she redid her hair, dispensing with the circlet of flowers and ribbons, plaiting her hair instead after the fashion of what Al'An had so curiously called a "sports braid."

Because of the gathering chill, despite the tent breaking the growing wind, Swan re-dressed quickly, donning sturdier petticoats and a dress of heavier, more densely woven fabric. It was dark green, round necked, long sleeved, laced closed at the front and devoid of any trim. A loop at the end of each sleeve allowed for her middle finger to be inserted through. Swan pulled on sturdier boots as well. There was no need of a sword, and her dagger was where it always was on her leg.

She donned a dark brown great cape, leaving its hood down. Lastly, she wound a long shawl of heavy brown-and-green yarn over her head and around her shoulders. It was a gift knitted by Bin'Ah's young wife.

Swan left the tent. The spray, colder than it had been when she'd entered the tent, immediately assaulted her, making her grateful for her sensible choice of wardrobe. The motion of the deck beneath her feet, because she had the horizon reference of the sea, was more pronounced to her.

The ship's prow plunged forward into each wave, as if the vessel were about to be engulfed, then rose again. Beyond the prow, there was nothing to see but the vast, whitecapped greyness of Woroc'Il'Lod stretching infinitely around them. All that there was to relieve Woroc'Il'Lod's emptiness, to reassure her mind and spirit that this was a reality and not a terrifying dream, were the other four ships of what Al'An called "Swan's Armada."

Woroc'Il'Lod frightened her, as it frightened everyone who set sail upon it.

The magical aura of the summer palace was gone as well. She could feel the emptiness of its absence. No longer would her magical energy be instantly renewed. She would have to be more cautious in its use.

Everyone seemed to be busily, almost frantically about his or her appointed task, adjusting sail, rowing at the oars, fighting the sea to keep it from claiming their lives. Hunching her shoulders against the rapidly growing cold and beneath the weight of the greatcape she clutched close around her, Swan moved to the stern rail. She was well aware that one chapter of her life was closing behind her. Another, which might be the final chapter, was beginning.

It was the ultimate bitter irony, she thought, her eyes focusing on a lonely whitecap far off to port. She ached for Al'An to touch her, hold her, make her his in every way, ached in body and soul to lie with him in the night, their flesh touching. Yet in order that the prophecy might be fulfilled, she must not be other than a virgin until she found the origin of her seed: her father.

Tears filled her eyes; she told herself it was the wind.

The whitecap she had been watching seemed somehow larger. It was an optical illusion, Swan decided. She kept watching it, however, even more intently.

Larger, still larger.

Swan worked the second sight, clutching at the handrail more tightly. "Al'An! Erg'Ran! Gar'Ath! Mitan! The Gle'Ur'Gya! The Gle'Ur'Gya are coming!" Swan shouted.

There was one obvious reason why the Gle'Ur'Gya had a reputation as always overtaking their prey on the high seas, one reason other than their considerably larger, better rigged, faster ships. The Gle'Ur'Gya were seafarers, and any other Creathan merely a landsman who happened to be caught woefully out of his element at the most impossibly wrong time.

Binoculars were unknown in Creath, as were telescopes, no requirement for advanced optics to be invented or even considered. If one needed to look at something far away, one merely second-sighted it. If one had no magic, the thing to do was ask someone who did to look. Alan Garrison had no magic. "What do you see?" Garrison asked. "What do you see?!" The size and rigging were all the detail that he could make out from his position along the stern rail, but Erg'Ran, Swan and Mitan could second-sight the rapidly approaching Gle'Ur'Gya vessel in perfect detail. Gar'Ath, whose face often read like a book for the visually impaired, had no magic either, except that which he needed for swordsmithing. And his face asked the same questions.

Mitan answered first. "It is clearly a single vessel only, Champion. That is the way the Gle'Ur'Gya usually hunt. I count as many as half our number visible on deck alone, and the Gle'Ur'Gya ships have spaces below the deck where weapons are cared for and food is cooked. There could be more Gle'Ur'Gya there."

"What kind of weapons?" Garrison pressed.

Erg'Ran spoke. "There are large fixed crossbows, of the type which are mounted to tripods and used in siege. They are affixed to the deck. I see twelve of them. They are cranked to the cocked position. Champion, no man, nor any Gle'Ur'Gya, is powerful enough to bend such prods. Their bolts are the size of short spears. A few strikes from one of these against our mast and it will be down, Champion."

Unaided by the second sight, Garrison was still able to gauge the height of the Gle'Ur'Gya's main deck as compared to their own. It was amply high enough that anyone aboard the Gle'Ur'Gya ship firing even conventional crossbows or longbows had a decided tactical advantage. "Those megacrossbows? How much elevation capability do they have, if they were firing downward?"

It took several seconds for a response. Gar'Ath answered even though he, like Garrison, could not have been able to see them. "I am familiar with such weapons, from the great siege of Kli'Il'Yer, where the Horde of Koth killed many of us, Champion. These weapons rotate upward easily, either freely moving at the will of the marksman or being capable of locking into position for repeated firings on the same target."

"How far do they crank downward, Gar'Ath?" Garrison was thinking of Renaissance-period warfare on Earth's high seas, positing that their five little ships might be able to stay under the Gle'Ur'Gya's artillery, if they could get close enough without getting sunk, first. That was the only encouragement, the sinking part. These were pirates and a ship gone to the bottom with cargo and gear intact was a prize lost.

Frantically, Garrison was trying to construct a scenario which would allow them some chance to combat the Gle'Ur'Gya's superior firepower. Gar'Ath spoke. "If your magic, Enchantress, can be used to shield us from the cold, a number of us can swim out from our ships and board the Gle'Ur'Gya vessel secretly, then fight them on their own deck."

"If we teamed that with longbow and crossbow firepower from our own decks, we might have something," Garrison remarked. "Trouble there is that we could hit our own guys just as easily as hitting them. If only we had something to use as an explosive. We could sink her." He realized that it would take a few precious seconds for the concept of what an explosive actually did to register, since they had no explosives in all of Creath. Perhaps, he thought, Swan could make something magically which—

"My mother." Swan spoke so calmly, so matter-of-factly that her simple words were suddenly terrifying.

Garrison looked away from the Gle'Ur'Gya vessel and stared at Swan. Her normally pale skin, her cheeks flushed with the cold, was now a deathly white. Garrison followed her gaze to the horizon off the port bow.

Erg'Ran, his voice almost a whisper, rasped, "The moons will not cross paths for—"

"It is not the moons doing this," Mitan solemnly intoned, interrupting Erg'Ran.

"I fear that you are right," Erg'Ran agreed.

Garrison still stared out toward the horizon. What he saw was miles away, but it gripped his soul. What he could not compel himself to look away from was one of the storms about which Erg'Ran had spoken, a tornado, but made of water rather than air. How rapidly it rotated Garrison could not guess. The velocity at its center would be even greater.

The cyclonic ocean wave was coming straight for them, as if it were hunting them. And Garrison knew that hunting them was exactly what it was doing. Swan's mother had sent it, sent it to destroy them before they could reach Edge Land.

Alan Garrison almost laughed. Eran the Queen Sorceress couldn't be all that all-knowing and all-powerful, despite sending this storm to annihilate them. She hadn't realized that the Gle'Ur'Gya had been about to spare Eran all the trouble of a magical storm and kill her enemies the old-fashioned way.

It was easy to forget that Swan—young, beautiful, willowy, feminine in every way—was, in reality, their leader. As she began to speak, Alan Garrison realized once again how fine a leader she was and he felt pride beyond measure to be with her. "We have few options," Swan told them, speaking logically, yet almost sweetly. "If the storm is not natural, which it cannot be because the moons are not crossing, either my mother used an unbelievably great amount of her own magical energy to create it or did so through the assistance of the Handmaidens of Koth." Garrison remembered them being mentioned as witches, an evil sisterhood serving Eran's will.

"In either case, it is of little consequence now. If we survive, however, it may be of great importance," Swan continued. "My mother wishes to win this struggle, whatever way she can. The Queen Sorceress would know full well that the only chance we might have to combat this storm is by the use of magic. If I use my magic directly against it, in an attempt to destroy it, even assuming that my magic would be powerful enough, my magical energy will be almost fully depleted. Even with my magic at full strength to use against hers at Barad'Il'Koth, we will have little chance of success. Without it, we cannot win against the Horde and we will die on the Plains of Koth. That is a certainty."

Swan gestured toward the rapidly approaching wave, the swells through which their ships made way already increasing in height and strength. "We have one chance. We must turn the ships, retreating into the magical aura surrounding the summer palace. The evil magic of the storm my mother sends against us will have no effect there and what magic I will need to get us there can be rapidly replenished." Swan looked toward the Gle'Ur'Gya pirate vessel. "The Gle'Ur'Gya are a powerful enemy, yet could prove a valuable ally. At any event, I cannot stand by and

abandon them to my mother's evil magic. Erg'Ran?
Do you know their tongue well enough that you could
offer them safe harbor inside the aura?"

Erg'Ran hesitated, then nodded thoughtfully. "I
believe so, Enchantress."

"Then do so now. Mitan, aid him with your magic
that his voice may be heard over the crashing of the
waves by the captain of the Gle'Ur'Gya vessel."

"Yes, Enchantress."

Swan looked at Gar'Ath. "See to it, Gar'Ath, that
Bin'Ah orders our ship turned toward the summer
palace. Signal the other four ships that they might
do the same."

"Yes, Enchantress!"

Swan turned her eyes to Alan Garrison. "Al'An,
please accompany me to the prow of our ship where
I will call forth the wind. I will need your strength
to support and sustain me."

Garrison nodded, honored. "Yes, Enchantress."

Swan touched his cheek as he fell in beside her.
They made their way rapidly forward along the rolling
and pitching deck, steadying themselves as need be
against the shoulders of the oarsmen. Raising her
skirts, Swan took the three low steps to the small
foredeck at the prow.

The cyclonic wave was getting nearer, a huge pillar
of gray so dark it was almost black, flecked with white
froth.

Gar'Ath's voice rang out. "Captain! Order the
oarsmen to ship oars. Trim the sail as needed. We
turn for harbor in the aura of the summer palace.
Then, raise full sail and order that the oarsmen row
as if their lives depended upon it. They do." Gar'Ath
pointed toward the cyclonic wave.

The Company of Mir's warriors were a brave lot,
fighting against impossible odds. From what Garrison had seen of them, they did not complain. If they
were rational, they feared, but they'd made no show

of it until this moment. Stark terror etched itself in their eyes, across the sets of their brows and chins and downturned mouths.

Bin'Ah, who was the son of a riverwater fisherman and one of the Company of Mir's principal talents when it came to shipwrights, gave the command. "Ship oars!" Immediately, the rolling of the deck beneath them increased, the growing swells hammering them broadside. "Hard left rudder and bring us about easy in the swells. Lower your sails until we find the wind. Oarsmen, be ready!"

Garrison looked at Swan.

Her greatcape open wide and fallen back, her arms were raised to maximum extension, palms outstretched. Over the din of the sea around them and the creak of ship's planking, Garrison heard Erg'Ran's voice, but the words he said were in a tongue totally unfamiliar. He was making the offer of a truce to the Gle'Ur'Gya.

Their own ship was coming about to port. The Creathan equivalent of a semaphore signalman worked his flags to the other ships. On either side of them, Garrison observed the other four ships of their tiny armada attempting to come about.

Garrison turned his eyes to Swan. Somewhere, at the back of his mind, he thought that he remembered the term for this part of a ship, the tip of the prow overlooking the water. It was called the pulpit. Swan stood there, as she had been, but now she was speaking in the Old Tongue. That much he recognized.

Garrison blinked. Balls of light were born from her palms, rolled over her hands; then, like lightning, the energy streaked from Swan's fingertips, racing toward the sky. The clouds above them, rapidly scudding heavy masses of grey, became luminous as the energy from Swan's hands penetrated them. And they began to change direction, to move toward the Land.

A wind rose up, strong and cold, Swan's skirts

billowing on it, the shawl which had been wrapped about her head blown back from her hair.

"All right, lads! Lower oars! Full sail and steady on the tiller, helmsman! Now, lads! Put your backs to those oars!" The rolling and pitching became almost instantly less pronounced, all lateral motion nearly ceased. The little ship was underway, back toward the magical aura which surrounded the summer palace. Garrison looked to port and starboard at the other four ships getting underway.

The Gle'Ur'Gya vessel was slowly coming about into their little armada's wake, under the circumstances its size a hindrance rather than an advantage. The Gle'Ur'Gya had accepted the offer.

The column of furiously spinning water a quarter mile wide or better, so tall that it seemed to connect the water to the sky above, roared relentlessly toward them.

"Help me, Al'An!" Swan rapidly descended the bow pulpit, Garrison beside her.

Swan wedged herself against the stern rail. "Hold me fast, Al'An! Hold me fast!"

Garrison braced himself behind her, the wind's force already buffeting them.

Swan raised her arms again, and the energy flowed from her fingertips, her hands beckoning the wind, like a symphony conductor summoning more from his orchestra, making the wind swell, rise to her demands. Garrison understood why she'd needed him with her. The wind forced her body back against him, his own hands white-knuckle-locked on the stern rail; his body was all that kept Swan from being blown down by the wind's force.

The cyclonic wave advanced inexorably, its speed seeming to increase.

Garrison looked behind him. The helmsman at the tiller—he'd lashed himself to its arm—shook with the force transmitted to him from the water through which their craft plunged. "Gar'Ath! Help the man at the tiller! The helmsman! Help him! Hurry!"

The helmsman's legs buckled and he stumbled, fell, the tiller arm swaying frighteningly. "Swan! Hold on as tightly as you can for a second!"

Garrison didn't know if she'd heard him, nor could he completely let go of her for fear that she'd be bowled over by the wind. But Garrison twisted round, bracing Swan with his back, one hand only clutched to the bow rail. He stretched his other arm as far as he could, at last fisting the tiller arm in his left hand. His body immediately began to shake from the force of the rudder. Garrison looked over his shoulder. Swan was not holding on, could not, he suddenly realized. She required both hands free in order to summon the howling wind to drive them on.

Garrison's hearing was nearly gone, the wind's shrieking wail filling his head, numbing his senses. He looked up. Gar'Ath clawed his way aft, hand over hand along the shoulders of the oarsmen. Gar'Ath's long hair whipped across his face, his cloak blown off his shoulders. "Coming, Champion!" Garrison thought he heard those words, but could not be sure.

Garrison's shoulder muscles ached with the strain from the tiller and his gloved hand was beginning to slip. The weight of the man lashed to the tiller arm pulled Garrison off balance. Garrison was hurtled to one knee as their ship crashed against a swell. He felt Swan's body shifting behind him. His muscles were tensed and stretching to the point of agony, but he held on because there was no choice.

"Hurry, man!" Garrison cried out to Gar'Ath.

"On my way, Champion!" Gar'Ath threw himself against the force of the wind, his body crashing against the tiller arm. Garrison released, nodded his thanks. Garrison pulled himself to his feet and around, wedging his body more firmly against Swan's.

Wind-hurtled spray blinded Garrison for an instant.

Struggling to reopen his eyes, what Garrison saw when he did was as frightening as the face of death. The cyclonic wave, obliterating all light above and behind it, was a wall of rushing blackness, bearing mercilessly down on their ships.

The Gle'Ur'Gya vessel had come about, was under full sail, and nearly passing them.

Garrison craned his neck to look forward and up. The square sail on their ship's single mast was strained full. His eyes tracked along its edges to the lines securing it to the spars. If one of those lines should snap, they were done for.

Swan heightened the tempo of the gale force winds she commanded, winds orchestrating five tiny ships and the full-masted Gle'Ur'Gya pirate vessel to water surface speeds Garrison wouldn't have thought possible. Her hands moved ever more furiously, the rush of air around Swan and Garrison tearing at clothing and the flesh beneath.

The deck planking under Garrison's feet was beginning to tremble and the handrail shook. Garrison looked forward. Their solitary mast vibrated like a tuning fork.

Garrison cast a glance over the side. Their tiny ship's wake was near tidal wave proportions, walls of white frothed water rising to port and starboard. He could imagine how it must have looked from the bow.

Faster and faster, the deck planking shuddering, starting to buckle. The roar of the wind was so intense that Garrison screamed against it, desperately trying to equalize pressure before his tortured eardrums burst.

Faster and faster, Swan's hands flew, drawing the wind to them, to the sails.

The Gle'Ur'Gya vessel had passed them all. In the same instant that Garrison looked for it, the Gle'Ur'Gya's aftmost mast snapped, flipping forward across the main deck, chopping down spars from the main mast, sails flapping wildly in the wind, tearing, blowing free.

Garrison wanted to cry out to Swan, call her attention to the plight of the crew of the Gle'Ur'Gya vessel. He shouted her name. If she heard him over the roaring air currents careening around them, she did not acknowledge it. Garrison looked to their own mast once more. It vibrated more pronouncedly.

The Gle'Ur'Gya vessel was slowing so dramatically that, within moments, it would be all but dead in the water, and precious few moments after that, the cyclonic wave would be upon it, consuming it.

Alan Garrison saw the thing more clearly than he wanted to. Around the base there was a trough, a plunging, white-capped chasm, the boundary between the cyclonic wave's suction and Woroc'Il'Lod's otherwise roiling surface.

The trough was perilously close.

But the trough was closer still to the Gle'Ur'Gya vessel, nearly even with it. Alan Garrison experienced an ironic, guilty happiness, engendered by the knowledge that he didn't possess the magic of the second sight, hence would remain mercifully blind to the agonized faces of the Gle'Ur'Gya as they met death beyond horrific imagining, their bodies thrashed and torn, broken limb from limb.

There was a moment when the Gle'Ur'Gya ship was all but motionless on the water's surface, what momentum it still possessed from before the collapse of its masts was equalized by the reverse current forming and reforming at the trough's outer boundary. Then the Gle'Ur'Gya were drawn inexorably back, into the advancing edge of the trough.

There were man-shapes, yet somehow different from men, hurtling themselves from the deck into the Woroc'Il'Lod, vainly, foolishly, heroically fighting for a last instant of life.

A lone figure, perhaps the vessel's captain, perhaps

its cook, stood on the high afterdeck, a sword raised in his right hand. It was possible that the Gle'Ur'Gya had lost his mind, yet even more likely that he was doing the only thing that he could do to keep his sanity. The figure began to execute a kata with his sword, ballet-like in its grace, the sword whirling in his hands as if it had a life of its own and it and the figure wielding it were in perfect harmony, communion.

In the end, as the crippled Gle'Ur'Gya vessel was about to slip off the edge and into the trough, to be devoured within the monstrous cyclonic wave, the Gle'Ur'Gya mariner manipulated his sword one last time. His right hand, which grasped the hilt, was almost beside his right ear, the sword's pommel angled rearward and slightly upward, the point of the blade stabbing aggressively forward. His left palm was open, fingers extended, his hand—at once a target and a shield—was thrust toward this enemy which he could not kill.

The Gle'Ur'Gya ship careened over the trough's edge and vanished. An instant afterward, fragmented portions of the vessel's hull were visible along the leading edge of the cyclonic wave, then gone.

Alan Garrison didn't know why his eyes sought out Gar'Ath's face but when they found Gar'Ath's face, he saw the swordsman's eyes swam with tears.

The Gle'Ur'Gya's fate would be theirs in moments, Garrison realized.

Faster and faster, Swan's hands flew with blinding rapidity, the speed of the wind which propelled their five craft increasing and increasing. Swan's greatcape was ripped from her shoulders, blinding Garrison for a second, then jerked away from his face. Her braid began to loosen, came apart, her spray-drenched hair whipping across Garrison's eyes. The sleeves of Swan's dress sheared, her bodice, her skirt shredding nearly to rags.

There were loud cracking sounds, one after the

other. Garrison twisted his neck around to look forward. Oars were snapping like matchsticks, wooden fragments caught up in the wind, firing along the deck. If enough holes were shot into their solitary sail, it would shred in microseconds.

Garrison turned his head, looking aft, his body wedged hard behind Swan's. Garrison squinted against the wind, and his lips were set wide apart, rictus-like. Wave after wave of spray launched over them, Garrison choking with it.

The cyclonic wave was frighteningly nearer, the trough's boundary readying its first kiss to their stern. Their wake was nearly eradicated by the reverse current into the trough.

Swan's body went rigid against Garrison, her hands and arms thrusting upward in one last summoning. The wind pushing them rose to her command. Garrison lost his grip, stumbling back. Swan's body hurtled past him. Garrison grabbed for her, caught her ankle. Her body slammed to the deck and both of them skidded along the spray-slicked planking. Garrison reached out with his other hand, clawing for a hold. He caught his fingers around a rail stanchion, his wrist breaking. He knew that he shouted with the pain, but he heard nothing but the roaring wind.

Garrison held on, wedging one foot against the ledge of an oarsman's well.

At last, he heard something over the shriek of rushing air, the sound he'd anticipated and most feared hearing. It was the thunderous crack of their mast snapping in two. Their square-rigged sail held its integrity for an instant longer, the mast's upper section rigidly suspended on the wind. The sail billowed outward, the broken segment of mast arcing backward, almost upright for a split second. Then, it snapped forward, like a thrown knife. Their little ship shuddered, the sail torn in two.

Garrison looked aft. All light was obliterated, the cyclonic wave towering over them.

The wind which had driven them in their desperate gambit, simultaneously ally and enemy, began to subside.

A new roar, louder than the wind, replaced its sound.

Garrison stared into the cyclonic wave. It seemed to be on all sides of them at once.

In his peripheral vision, Garrison caught sight of some of the oarsmen, trying to clamber back to their positions. Gar'Ath was slumped over the tiller, dead or unconscious.

The cyclonic wave edged nearer, and Garrison knew that their ship was slipping back, the reverse current dragging them into the trough. Garrison turned his head forward, for one last glimpse of Swan. He truly loved her; and, if somehow some part of them went on, he would love her even after death, he realized.

Garrison looked up. The sky, still cloud impacted, seemed oddly bright. He looked over the starboard rail. The other four ships were motionless on the water, the nearest only a hundred yards or so out. The Company of Mir crewmen were waving their arms, their oars, their swords.

"Holy shit!" Garrison gasped.

He let go of Swan's ankle, let go of the stanchion. Broken wrist or not, as he crawled forward on his knees, his eyes scanned the deck for something he could use as an oar. He found an actual oar, part of the shaft furthest from the blade broken away. Garrison plunged the oar into the water. He shouted, not knowing if anyone could hear him. "Row! We're nearly inside the aura! Row!" It was futile, one man gouging an oar's blade into the sea, but Alan Garrison did it anyway.

He thought he heard Swan's voice, but it could have been his mind playing tricks on him.

Garrison looked up from the water.

Her dress in tatters, left arm bleeding, hair plastered half across her face, Swan stood amidships, a broken piece of oar in her right hand, raised high over her head. She flung it into the air and it remained motionless. There was a flash of light, a vortex forming around the fragment.

And, oars, perfect and new, fell from the vortex, onto the deck. The Company of Mir oarsmen ran to them, picked them up, ran back to their positions, thrust them into their locks.

The little ship was moving, painfully slowly.

Pain consumed Alan Garrison, but also drove him on. Bone was visible through his skin, blood oozing down his hand from the puncture. With his armpit over the oar shaft, for added leverage, Garrison kept at it.

Lower.

Thrust.

Drag.

Raise.

Rotate.

Then again, and again, and again.

Garrison didn't look back for what seemed to be several seconds, but time in Creath followed other rules, rules he did not understand. Perhaps Swan was somehow controlling it, using time itself to aid them.

Lower. Thrust. Drag. Raise. Rotate. Again. Again.

Alan Garrison looked back.

The cyclonic wave was only a little closer.

Lower. Thrust. Drag. Raise. Rotate. Faster! Again. Faster! Again . . . again . . . again . . . again—

Garrison looked back once more. The cyclonic wave had gotten no closer.

Lower. Thrust. Drag. Raise. Rotate. Faster! Again. Faster! Again . . . again . . . again— "Al'An!"

No time to talk, he wanted to say, but there was no time to say even that.

"Al'An. We are safe inside the summer palace's aura. Evil magic cannot harm us here."

Garrison started to laugh. Someone had once told him that the first thing anybody usually did when they thought they were having a heart attack was to try to drive to the hospital. It was a way of going into denial. Hearing Swan's voice telling him that they were safe was his mind lying to him because his body hurt so much. He wouldn't take his eyes off the oar that he still moved to lower, thrust, drag, raise and rotate. He couldn't take his eyes off the oar or he would stop rowing and they'd die.

"Al'An, brave Al'An."

Alan Garrison thought he felt Swan's hand touch his brow, then darkness swept over him.

# Chapter Eleven

Swan blinked the sleep away from her eyes. The cyclonic wave straining uselessly against a magical barrier which it could not pass loomed over her, was omnipresent. Its roaring was and had been unceasing, but now she was only dimly aware of the cacophonous howl. The noise had not awakened her even once during the night, nor did it awaken Al'An, who slept beside her still.

She looked aft along the littered deck of their all-but-ruined ship. Bodies would heal—she'd seen to that—and structures would be repaired, by means natural or otherwise. What mattered was that the Company of Mir had survived her mother's evil magic one more time.

Swan was frightened, but not by the cyclonic wave, which would eventually dissipate, nor by her mother's power. This latter was dangerous beyond imagining; yet it was something she had long since ceased to fear. Fearing her mother's magic would have been an exercise in futility. Eran's evil was like a force of nature, always there, inevitable, waiting to strike. Rather, Swan respected its awesome capabilities and rationally chose to resist its tyranny.

What filled an inexorably expanding segment of Swan's consciousness with unreasoning dread was her own magical power.

Her magic was becoming stronger, draining from her less quickly, replenishing itself more rapidly. Swan didn't know why. Her wind summoning had amazed her, curiously terrified and intrigued her. She had enjoyed it for itself, beyond its being a necessity by means of which she might save all of their lives.

Like an angry beast at the end of some unbreakable tether, the towering cyclonic wave continued to threaten, glared back defiantly under her gaze. Yet it was unable to trespass within the aura of the summer palace, because evil magic was its very substance.

When she had first met Al'An, he might well have contended that there had to be some explanation other than magic for the wave, or for the creatures they'd battled on Arba'Il'Tac; after enduring all that had befallen them, she knew that he believed. Accepting the reality of that which was indisputably obvious was never a test of faith, of course, and magic was reality in Creath. Yet she was pleased that Al'An accepted this reality. In Al'An's realm, although magic surely existed, evidently its presence was not readily apparent to the untrained observer.

If, somehow, the cyclonic wave had been a naturally occurring anomaly, rather than the manifestation of evil magic, its strength would have rapidly depleted upon entering the aura, the phenomenon soon vanquished by the power of good magic. But the wave would have intercepted them just inside the aura, while there was yet strength enough remaining in it to destroy their little armada. The aura might have saved them from death, but Swan could not be certain.

Wrapped in two blankets and a borrowed greatcape, Swan and Al'An had huddled the night together against the stump of their ship's broken mast. Carefully, lest she awaken Al'An, Swan sat up, stood up.

Before taking her own rest, Swan had seen to the wounds of the Company of Mir, resisting the impulse of her woman's heart to first take away the pain of Al'An's broken wrist. There had been others more seriously injured, more needful of her magic. The energy necessary for her to magically transport herself to each of the other four ships in turn had drained her, almost more than she could bear. Unnatural magic was always the most fatiguing. Accelerating the healing of wounds, on the other hand, required virtually no magical energy at all.

A night's sleep at anchor within the summer palace's aura recharged her, however. Swan felt the magical energy coursing through her, strong and nearly full.

She never dreamed in the way that mortals dreamed. Her sleep was a perfect rest, especially within the aura. And, between exhaustion and having Al'An beside her, the sleep she'd taken could not have been deeper. Nor could any rest have better prepared her for what lay ahead: the attempt once again to cross Woroc'Il'Lod, then march on Barad'Il'Koth.

Swan was still attired in tatters, the greatcape clutched close about her for the dual purposes of modesty and warmth. She approached the portside rail. The two ships anchored some distance off the bow had raised no distress flags. As agreed upon, they would do so should any of the injured require additional magical attention.

The company of her little ship, save for a single warrior on watch at the stern, slept against the rails, in the oarsmen's wells, wherever they could. She had spellcast over all aboard the five ships that their sleep should be peaceful and long. As silently as she could, lest she unnecessarily rouse any of the exhausted,

Swan approached the starboard rail, ascertaining that no flags summoning her had been raised aboard either of the other two ships anchored nearby.

There was much to do and little time in which to do it.

Although the wave still taunted them, lurked in wait for them, it would eventually disappear. Sustaining the cyclonic wave required an enormous expenditure of magical energy. Even if the Handmaidens had assisted their Queen Sorceress in its creation, had formed their great circle six by six, only the Queen Sorceress herself could be maintaining the cyclonic wave for this long a time. In any case, when the cyclonic wave finally vanished, her mother's magical energy would be dangerously low, urgently require renewal.

Swan, too, had used precious energy, but not as much as she would have used had she attempted to dispel the cyclonic wave rather than outdistance it. And within the summer palace's aura, magical energy returned extremely quickly, even under normal circumstances. Her mother, Eran, did not have that advantage.

By the time that the cyclonic wave vanished, what Al'An called "Swan's Armada" would have to be fully ready to set sail for Edge Land, and at best speed.

If she was the Company of Mir's leader, the Virgin Enchantress, Daughter Royal, Princess of Creath, she'd have to see to it that she looked her part. Glancing toward the stern rail and reassuring herself that the warrior on watch was not looking her way, Swan shrugged out of the borrowed greatcape. She was nearly naked beneath it, her dress torn in places no maiden's dress should ever be torn.

Swan raised her hands, fingers level with the crown of her head, then envisioned the style of hair and raiment she desired. Drawing her fingers down slowly along her body, her hair arranged itself, her tatters vanished, replaced by attire nearly identical to what she had worn before the storm. Her new dress was deep maroon, rather than the dark green color which coordinated with the shawl made for her by Bin'Ah's wife; the shawl had blown overboard and was lost.

Again, Swan raised her fingers to the crown of her head, then drew them downward, and a black, fur-ruffed hooded greatcape spell-woven to protect her against the cold emerged. Swirling its skirt close about her, Swan tossed back its hood.

Theirs was the most severely battered of the five ships, and logically so. From this ship, she had controlled the wind and this ship had felt the greatest rush of its power. And this had been the rearmost of the five because it had been ahead of the other four prior to having to come about. Although the other vessels had sustained damage, it was minor. Hence, her own vessel—Al'An called it the Armada's "flagship"—would require the most rebuilding. There was little that Swan could do about repairing the ship immediately, however. Even by magical means, there would be a great deal of noise.

So she set about the ship doing little things: water-logged charts were restored, food and drinking water supplies were replenished, the processes of rust and corrosion attacking the metalwork of swords and spears were reversed, and such tasks were seen to.

While she was searching her memory for a spell which could produce wood to be used for deck planking, Erg'Ran came to stand beside her. He seemed at once physically rested, but on edge. "You realize that your magic grows more powerful each time that you must rise to meet the dangers your mother thrusts upon us."

"I have been thinking about that, yes. Do you know why, Erg'Ran?"

"All that I can say, Enchantress, is that I had anticipated it, with great expectation and great dread."

"You fear that I will become more and more like my mother as my magic becomes stronger and stronger."

"Yes, Enchantress. We need your magic if we are to win against her. Yet I cannot help but ask myself at what cost to you, to Creath's future, do we attempt to win? Do you understand?"

"I understand that you love me very much, and always have been concerned for my welfare, ever since you brought me to the summer palace for the very first time."

Erg'Ran set his weathered face, cleared his throat, then laughed. "How else should an uncle treat his niece, but with kindness and care to her well-being, Enchantress?"

They stood in the bow pulpit, and Swan sank against the rail. "You are—" So many things were suddenly confused, so many things clear as well, things which she had never understood. "That is why my mother hates you so? More than organizing the last of the K'Ur'Mir to resist her. More than getting them to use their magical energy to create the aura surrounding the summer palace. And even more than whisking me away from her before I reached womanhood! You are her brother, Erg'Ran?"

"Yes, Enchantress. I am her brother."

Swan threw her arms about her old friend's neck, pressed her cheek against his chest. "I love you, dear uncle!"

Erg'Ran laughed. "I never doubted that, Enchantress."

Swan pushed back from his chest, kissed him quickly and lightly on the lips. "To you, I should not be the Enchantress!"

"To me, dear one, you will always be the Enchantress," Erg'Ran confessed.

"How . . . what— How did—?"

Erg'Ran smiled down at her benignly. "And why did I choose this very moment to tell you? Is that another question for which you wish an answer, Enchantress?"

"Yes, Erg'Ran—uncle." She noticed his searching the pockets of his robe for flint and steel. Swan did not want him to be distracted, so she lit his pipe for him. Something dawned on her which she had never before considered. She asked, "Why is it that you will use magic not at all to aid yourself? You could light your own pipe with magic any time that you wished."

"That's part of the answer to the questions you've already asked of me, Enchantress." He puffed busily on his pipe for a short time, then looked at her across its bowl, smoke curling from his lips and nostrils, dragonlike. "I was a young man," Erg'Ran began, "son of the Queen Sorceress, brother to the Daughter Royal. Your grandfather, our father and my mother's husband, was the most respected man in all of Creath, for his mind and for his sword. Only man that I've ever seen as good as, perhaps better with a blade than our Gar'Ath.

"Creath was a happy place, then, Enchantress, and, like most young men, I was very full of myself. In those days, there was nothing really to do. Periodically, the Gle'Ur'Gya, who would raid coastal shipping whenever given the opportunity, would find themselves with a young chieftain who had conquest in his blood. And he'd come inland with his band. I longed for such times, so that I could have adventure, test my skill with a sword, feel the blood in my veins. My father and my mother preached to me that while it was every man's duty to be proficient at arms, it was also everyone's duty—female or male—to study the ancient prophecies, to learn all that could be learned of history. Even as a male, I was encouraged to study the use of magic. Some K'Ur'Mir men, in those days, Enchantress, could give a K'Ur'Mir female a good challenge in magic."

"I'd heard of such things," Swan told him.

"But, of course, the woman would always prevail, because magic is natural to the female. At any event, Enchantress, my father was most noted for his studies of the dark times before the coming of Mir. Much against my desires, I was persuaded by my parents to accompany my father on an expedition to what was suspected of being the site of one of the ancient cities. I consoled myself with the thought that such a trek might bring me a little of the excitement which I craved.

"And that, Enchantress, is how it all began, with that fateful expedition."

"How what began, Erg'Ran?" Swan inquired earnestly.

"Your mother's turning to the blackest of magic and the near-total destruction of the K'Ur'Mir." His pipe was going out and she not only relit it, but restuffed it magically. "Oh! Thank you, Enchantress." Erg'Ran leaned heavily against the pulpit rail, staring toward the summer palace, which was far too many lance-throws away to be seen, except with the second sight. He turned away from the unblemished surface of the sea and toward the cyclonic wave. "It was during that expedition that your mother first began to learn the arts which led to that! And," Erg'Ran tapped at his wooden peg, "this and all of the dark times which followed and will follow until she is destroyed utterly."

"Sit, uncle. Please?"

Swan dropped down to the second from the top step leading to the bow pulpit, gathering her skirts close around her legs. Erg'Ran—Swan knew that he would not want her to help, because of his pride—managed to seat himself on the top step. Swan gazed up at him, watching the smoke rising from his pipe, only to be swept away in the morning breeze. "Eran had already asked our father if she could come along. He was pleased that she wished to do so, worrying more gravely and more frequently than he would admit that she was obsessed with her study of magic. And, because both of her children were going, our mother decided to come, too. Of course," Erg'Ran chuckled, "mother and father were wildly in love, despite how long they'd been married as much taken with each other as young lovers sharing a first kiss."

That was a wonderful thought, a wonderful image that Swan wished that she had in her memories, her grandparents in each other's arms, deeply in love.

"So, Enchantress, we all set out with a retinue of assistants and a squad of palace guard, from the summer palace. Your grandparents, by the way, loved it there. Even before the aura was lain in place by the dying K'Ur'Mir, it had been a wondrous place to behold."

"Is that why you chose it, Erg'Ran? Is that why the summer palace was picked out of all of Creath?"

"Selfish of me, I know, Enchantress."

"No. It was sweet," Swan told him honestly. "It was very sweet. So tell me what happened next."

"Well, we set out, as I said, and we traveled overland for a great many lancethrows, eventually reaching Edge Land. My father, you see, always interviewed travelers who'd come from distant parts of Creath, always assembled every fact that he could concerning his studies. He'd come to the conclusion that one of the oldest cities on Creath, dating almost from the mists of time, was located there. Also that there had been a great civilization which had arisen there, only to be destroyed by some natural cataclysm. Over the years, he'd collected relics perhaps attributable to it.

"It was one of these relics, in fact, which had secretly ignited my sister's passion to accompany him in the search. She had her own agenda, Eran did, to which none of us was privy."

"There was something in that old city which would enhance her magical abilities?"

"Exactly, Enchantress." Erg'Ran drew heavily on his pipe, exhaled as he went on, saying, "Our mother, your grandmother, second-sighted for us, projecting it through birds and other creatures in an attempt to locate what still standing ruins or even blemishes on the ground there might remain.

"Edge Land was a harsh place, even in those gentler days, and the journey took its toll on us all. After some rather harrowing experiences—sandstorms, ice storms, an attack by witches—"

Swan interrupted. "Witches!" Incredulous, she repeated the word. "Witches? In those days."

"It was a happy world, but never perfect. There was a tribe of witches, warriors also, which had been rumored to have survived since before the coming of Mir." Erg'Ran's face looked suddenly odd, as if he were somehow embarrassed. "They were a female only society," he said. "At any event, at last your grandmother's second sight—"

"Tell me about this tribe of witches, first."

"You wouldn't really want to hear about them, Enchantress."

"Must I command that you tell me, Erg'Ran?" Swan felt awkward even saying it. "Please," she added after an eye blink's pause.

Erg'Ran shrugged his still powerful shoulders. "I suppose you'd have to hear about them anyway, Enchantress. Very well then. The witches were female only. Some of your mother's less pleasant tendencies when it comes to the men in her life may have something to do with their influence."

"She associated with them?"

"That was to be, yes. The witches needed males, of course, for the obvious reason of procreation. They would waylay travelers, slaughter the females and kidnap the males to be used—you get the idea. Most of

the male prisoners were killed, of course, after it was
certain that fertilization had taken place. A witch can
tell immediately, of course, if she's with child. Some
of the males—the less lucky ones, by my reckoning—
were gelded and kept as slaves. The witches didn't treat
their slaves well, and when these wretches would fall
ill or show the first signs of age, they were put to death.
There were stories—never substantiated—that the
witches ate human flesh. I don't believe those stories,
although there is truth to the tales that they would
consume the hearts of those who died bravely."

"How is it that I have never heard of this tribe?"
Swan wanted to know.

"I never thought it decent to tell you, Enchantress," Erg'Ran smiled, albeit a little awkwardly. "Now,
Enchantress, I pray that I might be permitted to
continue."

"Of course," Swan conceded, but there were more
questions about the witches, more answers that he
must know and she would pry from his memory.

"At last, as I said, our mother's second sight
prevailed and we were able to locate on a plain not
far from the very tip of Edge Land what appeared
to be the site of a long forgotten city. From the
subtle indicators along the ground, it had been very
large. There were a few monoliths standing, on one
of them a few lines of runes faintly discernible,
apparently in the Old Tongue, or something earlier.
Your grandfather was very excited; for the very first
time, I saw what had always so fascinated him with
learning. It was exciting! Of course, I wasn't about
to mention that, young as I was. But I think that
he realized my interest, because he made certain
that I accompanied him throughout the examination
of the area."

"And what did you find, Erg'Ran?"

Erg'Ran cocked his eyebrow as he exhaled. "More
than we'd bargained for, Enchantress."

His story-telling techniques perennially irritated her, Erg'Ran's flare for the dramatic always interfering with his narrative flow. But Swan endured it as well as she always had.

"So, with my mother's help and some considerable help from your mother, my sister, the few lines from the early dialect of the Old Tongue found on that monolith were translated. It appeared that we might have found the legendary Barad'Il'Koth—"

Swan gasped.

"—as, indeed, time has proven that we had. Several things happened almost at once. A messenger, who had taken up after us once it was no longer possible to send messages by arrow shot, brought word that a fearsome Gle'Ur'Gya chieftain whom I later learned was named Ag'Riig had decided to raid inland. My father was our greatest warrior, and duty called. I prevailed upon him that I might accompany him. Practicality dictated that three men—he, the messenger and myself—stood a better chance should we encounter the witches again. Your grandmother ordered that your grandfather and I should depart and the squad of guards from the palace would remain behind."

"And?"

Erg'Ran smiled. "We were off on another adventure, your grandfather and I. We managed to avoid the witches, thanks in large part to a spellcasting my mother made. To reach the shoreline where Ag'Riig's vessel would be awaiting his return, the shortest route was through the great wood which we had meticulously avoided on the journey to Edge Land, avoided at the cost of several days' travel."

Somehow, Swan knew what Erg'Ran was going to say. It was no magic, just an unpleasant guess. "When it was too late to turn back, we encountered the tree demons."

"Ugh!" A shiver of disgust ran along Swan's spine. "Don't tell me the details. Please!"

"I hadn't planned to, Enchantress. Suffice it to say, your grandfather and I were both injured, and our companion, the messenger, was lost. We escaped the wood with our lives, racing toward the Woroc'Il'Lod coast to rendezvous with our warriors and confront the Gle'Ur'Gya chieftain.

"But, meanwhile," Erg'Ran went on, "something far more important was about to transpire on the plain where my mother and sister had remained behind.

"Unbeknownst to us all, the artifact which Eran had discovered within my father's collection was the key which would allow her to unlock the secrets of the old magic from the days when Barad'Il'Koth was the center of power on Creath. She was about to take that power into her hands."

Erg'Ran stood up with some difficulty. Swan watched him as he paced about, his peg tapping rhythmically on the deck planking. She shifted position, perching now on the edge of the step, knees nearly to her chin, feet drawn under her, lost beneath her skirts. "Barad'Il'Koth ceased to exist as a city a very long time before the coming of Mir. What befell its inhabitants is still unknown. It is as if they vanished from the face of Creath. Perhaps some few remained behind and it was their legacy which Eran discovered. But whatever befell the evil ones of Barad'Il'Koth, a cache of tablets graven in stone was left behind. This legacy became our woe, yours and mine and all of Creath's.

"The tablets," Erg'Ran went on, "were the means by which Eran learned to heighten her magical powers to a degree unknown in Creath since ages before the coming of Mir, magic more evil than that which Mir himself dispelled."

"Didn't your mother try to stop her?"

Erg'Ran's voice caught, and she thought she spied a tear in his eye as he turned quickly away from her.

"Eran killed my mother."

Swan lowered her face into her hands. . . .

Alan Garrison awoke. He was cold, and his right wrist felt stiff. He raised his right arm from beneath the blankets and rolled back the knit cuff of his bomber jacket. His wrist had been broken, a compound fracture, bone sticking through his skin. There was no evidence of that now.

But what had transpired was not a dream. Looking aft along the deck, the sight of the cyclonic wave was an undeniable reality. It waited for them to venture out from the aura of the summer palace, waited to kill them. Since his right hand seemed to work perfectly, Garrison raised its middle finger and jerked it toward the wave. Somehow, he hoped, Swan's mother would be able to see it, know the meaning of the gesture, appreciate fully the words which would normally accompany it, were she only near enough to hear them.

His guns lay beside him on the deck, as did his knives. Swan had been busy. The guns were in seemingly perfect condition, despite being doused in seawater. Garrison pushed the button on one of the knives and the blade sprang out reassuringly. He closed the knife.

Since he seemed to be in one piece, he tried standing up. Aside from a little stiffness, the maneuver was completely successful. His pants were ripped along the right leg from the cuff halfway up the right thigh. Matter-of-factly, Garrison assumed that Swan would use her magic to fix the tear when she got around to it.

Garrison stretched, and turned to look toward the forward section of their little ship. He immediately started walking toward the bow pulpit, where Swan sat, face in her hands, Erg'Ran standing nearby. Most of the ship's company were still asleep, so

Garrison didn't call to Swan until he was nearly beside Erg'Ran. "What's wrong, Swan?"

Erg'Ran answered. "I just informed my niece that her mother murdered her grandmother."

Garrison just looked at the older man's face for a moment. "I came in late, remember?" Garrison looked at Swan, then dropped to his knees before her, raising her face in his hands. Her eyes brimmed over with tears.

Throughout the morning and the afternoon, Swan busied herself about their five ships, using her magic to speed the healing of the injured, facilitate repairs to the ships themselves and the attendant gear of the ships' companies, generally avoiding any sort of prolonged contact with Alan Garrison or her newly discovered uncle, Erg'Ran.

Food magically appeared at midday, but Garrison wasn't hungry, worried instead about Swan.

The most time Garrison spent with her was when she used her magic to see to his sartorial needs. "I'll make new clothes for you, but of the style you are used to." Swan led him forward along the deck. "You'll be naked for an eye blink as the new clothes replace the old." She placed her hands at the top of his head, then gradually drew them down along the length of his body.

Garrison's hair actually felt as clean as if he'd just washed it when her hands passed through it, magically combed as well. "This is nuts," he told her, but she only smiled. At least, he thought, he'd gotten her to shed her frown for a moment. There was a tingling feeling where his stubble had been growing, and in the next instant, his face felt clean shaven.

Her hands stopped moving as she asked, "Do you want your new clothes to be the same color as before?"

"Yes, please."

Swan's hands continued their motion along the length of his body, only very rapidly, the old T-shirt vanishing, replaced with a new one in the blink of an eye. She actually blushed a little and averted her eyes when her hands passed below his belt, but he never even felt a draft. Somehow, she was not only replacing old clothes with new, but cleaning his body as well.

Under different circumstances, what Swan was doing would have felt terribly erotic. At the moment, it was insanely frustrating.

The new boots felt good, and their leather positively gleamed.

"There." Swan turned away and left.

Garrison called after her with a superfluous, "Thanks," but she didn't turn around.

By late afternoon, Garrison took a break from helping Gar'Ath with rigging the new sail and took Erg'Ran aside, up to the bow pulpit. "What gives?" Garrison sat on the same step where Swan had sat that morning.

Erg'Ran seemed to ponder the question, then a moment later answered, "I suppose that I should tell you, Champion. She had to know. And, because of who you are, you should know as well."

"So, tell me."

And Erg'Ran did. Garrison had given up on the use of his wristwatch as anything other than an item of jewelry on Creath because of the way time seemed to move at differing speeds without any rhyme or reason. After what Garrison mentally gauged as an hour, Erg'Ran concluded by saying, "That is what I told the Enchantress, Champion." As Garrison was about to ask for the rest of the story, Swan joined them. "I saw the two of you speaking with one another."

"And?" Garrison inquired, looking up at her.

Swan shook her head resolutely. "I'm sorry that I

have been so much to myself. I just, uh—" Swan began to cry, heavy sobs from deep within her racking her body with tremors.

Garrison stood, swept her into his arms and just held her.

Gar'Ath cried out from the stern rail, "It's vanishing, breaking up! The wave is disappearing!"

Swan looked up. Garrison handed her his handkerchief, fresh like the clothes he wore and owing to the same magical manufacture.

Swabbing at her eyes, his arm still around her, Swan moved toward the rail.

Garrison was afraid to blink. Because, obviously, he'd never witnessed anything like this, he had no idea if there would be some enormous puff of smoke or what would happen.

The air around the cyclonic wave seemed to bend, ripple, twist, contort with an energy that was, somehow, more powerful than the wave itself.

The trough was shrinking, the wave expanding and contracting, as if it were breathing.

For an instant, the cyclonic wave grew, as if racing to obliterate all view of the horizon. Garrison had to blink. The cyclonic wave imploded, shrinking to nothing, vanishing into the contorted air surrounding it.

And the sea was calm, as if the cyclonic wave had never been.

A cheer rose up from their own ship and from the other four. Swan threw her arms around Garrison's neck and Garrison kissed her forehead.

"I love you," he whispered. He wasn't sure if she'd heard him, as the cheering grew louder and louder by the second.

But then he knew that she had. Swan turned her face up to his and—she had to be standing on her toes, he thought, or levitating herself with her magic—whispered into his ear, "I love you, Al'An."

"The heck with this cheering thing," Garrison whispered back. He had better things to do with his mouth. He kissed her and kept on kissing her.

The cheers kept up, grew louder still. After a while, Garrison realized that the cheers were no longer because of the disappearance of the cyclonic wave. The cheers were for the Enchantress and her Champion. When he stopped kissing her, Swan laughed and shouted to him, "Kiss me again, Al'An! Kiss me again!" He did. . . .

It was late that evening, after a hearty supper, that things were once again calm. In the morning, at dawn, they would set sail again for Edge Land, and Swan had promised them "a fine wind to carry us." Garrison could imagine from whose hands that wind would originate.

Swan brought cups of wine for Garrison and Erg'Ran. Once again, they sat on the steps leading to the bow pulpit. Globes of blue-white magical light swayed almost imperceptibly in harmony with the gentle lapping of the waves against the hull of their ship, similar arrays of light visible on the other four vessels of the armada.

The sky was particularly beautiful, Garrison observed. The sun was not yet gone from the horizon, both moons in ascendancy. For the first time since coming to Creath, Alan Garrison noticed that the two moons were apparently identical in size. There was probably a story about them. There seemed to be a story about everything in Creath, and the moons were likely not the exception.

But Alan Garrison was more concerned with the story Erg'Ran was finally continuing. "After my father and I escaped the wood, we made good speed toward the shore where we would meet with a company of our warriors and deal with Ag'Riig of the Gle'Ur'Gya before he and his men could reach their vessel."

Swan sat down beside Garrison, gathering her skirts close about her legs, a shawl around her shoulders against the breeze which blew fitfully across the water. With her head resting against his shoulder, Garrison felt her breath against his face when she looked up into his eyes. "At the time," Erg'Ran continued, "we, of course, knew nothing of what had transpired between my mother and my sister. All that might have alerted us was that my father seemed strangely tense, sad. He himself put it off to our experience in the wood against the tree demons and the tragic death of the young messenger.

"In fact, there was such a love bond between them, your grandparents, that the husband actually felt the death of his wife, in the very instant that it occurred, it would seem."

Garrison knew that this was painful for Swan, but they were committed to the story now and Swan seemed to want to know the whole story. So Garrison asked a logical question. "Did Eran just go to her mother and, well—just kill her?"

"It happened in the passion of the moment, according to the words of the few survivors from the palace guard. Oh, for a memory pool, that I could recall the details more clearly!" Erg'Ran lamented.

Erg'Ran continued his narrative. "My mother discovered Eran with the artifact taken from my father's collection. The markings—they were not runes, but something else, magical as well. They exactly matched the markings at the base of one of the stone tablets which had been uncovered after the clue translated from the runes on the monolith. Wisely, my mother had decreed that my father alone should be the one to translate the writings from the tablets, lest merely by writing or saying the words some magical incantation would be invoked. For a woman, there would be much greater risk, Champion."

"Gotchya," Garrison nodded.

"But my mother translated the tablets?" Swan suggested. "That's a stupid question. Forgive me for even asking it, uncle. Of course she did."

"Eran began to translate, and in the very act of doing so, her magical abilities increased. But she learned forbidden knowledge, as well, knowledge which she would use to magnify her powers beyond any seen on Creath since the coming of Mir, perhaps since the most ancient of days. That was her moral undoing, Enchantress, Champion."

"What kind of forbidden knowledge?" Garrison inquired.

Swan answered, and Garrison was surprised. "Before the coming of Mir, Al'An, a different kind of magic was practiced, the kind that my mother has brought back to Creath. It is the knowledge of this magic which was forbidden. In the earliest times, such magic was more powerful than any of us could imagine."

"Who forbid it? Having this knowledge, I mean. Mir?" Garrison queried.

"Not forbidden in that way, Al'An. Neither Mir nor anyone ever said that such knowledge could not be acquired, merely that it *should* not. It is magic which corrupts the user." And Swan leaned forward, taking Erg'Ran's hands in hers. "That is why you have chosen now to tell me these facts, isn't it, Erg'Ran?"

Garrison looked at the older man. "You're afraid that Swan's getting too powerful, and that she might go over the edge, like her mom did."

It took Erg'Ran a moment on the word "mom," but he responded, "Yes. As a member of the Company of Mir, as one of the comparatively few surviving K'Ur'Mir, as uncle to the Enchantress, yes. I fear for the Enchantress and I fear for Creath should the evil magic overpower her."

"He doesn't understand what we're really talking about, Erg'Ran."

"So, great! Now I'm the stupid guy, huh?"

After a second, Erg'Ran responded, "No one is saying that, but as a man from the other realm, you cannot comprehend fully the magnitude of power we're talking about, Champion."

"So give me an example."

Swan did. "What drove Mir to do what he did is unclear, simply because he was a complex person in a complex situation. But whatever else compelled him to change things in Creath, there was an immediate cause."

Garrison realized what she meant. If someone asked, for example, what started World War I, the classic—wrong—history test answer was the assassination of Archduke Francis Ferdinand. The actual cause traced back at least to the Franco-Prussian War of 1870, 1914's assassination in Sarajevo the immediate cause only.

Erg'Ran told Garrison, "Mir witnessed a duel, a fight to the death between the two most powerful sorceresses then living. The fight raged on and on between the two women, past many sunrises and sunsets, across vast distances. Many of those who had magic, female and male alike, were able to transport themselves out of harm's way. But countless numbers of ordinary mortals were consumed in the flames, cast into the vast crevices ripped across the ground, devoured by the beasts the two sorceresses created. Mir, despite his magic, which was well-developed for a male, was unable to stop them."

"Perhaps," Swan interjected, "if it hadn't been for that terrible time, well, perhaps those who became the K'Ur'Mir would not have listened to him, and things might have gone on as they were until we all eventually were destroyed."

"So there was a war," Garrison reasoned aloud, "but fought with magic so terrible that the sheer body count forced people to come to their senses."

"They followed Mir," Swan told him.

"What happened to the two sorceresses?"

Erg'Ran gestured toward the two moons.

Garrison looked at them, then at Erg'Ran, then at Swan. "Come on, guys! I may be the Federal flat-foot from Earth, and my SAT scores didn't go into the record books, but you expect me to believe—to believe—to believe—that!" Garrison stabbed his finger in the direction of the two moons.

"As the war progressed, and the ranks of the dead grew and grew," Swan recounted, "Mir sought out the most magically endowed of Creath. He reasoned with them, making them realize that neither of the war-ring sorceresses would win before the entire world was destroyed. But they could be defeated."

Garrison looked at Erg'Ran. "He did the same thing that you did when the aura was placed around the summer palace."

"Of course, Champion! Actually, I did the same thing which Mir did. It was his idea; I only copied it."

"So, Mir gets all the other people with magic to concentrate their powers on the two sorceresses. But don't give me this two moons stuff, guys."

"It's true, Al'An!" Swan insisted.

"How do you do that!? I mean, I've seen a lot of what I'd call impossible stuff since you brought me here, but how could anybody do—do that!" And, Garrison gestured again toward the two moons.

As if she were a teacher explaining a science experiment to some incredibly dense student, Swan explained, "It's really not that difficult, Al'An."

"You telling me that you could do that?"

"Yes, but I wouldn't want to. And I haven't the power to do such a thing to someone whose magic is as strong or stronger than mine. What Mir did was to combine the magical energies of those first K'Ur'Mir so that it didn't matter that the two warring sorceresses were individually unrivaled in their powers."

"It was a marvelous object lesson, too," Erg'Ran observed. "Had the warring sorceresses ceased in their attempts to destroy each other, their powers combined would almost certainly have been greater than those of all the rest of those who chose to follow Mir. In essence, they destroyed themselves with their hatred."

Garrison took a cigarette from his continually full pack and Swan lit it. "So how do you turn someone into a moon?"

"Mir knew," Swan said, "that in order to defeat the warring sorceresses it would be necessary to catch them off guard, to strike without warning. Once those he'd convinced to aid him struck, it would be imperative that the warring sorceresses could not retaliate. The only logical choice, Al'An, was to turn the women to stone."

"So, poof! They turn into stone?"

"What is poof? Is it like holy shit?"

"No. Never mind about poof. How do you turn somebody to stone?"

Swan seemed to be pondering something, then told him, "Place your cigarette on the deck a little distance away from your feet, Al'An."

"Should I put it out first?"

"There won't be time enough for it to cause a fire."

"All right." Garrison set his cigarette on the deck. Almost immediately, the glowing tip of his cigarette began to lose its color, its fire. The upward curling smoke seemed to pause.

Erg'Ran murmured, "Oh, very good!"

There were constant references by Swan and others to magical energy in the air, so it seemed oddly logical to Alan Garrison that the smoke itself was the first to begin to transform into stone, but in the blink of an eye the cigarette itself was stone as well. "After the object becomes stone," Swan said in a low, even voice, as if she were whispering to herself, "the object can then be levitated." The cigarette, smoke and all, seemed to shudder, then began to rise, floating upward to a level about even with Garrison's eyes. "In the case of the two sorceresses, because of their size as compared to your cigarette, it might have taken a few eyeblinks longer, Al'An." The cigarette just hung there. Tiny pinpoints of light, visible only because of the darkness around them, streaked toward the cigarette, moving at incredible speeds. Barely perceptible at first, the cigarette grew noticeably larger, beginning to lose its shape. "Then, mass is added to it, as I am doing now." Gradually, the cigarette lost all of its identity, becoming spherical. "In order to change something or someone to stone, it isn't necessary, of course, to alter the shape by adding mass. In the case of the sorceresses, Mir or the others with him must have planned to have them transform into the two moons from the very first. Nor, of course, Al'An, does one have to levitate the object or objects. I'm just demonstrating how I imagine that it was probably done."

"Thank you, professor," Garrison smiled.

Swan paused a moment, evidently determining the word's meaning, then blew him a kiss. "And then," Swan went on, "it was merely a matter of adding more and more mass, placing the two moons in the sky as they should be," and the stone ball that was once a cigarette rose slowly, steadily upward, floating over the stern rail, ascending until it was almost too distant to be seen, then seeming to descend rapidly. Garrison realized that the distance between the sphere and the water was not changing, that the sphere's size was increasing instead. It was about the size of a man's basketball or the first Soviet Sputnik when Swan said, "I think that's large enough to illustrate how it was done, Al'An."

"Now what?"

"I can't turn it back into your cigarette. I could transform the stone into a piece of stone in the size and shape of your cigarette, or even turn it into a real cigarette, but it wouldn't be the same cigarette. That is gone forever."

"So the two sorceresses," Garrison deduced, "aren't imprisoned inside the moons; they ceased to exist."

"Yes. And although Mir did not foresee the cyclonic waves which would form when the two moons crossed paths in the sky—as if, somehow, the sorceresses were still capable of creating a destructive force—it was wise that he did what he did," Swan told him.

Erg'Ran amplified. "Each night, since the coming of Mir, women and men have looked into the sky, known that the two moons were there, eternal reminders of the fragility of life and how the power of good overcame the power of evil."

"Evidently, Eran isn't much into moon watching," Garrison voiced, realizing how sarcastic his words sounded only after he said them.

"Yes," Erg'Ran agreed, the word drawn out so slowly that it was as if it had three syllables rather than one.

Swan swept her left hand gracefully toward the still floating sphere, and it augered downward into the water, making a great splash. Swan looked at Erg'Ran and urged, "Tell me the rest now, the rest of what happened. Please?"

Erg'Ran fumbled with his pipe, and in the next instant it was packed and lit by Swan's magic.

Garrison took another cigarette from his pack—the pack was full again—and Swan lit it, too. He sipped at his wine and smiled. Erg'Ran spoke. "My sister murdered my mother with magic when my mother forbade her to continue the translations from the tablets. Consider this, Champion," Erg'Ran digressed. "Our mother was the most powerful magic maker in Creath. Yet merely by translating the tablets, essentially just saying the words inscribed there, Eran was powerful enough—forgive me for being so blunt,

Enchantress— Your mother was powerful enough to cause our mother's heart to explode within her chest!"

Swan visibly shivered. Garrison folded her in his arm once again.

"And Eran discovered the secret to even greater power. Yet she was unable to either obtain or exercise that power at the time, and that enraged her. But the possession of that power, that continually renewing source of magical energy, was her goal. Eran never lost sight of it until it was hers.

"My father and I reached the shore, still ignorant of what had transpired between my mother and sister. We united with our warriors and intercepted the Gle'Ur'Gya chieftain and his men when they were about to return to their ship with their plunder.

"Ag'Riig was a fierce warrior and a talented tactician. The Gle'Ur'Gya fought bravely. Numerically, we were well matched, and both sides had endured similar journeys to arrive at the battlefield there along the shore. We may pass the site as we sail tomorrow.

"Many arrows were fired in fearsome volleys at the moment when the two forces initially sighted one another," Erg'Ran continued. "I was wounded, but only a graze along my thigh. I used my magic to stem the bleeding and was beside my father again in a matter of eyeblinks.

"The Gle'Ur'Gya had surprised us. Both forces really stumbled upon the other. Because of that, the Gle'Ur'Gya had the higher ground. They rained arrows upon us with great accuracy; and, although we responded in kind, they had the advantage. Only a small number of the Gle'Ur'Gya were ahorse, and in that we found our own advantage.

"My father broke our force in two," Erg'Ran enthused, "and honored me by placing me second in command of one of the elements, while he personally led the other. It was my company's lot to fight our way down the beach and past the

Gle'Ur'Gya position on the ground above, then find what way we could to reach the higher ground and harass them from behind, thus diverting a substantial portion of their force while my father led the main body in an assault against their position."

"We call that an envelopment," Garrison supplied.

"An envelopment," Erg'Ran echoed. "Yes. A good word for it."

"Then what happened?" Swan asked, caught up in the story.

"As I said, Ag'Riig was a fine tactician. He must have apprehended almost immediately that an, an envelopment was our intent. He dispatched a small body of his force to parallel the unit with which I rode, then position themselves to deny us access to the high ground. We didn't know this, of course.

"When our company had traveled fifty lancethrows or so, the leader spied a narrow channel heading through the sand and rock and toward the higher ground. Without dispatching anyone to scout for enemy archers, he wheeled the company toward the channel.

"The first volley fired by the Gle'Ur'Gya took him out of the saddle with an arrow through his throat. He had no magic, and no one with magic was able to reach him in time to stop the bleeding. He was dead by the time I'd swung down from the saddle.

"His death, of course, meant that I had command of the company. I had no experience as a leader, and none as a warrior. Hoping that the courage of Mir would guide me, I split my company into three elements. The first I dispatched still further along the beach, to find another way of reaching the high ground. The second I set to providing almost continuous volleys of arrows against the Gle'Ur'Gya's position above us. The third I led myself. Armed with pikes, a few crossbows, but mainly with swords and our shields, we stormed along the near side of the channel on foot.

"The Gle'Ur'Gya had not expected this, and the Gle'Ur'Gya warrior archers from the far side of the channel had gone on in pursuit of my maneuvering element which I'd sent along the beach.

"The fighting was fierce," Erg'Ran continued, "and I bloodied steel for the first time there amid the dunes. We took the high ground. Immediately, I dispatched archers to pursue the Gle'Ur'Gya who had gone to intercept my maneuvering element. With the very warriors who had accompanied me in the charge along the channel to the high ground, I took horse for the main body of Gle'Ur'Gya against whom my father would lead his warriors in less time than I cared to consider."

Erg'Ran's pipe went out, but Swan had it going again before Erg'Ran took notice of it. "We literally stumbled upon the rear guard Ag'Riig had established for just such a contingency. The fighting was nothing like I had imagined it would be. My hands became so sticky with blood, I could barely grip my sword's hilt. Both sides fought with the unremitting ferocity of tree demons, as if we spilled blood for blood's sake alone.

"My men acquitted themselves well, extraordinarily so. Ag'Riig was forced to divert some of his men from defense against my father's impending attack in order to hold us in check.

"It was then that my maneuver element and warrior archers joined us. We gave the agreed upon signal—a fiery arrow, then two more shot skyward after it—and my father's force began their assault.

"Ag'Riig held his ground, and when my father reached his position, the two men both ordered a cessation in the fighting, for all but themselves.

"My father's sword was a wondrous blade," Erg'Ran confided to them, "and I have never seen its like to this day. It had a single edge, the blade itself curved ever so subtly. Its hilt would easily accommodate two hands, but just as easily lent itself to use with but a single hand. The guard, very elaborately engraved in relief, was like a small shield, completely encircling the hilt.

"Ag'Riig's sword was almost equally magnificent, but of a different style and longer by several spans. My father and the Cle'Ur'Gya chieftain faced off and fought. The sun was nearly setting when they began their duel, and darkness was upon us in full measure when it ended, fires lit there on the high ground so that my father and Ag'Riig could see.

"Both were exhausted. When the firelight caught their faces, their expressions were grim, each knowing that the other swordsman could deal him death. They were an even match, you see. That is the most dangerous battle to endure, the most compelling to watch.

"Sparks flew in great showers as steel would contact steel. I've never seen such since. At last, my father's sword cleaved the blade of Ag'Riig, but the Gle'Ur'Gya chieftain fought on with half a blade, Ag'Riig's steel failing him but not his courage. My father offered to give quarter, or lend him another sword. Ag'Riig accepted neither.

"My father was clearly about to triumph. I felt that my father would spare the Gle'Ur'Gya chieftain because of such bravery and gallantry. I was never to know."

"What happened?" Garrison asked, unable not to interrupt.

"One of the Gle'Ur'Gya archers loosed an arrow. It pierced my father's eye and into his brain. He was dead before he fell, and no magic could have saved him. We all stood there, motionless for an eyeblink. Then Ag'Riig flung his broken sword across the darkness and into the chest of the Gle'Ur'Gya archer who had dishonored him.

"Everyone had his blades drawn, arrows nocked, crossbows cocked. Ag'Riig shouted out, speaking well enough in our tongue that he was understood, proclaiming that there had been enough blood shed here. Kneeling beside my father's body, I raised my voice and ordered that our warriors not be the first to renew the fighting.

"We did not clasp hands, or make some vow or another. We were not friends, perhaps more closely bound than friends, bound in honor. Ag'Riig took his Gle'Ur'Gya and I took my men, he to his ship, I to tell my mother and sister the terrible events which had unfolded.

"My father's body borne on a litter, we made our way to the encampment near the monolith. We traveled in sufficient force to risk the wood once again, and we traversed it unmolested by the tree demons.

"My heart was heavier than I thought then that it could ever be. But, upon reaching the encampment, I learned my mother's fate. What could be done was done for the guards. Enraged beyond enduring, with my father's sword I set out to find Eran. I have no idea if I would have killed her. As it was, I did not see her again until after you were born, Enchantress. I kept the sword for the day that I would avenge my mother.

"Eran established herself with the witches, became their leader. Not long before your birth, Enchantress, she at last obtained the ultimate power which she had so long sought. It is then that she began the destruction of the K'Ur'Mir in earnest. Yet already Creath was in the grip of violence and evil unlike anything known since before the coming of Mir. Eran was determined to make Creath still worse. And she has done so.

"Eran, whose curiosity was boundless, destroyed the person that once she was and nearly all of Creath as well. As you move against her, Enchantress, you must guard against the temptation which will present itself. You must use what magic needs be used in order to defeat Eran, then eschew its use, if you are strong enough. Eran has magic that no mortal or immortal was ever meant to know. In order to defeat Eran, you must learn this dark magic and then use it for purposes other than for which it was divined. Afterward, such magic must return to the darkness from whence it came.

"If you defeat Eran," Erg'Ran warned, "your greatest enemy will be yourself, Enchantress. Never forget that."

"Three questions, please," Alan Garrison requested.

"The first question, Champion?"

"The sword, your father's sword. You have it with you?"

"Yes. I hope to use it to take the life from Eran. While she lives, she will always be dangerous. But the important thing is not that I take her life, but that someone does."

"The tablets she translated. Where are they now?"

"Eran would have them closely guarded, at Barad'Il'Koth, Champion."

"Which leads to what is my third and presumably last question, Erg'Ran."

"It is?"

"How would Swan avail herself of the same magical abilities her mother has, which you say that she must learn if we're to win?"

Reading the older man's face in the light of the blue-white magical globe, Erg'Ran seemed to carefully weigh his answer. Finally, he spoke. "The magic grows within the Enchantress. When she controlled the wind, this was something which she could not have done as she did only a short while ago. Her magic grows and strengthens and it will be enough for now. When the time comes, all will learn the source of the Queen Sorceress's powers, and my

niece will know what to do. You will help her,
Champion."

"So, I unintentionally lied, Erg'Ran. Another question, sir."

"And?"

"How will I know how to help Swan if I don't
know what I'm supposed to do?"

"I was certain from the first, really. You will know
what to do because the answer which you seek is
already inside you, Champion. Circumstance will cause
you to know it. I can tell neither of you any more.
Should I do so, our mission would be lost. You both
must trust to me in this," Erg'Ran concluded.

Swan rested her head against Alan Garrison's chest.
Garrison took another cigarette. When he felt the
pack as he returned it to his jacket pocket, it was
already full again.

# Chapter Twelve

The second sight revealed that Swan, Erg'Ran and the Champion had set sail again with their pitiful band, this time crossing Woroc'Il'Lod on a wind of Swan's making. Swan was getting very good, and Eran could not help but wonder if her daughter knew the secret—yet.

Eran, skirts caught up in her clenched fist, stormed along the passageway toward its end. Her magic was so depleted from maintaining the cyclonic wave that she had to concentrate in order to make the chamber door open to her will.

She stepped inside, kicking the door closed with her heel.

"Things aren't going well?"

"Little do you care!"

"How old am I, Eran?"

"Such reckoning is meaningless, as is conversation between us. Will you submit willingly?"

"No."

Anger always increased her magical abilities, at least for an eyeblink or two. She willed herself naked and her clothes disappeared from her body. Walking across the room, Eran stopped in front of the glass, stared at herself. Her body was as firm now as it had been then. "How do you control yourself so?"

"With considerable effort, Eran, if that soothes your ego any. You're as beautiful as the day that I met you."

"Why, then?"

"My conscience. I have to refuse to help you, because you're a rotten, evil—"

"Silence!" His mouth still moved, but he made no sound. When he realized that, he stopped moving his mouth, only stared at her—but not at her body. He stared at her eyes.

Eran had set a number of spellcastings on him at the same time when she'd made the shackles appear on his wrists and ankles. Like the steel encircling his limbs, the spells were to control him.

"Would pain interest you?" She smiled. He collapsed to the flagstones in the next eyeblink. His mouth opened again in a mute scream, his hands grasping his abdomen, then his head, then his chest. "I got your attention, didn't I?"

Eran walked toward him. He writhed in pain at her feet. That was normally a pleasant sensation for her, watching a male suffer so. Under the present circumstances, it was a waste of her time. "I can leave you like this, or worse! Kiss my foot and the pain will stop."

Her foot was very near to his face. He would only have to move his head ever so slightly to obey. He did not.

"I can make you!" He knew that. And still he made no attempt to accede to her demand.

She had tried blinding and deafening him, left him that way when she went off on a campaign with the Sword of Koth. Periodically, she crippled him with unbearable pain. She had caused him to be gnawed upon by terrifying creatures throughout an entire night. Always, she healed him. Always, he continued to defy her.

Eran willed his pain to cease, and his speech to be restored.

He rose to his knees, and for a brief moment she thought that he might be about to relent. When he spoke, he said, "I wish that you'd kill me, Eran."

"Never. Never that."

Eran made her clothes reappear to cover her body, made the door open. She walked out and she left him there on his knees.

He knelt not in obeisance to her will, but in total exhaustion.

He had defeated her and she had helped him.

"'Déjà vu' means that something one sees or experiences seems to be something from before, happening all over again. It's a term in French, a language of Earth. My world has many principal languages, unlike Creath. Seems to me that the only major languages here are yours and theirs." Garrison jerked a thumb across the stern rail and toward the horizon, where a Gle'Ur'Gya vessel, identical to the one destroyed in the cyclonic wave, had just appeared.

"With the wind at my command," Swan told him, "we can outdistance them easily, despite their superior craft. But I would still like to secure them as allies against my mother."

"You're an interesting girl," Garrison told Swan truthfully. "It was a Gle'Ur'Gya who killed your grandfather, yet you don't seem to hold that against the Gle'Ur'Gya now that you know."

"I wish to do what is best for the people of Creath, Al'An. That includes the Gle'Ur'Gya, whether they appreciate my intentions or not, whether they like it or not. As Erg'Ran told us, it was the Gle'Ur'Gya chieftain himself who killed the one of his own who murdered my grandfather. My grandfather's death is past."

"You'll make a fine ruler here," Garrison declared.

"That is not my intention, Al'An. I wish for the people of Creath to learn to rule themselves. The Company of Mir can teach those who survive, teach them how.

"Now, what do you think that we should do, Al'An? Should we outrun the Gle'Ur'Gya, or should we try to speak with them?"

Garrison looked away from Swan and over the stern rail, the comparatively huge Gle'Ur'Gya vessel gaining on them ever so slightly. Swan would only have to summon up a few more knots of windspeed and the Gle'Ur'Gya would be left further and further behind, never overtaking them.

"Could you get me over to their ship? And set me up with a language spell so that we'd all be able to understand one another?"

"I can make it so that their tongue is intelligible to you, and yours to them. Understanding is another question entirely, isn't it?" Swan smiled. "Do you want to appear on their deck? Poof?"

"Touché. That's French, too. Yeah, let's go for poof."

"But not alone, Al'An. Gar'Ath and Mitan can accompany you. They are both fine warriors and Mitan has considerable magic, in the event that things go badly."

Garrison nodded his agreement, but said, "I just don't want this looking like a raiding party. I want the chance to talk before they react."

"I can fix that, too. Join me in a little while?" Swan smiled at him over her shoulder. She was already walking toward the bow.

What Garrison judged as about ten minutes had passed, most probably time enough for whatever Swan was doing in order to facilitate the planned talks with the Gle'Ur'Gya. Gar'Ath, whom Garrison had briefed concerning their intentions, had nonetheless undertaken to raise the armada's condition of readiness to what amounted to battle stations, just in case.

"It should be time, Gar'Ath," Garrison informed him.

Gar'Ath nodded agreement, made a remark to Bin'Ah, then snatched up his shield and fell in beside Garrison. Together, they made their way forward, toward the bow pulpit.

Garrison felt slightly ridiculous, carrying the golden shield which Swan had made for him out of his badge and an axe slung at his waist. But if trouble did occur, it would not be wise to let the Gle'Ur'Gya see his pistols in action unless absolutely necessary. His "firespitters" would be better held back as the hightech secret weapon.

Garrison happened to be looking at Gar'Ath when the ordinarily brash young swordsman's jaw dropped and his eyes glazed. Garrison stared at Gar'Ath for another moment or so before looking at whatever Gar'Ath was staring at. When he saw Mitan, he understood Gar'Ath's reaction immediately. Mitan, usually leather clad and striking in her warrior mufti, looked more beautiful than ever in midnight blue satin and white lace. Evidently, Gar'Ath had never seen her dressed any other way but as a warrior. Garrison felt almost sorry for Gar'Ath; what resolve the fellow had been able to maintain against becoming involved with Mitan had visibly just crumbled.

Swan announced, "The Gle'Ur'Gya know enough about our culture to appreciate the fact that those comparatively few women who are warriors do not dress for battle as Mitan is dressed now. Her appearance will place them at ease, if only slightly."

Mitan's appearance might place the Gle'Ur'Gya at ease, but it quite obviously had the opposite effect on Gar'Ath; he walked right into Garrison's shield as if he were unconscious. Mitan looked more properly dressed for a party than a diplomatic mission. Her neckline fetchingly low, the white lace there and at the belled cuffs of her three-quarter-length sleeves contrasted with the healthy glowing tan of her skin. Her dark brown hair was piled atop her head in an infinity of ringlets, a circlet of white flowers peeking out from within them.

"How do I look, Gar'Ath?" Mitan turned a full three hundred sixty degrees, skirt rustling round her ankles, a hint of white lace petticoat beneath.

Garrison shot a glance at Gar'Ath, the swordsman's face reading like a book again.

Swan broke the spell. "Language will not be a problem. I'll second-sight their deck from the moment you reach the Gle'Ur'Gya ship until the moment of your return. Erg'Ran will assist me." Without saying anything, Swan came into Garrison's arms and kissed him full on the lips, then stepped away. "Are you ready?"

"So we'll just be here one eyeblink and there the next? Poof?"

"Poof, Al'An."

"Then, you've gotta let me say this one word before we go. Okay?"

"Is it magical?"

"No. You wouldn't understand because you don't have TV here, yet. Someday, maybe. I can't pass it up, saying it."

"All right. Say the word and then poof."

Garrison felt a grin spreading over his face. He stood very straight, blew a kiss to Swan and summoned all the drama that he could into his voice. "Energize!"

There were no tinkling sound effect noises. Garrison was on the deck of their little armada's flagship, then he was on the deck of the Gle'Ur'Gya vessel. There was no in-between.

A voice which rolled like thunder and had the texture usually associated with too much whiskey and too many cigarettes startled Garrison's mind into reality. "Kill them!"

A half-dozen human-shaped creatures, the least powerfully built of them the size of a pro football nose guard, charged across the deck, swords and axes flashing in the sunlight. Leathery skinned, they had short hair—brown, blond, black—covering all that was visible of their bodies. The flowing hair on their heads and full beards conjoined to form what resembled a lion's mane.

Mitan interposed herself between the Gle'Ur'Gya and her companions, calling out in the Gle'Ur'Gya's language, "We come in peace! I am female. Am I dressed as a warrior?" The Gle'Ur'Gya were either stunned by Mitan's beauty or her talent for stating what had to be obvious even to them. Either way, Garrison realized, she'd halted the Gle'Ur'Gya's lethal headlong lunge for at least a second.

"We come in peace!" Garrison reiterated. The growing number of Gle'Ur'Gya surrounding them on the main deck narrowed their eyes, studying the three intruders, massive jaws set, their rippling muscles coiled springs. None of the Gle'Ur'Gya spoke. Garrison was tempted to say, "I am sent by the Great White Father in Washington! Harm us and the long knife soldier coats will come with many firesticks!" Garrison passed on that, recalling what happened to George Armstrong Custer. He told them instead, "The Virgin Enchantress, who fights against the Queen Sorceress for the freedom of all the peoples of Creath, has sent us to speak with your leader." So far, so good, Garrison thought. He said nothing else, waiting instead for one of the Gle'Ur'Gya to say something—anything—that wasn't an order to kill. Still, no Gle'Ur'Gya spoke.

Mitan, hands outstretched toward the six crewmen, the wind doing lovely things with her brown ringlets, implored the gathering Gle'Ur'Gya crew, "We were sent here to speak with all of you. Please! There is no time for us to fight. Your ship is superior to ours. Our magic is superior to yours. If we fight, there will be fewer who will be able to fight against the Queen Sorceress. That is all that a battle will accomplish. If we join together, though, we will all be stronger. Please! Who is in command here?"

"I am in command, fair lady!" It was the same voice which, moments earlier, had ordered them to be killed.

Garrison wheeled around. His nautical terminology was failing him again. He couldn't remember what to call the higher after deck where the wheel was located. It looked just like the deck from which Errol Flynn always made heroic speeches about fighting for England in all the old swashbuckler movies. The Gle'Ur'Gya who'd spoken might have been a pirate, and was quite imposing, but there the resemblance ended.

The commander seemed taller than the others, looming over them from the higher deck as he did, but that might have been optical illusion. Regardless of height, like the others he wore a garment similar to a Scottish great kilt, only it was faded black, girded around his waist and draped diagonally across his chest over a brown leather breastplate. His body was festooned with weapons: a sword was suspended from a baldric to his left hip, a long dagger in his belt, two additional and presumably shorter daggers carried one in each boot top.

"I am Alan Garrison, Special Agent with the Federal Bureau of Investigation, United States Justice Department. I work out of the Atlanta Field Office and have come from this place very far away to help the Virgin Enchantress fight the evil of the Queen Sorceress and secure freedom for the people of Creath." Garrison took a breath. "The lady to whom you just spoke is Mitan. She is K'Ur'Mir and has considerable magic. The third member of our party is Gar'Ath, a warrior of great renown. The Virgin Enchantress herself caused us to appear on your deck through the great power of her magic so that we might offer you a proposal."

"I am Bre'Gaa. There is no love lost between your Enchantress's people and the Gle'Ur'Gya. Leave now as you came, or die."

Garrison couldn't fault the Gle'Ur'Gya commander for a lack of directness. Under the circumstances, Garrison figured that he had nothing to lose by what he was about to say. "Then it doesn't matter to you that a ship of this size and its entire crew were killed in these waters only days ago by the magic of the Queen Sorceress?" There were a few unintelligible grunts from the crew. "I witnessed one of the Gle'Ur'Gya making the bravest gesture of defiance I have ever seen. A cyclonic wave, like you'd have when the two moons crossed paths, but made by Eran and sent to destroy us, intercepted one of your ships. When the ship was clearly lost, all of the crew dove into the water. They were just as doomed as if they'd stayed aboard. We couldn't turn back and try to rescue them without being destroyed ourselves. I think they knew that. But one of the ship's company stayed aboard. He drew his sword. He manipulated his sword with a grace unlike anything I've ever seen. He stood on the deck, like you're standing now, and met the cyclonic wave with his sword ready. Such bravery doesn't incite you to want to destroy the evil woman who caused his death? I'd heard that the Gle'Ur'Gya were great warriors. Perhaps those who told me this were mistaken."

Bre'Gaa's face was anything but inscrutable, the anger there unmistakable. Directed against whom, Garrison wondered?

From behind him, he heard one of the crewman mutter the name "Ag'Riig" and then another and another repeated the name. Garrison knew it, the name of the Gle'Ur'Gya chieftain who had fought Swan's grandfather, then killed his own crewman for interfering in the duel and murdering his opponent.

"Was Ag'Riig the swordsman who stood defiantly against Eran's magic?" Garrison shouted up to Bre'Gaa.

"Yes," Bre'Gaa answered. "My mother's oldest brother, the war chieftain of our clan. Ag'Riig taught me the use of the sword, gave me my first ship."

Gar'Ath spoke then. "If my uncle were killed fighting an enemy, that enemy would become my enemy, Bre'Gaa."

"I am not dressed as a warrior, as I told you. But even though I am a woman, I am a warrior. I wore these skirts to come here only so that you would know I came not to fight." Mitan announced. "And I echo the words of Gar'Ath, Bre'Gaa."

"Let's give the guy a little space here," Garrison told Mitan and Gar'Ath, then returned his gaze to Bre'Gaa.

The Gle'Ur'Gya captain's hands—huge—grasped the rail before him so tightly that Garrison thought it would snap into splinters. Bre'Gaa's voice so low that it was barely audible, he spoke. "The Queen Sorceress has never bothered the Gle'Ur'Gya, but only because she has no ships which can attack us and she uses her magic elsewhere. If she conquers the last resistance against her from among the Landers, she will find the time and find the means to bedevil us, dispatch her Sword of Koth to make war against us. But it is not my place to commit the Gle'Ur'Gya to warfare against the Queen Sorceress. That is for our Queen and her council to decide.

"I, as an individual, will fight." Bre'Gaa drew his sword and raised it over his head. "Who among you stands with me?"

From behind them, Garrison heard the Gle'Ur'Gya crew shouting and cheering. He heard the rattle of their steel. All that was missing was a trumpet fanfare.

Garrison turned around to look at the crew. He caught sight of Gar'Ath, instead, sweeping Mitan into his arms for what started out to be an enthusiastic hug, one comrade to another. The hug turned into their bodies molding against one another and Gar'Ath crushing Mitan's mouth beneath his, his hands hungrily grasping her body.

Gar'Ath had evidently overcome his shyness. Either that, or Mitan's courage and beauty had overcome it for him.

Mitan curtsied, and without rising said, "Virgin Enchantress, Daughter Royal, Princess of Creath, may I present to you the Chieftain Bre'Gaa, Captain Commander of the Gle'Ur'Gya vessel *Storm Raider*."

"I am honored, Enchantress," Bre'Gaa murmured, momentarily bowing his head. His left fist was clenched to the hilt of his sheathed sword; his right arm swept upward, its fist coming to rest over his heart.

Swan held her skirts and made a low courtsey to the Gle'Ur'Gya commander. "It is I who am honored, Captain," she declared, then raised her eyes to his. Like most Gle'Ur'Gya, his eyes were blue, but Swan found Bre'Gaa's particularly piercing and quite beautiful. They were, she thought, also a little nervous. With two of his lieutenants, she had magically transferred him from the deck of his vastly larger vessel to the deck of her tiny flagship.

Swan offered her hand. Bre'Gaa took it gently in his, lowered his eyes. "I suppose you know, lady, that I speak only for myself and my crew, and not the Gle'Ur'Gya as a people. That understood between us, I pledge my life and my sword to your service against the Queen Sorceress that I may take my revenge for the death of my uncle, Ag'Riig."

"I accept your pledge and am well-pleased by your wisdom and your courage, Captain."

Bre'Gaa relinquished her hand. Swan smiled. "May I present my uncle, Erg'Ran. He is brother to the Queen Sorceress and he is my most trusted advisor and oldest friend." She nodded her head toward Erg'Ran. "He witnessed the great duel between your uncle and my grandfather."

"You took many lives of the Gle'Ur'Gya, Erg'Ran. You were an enemy then, but your courage is still spoken of among the Gle'Ur'Gya." Bre'Gaa saluted Erg'Ran, fist again touching his chest over his heart.

Erg'Ran responded, "Although I was outraged at the death of my father, I was impressed with the great honor of Ag'Riig and how he so decisively dealt with my father's murderer. I shall forever be both impressed and grateful. I revere your uncle's memory and will be honored to fight beside you, Captain Bre'Gaa."

"Al'An you have met, Captain," Swan told Bre'Gaa. "He is my Champion. He is, indeed, come from the other realm where he is a great warrior. He has proven himself in battle here, as well, fighting heroically against my mother's magic."

"Al'An. Yes," Bre'Gaa said, bowing curtly to Al'An as he came to stand beside her. "What is the meaning of the strange runes which adorn your burnished shield, Al'An?"

Al'An responded, "As I have told you, in my own world I am an FBI agent. That is what these runes signify, Bre'Gaa."

"It is a fine shield. I have seen no finer."

Al'An nodded. Swan couldn't have been prouder of what he said next. "May my shield gather but one-tenth the honor in battle that I know your sword will win for us against the Queen Sorceress."

Bre'Gaa cocked one of his black bushy eyebrows and very deliberately nodded his great head.

❖         ❖         ❖

With the strong, steady wind Swan magically drew into their sails, the five little ships of her original armada, dwarfed beside the sixth vessel, continued on through the night across Woroc'Il'Lod. The Gle'Ur'Gya were gifted as seamen and could read the stars to guide their navigation. By late in the following day, Bre'Gaa had told them, they would reach the shore of Edge Land. The march on Barad'Il'Koth could then begin.

Swan—wisely Garrison thought—had determined that if the captain and crew of the *Storm Raider* were to be their allies they should be trusted fully. With that as the operating principle, Swan had asked Bre'Gaa if she could once again magically transport him to the flagship for a conference. That he came alone, that he drank wine with them, was equally demonstrative of his trust in the alliance.

Garrison and Swan, Erg'Ran with them, sat in the usual place, the blue white globes of light like captured stars illuminating the bow pulpit. In addition to Bre'Gaa, Mitan and Gar'Ath, all but inseparable since their kiss earlier that day, had been invited to join them.

Erg'Ran was saying, "I have the strongest reasons to believe the Enchantress's father still lives within the walls of Barad'Il'Koth. If I am correct in other matters, he will possess certain knowledge which will aid us in defeating the Queen Sorceress, my sister. And he may be able to provide direct aid to us, as only he can."

"What kind of help can he give us, Erg'Ran?" Garrison inquired.

"I cannot say until I am certain. It is my hope that before we even consider a direct assault against Barad'Il'Koth, a small group of us should get inside and find the Enchantress's father. If I am right, he has the power to confound Eran's greatest magical strength, if indeed he will cooperate."

"So, a commando raid on the castle," Garrison said,

thinking aloud. "How do we get past the armies she'll have surrounding the place, the guards within the castle itself, the magic of her witches, Eran's own magic? And assuming we do, how do we get out again? I wouldn't think that we could use magic to transport ourselves inside. Eran's gotta have some defenses against that, right?"

"Indeed, Champion," Erg'Ran responded. "We cannot use magic alone to enter and leave, but the Enchantress may be able to use magic along with a deception of some sort."

"I've been thinking a great deal about just what you propose, Erg'Ran," Swan announced. "I also feel that it is vital to our interests that I should find my father. And, of course, to fulfill the prophecy, I must. I hope that he still lives for many reasons."

Erg'Ran said nothing for a moment, merely stared at Garrison. Garrison asked, "What's wrong?"

"The time has come that I must reveal certain things to you, Champion."

"What certain things?"

"First of all," Erg'Ran began quite deliberately, "about your firespitters. They—"

"What are firespitters?" Bre'Gaa interrupted.

Garrison told him as best he could, "They are weapons which I possess. Like a bow, they fire a projectile, but not an arrow." Garrison drew one of the SIG pistols from beneath his jacket, removed the magazine, then cycled the action to empty the chamber. He closed the slide rather than leaving it open, lest Bre'Gaa inadvertently activated the slide release and catch his beard or something. Then he handed the .45 to the Gle'Ur'Gya Captain Commander. "They fire very small pieces of a lead alloy—a type of soft metal—but at very high speeds. One or two of these small projectiles will drop an average man in his tracks. Even a person your size would be seriously injured or killed by anywhere from one to just a few

of these." Garrison handed over the loose round he'd
taken from the chamber. "The front part there is the
bullet. That's the projectile."

"This is a marvelous thing, Al'An! May I try it?"

"It's quite noisy, so we'd best wait until tomorrow."

"Agreed." Bre'Gaa handed back the pistol, fingering
the cartridge in his enormous hand a moment longer,
then returning it as well.

"Firespitters are not unknown to Eran," Erg'Ran
said solemnly. "She may well have a spell which will
render them inoperable just when you might need
them most. You must not allow yourself to rely on
them as your sole means of defense, for yourself alone
or in your role as Champion to the Enchantress."

"Let's get in a little swordplay on deck tomorrow,
Champion. It might serve you well," Gar'Ath suggested.

"Fine."

"And, another thing that concerns you, Champion,"
Erg'Ran began again.

"Yeah?"

"You must firmly resolve that, should something
go wrong—"

"Gosh! How could anything go wrong?" Garrison
interrupted. He could hardly wait for more good
news. First, his pistols might suddenly become inoperable because of a spell of evil magic. What now,
he wondered?

"In the event of your imminent, unavoidable capture by Eran's forces or—the courage of Mir be with
you—by Eran herself, you must die fighting or, failing
that, take your own life. If you, because of your origin,
should fall victim to her power, all would be lost.
There would be no hope."

"Because I'm the Champion?"

"That is only a part of it. I can say little more until
we have entered Barad'Il'Koth and know what we
must know, Champion."

"That's just great! My guns might stop working at

the drop of a hat and I'm supposed to do the dutch act."

"Dutch act?" Swan repeated, apparently unable to make the connection between the languages, despite the spell she'd cast.

"It's kind of old slang for suicide—taking your own life." Garrison looked away from Swan and straight at Erg'Ran. "I wasn't raised to do that kind of thing, Erg'Ran, so if there's some compelling reason that I've got to, you'd better lay it on me and quick."

"I can promise you this, Champion. Barring the unforeseen, you will know all that you need to know before you might be required to slay yourself."

"This is supposed to be encouraging?"

Mitan spoke. "I agree with the Champion, Erg'Ran. Telling a warrior to take his own life while still the chance exists to resist torture—"

"Torture? How'd we get to torture all of a sudden?"

Mitan went on unfazed. "Telling the Champion that he must slay himself while still there exists the chance to fight again is a very strange thing indeed, Erg'Ran. He deserves a reason!"

Erg'Ran merely responded, "I would say more if I could, Mitan. I cannot. When I know, the Champion will also know."

The rationale behind Swan's saying, "I would like to discuss a possible plan," was obvious. She was attempting to defuse what might grow into an argument. Garrison let her do it. Erg'Ran's judgment was something which Garrison had come to respect; now wasn't the time to doubt it. "With the assistance of our new allies," Swan went on, "I think that we have an even better chance at success. I'm assuming that my mother's magical energy is not yet fully restored, and I hope that it will remain at less than full capacity until we have at least been able to reach Edge Land.

"By that time," Swan continued, "the Queen Sorceress should be wholly capable of attempting to

foil our best efforts against her. She'll quite possibly
have troops awaiting us when we reach the coast.
Even if my magic were somehow as strong as my
mother's, it would be impossible for me to combat
a wide range of enemy activity all at once.

"Thinking about that," Swan said, smiling, "is what
made me realize what our only chance might be to
get us into Barad'Il'Koth. My mother will have vastly
more troops standing ready to fight us than she would
ordinarily require to easily defeat a force of our size,
even augmented as it is by our new allies." She
nodded to Bre'Gaa. "She is counting on my magic,
which I suppose is oddly complimentary, all things
considered. If we can create a sufficient number of
diversions to preoccupy her, cause her to use her
magic, we have our greatest chance."

"You lost me a little," Garrison admitted.

Swan took his hand in both of hers. "You see,
Al'An, aside from maintaining spells and the like, it
is impossible to undertake more than one major
magical activity at a time. Remember that magic is
a natural phenomenon, whether used merely to accelerate a natural process or for something wholly
unnatural. Think of it like walking, Al'An. One cannot walk and run simultaneously. One must do one
or the other or something totally different entirely,
but one cannot do both at once because true walking and true running are mutually exclusive, one
precluding the other. Magic is not like thinking about
two things at once; it is like doing two things at once,
two things requiring almost total commitment."

"So, if we can keep her magic focused on some-
thing other than what we're doing, we're home free?
That is, except for the Horde of Koth, the Sword of
Koth, the Handmaidens of Koth and anybody else of
Koth hanging around."

Swan laughed.

Getting Swan to laugh had been Garrison's intent,

since there might be more than ample opportunity
for little else but tears later on . . .

Alan Garrison stood in the bow pulpit. The
morning was fresh and cold. Temperatures on
Woroc'Il'Lod the previous day had been deceptively
mild, but normalized overnight to a point where
Alan Garrison could better understand why this body
of water was so commonly referred to as the icy sea.
In the distance, what he'd at first thought might be
the sails of more Gle'Ur'Gya vessels on the horizon became recognizable as icebergs.

Garrison felt good, fit. After a simultaneously satisfying yet frustrating night—Swan had slept in his
arms, but he'd respected her insistence that she
remain a virgin—he'd awakened to an early morning practice session with Gar'Ath.

Garrison was pleasantly surprised that his limited
skills at swordsmanship had somehow improved. Or
perhaps what Gar'Ath had taught him in their sessions
at the summer palace had finally sunk in. He was not,
nor never would be in the foreseeable future, remotely
challenging to Gar'Ath, but Garrison felt confident
enough with a blade that he could fight an average
swordsman without being instantly killed or disarmed.
Considering the ability level at which he'd first taken
up the sword, he was vastly improved. At the conclusion of their session, he had asked Gar'Ath, "Is there
a sword to be had that I could carry when we go
against the Horde?" If a spell might be placed on his
firespitters, rendering them inoperable or ineffective,
a sword might come in handy.

Gar'Ath had smiled; and, in answer to his request,
Gar'Ath said, "You understand the basic techniques,
if not their finer points. At this juncture, the best
way—and the most potentially dangerous way—to
learn the sword can be when your life is in the
balance. If you keep your wits about you. Remember,

Champion, that the overwhelming majority of persons against whom you might bring a sword to bear will be no better than you, albeit to a degree experienced in actual life-and-death combat. There is a small number of fine swordsmen, and a smaller number still of great ones. Against the rest, you could make a good account of yourself if you keep your wits about you. You'll have a sword, Champion, a sword upon which you can wager your life if needs be."

They'd agreed to meet later on, which was rather silly, Garrison reflected. On a vessel the size of the armada's flagship, it would have been impossible not to meet later on, and frequently.

The wind was carrying their armada toward another armada, an armada of icebergs, the floating mountains of white in greater numbers than Garrison would have suspected usual or natural.

Mitan passed near the bow pulpit, wearing her alluringly skimpy warrior's garb and a heavy cape, the cape wide open, as if the cold didn't bother her. "Mitan?"

"Yes, Champion?"

"Do you know enough about these waters to even hazard a guess as to whether or not icebergs in such numbers are normal?"

She came to stand beside him at the rail. When Garrison glanced at Mitan, he could tell immediately that she was using the second sight; he'd come to recognize the look on the faces of those who had it. "I have no grounding in data concerning this, Champion, but the icebergs do seem oddly abundant, don't they?"

"Swan's mom, you think?"

It took Mitan a second, but when she looked back at him there was recognition in her eyes. "I will find out. Wait for me here, Champion." And she was off, sprinting across the deck.

"Killer icebergs. Wonderful," Garrison mused aloud.

By nightfall, if nothing popped up to slow them down, they would easily have made landfall. Of what would transpire after that Garrison was most uncertain. If Swan had a definite plan spelling out just what she intended as a diversion, she had not yet shared it with him. As far as he could understand magical theory, however, the broad outline of Swan's plan seemed sound.

Assuming that her mother's magical powers could be temporarily written out of the scenario, there were still military units and ordinary guards to contend with in order to penetrate the keep at Barad'Il'Koth. If his firespitters—"Guns," Garrison said aloud, chiding himself—could be relied upon, in and of themselves they would make tremendous equalizers. Their terror value alone against persons with what amounted to a late medieval European level of technology (at Garrison's most generous estimate) would be almost incalculable. He found himself wishing that somehow he'd been able to bring a Heckler & Koch MP-5 submachine gun along with him to Creath. With one of those and a half-dozen spare magazines, he could have taken on the entire Sword of Koth single-handedly.

There was another problem as well.

He was not some sort of commando, only a cop. The FBI academy didn't teach sentry removal techniques or any of the other requisite skills to penetrate an enemy stronghold. For that, Hostage Rescue or, if they were good enough, the local police SWAT Team got the call.

On Creath, there was no using a cell phone to call for backup.

Mitan rejoined him at the rail, and before either of them could speak, Gar'Ath was beside them as well. "I have that sword, Champion.

"And I have asked Swan to transport herself or Erg'Ran to the Gle'Ur'Gya vessel and ask Bre'Gaa if he will consent to being transported to our ship in order that he may confer with us concerning the icebergs and whether or not such a great number of icebergs could be natural."

"Here is the sword which I promised to you, Champion." From beneath his cloak, Gar'Ath produced a still-sheathed blade, then drew the blade from its scabbard. That the sword was clearly magnificent was readily apparent. "May you use it with skill and honor, Champion. It belonged to the finest swordsman I have ever met—next to my father, of course. My father was the man who made it. The previous owner was K'Ur'Mir, and he died fighting with this blade in his hands. When I came upon him as he lay dying, he asked that I find a worthy hand to wield it. Seven Sword of Koth—"

"I thought it was six," Mitan interrupted impishly.

"Six or seven. But, however many, they were Sword of Koth who fought him and he held against them, one man fighting harder and stronger than seven— or six. Neither heart nor swordarm nor steel failed him. The Queen Sorceress herself took his life, spellcasting that he saw his friends and family surrounding him rather than his enemies. In the eyeblink that he hesitated, the Sword of Koth stormed him as one. Even then, he took four of the seven—or six— with him unto death."

Garrison took the sword in his hands, looked at Gar'Ath, saying, "I'll care for it and, when this is over, return—"

"No, Champion. It is your sword to do with as you will, and not to be returned. I've found the hand worthy to wield it. You are no equal to his skill, but you have the same strength of heart."

"I don't know what to say, my friend."

"In those words, Champion, you have said enough." If the sword with which Garrison had practiced could be compared to a clunker off a used car lot, this was a Ferrari, yet much of its elegance was found in its simplicity. Its pommel was a solid wheel, brass like all the fittings and the lobed, drooping double quillons which formed the guard. Between pommel and guard the hilt itself felt as though it were made to fill his hand and no other. It was of wood, he supposed, seamlessly wrapped in black leather. Fullers, for lightening the blade on both sides, ran full length from the short, full thickness, brass-augmented ricasso toward the subtle spear point where the double edges met.

Gar'Ath's gift was reminiscent of an early sword used by the Scots, the antecedent of the classic two-hand claymores. Like the pre-claymore Scottish sword, because of its wheel pommel, it was more a hand-and-a-half sword, allowing two-handed use when required, yet—as far as Garrison's limited experience allowed him to judge—just as perfectly designed for single hand use.

As if he were reading Garrison's mind, Gar'Ath supplied the answer to an unasked question. "The tang of the blade runs full length into the wheel pommel, Champion, and is full width as far as it can go and full thickness throughout. My father built swords to survive combat; that's the only way the swordsman will survive, Champion." And Gar'Ath laughed.

"It's beautiful, Gar'Ath," Mitan declared, her voice low. "It's truly beautiful. You have a fine sword there, Champion."

Garrison only nodded. When he looked up from the blade, and over the rail and across the water, he couldn't help but notice the icebergs again. There seemed to be more of them now than there had been.

Swan's voice interrupted his worrisome thoughts. "Bre'Gaa graciously consented to join us."

Garrison looked around. The Gle'Ur'Gya Captain

Commander, much of his head obscured by the hood of his cloak, said nothing as he left Swan's side and went to the rail. He remained silent for several seconds, breaking his silence only to say, "That is a magnificent sword, Al'An."

"It was a gift from Gar'Ath."

"I watched your practice from my deck earlier this day. Such a sword will help with your confidence, thereby aiding you in rapid development of your skills."

"Thank you."

Bre'Gaa dismissed Garrison's thanks with a wave of his hand and what might have been a nod, then fell silent again, staring out to sea.

Bre'Gaa stared, and stared some more. At last, Gar'Ath demanded, "What do you see, man?!"

"Mitan or I can second-sight for you, if you like, Captain," Swan volunteered.

"That is unnecessary, Enchantress. My mind is already made up, was nearly so well before you invited me to your vessel. According to the legends of the Gle'Ur'Gya, generation upon generation ago, so long ago that the common seed of our peoples was still apparent among your race and my own, the great winter came upon Creath. Many creatures ceased to exist, unable to withstand the cold. The dragons which had once been so numerous all but disappeared as well. But a small number of them, which had been asleep as was their wont during the winter season, were trapped in their caves by the rapidly encroaching ice."

"We have this same legend," Swan told Bre'Gaa.

"When your mother brought the ice dragons from their great sleep, she did so with a spell which allowed the dragons to exit their icy lairs in order to perform her bidding, then return to their caves, to be frozen within again while they slept, remaining there until she should require their ferocity to serve her evil ends

once more or merely wish to see them wreak havoc
for her own amusement.

"If that story is true in all parts," Bre'Gaa continued, "then those great masses of ice can signal only
one thing."

"She has awakened the ice dragons from their
caves," Swan murmured.

"Yes. Once they are fully awake, they will hunger
and they will come for us. We must prepare with all
speed."

"I thought your mother's magic was probably pretty
much depleted," Garrison volunteered to Swan.

"Remember, Al'An? Magic which merely acceler-
ates that which is natural requires little magical energy
at all. The ice dragons are real, not a magical creation. Ice cracks and melts and falls away. Sleeping
beasts awaken. These are all natural occurrences,
Al'An, in our realm or in yours I should think. She
won't even need to send them against us, because it
is their natural instinct to hunt and devour flesh,
wherever they may find it. In ancient times, they
hunted over the Land. Upon awakening, they will go
there in search of prey. They will spy our ships along
the way and they will attack. That is the natural order
of things, Al'An."

Garrison asked a question which he considered at
once logical and extremely pertinent. "How many ice
dragons are we talking about, guys?"

Almost dismissively, Bre'Gaa responded, "It is
doubtful that more than a hundred or so of their kind
still exist in all of Creath."

"Would that mean we'll be facing a pack of a
hundred or so, Captain?"

Bre'Gaa shrugged his shoulders. "Hard to say,
Al'An. Have you fought a dragon before?"

"You have?"

Bre'Gaa nodded gravely. "Yes, on three occasions.
Loss of life was heavy. I have fought them, yes. And

it appears that I shall do so anon. I take it that you have not."

"We don't have dragons where I come from, so they didn't hit on it at the FBI academy."

"If you someday return to your realm, you might suggest that knowledge of dragon fighting can prove worthwhile."

"What sort of knowledge?" Gar'Ath asked. "An ice dragon destroyed the place where I was born, but I have never fought one, either."

"There is a saying among the Gle'Ur'Gya, young swordsman, that an amateur at ice dragon fighting can be the ice dragon's greatest weapon."

Garrison had always been fond of aphorisms and made a mental note to write that one down in case he needed it sometime. "What sort of special information might be useful to us if we're to have any hope of becoming more professionally competent at dragon slaying?"

"They are not mere brutes," Bre'Gaa explained. "Ice dragons have considerable cunning, even what might be called a degree of intelligence and sophistication. They are wholly capable of fighting independently of one another, or fighting as a group toward a common goal. You'll all find it most illuminating, an experience never to be forgotten, if survived."

Garrison had been hoping Bre'Gaa would tell them about some special spot on the dragons' bodies where they were inordinately vulnerable. That Bre'Gaa evidently didn't know of such a spot was most disquieting.

The typical ice dragon, Garrison learned, was the equivalent in Earth measurement of twenty-five to thirty feet in length, with a wingspan—when fully extended for soaring—of fifty feet or better. Like the terrestrial dragons of myth, they spewed fire (no one explained how that was possible) and their bodies were covered in razor-edged scales, the scales like pieces of interlocking plate armor. Even their genitalia was armored (nor did anyone explain how that allowed the conception of little ice dragons). The males had a great horn at the center of their foreheads. Color ranged from a sickly grey to jade green. Their sound or call, from what Garrison was able to put together from Bre'Gaa's descriptions of dragon combat and Gar'Ath's recollection of tales told to him during childhood, had no parallel with anything of Earth.

Erg'Ran, while most others aboard the flagship honed their blades or saw to their bows, sat on the steps of the bow pulpit and painstakingly studied an old scroll, the intensity with which he poured over it prompting Garrison's curiosity, "What is that?"

"It is a scroll, Champion."

"I know that, Erg'Ran! I mean, what is the subject? What are you reading about?"

"I predicted violent confrontation, with ice dragons particularly, as you may recall. In preparation for that," Erg'Ran went on, "I brought along certain scrolls and books of notes I have taken over the years in anticipation of the day that my niece, the Enchantress, would engage in battle against the forces of my sister, Eran. That is why I study this scroll, Champion. My axe is sharp enough. It is my mind which I must keen if we are to survive this encounter and go on."

"So, I should get lost and let you continue your reading?"

"As you say, Champion."

Garrison quit the bow pulpit and busied himself helping whomever he could about the deck. The armada still made good time toward Edge Land, and the icebergs, although closer, were still sufficiently distant that he really didn't worry about an imminent collision with one of them. However, this would not have been the time to sit on deck and casually regale his companions with graphic tales of the *Titanic* disaster.

Garrison saw Swan very little. She, too, was studying, not a scroll but one of her recopied spellbooks. She seemed thoroughly preoccupied and to have time for little else. Feeling somewhat like a child at a grown-up party, Garrison continued to busy himself helping wherever he could. But his thoughts were elsewhere, on the encounter which he considered inevitable.

Would the ice dragons be visible at a great distance? Would their cries boom like thunder?

Would his pistols work at all against the beasts?

Mitan sounded the alarm. "Ice dragons off the starboard bow!" All of Garrison's misgivings were about to be addressed.

Swan put away the spellbook and stood. Her body shook, the cold radiating from the water and the air only the smallest contributor to the chill which seized her body. She used the second sight in order to view the ice dragons in better detail.

They moved in a wedge formation, twelve of them. The apex was a male larger by far than any of the others, its great horn more than the length of the dagger strapped to her leg, half the length at least of a sword blade.

Swan had never been a good hand with longbow or crossbow. She pushed back the hood of her greatcape and drew her sword. Swan was uncertain if she knew the right magic to aid in defeating the ice dragons, and steel might be her only weapon against them if she did not.

Swan moved toward the bow pulpit, Erg'Ran already there, axe in hand. "What do you think, Erg'Ran?"

"I take it, Enchantress, that you are as uncertain as I concerning the use of magic against these winged beasts?"

"Yes, uncle. More uncertain than I would like. Our people have had so few encounters with them, and all of the spells are from so long ago. There's no way I can tell if they even worked."

"I considered that, Enchantress," Erg'Ran told her. "We could endeavor to use natural forces against them. What about lightning?"

"If it can be done. In order to summon lightning, I must summon a storm. I worry, out here, that we might then find ourselves forced to contend with high seas, wind gusts and heavy rains as well as ice dragons. And that will require a great deal of magical energy. If I deplete my energy too severely before we reach Edge Land, we may have even worse difficulties."

Erg'Ran nodded gravely. "Perhaps Mitan, if you taught her the summoning, could—"

"I don't believe that she currently has the capability," Swan told him. "Mitan has always had the potential, but she's expended little effort in the development of her magic, choosing the warrior way instead. And many's the time all of us have found ourselves grateful for her skills with blade and bow."

"Indeed. So, we must wait and see how well we fare against the beasts and then you will make the decision."

Swan nodded, looked past her uncle and out to sea. No second sight was needed now to see the ice dragons in all of their grisly detail.

Alan Garrison crouched by the starboard rail, beside an oarsman named Lii'Ku, a wiry fellow and shorter than the average woman, yet with muscles any bodybuilder would have envied. Like the other men in the wells, he rowed furiously, despite the wind.

Garrison warned him, "My firespitters are loud. Be ready for a very loud noise and ringing in the ears. When I use my firespitters, small pieces of brass are ejected after each shot. They can feel very hot against your skin. Just want you to know."

"I will be alert to this, Champion."

"Good." Garrison tightened position, on his right knee, his left elbow resting on his left knee. Because his "firespitters" were only handguns, and he wasn't an Olympic-quality marksman, and his targets would be moving, as was his firing platform—the flagship—Garrison had decided to abide by the old rejoinder, "Don't shoot until you can see the whites of their eyes." And, too, the eyes of the ice dragons would be his targets.

A dozen of the giant winged dragons were coming in at eleven o'clock, holding formation as if they were aircraft coming in for saturation bombing runs and their pilots had no fear of antiaircraft fire.

Indeed, what passed for antiaircraft fire was ready all around him. Gar'Ath had command of the fighters, and Garrison heard Gar'Ath's voice, calmly reassuring, saying, "All right, lads! When I give the command, we fire. If any one of us finds a vulnerable spot, all of us will concentrate on that spot on each of the other ice dragons." Because there were no ship-to-ship communications, all the vessels in the Armada, including that of the Gle'Ur'Gya, would await the flagship's opening salvo before commencing their own.

"Do they really breathe fire, you think, Champion?" Lii'Ku panted as he rowed.

"Beats me, pal. That's what everyone tells me."

"If one of 'em starts breathin' our way, can I hide behind that beautiful Golden Shield of yours?"

Garrison grinned, but didn't take his eyes off his target, the biggest of the ice dragons, a male with an enormous horn. "You can hide behind my shield only if you don't mind me hiding there with you."

Almost to himself, Garrison found himself humming. "What's that tune, Champion?" Lii'Ku got out between breaths.

"Richard Wagner's 'Flight of The Valkyries.' Great composer, shitty outlook on life. Terrific music, though."

"It seems to me . . . that a dirge . . . might . . . might be better suited . . . Champion."

"You might be right." The big, horned male was a good seventy-five yards out and closing fast. The hum of ice dragon wings beating the frosty air was growing to a roar. Garrison decided to ignore his own self-imposed range limits. "Gar'Ath!" Garrison shouted.

"Yes, Champion?"

"Permission to open fire with my firespitters."

"Aye, Champion! Whenever you feel that you should."

"Thank you!" Garrison sucked in a deep breath, let part of it out and locked the rest in his throat. He thumb-cocked the hammer of his pistol. Garrison held over high, settling his front sight just left of the horn's root and where, if ice dragons had eyebrows, its right eyebrow would have been. He took up the slack in the trigger, then squeezed.

"G'urg! That's loud!" Lii'Ku shouted.

A lot of people made a big deal out of .45 ACP recoil. Garrison thought they were silly. He knew slightly built women and comparatively young children who could fire a .45 without complaint. Garrison held, the pistol's muzzle barely rising. In the next instant, he knew the cry, the call, the ghastly sound of the ice dragons. He heard it.

His shot had no visible effect, but that it had caused pain or startlement was unquestionable.

A cheer went up from the people on deck. Gar'Ath shouted over it, "Open fire, lads!"

Garrison commenced firing in earnest, emptying the remaining seven rounds from the pistol toward the lead dragon's right eye. There were more hideous screams from the beast, but it kept coming.

A wave of arrows and crossbow bolts filled the air between the flagship and the ice dragons, more

projectiles launched from each of the other ships. As
Garrison changed magazines in the pistol, he glanced
toward the Gle'Ur'Gya vessel. If any conventional
weapons of Creath had a chance of inflicting serious
damage on the ice dragons, it would be the huge
deck-mounted crossbows of the Gle'Ur'Gya, their
harpoon-sized bolts already whistling through the air
toward the dragons.

Garrison made to fire again, but as he settled his
sights, he heard Swan shouting, "The fire breath is
coming!"

Garrison saw a tiny wisp of smoke coming from
between what would have been lips if the lead male
ice dragon had lips. "Holy shit! Lii'Ku! The shield!"
Garrison wrenched the Golden Shield of IBF up from
the deck beside him, interposing it between himself
and the ice dragons. Lii'Ku dove behind it, too.

Garrison had ventured into a burning building
once, many years before, having heard crying from
inside. He had nearly been burned himself when he
failed to feel a door for excessive heat, opened it and
a tongue of flame leaped toward him. The tongue of
flame from the ice dragon sounded the same. As it
had been years before, he escaped the fire, only
feeling the searing heat as it washed around and over
him, nearly suffocating him.

He'd survived the burning building, helping a
policeman to rescue what turned out to be a housecat
instead of a baby.

Despite the deck behind him being on fire, Garrison survived the first fiery blast from the ice dragons.

Lii'Ku whipped off his cloak, attacking the flames.

The nearest ice dragon—not the one Garrison had
fired at—was under twenty-five yards away, swoop-
ing over the water, wings fully outstretched. It would
loose its fiery breath in seconds, Garrison knew.

Garrison pushed his shield away, crouched and took

aim with his pistol. The underside of the wing, what would have been the wing stem had the dragon been an aircraft—it didn't look to be armored with scales. Garrison fired two shots, then two more. Garrison threw himself left, the ice dragon's wing spewing blood or bile under such pressure that Garrison knew he must have struck the equivalent of a main artery.

Peering out from behind his shield again, Garrison watched as the ice dragon tried desperately to beat the air with the one undamaged wing, skipping over the white caps like a stone flicked across the water by some gigantic child.

There was a shriek, horrible beyond anything Garrison had ever heard, clearly the sound of a mortally wounded creature, yet almost supernatural, like he imagined the screeching wail of a banshee.

But the creature was not dead.

Only as it writhed in the icy water could Garrison at last see the mouth of an ice dragon up close. Three rows of spike shaped teeth filled its upper and lower jaws. Fully open those jaws spanned more than six feet from the long, forked tongue to the roof of the mouth.

Garrison emptied his pistol into the ice dragon's mouth, firing down its throat. The ice dragon vomited a mixture of fire and blood across the water.

A cheer went up from the flagship, more cheers from the other vessels of the armada. Garrison changed to his last full magazine, looking skyward, knowing full well that the battle was just beginning.

The volleys of arrows and crossbow bolts began again, their targets the undersides of the ice dragons' outstretched wings, where wing and torso met. Garrison happened to be looking the right way as one of the harpoon-sized bolts fired from the deck of the Gle'Ur'Gya vessel struck its mark, the ice dragon struck with such force that its untouched wing folded and the creature rolled over onto its spiny back. Spewing fire toward the Gle'Ur'Gya vessel, almost as a final act of hatred, the creature augered downward into the sea. It struck with the force of a missile. A concussion wave started from impact zero, rolling the sea outward in a full circle around it. The flagship and the other four small ships rolled as it struck them broadside, only the more massive Gle'Ur'Gya vessel seemingly unaffected.

Fire belched from above and Garrison ran for his shield as flames crackled along the deck behind him. There was no time to look up and back; he knew an ice dragon was chasing him. Flames outdistanced him to his right, Lii'Ku consumed by them and he changed directions. As Garrison was about to run out of deck— he was nearing the bow—at the far edge of his peripheral vision he caught a glimpse of Gar'Ath and Mitan. They fired longbows in almost perfect unison, then dove over the rail.

Garrison hit the bow pulpit, ran the three steps, jumped the rail and plunged into the frigid water, clutching his pistol tight in his fist. The water above him vaporized into steam.

There'd been no time for a huge gulp of air. Garrison was forced to the surface. As his head broke the water, he saw the ice dragon. one wing crippled, but if there was any great bleeding, it was not immediately apparent.

Treading water, Garrison tucked his pistol into the double shoulder holsters, secured the thumb break safety strap, hoping it would hold, soaked as it was.

His eyes focused hard on the ice dragon. It flapped both wings, propelling itself through the water, belching a stream of fire which streaked a good twenty yards over the water. Not far beyond the flames were Gar'Ath and Mitan. They would never outswim the beast.

"Aww, shit!" Garrison snarled, cursing his own

stupidity. But, Gar'Ath or Mitan would have done the
same for him. They had, in fact, when they'd loosed
arrows at the beast. Garrison started swimming toward
the dragon. He would empty his pistols into the beast
at close range, and if they didn't stop the creature,
his only viable recourse would be the axe which hung
from his belt. Both the sword and the Golden Shield
of IBF were back on board the flagship. The shield
would have been only a burden under the circumstances, but the sword could have proven itself useful. He hoped that he wouldn't need the axe.

Ten yards from the dragon, Garrison drew the
pistol he'd just reholstered. He swam closer, wanting to be as close to point blank as possible before
opening fire. In theory, his ammunition would still
function, if Swan's duplicates of his original ammunition were as perfect as they seemed to be. Seven
rounds loaded, the distance six yards or so, he didn't
bother thumb-cocking the pistol. Both he and the ice
dragon bobbed too much in the water—and, the
water's temperature was progressively numbing Garrison. Pinpoint accuracy, even at such a short distance,
would be impossible.

He waited, waited, for the ice dragon to get past
him, leaving the underside of its damaged left wing
exposed.

The ice dragon exhaled fire again. A tongue of
flame licked lustfully across the water, stopping less
than a yard from Gar'Ath. The young swordsman had
interposed his own body between that of the woman
he loved and the dragon.

The ice dragon swam relentlessly forward. When
it next loosed its fire, the flames would engulf Gar'Ath
and Mitan, no matter how rapidly they swam.

Garrison saw the arrows, still stuck in the underside of the dragon's left wing, so close to the torso
that one or the other should have pierced the artery.
Neither had. Using the arrows as his aiming point,

Garrison fired once, then again and again and again. All four bullets impacted, but he saw no effect. Garrison emptied the last three rounds into the creature.

There was still no noticeable effect. It didn't even turn its head toward him.

Garrison inhaled and ducked under the waves, twisted his body so that he was on his back. Still under water he reholstered the pistol, then drew its match from the second holster.

Garrison surfaced. With a full magazine and one in the chamber, the pistol had eight rounds. Garrison fired twice, then twice more. He was closer to the artery, had to be, Garrison told himself.

Only four more rounds remained and he'd be down to the little .32 in his pocket and his two knives.

Deliberately, Garrison disregarded the arrows. If they had not struck the artery where they had hit, it had to be for a reason. There were some few human beings born with their hearts in right sides of their chests. Could an ice dragon have been born with this main artery between the wing and the torso either further forward or further rearward?

Garrison had four shots left with which he could find out.

Treading water, steadying himself as best he could, Garrison opened fire, two shots further forward along the underside of the wing, two shots further back. The first two shots achieved nothing. Nor did the third shot. The last shot struck the artery, and the ice dragon shrieked in anguish and rage. The pressure from the ice dragon's great heart pumped blood toward Garrison with the force of a fire hose. Garrison was knocked back and downward, under water, no air in his lungs, his hand barely able to still grasp his empty pistol.

Garrison was going down, blackness and cold enveloping him. He thrust his empty hand upward, felt the chill of wind on his fingertips. With his last iota of strength, Garrison heaved his body upward, gulping air the instant his mouth broke the surface. He choked, his lungs cold and on fire at once.

The monster shrieked one last ear-splitting cry and its head bowed over, great red-rimmed eyes open as sea water washed across them.

Alan Garrison's body was getting seriously numb. Somehow, he fumbled the empty pistol from his hand and into its holster beneath his sodden bomber jacket. Between the jacket and his cowboy boots, his body felt as if it weighed a ton. Forcing himself, Garrison started to swim. The vessels nearest to him and to Gar'Ath and Mitan were the flagship and the Gle'Ur'Gya *Storm Raider*. Gar'Ath and Mitan were already being thrown lines from the *Storm Raider*.

As Garrison fought to swim on he saw nine ice dragons were still in the sky, including the big horned male. Then he heard two splashes nearby. Looking around—his neck hurt when he did—Garrison noted that there were two men swimming toward him from the flagship, one of them Bin'Ah.

Garrison tried to swim toward them, his arms leaden, his legs not responding.

Erg'Ran peered over the side, the Champion floundering in the waves, but two men of the flagship nearly to him.

"Will he—"

"You will need your magic, Enchantress, lest he lose a limb. Waters as frigid as these can do much damage, and not only to the limbs, but can kill a heart, even one so great as that of the Champion."

"Yes, Erg'Ran. I will see to—"

"See to him quickly, I suggest, Enchantress. Our best warriors are unable to continue the fight, and nine of the ice dragons still continue at the attack. That three have perished without the aid of magic is beyond anything that we could have hoped for, Enchantress. If they change their tactics and come in a group against one ship at a time, we will surely perish."

"You are right," Swan agreed, her eyes not meeting his. Erg'Ran knew that she was looking toward the water, and he knew why.

His niece would likely have to expend a considerable amount of her magical energy, not in summoning the storm, which was only a natural phenomenon, but in controlling the lightning.

If her magical energy became so depleted that it would take some time to restore itself, he would find himself on the horns of a terrible dilemma. If he shared with the Enchantress and her Champion his strongly held theory concerning the origin of her mother's vast magical energy, Swan might be tempted to try tapping into that source herself. And, indeed, she might then have magical power as great as or exceeding that of her mother. If she did so, however, the prophecy could not be fulfilled.

But what if the prophecy was wrong?

Her magical energy seemed to return to her more quickly than it had. And her magical abilities were strengthening, expanding, deepening.

Erg'Ran did not know what to do, and only hoped that he would not have to make the choice.

Alan Garrison looked up into Swan's eyes. "How am I doin'?"

Swan only smiled. Her hands passed slowly over his body, and he felt warmth returning to his legs and arms as her fingertips touched them. But warmth also radiated from the very core of his being, coursing through his veins. She was healing him, staving off the almost inevitable results of the hypothermia which had gripped him in the icy waters.

"Gar'Ath and Mitan?"

"They will be well. Such healing as this is simple, the simplest kind of natural magic. Mitan is well-versed in it. She will have been able to heal herself, without even consciously trying, and will be attending Gar'Ath as I attend you. Bin'Ah and the other of our company who went into the water after you were not so seriously affected. I will see to their needs very soon."

"What about the little guy with the muscles? Lii'Ku?"

"My magical energy is sufficient that I could cause him to move about, even talk, laugh. But, it is not for my magic nor any magic to restore life to a body once life has slipped from it. He is dead, Al'An." Swan touched her lips to Garrison's forehead, as tenderly, he thought, as a mother might kiss a small child. Swan whispered, "That is why I took the essence of you from your body and placed it in the bird at Arba'Il'Tac. Had the life slipped from your body when you crashed to the rocky ground, I could not bring it back, with magic or any other way."

"I understand," Garrison answered.

"The ice dragons still attack." As if to emphasize her words, there was the whooshing sound of a volley of arrows being launched against the beasts. "I must quickly see to many things. When you feel strong enough, bring your sword and the Golden Shield of IBF and attend me at the bow pulpit, Al'An."

"I will," Garrison promised. "Soon."

She rose from her knees, Garrison watching her from where he lay near the mast. Swan stopped, her skirts lifted delicately in the fingertips of her left hand, her right hand first touching to Bin'Ah's chest. After what would be called in Creath only a few "eyeblinks," Swan touched the other of Garrison's rescuers.

Garrison totally trusted to Swan's magic and her goodness. Without being told, he knew that both men were healed.

Very quickly then, Swan walked forward, side-stepping still smoldering decking, making her way to the bow pulpit. Erg'Ran dropped to a crouch beside Garrison the next instant. "The Enchantress will summon forth a great storm. We must all be prepared. She will use her magic then to draw out the lightning, make it yield to her will. She will use the lightning to repel the ice dragons. It is our only hope if we are to survive."

Garrison trusted to Swan's magic, yes, but promised himself that as soon as the tingling was gone from his fingertips, he would load fresh cartridges into his fired out magazines, then reload his empty pistols. Just in case.

Swan ascended the three steps to the bow pulpit.

Her hands emerged from beneath her great cape, raised upward, arms fully extended.

There wouldn't be time to reload his pistols. "Help me get to my feet, Erg'Ran."

"Slowly, Champion."

"Right. Help me."

Erg'Ran stood, leaned down, offered Garrison his hand. Garrison clasped it nearly collapsing against the older man. "You'll recall, Champion, I cautioned that you stand slowly."

"I recall, already," Garrison nodded, catching his breath from the exertion. "I need my sword and my shield."

"I will bring your shield. Bin'Ah?" Erg'Ran called out along the deck.

"Yes, Erg'Ran?"

"The Champion's sword and golden shield."

"Yes, Erg'Ran."

Garrison steadied himself, tried walking a step, nearly made it. Erg'Ran held on to him.

Volley after volley of arrows had sailed overhead, but none flew as Garrison stood on the flagship's deck. The ice dragons had temporarily withdrawn to what

Garrison mentally labeled as the west, swarming like hungry insects, circling the almost gently gliding horned male who appeared to be their pack leader. It was as if they were somehow conferring, via body language. And, perhaps they were, Garrison granted.

His sword was brought to him, on a baldric of wide dark brown leather. Erg'Ran helped him to slip it over his head and left arm.

The acrid smell of still smoldering deck planking merely added to Garrison's lightheadedness. But Garrison felt steadier than he had and ready to walk, albeit slowly and quite carefully. Erg'Ran carried Garrison's shield and walked beside him, close enough to catch him, Garrison noted with some reassurance.

Ahead, at the very prow, Swan's hands moved rhythmically through the air, swirling, gliding. In the distance, Garrison spotted a small, dark cloud. Garrison's eyes followed Swan's hands, moving with such grace that the motion was erotic. When he felt less than himself, he'd discovered over the years that he seemed to find humor in the oddest things. Such was the case as he continued forward along the deck, Erg'Ran still beside him. "Figured out why K'Ur'Mir men don't get into magic very heavily. It's not the thing that women just have more of it."

"Oh! Really, Champion? Prithee, why, then?"

"Simple. All the hand movements and gentle touching and stuff like that?"

"So?"

"If a guy did that, he'd look like a sissy." Erg'Ran obviously pondered the meaning of the word for an eyeblink or so, then slowly responded, "That is an interesting observation, Champion. I'd prefer to consider the full implications of your remarks before commenting, if I may."

"Hey. Not a problem, Erg'Ran. We can talk about it later."

They were nearly at the bow. No volleys of arrows

were being fired. Men stood on the deck, some with spears ready, some with hands on the hilts of their still sheathed swords, some with the prods of their crossbows cocked, all waiting for the dragons to strike. Garrison looked toward the *Storm Raider*. He thought that he made out Gar'Ath and Mitan on the afterdeck, but was certain that he saw some of the Glc'Ur'Cya setting their massive deck-mounted crossbows, preparing for the ice dragons' imminent assault.

The little dark cloud Garrison had spied to the north was larger now, growing noticeably even as he watched it, expanding in height and width along the horizon. The wind was picking up. The icebergs seemed to be moving, too.

From within the darkening cloud, Garrison saw a flash of light.

Swan was building her weapon, one which would destroy the ice dragons, and just possibly might destroy them.

Swan's hands moved still more rapidly, as they had when she summoned the winds which saved them from the cyclonic wave, but somehow differently, as if each manifestation of her magic had subtle differences, like the intonations in speech or song.

Her hands moved with a flourish which Garrison had never witnessed before, palms outward, willowy fingers splayed. Yellow-white chain lightning crackled from the ever enlarging cloud bank in rhythm with the movements of her fingers, firing right and left, striking into the sea. The booms of thunder eyeblinks later were louder than any thunder Garrison had ever heard.

A gust of wind, colder than cold, swept across the ship, and Garrison's bones all but rattled with its icy touch.

"Prepare you!" Erg'Ran shouted out across the deck. "Send forth signals to the other ships, Bin'Ah. Make it known to all the Company of Mir and to our

Gle'Ur'Gya allies that a storm, in its relentless intensity unlike any that they have ever endured, is visited upon us! Its lightning will smite the ice dragons, ripping them from the sky, plunging them to their destruction in the icy deep!"

"Whew," Garrison whistled under his breath. Erg'Ran's speech struck him as awfully long to send as a semaphore style message, but Garrison kept that opinion to himself.

He turned his attention, instead, toward Swan, her hands and the weather that she undeniably, masterfully commanded.

The dark cloud totally obscured the horizon and seemed to cover half of the ocean itself. Inexorably, it devoured the distance still dividing it from the armada, rolling across the sky and sea, engulfing all before it.

Lightning. Thunderclaps. And the fair wind which had propelled them so faithfully over Woroc'Il'Lod was risen into a howling gale. The very air surrounding their vessels turned to luminescent green, electrical energy flickering everywhere around their ship and the other ships of the armada. The suddenness of the storm's grip closing on them nearly robbed Garrison's breath, sending a shiver along the full length of his spine.

Rain fell, at first a mist, an instant later a downpour, and an instant after that wind-lashed torrents, each enormous frigid drop stinging the skin like a needle prick.

The ice dragons, all nine of them, chose this very moment to strike, vectoring their attack against the flagship. Garrison had no idea of the ice dragons' level of intelligence, but they clearly realized in some element of their consciousness that the female standing in the prow of the flagship had something to do with the storm. That was obvious as the ice dragons started their dive.

Erg'Ran cried out over the keening of the wind. "Concentrate your arrows and bolts on the leader! Fire, lads! Fire now!"

Garrison's pistols were still empty and there was no time to reload. The .32 in his pocket would be useless for such work. Summoning all of his strength to ascend the steps to the bow pulpit and stand beside Swan, Garrison unsheathed his sword and raised the Golden Shield of IBF.

"Can you still command the storm if I shield you, Swan?"

"Yes, Al'An."

"Then be ready!" The exertion required to ascend the steps and bring sword and shield to bear had, rather than exhausting Garrison, somehow reinvigorated him.

And he had confidence that the shield would protect them from dragon fire.

Strange words—the Old Tongue, Garrison assumed—issued from Swan's lips like a cry, yet unmistakably a command. A bolt of lightning, brilliant yellow-white, streaked from the nearly black clouds. One of the nine ice dragons diving toward the flagship was struck. The rumble of thunder was deafening. Garrison's ears pulsed with it. The colossal winged beast's vile grey body exploded into flame, a rain of blood and tissue and fire cascading from within the explosive cloud, and an eyeblink later the fireball itself totally dissipated on the driving wind.

Cheers rose from the flagship, hurrahs echoing across the water from the other ships as well. But any human sound was barely discernible as little over a whisper. The relentless shrieks of the ice dragons, the nerve-shattering rhythmic thrum of their mighty wings and the howl of wind and roar of waves vanquished all other sound, penetrated the human soul to its innermost redoubt.

Soaked, freezing, the enormous breakers which

crashed over the prow of the flagship pummeling him,
Garrison braced himself and stood, offering what
protection he could to the Virgin Enchantress whom
he loved and served. The nearest ice dragon made
what Garrison mentally classified as a strafing run,
soaring over the flagship's deck, fire rolling from its
wicked mouth. Garrison wheeled, lifting his shield
higher, drawing Swan close against him. The flame
washed over them, stealing their breath for a microsecond, the beast's left wing grazing Garrison's left
cheek, ear and shoulder.

Garrison felt the slick hotness of blood. Shoving
Swan aside, but still shielding her, Garrison stabbed
upward with his sword. His blade skated over the
creature's scales, its tip finding a spot of flesh. As the
great monster passed, a spray of gore spewed from
beneath its wing.

Garrison staggered, his sword hand shaking, his
blade dripping a greenish yellow puss-like liquid onto
the deck. The next wave to crash over the ship's bow
washed the ichor away. The whole left side of Garrison's
face and upper body ached beyond any pain he'd ever
known.

The ice dragon had gained altitude, was cutting a
tight arc, its wings flapping incredibly rapidly. In an
eyeblink, it dove toward them, slavering spike-toothed
jaws open wide.

Fire.

Garrison raised the Golden Shield, drawing Swan
into his sword arm.

The decking around their feet was aflame. Swan
didn't scream, but shouted, "Al'An!" Her skirts had
caught fire. Garrison cast his shield against the bow
rail, threw himself to his knees and smothered the
flames with his body.

"I am all right, Al'An!"

Garrison looked up from his knees, saw her hands
moving again. His eyes were blinded by the flash as

lightning forked from the black cloud across the green air. There was a dragon sound louder than any Garrison had yet heard, and as his eyes recovered from the flash, he saw the creature spiraling down in flames just off the port bow. His ears rang from the thunderclap.

Seven ice dragons remained.

Bleeding heavily, Garrison staggered to his feet. Magic might not help these wounds, if Swan had any magic left after this, if they survived at all.

Garrison's left arm was numb, and he refused to look at it. He thrust his sword deep into the decking, keeping it to hand while he once more raised the shield.

Hails of arrows and crossbow bolts filled the air overhead, ice dragons circling there. If the creatures were hit, Garrison couldn't tell.

Swan had inched forward to the very prow once again, her body wedged into the apex of the port and starboard rails.

Swan's cape was gone. Her auburn hair wildly tossed in the wind and spray, her arms at maximum extension, Swan's splayed finger tips drew electricity from the air. A halo of light and energy surrounded her, glowing all about her.

"Swan! No!" Garrison shouted, starting to reach for her.

Swan's arms moved, describing ever enlarging concentric circles. Her left hand flung suddenly upward, outward, palm upraised, a ball of electricity firing from her fingertips, striking the nearest of the remaining dragons.

Thunder reverberated around the ship, shields ringing like bells, swords like tuning forks.

Her right hand. Light and energy. A ball of lightning streaked from her fingers to its mark. Again and again the energy soared from her fingertips and again and again the ice dragons were struck and incinerated.

The last ice dragon, the great horned male, quit the attack.

If it got away, Garrison told himself, it would find other Creathans to feed on.

Swan clapped both hands together, then flung her palms open, the halo of energy surrounding her pouring into her, through her, spewing from her fingertips in a streak of blinding light and an explosion of sound.

Garrison shielded his face, but risked his eyes to look.

Somehow, the great male ice dragon must have sensed that the frail girl on the pitiful ship was not through with him.

The ice dragon looked back.

The energy summoned through the body of the Virgin Enchantress flashed round the beast and devoured it.

They were through now, the final ice dragon accounted for and dead. Alan Garrison turned his eyes to his left shoulder and arm.

The sleeve of his jacket was gone. A dragon scale had completely pierced his upper arm. He could see bone when a wave crashed over the bow and washed the blood away. He didn't want to feel the left side of his head, because he was certain that his ear had been torn away.

Swan turned away from the prow. Even if his left ear was still where it belonged, Alan Garrison couldn't hear her because of the thunder which still rang within him. But her lips formed a word he was certain he recognized, "Al'An?"

"I love you." Garrison didn't know if Swan could hear him, either. A wave crashed over the bow and brought blackness with it which engulfed him. There was nothing left to worry about.

# Chapter Thirteen

When he folded back the blanket covering him and looked at his left shoulder and upper arm, he asked Erg'Ran, "Did she do as good a job on my jacket as she did on me?"

"Oh, yes, Champion. When you have the chance, you won't see a thing wrong with your left ear, either. It was partially torn away."

Garrison raised his left arm. It was a little stiff, but worked. He held his Rolex next to his left ear. He could hear it ticking.

"We are where?"

"Edge Land. Just off shore. It will soon be dawn."

"Swan, I take it, is—?"

"The Enchantress's magical energy is very much depleted, and she's a very physically exhausted girl. There were more than fifteen seriously wounded to whom it was necessary to attend."

"How many dead?"

"Just the one of whom you know, Champion— Lii'Ku."

"Any sign of a reception committee?"

Erg'Ran puzzled over the phrase for an eyeblink

or so, then answered, "So far, we are unmolested. Either the magical energy of my sister is still very much depleted, or she has lain a trap for us."

"Could be both," Garrison noted. "You're good with this sort of stuff, I imagine. Am I okay to get up and around?"

"You may feel a tad debilitated, lacking in strength for a short time, but you will soon feel your normal self."

"Nothing has been normal at all since I came to Creath, Erg'Ran."

The older man's face seamed with laughter. "True enough, I suppose, Champion. True enough. It hasn't really been a happy time for any of us."

"I disagree. I've been happier here than I've ever been where I come from. I know; I'm strange."

"You love the Enchantress a great deal, Champion."

"You're supposed to be the resident smart person, Erg'Ran. Doesn't take a genius to figure out that I'm nuts about your niece. By the way?"

"Yes, Champion?"

"When I get around to asking Swan to marry me, you being her uncle and all, do I need to ask your permission?"

"Swan is the only one who can give the permission you will seek. But, for what it is worth, you already have my blessing, Champion."

"Jeepers! Can I call you Uncle Ergy? Huh?!"

Erg'Ran's hearty laughter filled the room. Garrison suddenly thought to ask, "Where the heck are we, anyway?"

"The Enchantress felt that you would rest more soundly aboard the *Storm Raider*. And, your Gle'Ur'Gya host provided you with his personal quarters, Champion."

Garrison looked about the room, correcting himself to think of it as "the captain's cabin." As one would have supposed, an enclosure which would comfortably house a Gle'Ur'Gya was proportioned about ten or fifteen percent larger than ordinary human scale. A backless chair by a chart desk at the center of the cabin seemed halfway between the height of a normal chair and a high chair, and the desk itself was closer in height to a kitchen counter than a table.

There was no knock, but the oversized door opened and Bre'Gaa entered, ducking his head to avoid the top of the doorframe. "Al'An! You have returned to the living!"

"Apparently so."

"Excellent. I am personally glad that your Enchantress is so skilled in her healing. I would have missed having you as someone with whom I might confer."

"I'm flattered, Bre'Gaa, but I don't follow you."

Erg'Ran smiled. "What the good Captain Commander Bre'Gaa means, Champion, is that as someone from the other realm, he considers your opinions a little more evenhandedly arrived at." And, Erg'Ran stood and faced Bre'Gaa. "Is that not true, Captain Bre'Gaa?"

"Quite true, brave and learned ally. Quite true, indeed."

"Thank you for the loan of the cabin, Bre'Gaa."

Bre'Gaa bowed slightly and flung back the hood made from the upper portion of his great kilt. "The weather is cold, even for a Gle'Ur'Gya. I came for my cloak. You are both welcome to my cabin as long as you wish, or to join me on deck."

"I think I'd like that," Garrison told him honestly. Enclosed as they were, Garrison felt the motion of the sea more pronouncedly. And, still feeling a little weak, he had no desire to experience nausea.

"Excellent," Bre'Gaa declared. He ducked his head again, this time to avoid an overhead mounted oil lamp, as he crossed the cabin floor to an armoire. He opened one of the doors and pulled out a hooded cloak. "Your swordsman friend and his lovely lady are on deck and I am certain that you'd be interested to know that the Enchantress is supposed to arrive shortly. At least as far as I am able to ascertain from her flagship's signals. By the way, I was very impressed watching your firespitters against the ice dragons. You must let me try them at our first opportunity."

Garrison sat up too fast, his head reminding him of that fact. "Yes, I will—both join you on deck and let you try my firespitters. Thank you for your hospitality."

"Anon, then." Swirling his cloak about his shoulders, Bre'Gaa was at the cabin door in two strides, ducking through the doorway and gone in another.

Garrison swung his legs over the side of the berth. His feet didn't touch the cabin floor. "These guys are tall," Garrison observed to Erg'Ran.

"Let me help you, Champion."

Garrison let him help. He clambered down from the bed to his feet, unsteady the moment they touched the cabin floor. "This is getting to be a habit with us, Erg'Ran, you helping me to keep from falling down."

The older man merely smiled, then, after a moment, suggested, "I think that you ought to lean against the bed here for an eyeblink or two whilst I get your things. Save your strength until you have a good feel for your legs under you, Champion."

"Good advice," Garrison agreed.

Erg'Ran went to a second, matching armoire on the opposite side of the cabin, opened its double doors and began rummaging about inside. "The Enchantress has restored your weapons as they should be. Your bombing jacket—"

"Bomber jacket, Erg'Ran. Not bombing."

"Ahh! Bomber jacket. Yes. It has been seen to as well, Champion. But, I fear you'll need a cloak, considering the cold weather. The Enchantress anticipated your requirements and has provided one for you."

"Question?"

"Yes, Champion?" And Erg'Ran turned away from the armoire and looked Garrison in the eye.

"Are you really as afraid as it seems that Swan could turn evil, like her mom did?"

"Just a casual question, I see. One of little import. Yes, well . . . You see, Champion, my niece is as fine as fine could ever be. Yet, you saw yourself how she resolved the issue of the ice dragons. Indeed, I encouraged her to bring on the tempest, to use the lightning. Lightning was all that either of us could think of as a weapon which would destroy the ice dragons. But my niece surpassed anything I had imagined as possible. You heard the Old Tongue words come from her lips? You saw the energy form around her, flash through her? I would doubt that my sister could do that in quite that way, with so much power.

"In short," Erg'Ran concluded, "if the Enchantress should succumb to the enormity of the power which she can already wield and were to become obsessed with possessing still more—and she will have that opportunity—she would have greater magic ability than anyone Creath has ever known or had, more magic than all of the K'Ur'Mir who have ever lived combined. Such power cannot help but seduce even the Enchantress, make even the best of us teeter on the brink of falling victim to temptation. Should the Enchantress succumb, she would lust for more and more power until becoming so lost within her personal desires that she would have become oblivious to her own evil. I fear for her because I love her. And, because you love her, Champion, do not forget what I have told you."

"You never give simple answers."

Erg'Ran returned to getting things from the cabinet, but said over his shoulder, "Where you come from, are there simple answers to complex questions, Champion?"

"I suppose not."

"Then, I shouldn't expect that you would hope to find simple answers here, either."

"Can't blame a guy for trying, Erg'Ran."

The older man was through with his search. His arms weren't laden with its results—Garrison's pistols, his sword and the golden Shield of IBF, the bomber jacket, a cloak. They floated in the air beside him.

"Magic? You?"

"You'll note that it serves you, not me."

"But, your magic, although it levitates *my* belongings serves *your* ends, means that you don't have to carry my stuff."

"That is a good point." Erg'Ran let the items slowly sink to the cabin floor. "When you're ready, then. I'll see you on deck, Champion. No rush."

Erg'Ran walked to the doorway and left.

Alan Garrison lit a cigarette the old-fashioned way, albeit with considerable difficulty. Because of the strength of the wind which whipped over the *Storm Raider*'s deck, he was forced to shield his windlighter in his cupped hands and still screen it within the cowl of his hood. After all of that, it took three tries.

The temperature felt bitingly cold, despite the heavy outer shell and lining of the cloak he wore and the bomber jacket underneath.

To what Garrison mentally labeled the east, he saw the faintest hairline of sunrise on the horizon.

He was rested enough, he supposed. He was hungry, but there'd probably be food forthcoming. He had looked at himself reflected in a sheet of brightly burnished copper which was hung like a mirror over a wash basin in Bre'Gaa's cabin. He was clean shaven—Swan had seen to that—and there was no trace of a mark or scar where his ear had been partially ripped away by the dragon scale.

Despite the dangers and resultant injuries, Garrison was having the time of his life. Every day was a new challenge, a new adventure, just what he'd hoped to find in life "in the other realm" and never had. He was living the novel he had always wanted to write, and the willowy, drop-dead gorgeous heroine of the story was his girl.

Garrison inhaled on the cigarette, staring out to sea.

He'd slain a dragon, fought monsters, been instructed in the use of a blade by a master swordsman, done all kinds of neat stuff and met the greatest girl ever. The business of almost dying twice he could have done without, but one had to take the bad with the good.

By the same token, the venture in which he was engaged was deadly serious business, the fate of all of Creath in the balance, not to mention his own life and, most importantly, the life of the woman he loved.

"The woman I love," Garrison murmured to the dark waters, saying the words very slowly so that he could savor them.

From beside him, he heard Swan's voice. "Who is she, the woman that you love, Al'An?"

Garrison snapped the cigarette into the water, turned around and took Swan into his arms. "Who is she! Are you going to just magically appear without warning all the time? And, this virgin thing. Let me tell you! It's driving me nuts, Swan. Who do you think's the woman I love?"

"Me?"

"You know it, darling," Garrison whispered to her. He drew Swan's body tightly against his own, looked into her eyes, then put his mouth to a better use than talking.

"The six of us are all that will be required, and any more people will just get in the way. That's assuming, Bre'Gaa, that you really do want to come."

"If you wish me to, Gar'Ath."

"You'd be an asset," Mitan declared. "A definite asset."

"Then we are six," Erg'Ran announced.

Garrison took a cigarette from his pack, but replaced it before Swan could light it or the pack magically refilled itself. There was no ashtray in Bre'Gaa's cabin. "If there were seven of us, we could saddle up and go out and save a Mexican village from banditos. But I'm not gonna be the guy who shaves his head."

Erg'Ran just looked at him. "What in Creath are you talking about, Champion?"

"Cross-cultural reference to my world. You couldn't be into Yul Brynner movies, so don't worry about it."

"As you say, Champion. I shall not worry, nor do I believe that any head shaving will be required."

"Then, I won't worry either." Quickly trying to redeem himself after the absurdly obscure reference to the classic western had made him sound like an idiot, Garrison asked, "Is everything planned for the diversions? I missed a lot while I was recuperating."

"See this chart, Al'An," Bre'Gaa said, rolling it out across the nearly waist high table at the center of his cabin. "We ply these coasts regularly looking for whatever we may find to plunder." Bre'Gaa's middle finger, nearly as long and thick as a small banana, traced along an impossibly rugged looking outline of Edge Land. "My crew knows every inlet where there's depth enough that the *Storm Raider* won't run aground. All of the tides—high, low, neap—are as familiar to us as our names. My first officer is working with your Bin'Ah and the commanders of the Enchantress's other vessels. Short of the use of powerful magic against a widely dispersed array of targets all at once, which the Enchantress tells me is impossible, Eran will never be able to catch us. She can second-sight us all she wants, and I hope that she does. That will just keep her infernal Horde of Koth in constant motion. The Queen Sorceress will have no way of knowing where we'll strike, where we'll land, if we'll strike or if we'll land."

Garrison was concerned about what seemed to him an obvious flaw in the plan. He asked about it. "Bre'Gaa mentioned the second sight. I've been thinking about that. What if Swan's mother second-sights every ship in the armada and doesn't find her daughter, or Erg'Ran—doesn't find any of the six of us? Isn't she going to get suspicious?"

"My sister probably will be suspicious," Erg'Ran agreed. "However, not to worry, Champion. First of all, as you may have noticed or may not have realized, the second sight allows one to view at great distances in exquisite detail. It does not allow one to see through walls, however. Even if Eran were to use a bird through which to project her second sight, to see inside this cabin aboard this ship the bird would have to be inside the cabin. The only exception to that would be if the structure—in this case, the *Storm Raider*—were protected by a guarding spell. Only the person who had initiated the guarding spell would then be able to second-sight through walls."

Garrison nodded. "I get it, then, I think. We make it obvious that the six of us are inside this cabin, in the hope that she does second-sight us, or is second-sighting us now. Then, somehow, we slip out the back."

"Actually, with magic, which I will be able to use because my mother's attentions will be so much divided and her magic cannot be used to accomplish two tasks at once," Swan supplied.

"Aye, and we hope that our naval diversions keep the Queen Sorceress so busy that indeed we can get inside Barad'Il'Koth and get ourselves out again," Gar'Ath declared. "At least, it sounds simple. I like that."

Garrison laughed. "Everything sounds simple, unless Erg'Ran is telling us about it."

"Champion!"

Garrison clapped the older man on the back. "Only joking, my friend. Only joking." He looked at the others, then threw out the question, "How's this little raid of ours supposed to work, guys?"

"My magical energy," Swan began, "was severely depleted, as you know, but is almost completely restored; this occurred much more rapidly than I had supposed that it might, Al'An. I have no idea why. But it should be easy enough for me to place shift us from Bre'Gaa's cabin to Barad'Il'Koth, although whether or not I will be able to place shift the six of us all at once remains to be seen.

"Despite the diversions," Swan went on, "my mother might still sense us arriving; but I doubt that she will be alert to what we are about. She should be too busy to notice."

"How about getting out of Barad'Il'Koth when we've done what we need to do? Especially if—by some quirk of circumstance, let's say—your mother somehow does catch on to us being there," Garrison persisted.

"We will have some options, Al'An," Swan assured him. "Magic would certainly be one of the options. Others may prove more viable. We'll simply have to determine our means of escape after we've accomplished what must be done."

Garrison told Swan and the others, "There's a wonderful old expression where I come from, about doing something by the seat of the pants." Garrison looked around the cabin before saying anything else. Bre'Gaa wore a great kilt, Erg'Ran a monkish robe. Gar'Ath was dressed in a brown leather jerkin, dark green tights and knee boots. Mitan was attired in next to nothing, as usual (a bra-like top and matching short skirt of brown leather, boots to her thighs and lots of edged weapons). Swan wore a full-skirted, floor-length charcoal grey dress.

"By the seat of the pants?" Erg'Ran repeated quizzically.

"Oh, never mind."

Swan could not bring herself to be as scantily attired as Mitan. Mitan looked wonderfully pretty that way, but Swan would have felt so self-conscious that she wouldn't be able to think straight. And think straight she must if they were to accomplish their mission at Barad'Il'Koth and have any hope of getting out alive.

Swan compromised, magically attiring herself in traditional male clothing. She wore a full-sleeved white blouse, a black leather jerkin, black stockings and black knee boots. Swan belted her sword at her waist, swinging aside her hair, which was done in a single heavy braid extending well below her waist.

Using a little magic which she hoped that she could spare, Swan made a full-length looking glass appear. Dressing like a man made her feel silly, but it was practical under the circumstances. And there was a certain kind of almost wicked fun just in doing it.

The dagger which she usually carried under her skirts, she sheathed at her right side in such a manner that it could be drawn conveniently with either hand.

Swan wheeled around so that she could see herself more fully, trying to convince herself that at least, had she really been trying, she could have made a convincing looking boy—except for the braid, of course. Resignedly, Swan just shrugged her shoulders. Even her shoulders looked obviously too little. She looked like a girl, a girl trying unsuccessfully to look like a boy. "Oh, well," Swan sighed acceptingly.

Swan still felt self-conscious about her legs. The stockings revealed every curve and contour of them. She made a long black cloak appear, which she threw over her shoulders. "That's better." The cloak restored at least a glimmer of decorum and made her look a little bigger in the shoulders (she tried to convince herself).

Swan made the mirror vanish.

She'd used Bre'Gaa's offered cabin in which to change, and she wandered about it while she waited for the others to arrive. The diversions were already underway, all six ships moving to different positions along the coast of Edge Land.

The Gle'Ur'Gya vessel was certainly much more comfortable than the tiny ships to which she was accustomed. That one person aboard the vessel could have living quarters as comparatively capacious as these was fantastic. There was a comfortable looking bed; she'd seen to Al'An's healing while he'd slept in it. There was a chamber pot, a washbasin. She glanced casually at her reflection in a burnished copper plate over the basin. There were cupboards and cabinets. There were books aplenty, and scrolls. The map of Edge Land's coast was attractively illuminated. The Gle'Ur'Gya weren't the uncivilized brutes she'd always thought of them being.

Swan had never tried place shifting six living things at once, and she still felt a little nervous about something going wrong. Inside her head, she rehearsed what she must do, but her eyes were wandering over charts and instruments used for plotting courses. The Gle'Ur'Gya were talented seafarers, to be sure. After what was about to transpire, if she lived, she would make it her business to once and for all see to it that there was peace between the Gle'Ur'Gya and her own people.

There was a polite knock at the door. "Please come in," Swan called out.

Mitan entered, followed by Gar'Ath, Erg'Ran, Captain Bre'Gaa and Al'An, Al'An wearing his sword and carrying his shield, but without a cloak. Before leaving her alone to change, Al'An had asked, "If I gave you a description, do you think you could make me something called a sweater? This greatcape is nice and warm, but I'm not used to moving around in one."

The "sweater" turned out to be easy enough to magically fabricate for him. Once he described the process—he called it knitting—by which it was made, she had the general idea clearly in mind. Although she hadn't mentioned her observation to Al'An, she felt that the green sweater went rather poorly with the rest of his clothes (which were blue), not to mention clashing with the leather harness for his firespitters.

Al'An came up to her, kissed her lightly on the lips, and, as he held her, whispered, "You look cute." It took an eyeblink to comprehend "cute" and, when she did, Swan smiled.

They all assembled at the center of Bre'Gaa's cabin. "I don't think that we'll have any problems," Swan told them, "but I'd be remiss not to remind all of you that I've never performed a place-shifting spell for six people all at once. If I have any reason to believe that there will be any problems, I'll stop at once and send us out two or three at a time."

"Do you have any idea where we'll arrive?" Mitan asked.

Swan answered, "We all studied the sketch which Erg'Ran made for us of the interior of Barad'Il'Koth as he remembers it, and you, Mitan, as well as Erg'Ran and I have second-sighted Barad'Il'Koth's exterior. I think that I can make us arrive somewhere safe. I'm hoping that we'll be in the anteroom to my mother's great hall. From there, if Erg'Ran has recalled correctly, we will have direct access to all of the main passageways within the keep."

"I believe that I speak for us all," Erg'Ran announced. "We are ready."

Swan merely nodded.

Swan outstretched her arms, her hands grasping

for the magic in the air around her, feeling its current surging through her body, strengthening her. She uttered the words of the place-shifting spell. Swan pressed her palms together between her breasts, becoming one with the energy around her.

Light, dazzlingly bright, filled her, exploded from her. There was a sound, soft, like the rumble of thunder heard at a great distance.

A darkness that glowed like light but was neither light nor dark was all around Swan and the others. The glowing darkness lingered, nothing replacing it. For an eyeblink, Swan's concentration nearly failed her, as she feared that somehow, in some way, she had made a mistake. There was a light again, and Swan beheld bleak stone walls on either side of her, smoldering tapers going on and on, endlessly into darkness. When she looked around, Al'An, Erg'Ran, Mitan, Gar'Ath and Bre'Gaa were with her.

They were inside Barad'Il'Koth, but not where they should have been.

"Where are we?" Mitan whispered, voicing Swan's own concern.

"Not the anteroom," Erg'Ran declared. "This is the passageway leading between the barracks for the Horde of Koth household guard and the keep itself. Down a hundred swordlengths or so there is an additional passageway, which leads to the barracks for the Sword of Koth. That is on the right. On the left, another passageway leads to the main stables. The passageways are here in order to facilitate movement between the principal structures within the fortress in the event of attack. They are chiefly used, however, when the snows are too heavy above."

Gar'Ath, sword in hand, asked, "And, to the keep?"

"That way, swordsman." Erg'Ran jerked his thumb in the opposite direction from which they were faced.

"I'm sorry," Swan announced. "I must have misjudged."

Al'An took her hand, telling her sincerely, "Hey, we're inside, we're not surrounded by bad guys and we know which direction to go in. You did great, darling."

Swan smiled and kissed Al'An's cheek, then drew her sword.

They began moving along the passageway, Swan following close behind Erg'Ran who led the way, Al'An beside her. Erg'Ran's axe was lashed to the girdle at his waist, a sword in his right hand. For the first time, Swan truly noticed the sword. She touched at Erg'Ran's shoulder and he glanced back at her. "Is that your father's sword, uncle?"

"Indeed, Enchantress. The very same."

Swan understood why he carried it, and a chill ran along her spine at the very prospect of encountering her mother.

Periodically, as they crept along the dank passageway, they would stop, Swan and Mitan second sighting ahead and behind them. Each time, they spied no sign of life and continued along their route.

"We near the keep, Enchantress," Erg'Ran announced after a time.

Gar'Ath whispered hoarsely, "Let Mitan and me go ahead, Enchantress. She can second-sight for danger, and if there is any . . ."

Al'An volunteered, "That's a good idea, but I'm going with. If there is a trap, my firespitters might be the only way out, assuming that they work." Al'An didn't wait for her approval, and Swan secretly liked that. "Bre'Gaa?"

"Yes, Al'An?" Bre'Gaa responded.

"Would you keep an eye out behind us? If there's a trap, the logical thing would be for them to close us off from both ends of the corridor."

"The minions of the Queen Sorceress will only reach the Enchantress over the corpses of Erg'Ran and myself. Be assured of that."

"You guys wait a little while so that we have a head start," Al'An told them.

"Al'An—be careful," Swan heard herself saying to him.


When they were still fifty yards or so from what looked to be the end of the passageway, Garrison, Gar'Ath and Mitan stopped, so that Mitan could second-sight. "There is a chamber beyond the passageway," Mitan whispered. "This is very bad, very bad."

Alan Garrison failed to grasp the cause for such enthusiasm. "What do you mean?"

"Come ahead, but quietly, Champion, and you and Gar'Ath will see."

They continued to the end of the passageway. It had seemed to go on forever. Looking at his watch was useless in Creath, of course, but Garrison guessed that Swan, Erg'Ran and Bre'Gaa would be about ten minutes behind them.

The passageway opened onto a low-ceilinged, pie-wedge-shaped chamber—narrow where Garrison, Gar'Ath and Mitan lurked in hiding, gradually widening toward a very high, arched opening at the far side.

There was absolutely nothing on the chamber's floor. But, at regular intervals along the chamber's walls were mounted a succession of sculptures, grotesquely shaped icons which resembled horribly shaped miniature humans about the size of small monkeys, all of them naked, with huge, bulging eyes.

"I had heard that the Queen Sorceress had done this, but I was unbelieving of it."

Garrison looked at Mitan. "Unbelieving of what? They're just ugly little statues, right?"

Gar'Ath answered for her. "They are Tree Demons which the Queen Sorceress has spell-changed."

"She turned them to stone?" Garrison asked.

"Yes, but they still live and will know when we pass them and they will attack us," Mitan told him.

"Tree Demons were the things which nearly got Erg'Ran and his father years ago, right?" Garrison asked.

"They are some of the evil creatures which, before the Queen Sorceress undertook to destroy Creath, lived only in the deepest recesses of the forests," Gar'Ath informed Garrison. "I was attacked by such creatures, as you know, but was able to speed past them, suffering little injury."

"What do they do? Bite?" Garrison queried.

"Worse than that. They will bite, but their goal is to sink their teeth in so deeply," Mitan recounted, a shiver visible as she spoke, "that they cannot be torn free without the victim ripping away a large piece of his own flesh. They eat anything living, but are especially fond of human flesh."

"Oh, wonderful!" Garrison said, shaking his head. "And, if I get this right, when we walk past them, they'll come alive and attack us?"

"Yes, Champion," Gar'Ath nodded gravely.

"Anybody have any brilliant ideas?" Garrison looked at Mitan, then at Gar'Ath. Neither of them seemed ready to volunteer. "Okay, we can't go in a different direction without walking into troops. We can't magically transport ourselves past here, I imagine, because if there was a remote chance that Swan's mom would somehow sense us entering the castle, using magic to transport ourselves within the castle would probably be a dead giveaway, right?" Garrison looked at Mitan.

"Correct, Champion." Mitan nodded.

"If we make too much of a racket fighting these ugly little guys, we'll alert some of Eran's troops— probably. Right?"

Gar'Ath answered, "That is true, Champion."

Mentally, Garrison stepped back from the problem. The petrified Tree Demons were being used like motion sensors in an Earth-style alarm system. "That's it!"

"What is it?" Gar'Ath asked him.

"Question, Mitan?"

"Yes, Champion?"

"Could Swan use magic which didn't involve place shifting, just natural magic, the low-energy kind, without a great risk of alerting her mother?"

Mitan seemed to ponder Garrison's question before responding. At last, she told him, "There must be magic in use throughout the entirety of Barad'Il'Koth. There are witches here, who are magic users, of course, and she would have guarding spells in place, other types of magic in constant use. No, I don't think that the Queen Sorceress would sense a reasonable amount of natural magic. Otherwise, she would be constantly interrupted by the magic all around her."

Garrison still had to work out whether the answer was heat or cold. . . .

Her skirts bunched in white knuckled fists, Eran ran along the passageway toward the closed chamber door at its far end. Her magic had almost been fully restored when the naval maneuvers along the coast of Edge Land began, but, in a very short time, between whisking entire units of Sword of Koth from one point to another and second-sighting six separate ships, it had become sorely depleted once again. It was obvious that this was her daughter's plan, to exhaust her magical energy. It was working.

"Damn her I will!" Eran screamed. The masked Sword of Koth was barely able to drop to one knee and bow his head as she streaked past him.

Normally, the shackles and her spells were sufficient to secure the chamber's occupant, but she could take no chances with her daughter's followers afoot. Eran stopped at the doorway and willed the door to open, ran through and kicked the door closed behind her.

"You're upset again, Eran."

"This is your last chance, Pe'Ter! I have had enough of your insolence!"

"What are you going to do? Kill me? Turn me into something vile and disgusting? Oops! I forgot. You already did that, when you decided that there was only one thing you needed from me."

"I want an answer, not philosophy, Pe'Ter!"

"I'd give you an answer the way you deserve to hear it, but you'd think it was an invitation."

Eran thrust her right hand toward him and willed him to be seized with pain throughout his entire body.

Pe'Ter had been standing beside the solitary window when she entered the room and confronted him. Now, he writhed beside the window, collapsing to all fours, then rolling across the floor in agony.

Eran cleared the spell. Breathless, Pe'Ter looked up at her from the floor, whispered, "You are afraid, aren't you, Eran?"

"You will be, Pe'Ter. You will be." Eran had done what she was about to do only once before in order to force Pe'Ter to cooperate, bend his iron will to her own needs. But it pained her to do it, making her recall feelings she did not wish to remember that she had ever had. And it was particularly dangerous at this juncture, because she would consume all of her remaining magical energy in order to achieve the result which she so desperately needed. . . .

Peter Goodman fingered his pack of Luckies, his eyes focusing on the green on the package. "You think she'll come?"

"She'll come, lieutenant."

Goodman stared at the cigarettes. "Ya know, my mother used to tell me that smoking cigarettes would kill me, Dave. My dad used to call 'em coffin nails. He smoked Fatimas till the day he died."

"Look, lieutenant. The way I figure it, if some damn Nazi shell don't fall on us or GI food don't poison our guts out, we got life by the tail. I ain't even seen my littlest kid, 'cept them box Brownie Kodaks Betty sends me in her letters. And I got the garage waitin' for me. I'm gonna live to be a hundred. And I'll still be smokin'."

Goodman offered Dave Spaulding a Lucky and he took it.

"You really think she'll come, Dave?"

"I really think she'll come, Pete."

Peter Goodman sipped at his wine, shrugged his shoulders. All his life, he'd heard about how terrific French wines were. Evidently, whoever had started those rumors had never drunk wine in this village. "This wine is the pits."

"Man, I tell ya'. What I wouldn't give for a bottle of real American whiskey, lieutenant!"

"You've been reading my mind again, Dave."

"A good platoon sergeant's s'posed to read his platoon leader's mind, sir."

"So that's the reason we got off Omaha Beach alive, huh? Glad you told me, Dave. And here I figured the Germans were just lousy shots last June."

Dave Spaulding laughed.

Peter Goodman swallowed some more of his wine. With the three day pass, everybody else in Second Battalion C Company had hit the road for Paris. Spaulding, for all his tough talk, was a quiet family man with a wife and two more kids besides the little one, all living in a little house right next door to his repair shop in New Jersey.

When all the guys hot-footed it to Paris, Spaulding—who was also Goodman's best friend in this part of the world—confided to him, "I'm not goin' to no Paris, Pete. See, lieutenant, it's like this. I ain't been near no woman in so long, I'm afraid I'd do somethin' damn stupid runnin' loose in Paris and all. These French ma'amselles wanna make every GI feel like he liberated Paris all on his own. Know what I mean, lieutenant?"

"Hell, we didn't liberate Paris anyway. It was Ernest Hemingway who led the first troops in. Remember?"

"Yeah! How'd'ya like that guy! A damn reporter leadin' the army into the city like that! What a crazy thing to do, huh, lieutenant? Beatin' all them big-shot officers to the punch like that. Gosh! He's gonna have some swell stories to tell."

"He already tells some swell stories, that Hemingway guy. So, what you gonna do with three days if you're not going to Paris?"

Spaulding figured that if he went to Paris he'd be too weak-willed not to cheat on his wife, and cheating on his wife would be wrong. There she was, working in a defense plant, raising three kids and writing him letters all the time about how she missed him and everything.

Spaulding wasn't going to go to Paris, no matter what.

There was no wife or sweetheart waiting back home for Peter Goodman, but he stayed behind anyway near the little village fifty kilometers outside of Paris, just to keep his friend company.

But a curious thing happened this night. He and Spaulding were tooling down the dirt road into the village in their borrowed Jeep—just like they had planned—when both of them spotted a bright flash of light from just inside the treeline in the woods, just to the north.

After exchanging a couple of worried looks, they stashed the Jeep by the side of the road. Dave had rigged the Jeep's battery cables so that he could pull the positive one and drop it in his pocket. That way, whenever they parked the Jeep, they didn't have to worry about a downed German aviator or even an ordinary car thief stealing it. Back in England, before the invasion, the Brits were taking the rotors out of their cars for the same reason, but it was rumored that German pilots were carrying spare rotors that would work in the most commonly encountered English automobiles.

Goodman and Spaulding crossed the road and started into the woods. Spaulding clutched the Rock-Ola M1 Carbine (lighter and handier than his own Garand) which he perennially borrowed from Peter Goodman, Goodman his genuine Colt 1911A1 .45. Armed but hardly ready, they entered the woods.

"If that's some sorta Kraut signal flare, lieutenant, then—"

"Yeah, I know. We could be looking at a paratroop regiment crawlin' up our butts in five minutes. Just keep your eyes peeled, Dave."

The night was particularly dark, only a few stars peeking out from behind the overcast and no visible moon at all. Goodman had his anglehead flashlight stuffed in his field jacket pocket, but wasn't about to turn it on and reveal his position, just in case there were Germans in the woods and one of them was looking for a target.

But when they reached the spot where they'd seen the flash of light, they found nothing. Goodman ordered Dave Spaulding, "You circle around to the right. I'll cut around left. Meet ya back here. Be careful."

"My middle name, lieutenant."

Goodman only nodded, but racked the slide of his .45 just in case.

After a solid, scary fifteen minutes stumbling on broken branches and sidestepping deadfalls in the darkness, Goodman and his sergeant returned to the road.

That was the first time Peter Goodman saw Eran.

Eran was striking, the green of her eyes visible despite the darkness, as if they shone with a light from within. Her hair—it was past waist length—was blacker than the night surrounding her. Her skin was perfect, almost luminescent. She was dressed rather oddly, Goodman thought at the time, her clothes looking more from some style of hundreds of years ago instead of 1944.

She was standing beside their Jeep, looking at it as if she'd never seen something with an internal combustion engine before.

"Parlez vous English, ma'amselle?" Dave Spaulding sang out.

She just looked back at them, saying nothing at all. Goodman tried a significant amount of his paltry French, asking her name, what she was doing on the road after dark, if she were in trouble. For several moments, she said absolutely nothing in response.

Goodman finally said, "Je ne comprens pas Francais tres bon," which he was sure that he hadn't said quite right. He followed that up with, "Do-you-speak-any-English?"

She was totally silent.

"I don't think this little cupcake speaks no English, lieutenant. And your French must be worse than we thought."

"She could have been injured during the Nazi occupation, maybe deaf or something. Maybe she's just afraid, Dave."

"She's a looker though, ain't she, sir?"

"Yeah, she's a looker." And he looked at her, asking one more time, "Do-you-speak-English?"

"Yes, I do. Who are you?"

Goodman was totally lost. "Look, lady, I gotta ask who *you* are! Who are you and what are you doing here?"

"My name is Eran, and I am looking at this." She gestured toward the Jeep.

"No, I mean, I can see that. How'd you get here?"

"I was looking for something. I think I found it."

The conversation went like that for some time, Peter Goodman unable to take his eyes off her, Eran looking prettier by the minute. But he got no information.

When pressed for a last name, Eran told him that it was "something-Mir" that he didn't quite catch, but he assumed was French.

"I'm First Lieutenant Peter Goodman, United States Army. This is Staff Sergeant Dave Spaulding."

"Pe'Ter. I like that name."

"Thank you."

Peter Goodman knew procedures, and he should have hunted down the Provost Marshall or found some MPs at least. She didn't have any ID, he assumed, and she didn't even offer an explanation for being on the road at night. Maybe her bicycle broke down or something. He didn't put her under arrest. He made her an offer, instead. "Need a ride to the village, miss?"

"I would like a ride to the village. Have you a horse nearby, Pe'Ter?"

Goodman laughed. "No, but the Jeep works fine. Get in."

Spaulding chuckled under his breath, "Pe'Ter! Well, la-de-da."

"See to that battery, sergeant."

"Yes, sir!"

Spaulding popped the hood, replaced the cable and they were on their way. It was a short drive to the village, but Goodman had time to ask, "What was that light out in the woods?"

"I saw it, too."

"How did you learn to speak English so well?"

"I was always very interested in translating things from one language into another."

"So, you're just good with languages, huh?"

"Yes, good with languages."

Goodman couldn't help asking the next question. "Can I see you later? I mean, I know we just met five minutes ago, but—"

"Where will you be later?"

"The inn down there in the village. Have a glass of wine with me, Eran?"

"Yes." When she smiled at Goodman, his heart melted. They dropped her near the village fountain and she disappeared into the shadows between two buildings and Goodman and Spaulding found a table at the inn.

Goodman's thoughts returned to the present. "You think she's coming?"

"She'll be here, lieutenant. Relax, already."

Peter Goodman looked down at his hands, his fingers beating a tattoo on the table top.

"Yo! Here she is, lieutenant! Snazzy!"

Peter Goodman nearly fell out of his chair. "Holy smoke!" There were maybe a dozen GIs at the inn that night and, if eyes could really pop out of their sockets, there would have been two dozen funny looking marbles rolling across the floor.

"I shoulda gone to Paris!"

"Down, boy. Down. Remember New Jersey."

Peter Goodman stood up and walked across the room, at least three other guys—two sergeants and a major—doing the same thing. But Eran walked right past everyone else and stopped just in front of Goodman. "Pe'Ter."

"Eran. You are beautiful."

"You are beautiful."

Goodman swallowed hard and licked his lips, which didn't help because his tongue was dry. "Uh, we've—we've got a table. It's over there." Goodman pointed toward the table with fingers which felt thick and stiff.

"Will your friend the sergeant be with us all night?"

"What?"

"I wasn't sure of the customs."

"What?"

"I want to be alone with you."

"You—all right." Goodman ushered her back to the table, made eye-contact with Dave Spaulding and announced, "You'll see to bringing that Jeep back for me sometime tomorrow then, sergeant. I'll be spending the— I'll stay in the village tonight."

Dave Spaulding's grin went from ear to ear. "Yes, sir! Very good, sir! With the lieutenant's permission, then, sir! I will take my leave, sir!"

"Very good, sergeant. That'll be all."

"Yes, sir!" Spaulding grabbed his steel pot off the table, put it on and saluted. Goodman returned the salute. As Spaulding walked past him, Goodman heard him mutter, "Lucky son-of-a-gun!"

"May I sit down, Pe'Ter?"

"Oh! Yeah!" Goodman stopped just standing beside the table and pulled out a chair for her, helped her into it, then sat down opposite her. He already had a glass for her and poured wine into it, nearly spilling the dark green bottle as he reached across the table.

Eran was dressed totally differently, in a white blouse kind of off one shoulder, a simple dark blue skirt and a shawl around her shoulders which partially covered her bare arms. "It's kind of chilly tonight. You must be warm-blooded," Goodman said lamely.

Eran smiled at him. "You are the man that I want. Can we drink wine later?"

Goodman didn't know what to say.

Eran spoke again. "Is there someplace that we can go?"

"Uh—"

"If that is what you want, of course, Pe'Ter."

Goodman blurted out, "Look, I think you're the

swellest looking girl I've ever seen in my life. But we just met."

"Then, let's drink wine first. And then can we go someplace to be together?"

Goodman heard himself saying, "Yes."

They each drank a glass of wine and Goodman left the table for a few moments, found the innkeeper and paid her twenty dollars US over the cost of a room and threw in two packs of American cigarettes.

When he went back to the table, a major was drifting toward it and Eran, but vectored off. "I got us a room."

"A room is what we need?"

"Yes. I mean, if you still want—"

"You are very sweet, Pe'Ter." Eran started to stand up and Peter Goodman got her chair, then ushered her from the table to the stairs just outside. "This way?"

"Yes, Eran."

Eran started up the stairs, Goodman right behind her. They had room number five. The lock worked— sort of—and they went inside, Goodman lighting the oil lamp beside the doorway before closing the door. Heavy bombardment drapes were hung over the window.

The bed looked clean. Peter Goodman looked around for a place to put his helmet, then started to unbuckle his pistol belt.

When Goodman turned to look at Eran, Eran stood naked before him, but there hadn't been time for her to undress. "How did you do that?"

"Magic," she smiled. . . .

Eran screamed, "Pe'Ter! More! More! Fill me!" Pe'Ter's body thrust against her, within her, then rested over her, still lying between her thighs, his heartbeat strong against her breast.

When his eyes met hers, they hardened and he pushed himself away. "You rotten—"

Eran laughed. "You gave me what I needed, Pe'Ter. Think of it this way: for a short while you were free of this place."

"Damn you!" Pe'Ter clambered out of the bed, staggered toward the window overlooking the courtyard below. He was staring at the shackles on his wrists. "How could you do that to me?"

"As you told me, Pe'Ter, there is only one thing which I need from you, and you just gave it to me. Admit it! You enjoyed it."

Pe'Ter, his voice controlled, even, said to her, "That's just the point, Eran. There's only one thing you need from me, but I actually loved you that night. And despite what you are, I still love you."

"Then why must you resist giving me what I need, Pe'Ter?"

"Loving you doesn't mean I condone what you do, Eran. When you came to me, a million guys just like me were fighting a lunatic, a goosestepping madman, a dictator who didn't care how many people he killed, who he stepped on. Like some cheap gangster, but with an army behind him. I don't know how long it's been, what's happened back there, but I know one thing. If we haven't knocked out the Axis by now, then we're still fighting. Americans, Englishmen, Canadians, Free French, Aussies, Norwegians. It doesn't matter. We're still fighting and we'll keep fighting. And you're just the same as Hitler. You want everybody to bow down before you and you don't care a hoot who you hurt or how many you kill. You don't care about love or honor or human decency. You just care about Eran, and all the power you can get your dirty hands on.

"But the people here are gonna stand up against you someday, too. Just a bunch of ordinary joes and janes, and they'll come after you and keep fighting you until you and all you stand for is nothing! Nothing, hear me!? Nothing!"

"Are you finished, Pe'Ter?"

"Why don't you kill me? Let's see some of that power you've got, Eran. Come on! You can do it. Let me have it. Kill me."

"Never. If it's true that you still love me, Pe'Ter, then I've found the perfect torture for you, haven't I? Killing you would be merciful, and I don't deal in mercy."

Pe'Ter turned his face away.

Eran felt the power surging within her as it had not for longer than she wanted to remember. And she began to laugh, just considering all of the truly marvelous possibilities. . . .

"I have spells for whatever phenomenon that you might wish," Swan told Al'An. Her eyes were not gazing at the man she loved, but at the disgusting stone creatures instead. "Whether it is heat or cold, couldn't we use such a spell directly on the Tree Demons?"

"I mean, I don't know for certain, Swan, but if these things are at all analogous to what are commonly called motion sensors, where I come from, then changing their temperature would create the opposite effect from what we want. We want those yucky-looking little guys to be unaffected by temperature.

"Now, if somehow they're able to see through those stone eyes, my plan won't work at all, regardless of heat or cold. But if they work like I hope that they do, we can fool them."

Swan, Al'An and the others stood within the passageway, well back from the sculptures. Bre'Gaa asked, "Do you believe that they will feel us as we cross before them rather than see us?"

"Eran needs something that can be relied upon as an intruder defense, but doesn't require constant monitoring," Al'An answered. "If it were visual, even with magic, the problem would be the same as where

I come from—either a human being somehow monitors what the statues see or there's some machine to do it. You guys don't use machines for most things, and I don't see one guy or a group of guys looking out for what the little stone creatures have passing in front of their eyes. If that were the case, Eran would be just as well off cutting the cutsey crap and having live human guards instead of stone Tree Demons.

"There's got to be some sort of trigger which awakens the creatures from the spell. Visual, maybe. But, like I said, very doubtful. Could be smell, but even in a technology based society, that would be quite complicated and not too reliable. Temperature is the best guess I can come up with," Al'An concluded.

"Then how shall we accomplish things in order to obfuscate the capability of the stone Tree Demons to sense temperature?" Erg'Ran asked.

"Where I come from, again, the normal human body temperature is ninety-eight point six degrees Fahrenheit."

"What?" Gar'Ath asked.

"How hot it is inside your body, or mine, or Mitan's or Swan's."

"Why would one care to know this, Champion?" Gar'Ath asked Al'An.

"For medical reasons," Al'An responded. "If the body is a little too hot or too cold, the body may sicken. Very hot or very cold and the body can die."

"I am familiar with this concept in the treatment of bodily ills, but we gauge the heat of the body differently. Be that as it may," Erg'Ran went on, "I take it that you intend to prevent the air which surrounds our bodies from radiating the heat of our bodies.

"Two ways of doing it," Al'An declared. "Whichever one is most handily accomplished magically would suffice."

"And, Al'An, what are these two ways?" Swan asked him.

"The first would be the more common technique, in my realm, at least. Each of us would need some kind of suit, a suit which completely covered the body from head to toe, and filtered our exhalations to cool them, either that or had its own self-contained breathing apparatus."

"What?" Gar'Ath asked.

"Like a container that you draw the air from when you breath and another container which would capture the air you breathe out. That air will be heated by our body temperatures," Al'An explained.

"The other method?" Swan persisted. She understood Al'An's words, and the basic idea behind them, but had no idea herself how she could magically fabricate what he described in such a manner that the suits would work. Swan hoped that his other alternative would be simpler.

"The other way," Al'An told them, but looking at her, "is to construct some sort of barrier which would seal around the stone Tree Demons, preventing them from sensing our body heat. It has to be a perfect seal, air tight. If they're not alive, at the moment, they're not breathing. If we seal them in something, we shouldn't trigger a response."

This latter alternative Swan easily comprehended; and, almost before Al'An stopped speaking, she was recalling the spells and formulating the technique by which she could transform Al'An's idea into reality.

Using the second sight, Mitan accurately gauged the dimensions of the stone Tree Demons. Garrison, familiar by now with spans, warblades and lancethrows as a system of measurement, learned a new term: thumbnail. The thumbnail was used analogously to the inch, although (judging by eye) a little less than three quarters of an inch in length. Each of the Tree

Demons measured twenty-three thumbnails in height and thirteen thumbnails around the slightly potbellied midsections. For the sake of his own sanity, Alan Garrison tried to think of the disgusting looking little things as approximately sixteen and one-half inches tall, as opposed to twenty-three thumbnails.

The dimensions determined, a by-now-familiar vortex appeared out of thin air and, spilling forth from within the vortex, as uniform in appearance as if rolling off an assembly line, were little coffin-shaped foot-and-one-half-long boxes, open on one side. They reminded Garrison of unnaturally dark green peanut shells, but split in half. Garrison touched one. It was neither hot nor cool, and felt unlike anything he had ever put his hands on. The material was similar to plastic—almost weightless, too—but somehow seemed organic. The darker green edges, where presumably the shells would contact the wall surface to which the Tree Demons were somehow affixed, were soft, pliable, conformed to Garrison's fingertip as he touched them. When he took his finger away, the edges returned to their original shape.

"I'd take off my hat to you, if I were wearing a hat," Garrison told Swan. "You are a genius, lovely lady. These edges are so that the little shells will exactly conform to the rough stone and give a perfect seal. Right? Marvelous!"

"Thank you, Al'An."

"How do we get them over the little Tree Demon guys and how do we make them stick?"

Swan smiled. "Do you recall, Al'An, what I did with your cigarette when you asked me concerning the formation of the twin moons?"

"Yes," Garrison told her, remembering quite clearly how she had transmuted his cigarette—curling smoke and all—into stone, levitated it, then encased it in more stone, then levitated it still higher. "You're going to levitate these into position."

"Yes. But I cannot form stone around the shells, as you call them, even at the edges, since such magic generates a modest amount of heat, and heat would defeat the purpose of our enterprise. So, I will hold them in position with magical energy while we pass, then release the shells, levitate them to the other side of the chamber and back into the vortex within which they were formed."

"You're good, Swan, really good," Garrison informed her, as if she didn't already know that. And, he was proud of her, like a father would thrill to the accomplishments of a child, or a husband would to the success of—Alan Garrison wanted Swan for his wife, very badly, he realized. If that meant never returning to his own world, so be it.

"How can we aid you, Enchantress?" Bre'Gaa inquired, interrupting Garrison's thoughts.

"Merely be ready to cross the chamber when the last of the shells is in position, and be vigilant lest my magic should somehow fail and we would be forced to fight these terrible creatures, Captain. I have never attempted an endeavor quite like this with my magic."

"So it shall be, Enchantress," Bre'Gaa declared.

There were fifty-six of the horrific enchanted beasts. Gar'Ath had warned Garrison only moments before Swan had made the shells materialize from the air, "Should the Tree Demons come alive, they will attack instantly, swarming. Fighting them with a sword is no good, nor with any blade, unless they are being held at bay. Once they are upon you, you must tear them from your flesh, throttling the life from their bodies with your hands, stomping them to death with your feet, ripping them limb from limb. Even if a sword could be employed without risk of the blade sundering your flesh from your bones, in quarters such as these through which we must pass, there would be too great a risk of your blade rending the flesh of one of your companions."

With Gar'Ath's vivid admonition still in mind, Alan Garrison hoped that Swan's plan would work and that her magic would not fail as she undertook what Garrison judged to be a "test flight" with one of the shells. The object moved slowly, easily upward, downward, side to side, then hovering. Garrison watched the concentration in Swan's eyes, etched across her face.

Gar'Ath and Mitan nocked arrows to their longbows. Bre'Gaa did the same. Garrison took the hint, drawing one of the SIG-Sauer .45s.

Garrison felt Erg'Ran's hand clasp to his shoulder. "It is wise to plan for any contingency," the older man whispered. "The Enchantress will be attempting a complexity of magical use unlike any which I have ever witnessed. You must, even as you plan for the possibility that she might not succeed, have faith that she will."

"I do," Garrison replied honestly.

"I am ready to begin," Swan announced.

Garrison looked at Swan and made his best encouraging smile. Swan smiled back, then all expression left her face and Garrison readied himself. The first of the shells took flight.

Garrison tracked the first shell over the sights of his pistol. As he did so, Garrison discovered something in Swan's character of which he had not been aware, but it endeared her to him even more. Rather than setting the first shell over the nearest of the stone Tree Demons, Swan tackled the farthest one first, so that each successive placement would be easier—even slightly—than the last.

The dark green shell glided onward, along the length of the chamber, the chamber walls farther and farther apart because of the wedge shape. At last, the shell stopped, hovered, then advanced on the stone Tree Demon, its leading edge angling upward until, mere "thumbnails" from the icon, the shell had completely reoriented from horizontal to vertical. Very slowly now, the shell moved forward, raising slightly, lowering slightly, then closing over the stone Tree Demon.

Garrison let out his breath.

"One down, fifty-five to go," Garrison rasped to Erg'Ran beside him. The next shell took flight in the same instant. . . .

"Fifty-five down, one to go," the Champion called out softly. Erg'Ran held his breath. All had gone perfectly, and that was why he felt nervous.

The last of the coverings sailed from where it hovered near the Enchantress and toward the closest of the ghastly figures. It uponded, then settled over the statue. "Now, Champion, we shall discover whether or not your supposition was the correct one."

"Thanks for reminding me, Erg'Ran." The Champion shifted the firespitter which had been in his right hand to his left hand, with his right hand drawing his sword. "We ready?"

"I will be last," Bre'Gaa announced.

"And I with him," Erg'Ran added.

Gar'Ath and Mitan stepped from the passageway and into the chamber, nearly—but not quite—standing in front of the first of the stone Tree Demons. Mitan started to move, and Gar'Ath placed a hand on her arm. "Lest the Tree Demons should come to life, stay behind me."

"Yes, Gar'Ath," Mitan answered softly.

Gar'Ath took one step, then another, ignoring his own advice, his sword at the ready.

The young swordsman stood before the first icon, stared at the shell covering. Nothing happened. He flashed his left hand back and forth in front of it. Nothing happened.

Mitan walked up to Gar'Ath and kissed him. They started forward once again, walking quickly.

"Champion! You will escort the Enchantress?"
Erg'Ran suggested.

"I'm on it," the Champion responded, going to stand
beside the Enchantress. Very slowly, her countenance
still expressionless, the Enchantress began to walk out
of the passageway and into the chamber.

Erg'Ran lifted his axe from the ring at his belt.
"Ready, Captain Bre'Gaa?"

"Indeed, my learned ally."

Side by side, Erg'Ran and Bre'Gaa left the passageway and entered the wedge-shaped chamber, Bre'Gaa's
arrow quivered, his bow in his left hand, his great sword
in his right. To a Gle'Ur'Gya, such a sword was not a
great sword, Erg'Ran reflected, smiling at the thought,
but merely a conventionally sized broadsword.

Into the chamber, they passed the first of the icons,
then the next and the next. The concentration necessary in order to keep in place the fifty-six shells, as the
Champion referred to them, was beyond anything
Erg'Ran would have considered magically possible for
anyone—except his niece.

The magical ability grew within Swan, deepened
and broadened to a level surpassing anything which
Erg'Ran had considered even conceivable without that
special power of which he was certain Eran periodically availed herself. Could Eran still rely on it,
however? Erg'Ran wondered.

The Enchantress, her Champion and lover beside
her, was at the midway point within the chamber. The
Champion's firespitter was still in one hand, sword in
the other. Erg'Ran caught a glimpse of the Enchantress's face. As before, her countenance bore no expression, but there was a barely discernible twitch near her
right eye. "Hasten, Bre'Gaa!" Erg'Ran urged. In as
loud a whisper as he dared, he called out to Gar'Ath
and Mitan, "Be quick, young warriors! Be quick! Then
be ready!"

There was a story known throughout Creath,

apocryphal almost certainly, of a young K'Ur'Mir lass who held back a torrent of water with but a finger. She lived in a humble coastal village, so the tale was told. A wall was erected generations before her time in order to hold back the high tides which periodically arose when the twin moons crossed. Unbeknownst to the people of her village, the wall had developed a crack. The young lass spied the antique wall's imperfection even as water began spilling through it. Unchecked, the water would widen the fissure and demolish the wall and let the tide wash across the village beyond. The lass stuck one finger into the breach, the lad with whom she had been playing going for help. Had she removed her finger from the chink in the wall, all beyond would have been destroyed.

The concentration evident in Swan's dear face could not help but remind Erg'Ran of the young maid in the old story. Only Swan's mind held back destruction.

Gar'Ath and Mitan reached the far side of the chamber, by the tall arched opening. Mitan would be second-sighting beyond it, looking for any evidence of more dangers. Gar'Ath had already sheathed his sword and readied his longbow.

Erg'Ran licked his lips.

"I don't like this, learned ally," Captain Bre'Gaa hissed through clenched teeth. "If your Enchantress's concentration slips—"

"It won't." Erg'Ran cut him off. "We will pass them, so that once we are clear of this place, the Enchantress will have none to concern her save for herself and the Champion."

"Aye, Erg'Ran."

In the next few strides Erg'Ran and Bre'Gaa overtook and passed the Enchantress and her Champion, neared the archway on the chamber's far side. Erg'Ran's eyes alternated their gaze between the

Enchantress's face and the green shells which covered
the stone Tree Demons. The twitch near Swan's eye
evidenced itself once more and Erg'Ran's eyes flickered toward the chamber wall. Two of the shells moved
almost imperceptibly.

Erg'Ran quickened his pace, nearly running,
Bre'Gaa striding beside him.

They reached the tall archway. "Now, this is a
proper height through which a Gle'Ur'Gya can pass
without hunching his shoulders!"

"I'm happy for you, Captain Bre'Gaa," Erg'Ran
replied dismissively, his eyes on the Enchantress.

"Do you think the Enchantress'll make it, old
friend?" Gar'Ath whispered hoarsely.

"Aye, lad. But be vigilant nonetheless."

The Enchantress and her Champion were nearly
to the archway. Just a few more paces remained. If
one shell fell away, her spell would collapse and all
of the shells would drop off. The vile little carnivores
would swarm over anyone in their path. The six of
their little band would be powerless against fifty-six
of the Tree Demons, nor would there be time for any
magic to be used against the creatures.

The Enchantress took another step, swayed slightly.
The Champion tucked the firespitter from his left
hand into his belt, his left hand moving to support
the Enchantress at her waist.

Erg'Ran was about to speak as Mitan whispered
in his ear, "There is someone coming, Erg'Ran."

"G'urg," Erg'Ran muttered under his breath, turning
away from the interior of the chamber and looking into
the passageway beyond. There were two Ra'U'Ba just
entered into the passageway. He second-sighted quickly
on the figures, neither helmeted—which meant that
they could be killed—and neither carried the characteristically enormous shield. Both wore skirts that were
an incongruous blend of sickly green, faded red and
washed out grey, combining to compose an entirely

alien color which was disgusting looking in the extreme. Both had full weaponry. Ra'U'Ba always looked odd, but these two moved more oddly than Erg'Ran considered normal even for Ra'U'Ba.

"They are drunk, I think!" Mitan exclaimed in a soft whisper beside Erg'Ran's ear.

"I think you are right, pretty one." As if to confirm the analysis of their behavior, one of the two promptly fell down, his enormous tail slapping into the wall. The other laughed. "Hide," Erg'Ran ordered.

There was no reason to suppose that an inebriated Ra'U'Ba would be less capable of communicating his thoughts over great distances to his fellows than a sober one. The Ra'U'Ba had to be killed before they noticed that they were not alone and could reveal the information to other Ra'U'Ba within the keep. It was, at least, clear that the two Ra'U'Ba were not alert to the fact that they were being watched, because Erg'Ran still second-sighted them and the Ra'U'Ba had the peculiar proclivity for blocking the second sight. Erg'Ran had never quite understood how this could be possible, but it was fact, nonetheless.

"We can't stay here forever, old friend," Gar'Ath whispered, stating the obvious.

"Aye, lad, I'm thinking." Erg'Ran glanced over his shoulder. The Enchantress and her Champion were nearly through the chamber. In only a few eyeblinks, the Enchantress would be able to release the spell which so visibly exhausted her, but could not as long as it was necessary to hide on the chamber side of the archway from detection by the Ra'U'Ba. "Ra'U'Ba disgust me, and always have," Bre'Gaa announced.

"We are in perfect agreement, Captain Bre'Gaa. At the moment, however, the issue is to contrive a manner in which the two Ra'U'Ba in question can be killed extraordinarily quickly, before they would be able to communicate our presence here to their fellows."

"The exposed portion of the brain, where it looks like a third eye," Bre'Gaa suggested. "That nauseating-looking yellow protuberance is an excellent target. An arrow might—"

"It will have to be an arrow," Gar'Ath interrupted. "The distance is too great to hurl a dagger with certainty."

"I don't like it, but we have no alternative but to try," Erg'Ran acquiesced.

"What's goin' on?" It was the voice of the Champion.

"Ra'U'Ba. I believe you encountered other specimens in company with Gar'Ath behind the Falls of Mir, Champion. These seem to have partaken a bit too much of intoxicants."

"What are we going to do, Erg'Ran? Swan can't hold the spell much longer without passing out, and then it breaks anyway, right?"

"You're correct in your assumptions, Champion. We are going to endeavor to kill these Ra'U'Ba very shortly. Do your best with the Enchantress."

"I will," the Champion told him.

Mitan, Gar'Ath and Bre'Gaa had their longbows ready, arrows nocked. "Give the word, old friend," Gar'Ath said.

Erg'Ran was about to speak, but as he looked at the Ra'U'Ba, the one who had fallen down a moment earlier howled with laughter and flung something from his six-fingered right hand.

"Fire!" Erg'Ran commanded, hoping that it was not too late. In their drunken condition, perhaps they had not already communicated their discovery.

Mitan's and Gar'Ath's bows were already drawn, their arrows flying to target in the eyeblink after Erg'Ran spoke, but Bre'Gaa's bow string had not been taut. Bre'Gaa drew, but in the eyeblink that he released, a Ra'U'Ba star dagger struck the Gle'Ur'Gya Captain's bow. Bre'Gaa's arrow loosed, but upward, striking the archway, ricocheting off the rounded surface of the stone and flying wildly back into the chamber.

Bre'Gaa cursed, nocked a fresh arrow.

Erg'Ran's eyes flickered toward the two drunken Ra'U'Ba. Arrows were buried half to the fletching in their yellow brain protuberances, their bodies falling dead to the stone floor of the passageway.

Behind Erg'Ran, there was the shriek of a Tree Demon.

Erg'Ran wheeled toward the sound, nearly falling on his peg leg.

An arrow—from Bre'Gaa's bow—whizzed past Erg'Ran's face and impaled the body of the Tree Demon, killing it in an eyeblink. One arrow would not be enough. The shielding green shells were falling away from the remaining fifty-five Tree Demons, the Enchantress was on the chamber floor with the strayed arrow piercing her left hand and the Champion was reaching down to her.

Too many things happened all at once for Erg'Ran to calculate the next logical move. The Champion swept the Enchantress up into his arms. The Tree Demons—one after another—streaked from their positions on the wall and toward human flesh. Gar'Ath lunged past Erg'Ran, snatching the axe from Erg'Ran's belt as he went.

A Tree Demon jumped for Swan's throat and the Champion skewered it on his sword. Gar'Ath swung the expropriated axe, killing two Tree Demons in midair.

Another arrow took flight from Bre'Gaa's bow, another Tree Demon down.

Mitan, who had never developed her innate magical abilities, shrieked what Erg'Ran recognized as a shielding spell. "Good idea!" Erg'Ran called out to her, taking up the incantation in the next eyeblink. As the Champion, with Erg'Ran's niece in his arms, vaulted from the chamber, the air between the archway and the rest of the chamber began to shimmer.

"Out of there, young swordsman!" Bre'Gaa shouted to Gar'Ath as Gar'Ath accounted for three more of the Tree Demons with the axe, then turned to run. Three Tree Demons fell upon him, one at his neck, two at his stockinged legs. Gar'Ath stumbled, fell, a dozen more of the Tree Demons swarming over him.

Erg'Ran heard the Champion shouting, "Take her, Bre'Gaa, and guard her with your life!" As Erg'Ran turned to look, the Champion rested his Golden Shield of IBF against the archway and raced past him, staggering as he passed through the still and too slowly forming shield of magical energy. A Tree Demon jumped for the Champion's right cheek, the Champion's left hand grasping the creature, flinging it with terrible force against the wall from which it had sprung.

The Champion skidded to his knees beside Gar'Ath, whose hands tearing at the Tree Demons as they tried to devour him alive. A Tree Demon attached itself to the Champion's neck. The Champion either didn't feel it or ignored it. A very tiny firespitter, its gleaming steel polished like that of a swordblade, emerged from his right pocket. The Champion put the firespitter flush against a Tree Demon which had begun to gnaw on Gar'Ath's right thigh. There was a terrible noise, and the Tree Demon disintegrated, its blood and gore sprayed across Gar'Ath's lower body.

"Get the Enchantress out of here, Bre'Gaa! Hurry!" Erg'Ran commanded. The shielding spell was not building fast enough, his magic and even that of Mitan, a female K'Ur'Mir, too meager in power. The far stronger, extraordinarily complex magic which had enchanted and still sustained the Tree Demons could only have been directly combated by magic which was its equal, such as the Enchantress possessed. And she could not aid them.

The Champion's tiny firespitter spoke again, another of the Tree Demons exploding.

That firespitter was so much smaller than the other firespitters. "Of course!" Erg'Ran shouted. "Smaller was better in this situation," Erg'Ran announced to anyone listening. "And, sometimes simpler is better, too." Erg'Ran called to Mitan, urging her, "Forsake the shielding spell! You can levitate; I've seen you do it. My cloak! Levitate my cloak!" Erg'Ran snatched the cloak from his shoulders and hurtled it into the chamber, then employed one of the most basic of all spells . . . to make fire. The cloak was ablaze as Mitan began the levitation. "Now, propel my burning cloak toward the Tree Demons and burn them to death!"

Gar'Ath was to his knees, tearing Tree Demons from his body, his face and legs and hands covered in bleeding bites. The Champion, his exposed skin having suffered much the same abuse, flung a Tree Demon from his face, then killed it with another blast from the tiny firespitter. There was one of the Champion's odd knives in his other hand, and he hacked through the air with it, missing one Tree Demon and slicing the arm off another. Five Tree Demons, slavering jaws snapping, attacked the Champion's head. The Champion cried out in pain, but did not surrender.

Drawing his father's sword from its scabbard, Erg'Ran hobbled into the chamber, to aid the Champion and Gar'Ath. The burning cloak sailed about the chamber, trapping Tree Demons within its folds, setting them afire. The vile things, skin in flames, ran wildly about, hurtling themselves into the air, smashing against the chamber walls, rolling about on the chamber floor. The Tree Demons' howls of pain echoed off the stone, pulsed within Erg'Ran's ears.

If the burning cloak could combat and kill the rest of the Tree Demons, there were still more than half a score of Tree Demons attacking the Champion and Gar'Ath. These could not be dealt with by means of magic.

Erg'Ran's father's sword was unlike any which he had ever seen in all of Creath. And, its single edge could be to be sharpened more finely than any steel even Gar'Ath could fashion.

Erg'Ran grabbed with his left hand at a Tree Demon which gnawed at the nape of the Champion's neck, tore it free and flung it into the air. Erg'Ran's father's sword was already in motion as his left hand closed behind his right on its hilt. The Tree Demon was still in the air as steel met foul flesh and cleaved that flesh in twain.

Gar'Ath was to his feet, axe in hand. Wrestling a Tree Demon from his left cheek, Gar'Ath hurtled it into the burning cloak, the tiny beast's skin ablaze in an eyeblink. As the Champion tore a Tree Demon from his neck, Gar'Ath's borrowed axe cleaved through it, burying its edge into the stone wall.

A Tree Demon jumped for Erg'Ran's face, and in his terror in the instant that the creature's teeth clamped to his cheek, Erg'Ran nearly hacked at it with the sword. Had he done so, he would surely have sliced off half his face. Another Tree Demon bit into Erg'Ran's left hand. Erg'Ran smashed his left hand toward the wall, crushing the Tree Demon's skull, leaving his bleeding left hand free to claw at the Tree Demon on his face.

The thing was coming for his eye. Erg'Ran could see its yellow-brown eyes, feel its exhalations against his skin. Bile rose from Erg'Ran's stomach and into his throat. In the instant that the Tree Demon's humanlike hands grasped for his nose and left ear and its teeth let loose from his cheek to clamp into his eye, Erg'Ran jerked at the creature, tearing away his own flesh as he freed its claws. The creature fell to the floor. Erg'Ran staggered with pain, and in that eyeblink, his peg leg lost traction in a puddle of blood and slipped from beneath him.

As Erg'Ran fell, the Tree Demon lunged toward

him again. There was the earsplitting crack that was
the thunder made by the Champion's tiny firespitter.
The Tree Demon burst into a puddle of blood and
gore.

Erg'Ran tried to stand up.

Gar'Ath, a Tree Demon on his neck, wrenched free
his axe, pulled the Tree Demon free and flung it
against the wall. With the flat of the axe, Gar'Ath
smashed at the vile creature, crushing it.

The Champion, his face all but obscured by bleeding wounds, tore a Tree Demon from his left hand,
threw it to the floor and stomped it beneath his boot.

Gar'Ath had the last of them in both hands, its
arms outstretched, legs gyrating wildly. "Die, you little
piece of g'urg!" With that utterance, Gar'Ath snapped
his own arms outward and tore the Tree Demon's
arms from their sockets. The beast fell to the floor,
writhing in pain not unlike that which it inflicted upon
its victims. Blood spurted from the arm sockets, slick-
ing the floor. And the Tree Demon died.

Erg'Ran said two things. "One of you help me up.
We'll have Sword of Koth swarming over us next."

"Aye, old friend!" Gar'Ath held out a blood covered hand and so did the Champion.

Erg'Ran took both offered hands, then said, "One
of you, my father's sword, please. There, on the floor."

There was no more use for the burning cloak with
the Tree Demons all accounted for. Mitan ran from
the archway, then drew Gar'Ath into her arms, his
blood smearing her skin. . . .


Swan, her magic all but depleted, told Bre'Gaa,
"Break the arrow, Captain, so that you may pull it
from my hand."

"I will never forgive myself, Enchantress."

"It was not your fault. Break the arrow. We must
hurry, I fear."

Bre'Gaa snapped the arrow's shaft, and Swan

winced but did not cry out. She nodded her head and
Bre'Gaa placed one enormous hand over her wrist,
so that she could not move her hand. He told her,
"You are brave, Enchantress. There is a little of the
Gle'Ur'Gya in you." He smiled, then wrenched the
shaft from her flesh.

Swan sucked in her breath, so quickly, so strongly
that it sounded like a scream, but she assured Bre'Gaa,
"That was not a scream, Captain. It only sounded like
one."

"I never assumed otherwise, Enchantress. You are
bleeding, of course."

"That will stop—now." Swan willed the bleeding
to cease and for the wound to begin to heal. Her
hand still pained her, but that would pass shortly. "We
must aid the others." Already, there was a warm,
itching sensation in her hand and the broken skin was
starting to scab over and close. Swan began to get
to her feet, Bre'Gaa assisting her.

Swan was going to tell him that he should run back
and that she would follow, but as she looked along the
passageway, she saw Mitan, an arrow nocked to her
bow, and, behind Mitan, Al'An, Erg'Ran and Gar'Ath.
The three males moved as though gravely injured.
Mitan was covered in blood. Quickly second-sighting
her, Swan detected no evidence of wounds, but second-
sighting the others revealed just the opposite.

"Help me, Captain. I am weak, still, but I must
see to their healing."

"Your will is my command, Enchantress," Bre'Gaa
whispered. . . .

There had been the sounds of pistol shots within
the keep. Swan and her other realm man were within
the keep. And Eran knew why.

That first night when she took Pe'Ter Goo'D'Man
into her, Eran realized that the tablet which she was
directed to by the monolith had spoken truly to her.

All of the power in the universe would, one day, be hers alone.

Eran stared from the windswept parapet, beyond the stone walls and across Barad'Il'Koth. Second-sighting, she could see Woroc'Il'Lod, white caps rising at the command of the currents of frigid air. She threw back her cloak. With a toss of her head, its hood fell away and the cold embraced her naked body and the wind from the icy sea toyed with her hair.

She felt beyond wonderful.

It was clear to Eran, as she considered the current state of affairs, that the naval maneuvers along her coast were something with which she could easily deal when she felt that the time was right. They required no urgent action. After she had dealt with her daughter, the other realm man, and her brother, she could afford to waste magical power and summon, once more, the Mist of Oblivion. Watching it devour the ships and the arrogant fools aboard them would be a delight.

It was also clear to Eran that a trip to the other realm would soon be required. Pe'Ter was becoming more and more difficult and she tired of the memories she had to re-create for him. When Swan was gone and Pe'Ter was gone, it would be the end of a chapter in her life and she could move on.

And little time remained until Swan's end.

Moc'Dar whined, and Eran gazed down at him. He cowered beneath his too-small cloak, his twisted body within its repulsively splotchy skin curled into a ball near her feet. He wanted to lick her boots, which made him feel secure. Because of that, she rarely relented to his simpering urgings. The time was, Eran mused, when Moc'Dar's mind would have been engaged in more interesting pursuits. He'd been very handsome and clearly wanted her. Naked save for her open cloak and riding boots, gazing at her would have set his blood racing; hers, too.

Instead, Moc'Dar, the once magnificent and courageous Captain of the Sword of Koth, was something
totally different than anything else alive, a freak of
her own design.

Eran had changed many males—sexual partners
with whom she had become dissatisfied—into beasts,
broken them with the whip to the saddle and the bit.
She had ridden them over the hills and plains of
Creath until they no longer pleased her, personally
gelded them and left them with their still human
minds to sink deeper and deeper into total madness.
Eventually, they would die.

But, somehow, as she looked at Moc'Dar, Eran
regretted what she had done. She could use Moc'Dar
as he had once been.

"You pitiful thing. Get to your knees. Now!"
Moc'Dar, his disgusting body trembling, groveled
before her. "I gave you a command!"

Shaking as would a leaf in the wind which caressed
her skin, Moc'Dar rose clumsily to his knees.

"Raise your eyes so that I may look into them."

Hesitantly, obviously terrified, Moc'Dar obeyed.

"My power is without limit, Moc'Dar. Soon, my
power will be all of the power in the universe. The
punishment I made for you has sufficiently terrified
my other officers. Perhaps, I can further instill fear
and wonderment by demonstrating that I do not only
punish with the greatest severity, but likewise show
the greatest munificence." With those words passed
from her lips, Eran took a step closer to him, drew
her cloak forward in her fingertips and swathed its
folds around Moc'Dar.

As she did so, her flesh touched his.

"I return to you your former shape and strength
and visage, the power of speech and rational thought,
the courage with which you were once imbued. I
return to you all that you once were, Moc'Dar."

Eran opened her cloak, flinging it back. Naked

before her knelt Moc'Dar the man. "Speak, Moc'Dar, but choose your words wisely."

"Queen Sorceress, Mistress General, I am yours to command."

Eran smiled. Moc'Dar had always had a way with words. "You will uniform yourself at once; I will facilitate that." With a thought and a wave of her right hand, Moc'Dar was dressed as a Captain, his black leather mask totally obscuring his face except for his eyes and mouth and the holes for his nostrils. With her left hand, she made fine weapons—firesword, dagger, crossbow and quiver of bolts—appear.

"You will lead the Sword of Koth to the chamber where I keep Pe'Ter. You will find my daughter and perhaps several others there, or they will have just departed. If they have departed, you will pursue them. You will find them. You will kill all who may be accompanying my daughter except for the old fool Erg'Ran and another whom you will recognize because he is not of Creath. You will bring Erg'Ran, the other realm male and my daughter to me, if at all possible. I wish to deal with them personally. However, should you find my daughter in the embrace of the other realm male, you are to kill them both by whatever means necessary and as quickly as possible. Do not indulge yourself and risk my wrath.

"If my daughter attempts to use magic against you and no other viable alternative presents itself in order that you may serve my will, even if she is not with the other realm male, you must somehow kill her. I cannot overemphasize the importance of your understanding this quite clearly, Moc'Dar. As much as I wish the pleasure of my daughter's destruction for myself, at any cost Swan must be prevented from accomplishing her purposes.

"Six of my most gifted Handmaidens will accompany you and your men. The entire Sword of Koth and, indeed, the Horde in all its numbers will be at your disposal for the sake of this mission's successful resolution. If you fail, your only recourse will be to take your own life. What I did to you the last time would be merciful by comparison to the punishment I should mete out if you fail me again."

Moc'Dar said nothing, merely lowered his eyes.

Eran made her spell bag appear from the air around her, and from within it drew the pistol which Pe'Ter had carried before she had brought him to Creath. Moc'Dar visibly recoiled just seeing it.

Eran spoke in the Old Tongue, a summoning to alter the universal bonds within the natural elements which burned and caused the projectile to spew forth toward its target. She looked at Moc'Dar and told him, "That which was consumed in flame behind the projectiles within this firespitter and all others in Creath will burn no longer. No firespitter in Creath will function. If a firespitter is pointed at you, Moc'Dar?"

"Yes, Mistress General?"

"Laugh."

Eran saw a gleam in Moc'Dar's eyes. . . .

Garrison's face and hands itched, as did his neck, The dozens of bites he'd received and the gouges where chunks of flesh were torn from his body were healing so rapidly that the process was almost beyond his powers of belief.

Swan walked beside him through the upsloping passageway, seeming not only depleted in magical energy but so exhausted that she could barely move. Likely, Swan still possessed adequate magic to heal wounds, or for something as silly as lighting his cigarette were there time to smoke one, but the more spectacular magic which might be required to get them out of a tight spot would not be available for some time. Somehow, the only word that Alan Garrison knew in the language spoken by Swan's people was perfectly appropriate: g'urg.

Nagging at the back of his mind was the unpleasant thought that, if they survived, getting out of Barad'Il'Koth would be a lot tougher than getting in. And he was worried that his pistol shots with the Seecamp had not attracted any response. The keep was a very large structure indeed, but hardly so enormous that the reports from the .32 hadn't been heard by somebody. The two drunken Ra'U'Ba whom Mitan and Gar'Ath had killed quite possibly had the time to communicate telepathically with other Ra'U'Ba.

One way or the other, Garrison was certain that their presence in the keep was known, and that a trap would be awaiting them.

As they neared the end of the passageway and were about to reconnoiter the area beyond, he heard the sound of running feet behind them. Mitan spun around, drawing back her bow. "I can't see anyone yet!"

Bre'Gaa, brandishing his sword, declared, "I'll look ahead," then ran toward the end of the passageway.

Garrison drew both SIG .45s.

In the next instant, Garrison spied two black-uniformed soldiers, then two more, then more and more, coming into view round the nearest bend in the passageway, less than a hundred yards behind them.

"Ordinary Horde of Koth," Erg'Ran labeled them. "They'll kill us just as dead as their elite brethren in the Sword of Koth. Come on!"

Somehow, the immediate danger seemed to reinvigorate Swan. When she broke into a dead run toward the end of the passage, it was as if the exhaustion which she had evidenced only moments earlier had completely fled. Garrison hung back in order to support Mitan as Mitan loosed an arrow, dropping one of the Horde of Koth troopers with a solid hit to the chest. Mitan was already nocking another arrow, a third arrow clenched in her teeth.

Garrison stabbed both pistols toward the still charging enemy and fired—or, tried to. The hammers rose and fell, but neither pistol discharged a round. "Aw, shit!" Accepted procedures for hangfires not withstanding, Garrison thrust one pistol into his belt, freeing his left hand to rack the slide of the pistol in his right. A fresh round chambered, Garrison touched the trigger. "Shit!"

Mitan loosed another arrow. A third soldier went down.

Garrison told himself that maybe the only ammunition which had been magically rendered useless was the ammunition Swan had produced for him magically in the first place. Garrison pulled the .32 from its Pocket Natural holster. Pointing the little pistol in the direction of the enemy, he pulled the trigger. There was no sound except for a loud click.

"Shit! Shit! All right! Run for it, Mitan!" Garrison grabbed Mitan's shoulder the instant an arrow flew from her bow. "Come on!"

Mitan took his advice, sprinting toward the end of the passageway, Garrison at her heels, holstering his now useless ordnance as he ran.

Bre'Gaa was shouting, "A high-ceilinged chamber and a staircase beyond. A small force of Horde of Koth is coming down the staircase."

Swan had stopped beside Bre'Gaa and Gar'Ath at the end of the passageway. Erg'Ran told her, "I'll stay behind and hold off the Horde behind us. I'm too slow afoot with this cursed peg leg."

"Yeah, and you'd die, too," Garrison told him. "We all go or we all stay, right?"

Everyone nodded or grunted agreement. Swan said, "I would never leave you to die. You were always my dearest friend, and you are my uncle. Without your wise counsel, if we were to succeed, we would still fail."

Was long-windedness in times of emergency a

family trait? Garrison wondered. Swan was beautiful, intelligent, compassionate, forthright, courageous and loving. "So, who's perfect?" Alan Garrison almost said aloud. Instead, he urged, "Can we get going here?"

"To the staircase!" Swan commanded.

Mitan hung back with Erg'Ran, Garrison handing off his Golden Shield of IBF to the older man. "Carry this for me, please, for a while? I never learned how to fight using a shield and it might come in handy for you."

Erg'Ran started to reply, but Garrison had no time to listen. Swan charged toward the staircase, sword in hand, a cry on her lips. "Death to the Horde!"

Garrison was right beside her, his sword drawn, Gar'Ath and Bre'Gaa outdistancing them, reaching the base of the staircase, then running up.

Garrison paused for an eyeblink. Swords flashed, steel clanged. This was just like something out of a movie. If he'd squeezed his eyes tightly, Garrison could have almost convinced himself that Errol Flynn and Basil Rathbone were battling to the death, with cold steel in the brisket as the price of defeat.

Without realizing it, Garrison was in motion, running up the stairs, Swan beside him, sword arcing over his head as he shouted, "Death to the Horde!"

In the next eyeblink, Garrison was locked in mortal combat with two black-uniformed ugly guys with mean faces and big swords. The one to Garrison's left—tall, broad in the chest—brought his blade around in a sweeping arc on level with Garrison's throat. Garrison ducked, backstepped and nearly fell down the stairs. But the blade missed him.

The Horde of Koth soldier to Garrison's right—shorter and wiry seeming—lunged with his sword.

Despite the fact that Garrison had little experience with a blade actually in his hand, he had a considerable reading knowledge of swords, sufficient for him to realize that the Horde of Koth issue sword was not designed for cut and thrust, but for cutting alone. The curve of the blade made accurate thrusting difficult for all but the most gifted of swordsmen, and only as a setup where the opponent was enticed into an open position. Garrison's sword, on the other hand, was made for both cutting and thrusting.

Alan Garrison thrust with his sword as he dodged the thrust aimed against him. The tip of Garrison's blade glanced off a link of mail.

"Try again," Garrison encouraged himself. Side-stepping along the stair tread, Garrison thrust for his opponent's hip, where there was no armor. Garrison missed the hip, but stabbed through the left cheek of his opponent's rear end.

There was a terrible cry of pain. The shorter Horde of Koth trooper fell forward and slid down the stairs, leaving a trail of blood in his wake.

The other of the two, the tall one who had first attacked him, came at Garrison again. With his sword in both hands, the enemy soldier ran down the stairs at a diagonal, blade smashing downward as he charged.

Garrison remembered something that Gar'Ath had taught him. hilt clenched in both hands, Garrison brought his sword back over his left shoulder, stepping rearward with his right foot and flexing his outstretched left leg at the precise moment that his opponent's blade crashed downward. Parrying the edge of the tall soldier's blade with the flat of his own, Garrison took another step forward, letting his opponent overextend his balance as their blades slipped apart. It wasn't the right procedure, Garrison knew, but as he moved he pulled his blade across his opponent's right thigh in a deep drawcut.

The tall soldier staggered. Garrison flicked his blade up, cleaving counterclockwise with it toward the man's neck, drawing back on the blade as it struck flesh. Garrison opened the Horde of Koth trooper's throat from earlobe to adam's apple. Blood sprayed everywhere.

Bre'Gaa was hurriedly scrounging arrows and cross-bow bolts from the dead on the stairs. Mitan was firing her longbow, Erg'Ran his crossbow. Their arrows and bolts only ephemerally stemmed the tide of Horde of Koth troops surging in the passageway. But Alan Garrison allowed himself one instant.

He looked at his sword.

Garrison took no pride in the blood which stained its blade, but rather in its strength and that he had used it to fight for his convictions against that which he perceived as evil. What Garrison felt was that link between a man or woman and a weapon, so often misconstrued by the misinformed as bloodlust, which was, in reality, a part of the very essence of being human, inextricably interwoven with honor, pride and the will to persevere.

Swan, her sword bloodied as well, leaned against the staircase wall. "We'll need to hold them back while Erg'Ran and one or two others with a bow reach the height of the staircase."

"I know," Garrison agreed.

"We have to get the Enchantress out of reach of the Horde if she's to have any hope of finding out whether her father lives or not," Gar'Ath announced, his breathing still coming hard.

Garrison suggested, "Why don't you and Erg'Ran take the stairs along with Swan, Gar'Ath. We can alternate fire and maneuver elements." He'd originally heard the terms in a war movie, then looked them up. "You guys go up and cover us as we move to your position. We leapfrog it."

Swan asked, "What about frogs?"

"It means when one group moves, the other stays put, and so on. That way, we've always got some protection with your bows, Erg'Ran won't have to run for it any faster than he can manage, and Bre'Gaa and Mitan can cover you with their bows while you guys move up. If you bump into troops as you progress along the stairs, Gar'Ath, then you and Swan can brace them with your swords while Erg'Ran can still provide some cover for us. Sounds like a plan, huh?"

"Aye, Champion. It does, indeed."

"These arrows are shorter than my own," Mitan said, having just reached the stairs and taking well over a dozen arrows from Bre'Gaa's hands. "They'll be a little less powerful on target."

"Like .38s out of a .357 Mag," Garrison observed. When Bre'Gaa, Swan, and Mitan all looked at him oddly, Garrison just said, "Never mind, guys. I'll explain it to you later."

"Good fletching," Mitan said to no one in particular.

Garrison asked, "Good what-ing?"

"Never mind," Mitan smiled wickedly. "I'll explain it to you later."

Bre'Gaa launched an arrow, then another and still another toward the mouth of the passageway. "We should be on our way," he announced.

"Bre'Gaa. Mitan. You guys are with me," Garrison informed them. "We hold back the bad guys."

"Come, Erg'Ran," Swan urged. Gar'Ath was already taking the stairs three at a time in a run. "Be careful, Al'An—all of you!" Swan called after her.

Bre'Gaa handed out more arrows to Mitan, both of them nocking arrows to their bows and waiting for the next Horde of Koth target to show itself coming out of the passageway. Garrison picked up one of the swords lying on the stairs. The Horde of Koth swords were heavy, almost the heft of a Civil War cavalry saber. "Do these guys fight a lot from horseback, Mitan?"

"Yes. Why do you ask?"

"Their tactics, hanging back like that, waiting to

charge in a group. And the heavy swords they carry. It all smacks of cavalry."

Garrison looked up the stairs, actually taking note of them for the first time. The staircase extended straight upward to an almost dizzying height, matching the elevation of the chamber. There was, presumably, a landing or some corridor or another, leading to more stairs. Swan, Erg'Ran and Gar'Ath were almost in position to provide covering fire for Garrison, Mitan and Bre'Gaa.

"Mitan?"

"Yes, Champion?"

"Why don't you run up about halfway along the height of the staircase and you can help to keep us covered. As soon as you're in position, give us a shout and Bre'Gaa and I'll start up."

"I will, Champion, but first a short volley, I think."

"Good idea." Garrison, a sword in each hand, waited while Bre'Gaa and Mitan each fired two arrows, just as reminders to the Horde troopers in the passageway that if they stuck out a head, they'd wind up dead.

As the second arrow left Mitan's bow, she turned and raced up the stairs. "A pretty one, that," Bre'Gaa offered.

"She is indeed," Garrison answered. "Nice girl, too."

"Your Enchantress. She is exquisite. You must meet my wife, sometime, Al'An. There is nothing like a Gle'Ur'Gya female. Her fur is soft. When we are in each other's arms, and her mane falls over my face, the feeling is indescribable."

"You sound like a happy man," Garrison said honestly, his eyes on the mouth of the passageway.

"I'd be the happier if I saw her the more, truth to tell. A mariner's life is wearisome at times. When these Horde of Koth emerge," Bre'Gaa said, changing the subject without missing a beat, "I say let them come. We kill a few here on the stairs, then run while

Mitan covers us and the others cover us from the top of the stairs. If we can get the enemy into the open, our arrows and bolts should slay many of them."

Garrison couldn't truthfully say, "I like it," but he could say, "That's a sound idea, Bre'Gaa."

As of yet, there'd been no evidence that the Horde troopers who would be charging toward them at any moment had longbows or crossbows available to them. Had there been enemy archers in any number, the situation would have been radically altered for the worse.

"By the way, Al'An?" Bre'Gaa unstrung his bow, slipped it under a pair of slots built into his quiver, and he drew his sword.

"Yes, Bre'Gaa?"

"In the event that I should die—"

"Hey, man! Don't talk like that!" Garrison interrupted.

"In the event that I die in combat against our foemen, or some other fatal event should befall me, I would crave two boons from you."

"Boons? Oh! Boons. Yeah. What?"

"I would ask that, as is the custom of the Gle'Ur'Gya, I should be buried with a sword, and a good one. After all, a dead Gle doesn't really need that much of a sword, so certainly no noble gesture such as placing your sword or Gar'Ath's with me. An enemy sword, even one of these disappointing things the Horde uses, will suffice. But see to it that it's sharp and of decent steel. Among the Gle'Ur'Gya, a warrior is only buried with his personal sword should he have no warrior son or warrior daughter to whom the blade can be passed. I have both, and my son and my daughter can fight over who gets the blade.

"Which leads me to the second boon I would seek."

"Which is?"

"Well, someone needs to return the sword to my family. I think that it should be you. And at the same time, you can relate in exacting detail how I perished so valiantly."

"Don't die, okay?" Garrison requested.

"I will endeavor to honor your wish to the best of my ability, Al'An—trust to that!" And Bre'Gaa laughed.

Garrison's eyes narrowed. The Horde of Koth unit which had been bottled up in the passage was, hesitantly, venturing into the chamber. In the next eyeblink, the inevitable happened.

The Horde of Koth, swords raised, bloody curses on their lips, charged. Garrison's stomach suddenly felt like he'd eaten spoiled chili and his palms sweated and he was exhaling more than he inhaled, or so it seemed to him.

"There's a trick, Al'An. Make the enemy think that you are insane for combat and desire their blood on your sword with every fiber of your being! The more you make them fear you, the less time you'll have to fear them."

"Thanks for the advice, pal."

"Take it for what it's worth," Bre'Gaa told him.

The Horde unit came in a dead run. Garrison counted thirty soldiers before he stopped counting and started shouting, "Come on, you chickenshits! Let's see how tough you really are! Your mothers sew dirty socks! Your sisters wear men's underwear and have to shave their upper lips! Come on, you wimps!" Garrison looked at Bre'Gaa. "That's the kind of thing I should be saying?"

"The very words I would have used, Al'An. Yes! Such epithets will strike terror into their hearts and fine hone the steel of your resolve."

Garrison didn't waste his energy waving his sword. There'd be plenty of opportunity for exercise in another moment or so. . . .

Swan wished that she had studied archery, but she had not. She wished that her magical energy would return more quickly, but it would not.

Midway along the staircase, Mitan readied her bow. Flanking Swan, Erg'Ran's crossbow was cocked, a bolt readied to fly from the slot. Gar'Ath's longbow was drawn, an arrow nocked, two more arrows clenched in his teeth.

"You should not fire until Al'An and Captain Bre'Gaa run up the stairs. There would be danger to Al'An and Captain Bre'Gaa if you fire prematurely. They are drawing the Horde out, toward them, so that there will be nothing behind which the Horde can hide and thus evade your missiles. Be patient."

"It was Mir who said that one should not loose one's bolt prior to confirming that the whites of the enemies' eyes were readily visible," Erg'Ran reminded them.

"The wisdom and courage of Mir will inspire us," Gar'Ath agreed.

Swan's eyes gazed at her heroic Al'An. Al'An's courage—standing there, fearlessly, a sword in each hand, hurling curses at vastly superior numbers of the enemy—filled her soul with love and pride beyond any measure, flushed her cheeks with desire. "My Champion," Swan sighed, and she sniffed back a tear of happiness.

An eyeblink later, she sucked in her breath from fear. The Horde was upon Al'An and Captain Bre'Gaa. Al'An hacked and stabbed with his sword, parrying enemy swords with the flat of his own, making a fine account of himself. Under the pressure from Al'An and Bre'Gaa, the first rank of the Horde fell back. From beside her, Swan heard Gar'Ath remark, "He learned well, your Champion, for true he did, Enchantress!"

She glanced at Gar'Ath, smiled her thanks, then looked back down the length of the staircase. Al'An and Bre'Gaa feigned another onslaught against the Horde's front rank. Al'An flung the enemy sword from his left hand, impaling one of the Horde through the throat. Then Al'An and Captain Bre'Gaa turned and vaulted up the stairs, taking the treads three at a time.

"Now! Open fire!" Swan commanded.

Gar'Ath and Erg'Ran let fly. Mitan launched her first arrow, then a second and a third; arrows from both positions filled the air over the staircase.

As Al'An and Captain Bre'Gaa reached Mitan's position, Bre'Gaa handed his sword to Al'An, shouted something Swan could not hear. In the next eyeblink, Bre'Gaa had his bow strung and an arrow nocked. He fired.

Bodies of dead Horde of Koth littered the stairs. Those few who managed to escape the rain of arrows and crossbow bolts charged Mitan, Al'An and Bre'Gaa. Al'An stepped down a few treads, met the first foeman and ran him through. One of the Horde soldiers cleaved downward with his wickedly curving blade, Al'An intercepting his foeman's steel by crossing the flats of his sword and that of Captain Bre'Gaa.

Bre'Gaa shouted something and Al'An sidestepped, drawing his foeman off balance. Captain Bre'Gaa fired an arrow, impaling Al'An's foeman through the left eye.

Those few men of the Horde who had ventured past the hail of arrows and bolts now fell back, escaping down the staircase. In the same eyeblink, Al'An, Captain Bre'Gaa and Mitan began to run up the staircase as rapidly as they could.

"Hold fire!" Swan ordered.

Swan looked away from the stairwell and second-sighted along the wide hallway and to the staircase beyond. She needed to see beyond the confines of line of sight, and she could not employ a guarding spell because Barad'Il'Koth might already be under a guarding spell of her mother's making. She could not see through walls, but there was the spell which she had used to enhance the second sight, and thus

see around corners. It was the means by which she
had enabled herself to search the passages and halls
of the magnificent place in Atlanta for the evildoer
whom Al'An had sought to foil.

As Swan considered it now, she experienced a
remarkable epiphany. In the other realm, her magical abilities had returned to her much more quickly
than she'd had any right to think that they would.
And borderline magic, which was neither natural nor
unnatural, but an unnatural utilization of the natural, had been quite simple in the other realm, vastly
moreso than it was in Creath.

There was a sudden queasiness in her stomach, and
she looked back, along the staircase. Al'An was coming. "No!" Swan hissed through her teeth. Was it the
other realm which held the real magical power, and
had her mother somehow captured this power and
returned with it to Creath? Was this the secret behind
her mother's unparalleled magical abilities?

And, Swan asked herself, was the very nearness of
Al'An the cause for her own continually heightening
magical power? Throughout nearly all of the wind
summoning, Al'An had been touching her. Al'An had
kissed her—quite a lot, and she felt her cheeks red-
den at the thought—before she had summoned the
storm with which they'd combated the ice dragons.

Al'An reached the head of the staircase. "Al'An?"

"Yes, Swan," he responded, out of breath.

"Hold my hand?"

Al'An smiled, took her in his arms and kissed her
forehead. Then, he took her right hand in his left and
merely looked into her eyes. "What's the matter?"

"I need to try something." Swan hoped that she
would fail, knew that she would not. She second-
sighted, without the use of any spell, and she was able
to see to the end of the hall, up the much narrower
staircase which wound ever upward toward the tower,
along a passageway there past many great doors and

to a doorway at that passageway's very end. "My father is behind that door, I think."

"What door, Swan?"

"The door which I second-sighted." Swan took her hand free of Al'An's hand and the second sight drew in on itself, almost imperceptibly. In a few eyeblinks, she could no longer see beyond the hall. Swan looked at Erg'Ran. "He is the magic for me, and one like him for my mother?"

Erg'Ran said nothing, merely nodded gravely.

"You are certain, Erg'Ran?"

"I am almost certain, Enchantress. There is only one way to know about the source of your mother's power; that lies before us. And there is only one way to know the answer to that other question which so vexes you. That answer lies within you, Enchantress, and your Champion."

"What are you guys talking about?" Al'An asked.

Swan did not answer, only swayed slightly in her mannish boots, nodded her head very slowly, all hope of lasting happiness gone. . . .

They moved rapidly—as rapidly as they could considering Erg'Ran's peg leg—across the high-ceilinged hall. They kept watch that the force of the Horde of Koth might be in pursuit. Swan clung to Garrison's hand, sometimes holding his hand in both of her hands. As they climbed the corkscrew shaped winding staircase toward the tower, Swan asked him, "Would you put your arm around me, Al'An? And don't let go?"

"Alright." At the back of his mind, Alan Garrison felt that something had changed, but he didn't know what or why.

The staircase wound upwards within what, for lack of a better term, Garrison mentally labeled a chimney, the various levels through which they passed accessible by passages veering off from the staircase. The effect was much like that of riding an elevator, passing one floor after another while ascending to the penthouse.

About halfway up the staircase, Swan remarked, "I am second-sighting the doorway leading into my father's chamber. There is one Sword of Koth guard visible, but there are so many other doorways along that passage that I fear more Sword of Koth will lie in ambush for us."

"What are their fireswords like?" Garrison asked her, tangentially redirecting the subject.

"The swords are enchanted, Al'An. When they are drawn in combat, they glow red hot, even white hot. Such steel as they are made from and enhanced by the spells placed upon them, they will cleave through any sword which is not, itself, magical. Your sword belonged to a K'Ur'Mir of great skill and valor, and was made by Gar'Ath's father. Gar'Ath's father was not K'Ur'Mir, but he had magical abilities as concerned the weaving of metals into fine steel. A Sword of Koth firesword will be neither more nor less deadly against your sword than any other. But be careful."

"I always try to be careful. But, of what?"

"The Gle'Ur'Gya use no magic, so Captain Bre'Gaa's sword could be broken by a firesword wielded properly. He knows this, of course. I offered magical protection for his sword, but Captain Bre'Gaa refused. And the swords of the ordinary Horde of Koth are also vulnerable. Likewise, they too would be broken by a firesword. Your mechanical daggers—"

"Benchmade automatic folders," Garrison corrected her. "You made them magical, I know."

"Exactly, Al'An," Swan said.

At last, they reached the height of the staircase, Erg'Ran bringing up the rear, Mitan with him, the sounds of Erg'Ran's labored breathing mingled with what could only have been a sigh of relief. Another few yards and there was a right angle bend in the passageway. Beyond that lay violent trouble.

Her voice little over a whisper, Swan asked Garrison, "Will you kiss me, Al'An? Will you kiss me harder and longer than you have ever kissed me? Will you do that now? For me?"

Garrison looked into her eyes. He wanted to ask Swan, "Why?" But he didn't. Instead, Garrison curled his left arm around Swan's waist, drawing her close against him. Her head cocked back, mouth offered to him, eyes wide. Garrison lowered his lips to hers; and when their lips touched, his body tensed with the need for her, desire he had never known existed. Her hands caressed his face, his throat, her body molding against his own. He let go of her, turned away for an instant, to get himself under control. "Are we gonna make it, Swan?"

"You mean—"

"I mean you and me. We'll make it out of here, or die trying. I mean after that, you and me?"

"There is more to 'you and me' than might be readily apparent, Al'An."

Garrison told her honestly, "I don't care. I love you."

"And I love you, Al'An. Shall we go to meet our fate, then?"

Garrison turned back to look at her. "There's an apropos line about that in one of the songs in Gilbert & Sullivan's *The Pirates of Penzance.* I'll tell you about it, sometime. Remind me." It was better, Garrison thought, not to mention that the line alluded to considerable trepidation concerning just exactly what that "fate" might be.

His sword was already drawn.

Garrison started walking.

This was a Hogan's Alley, Garrison told himself, but with swords instead of guns, and the targets fought back.

"I second-sight one Sword of Koth. He waits nervously near the end of the passageway," Swan whispered. Mitan and Gar'Ath nodded. Bre'Gaa and Erg'Ran seemed emotionless.

They rounded the right angle bend in the passageway, weapons ready.

When the Sword of Koth guard looked their way, he drew his sword, turned toward them, brandishing the weapon. It had already begun to glow red hot. That he sounded no alarm, issued no verbal challenge was clear evidence that they were walking into a trap, Garrison deduced. The logical question, he knew, was why were they doing this? The bitter answer was that they had no choice.

"Lay down your weapon!" Garrison advised the solitary Sword of Koth. "Put it down and you won't be hurt."

As Garrison had known that he would, the Sword of Koth ignored the warning.

Garrison inhaled, then exhaled very slowly. "I just hope you can get us out of that chamber once we're inside," Garrison told Swan. "Any chance of that?"

"My magical energy is replenishing itself extremely rapidly."

"I knew that," Garrison told her. For a second, their eyes met. Over his shoulder, Alan Garrison asked, "Who wants to nail that Sword of Koth guy with an arrow, huh?"

"Would a dagger do, Champion?" Gar'Ath volunteered, shifting his sword to his left hand, drawing his dagger, flipping it in the air and catching it safely blade first. The dagger flew from his hand, made one and one-half revolutions and buried itself in the throat of the hapless guard. The man fell over, dead before his blood spurted all over the stone floor of the passage.

Garrison walked on, Swan holding his left hand with her right, her sword in her left hand. She would be relying on magic more than that sword, Garrison realized. Somehow, touching him had something to do with her magic, as had their kiss.

"Any moment, now," Erg'Ran observed.

"Aye," Gar'Ath seconded.

Bre'Gaa complained, "Why don't they strike?"

"They will," Mitan told him. "In their good time, they will strike."

"There will be a magical barrier at the door to the chamber," Swan told them. "I must break it."

"I have confidence in you," Alan Garrison said truthfully, but realizing after the words left his mouth that he sounded unintentionally sarcastic. "I really do," he added.

Swan's hand squeezed his harder. He raised her hand to his lips and kissed it gently.

"When they hit," Garrison advised his companions, "it's important for Swan, Erg'Ran and—I guess—me to get through that doorway."

"Aye, Champion. That is understood," Gar'Ath responded.

They kept walking.

The doorway at the end of the passage was fewer than fifty paces away. Other doorways flanked them, ahead and behind. If the Sword of Koth had any plan other than nailing them with sheer force of numbers, Garrison surmised, it had to be to get them trapped by the magical barrier leading into the chamber. If Swan couldn't break the barrier which her mother would have so thoughtfully placed there, the passage would be transformed into a blind alley.

For some reason, Garrison recalled a frequently recurring episode from his boyhood. He was sitting in front of a television set with a glass of milk and some chocolate chip cookies, watching a masked Clayton Moore and his faithful American Indian side-kick Jay Silverheels as they fought fearlessly for justice on the frontier and, coincidentally, made a social statement about brotherhood and loyalty which Garrison had never forgotten.

In the next instant, Garrison was overcome with a sudden sinking feeling in the pit of his stomach. He realized why he'd recalled those happy memories at this particular moment in his life. It had to do with a group of Texas Rangers who died in a box canyon.

"What is that sound you are making with your lips, Al'An?"

"It's called whistling," Garrison told her, not even realizing he'd been doing it until she remarked about it. "Where I come from, people whistle if they're happy; or, sometimes, they whistle when they're afraid. The tune's from 'The William Tell Overture.' But, I wasn't thinking about William Tell. I was thinking about some Texas Rangers."

"Who was William Tell? Was he a Texas Ranger?" Swan asked.

Garrison smiled, "Tell you later, darling."

They kept walking. They were about twenty feet from the doorway leading into the chamber which they were so intent upon entering.

Most of the other doorways lay behind them.

There was a shouted command. Those doors opened, and spilling from them were more than three dozen Sword of Koth, fireswords drawn. With them, more menacing appearing somehow than the soldiers in their black leather face masks and black coats of mail, were six women.

"Witches! Evil personified!" Bre'Gaa snarled.

Everyone in the passage stood still, waiting.

"I am Moc'Dar. When last we met, I was Captain Leader of the Third Company Sword of Koth, Elite Guard to the Mistress General of the Horde. Then, much evil befell me because of all of you—evil unspeakable."

Garrison shrugged his shoulders and smiled. "Sorry about that, man."

Moc'Dar continued. "I have been charged with bringing you before my Mistress General, the Queen Sorceress, either living or dead."

"If you're gonna give a speech like this, Moc'Dar, you oughta get the terminology straight. The expression is 'dead or alive,' not living or dead. Sounds very tacky that way. Trust me."

"You, of the other realm, and you, Virgin Enchantress, and you, old one—"

"Seasoned and true is more flattering a description," Erg'Ran suggested, getting into the spirit of the thing.

Unrattled, Moc'Dar said, "You three my Mistress General has interest in seeing alive." Moc'Dar looked at Mitan, Gar'Ath and Bre'Gaa. "You three, she wishes to see only dead."

"You forgot the part about how I should know the name of the man who kills me," Gar'Ath reminded Moc'Dar. "Just like last time. Remember?"

Six Handmaidens of Koth extended their fingertips from within their long, flowing sleeves. They were veiled from the crowns of their heads to the hems of their ankle-length black robes in translucent black cloth which cast the planes and angles of their faces in eerie shadow. They formed a circle, hands clasping as they began to chant.

Garrison cracked, "I think the one second from the left is the ugliest, Bre'Gaa. What do you think?"

"It is hard to choose, Al'An, but you may be right. However, that one on the far right, I do believe, is even more unattractive."

Garrison looked at Swan, loosed her hand and raised her chin with the tips of his fingers. He kissed her hard on the mouth, then whispered, "I hope it helps; we're gonna need your special talents, darling."

Swan smiled up at him. "Tell me when, my love." Inexplicably, Alan Garrison felt considerably better. He looked at the six witches, at Moc'Dar, at the other Sword of Koth warriors, their eyes glowing slits of hatred beneath their black leather battle masks. "That can't be good for your complexions, guys," Garrison began, walking slowly toward three Sword of Koth who blocked him. "I bet you guys get blackheads like crazy wearing those masks. Back where I come from, we have television. Well, I've seen these commercials for these strip things you put on your nose? Snags the blackheads out like that!" Alan Garrison flicked up the point of his sword and ran the first six inches of its steel into the nearest of the three Sword of Koth.

As Garrison stabbed the man he shouted, "Now's the time, Swan! When!" As the words left his lips, in the same eyeblink Alan Garrison shoved the dying Sword of Koth warrior off his blade and toward the circle of six witches, using the soldier's body like a battering ram. The circle of hands was broken.

Garrison sidestepped, a firesword, burning red hot, just missing Garrison's right shoulder. There was a second flash of steel, past Garrison's face. Mitan's blade thrust forward and into the throat of Garrison's attacker. Garrison arced his own sword right and up, catching another Sword of Koth behind the thighs, draw cutting, then stabbed his blade forward, into the Sword of Koth's face mask.

There was a shout from Gar'Ath. Garrison wheeled toward the sound. Four Sword of Koth formed a semicircle around him, Gar'Ath beating them back, but not that easily. Garrison leaped toward the melee, spinning his sword like Errol Flynn had done when he'd starred as Robin Hood. Garrison caught one Sword of Koth's blade, deflected it, then hacked downward, gouging steel into flesh where the man's neck and right shoulder met. Garrison averted his eyes from the arterial blood spray, ducking as another sword whistled through the air where his face had been a split second earlier.

Garrison thrust, his blade hesitating for an eye-blink, then punching on, puncturing the Sword of Koth's coat of mail, skating past ribs and up into the right lung.

Garrison was suddenly aware of a whistling sound. As he deflected another foeman's blade, he glanced to his right. There was a vortex formed near the chamber door, hailstones flying from within it at stupendous speeds, Swan's hands gestured toward this target and that, and the marble-sized balls of ice struck at witches and Sword of Koth, driving them back along the passage, into the doorways from which they'd emerged.

Erg'Ran's father's sword sang through the air, severing the head of the last of the combatants against whom Gar'Ath fought.

"This way!" Swan called out, gesturing with a nod of her head. Garrison, Erg'Ran and Gar'Ath ran behind the vortex, Garrison and Gar'Ath half-carrying Erg'Ran as they propelled him forward.

Swan ordered Mitan, "Take over the vortex. All you need now is to maintain it."

"I'll try, Enchantress!" Hesitantly, Mitan began to move her hands, her eyes focused on the vortex. "I should look in the direction in which I wish the hail to flow, shouldn't I, Enchantress?"

"You're getting it," Swan reassured her.

There was something like a stutter, the vortex's shape contracting, then expanding again to its original size, the flow of hailstones, interrupted for an eye-blink, renewing itself.

"Gar'Ath and Captain Bre'Gaa—please stay with Mitan," Swan ordered as if she were making a request.

"Yes, Enchantress," Bre'Gaa responded, snatching up a partially ice-encrusted firesword from the passage floor. As his hand closed around it, the blade began to glow, the ice turning to steam.

Swan faced the doorway, extending her hands toward the door itself.

The door seemed to vibrate, its shape shifting almost imperceptibly. Swan sagged back, almost fainting and Garrison caught her in his arms. "My mother's magic is very strong."

Garrison stared into Swan's eyes. "Tell me what to do."

"Fold your arms about me and stand very close."

"Yes," Garrison nodded, doing as she'd requested.

Again Swan tried to break the spell which sealed the doorway, only this time Garrison felt a tingling sensation throughout his entire body, felt his own strength draining from him. His knees beginning to buckle, he held on to her, more tightly.

The vibration of the door increased. Over the constant whistling sounds of the ice pellets spraying from the vortex, Garrison detected a very faint, almost mechanical sounding hum.

There was a flash of energy, visible as yellow light, like the popping of an old camera bulb but the wrong color. Swan sagged against Garrison and Garrison himself nearly fell.

The draining of his own energy had stopped. Erg'Ran reached for the door's round handle, lifted it and twisted it. The door swung inward.

Garrison glanced behind him. Ice pellets had formed a ridge almost a foot high in some places and coated most of the passage floor. Gar'Ath and Bre'Gaa flanked Mitan as she continued to orchestrate the hailstorm which Swan had begun.

Barely able to hold himself up, Garrison assisted Swan forward, through the doorway and into the chamber beyond.

The chamber was surprisingly well lit, tapers burning in sconces spaced evenly along three of the walls, a large window dominating the fourth. Lying face down on the bed was the figure of a man. He wore a monkish robe of heavy grey cloth, cowl turned down. He didn't move and for an eyeblink, Garrison thought that the man might be dead.

Swan, sounding very much like a little girl, began to sing softly, "L'Ull B'Yan G'Ite . . ."

The words sounded strange to Garrison, and with Swan's language spell they shouldn't have. But, somehow, Alan Garrison knew that he should know their meaning, recognize them as something heard long ago.

As Garrison was about to ask Swan why she sang them, the figure on the bed moved, sat up.

In the next eyeblink, in a voice choking in emotion, the man on the bed sang back, "Lullaby and good night, with roses—" This time, the opening words to Brahms' "Lullaby" were unmistakable. The man was singing in English, American English.

"Father!" Swan gasped.

"Swan?" The man stood up from the bed. "Swan? Swan!" Whatever energy Swan had remaining to her went into the few steps that she took before falling into her father's waiting arms.

He kissed her forehead. She kissed his cheek, her arms encircling him. His arms closed around her like a shield and rocked her gently back and forth, as if, somehow, the notes of the lullaby still echoed within them both.

Alan Garrison cleared his throat and sniffed. "Sir?"

The man who held Swan in his arms looked up. "Did you just speak to me in English?"

"Yes, sir. I'm Alan Garrison. I'm from back home, sir."

Swan's father closed his eyes and turned his head. When he looked back across the chamber, tears streamed from his eyes. "I recognize that jacket you're wearing. A-2 bomber jacket. You a flyboy, fella?"

"I took some flying lessons; but, no, sir. I'm a Special Agent with the Federal Bureau of Investigation."

Swan's father shook his head wearily, sighing, "This has gotta be one of Eran's tricks." He cleared his throat. "I knew you G-Men had a long arm! But, it can't be this long, from one world into the next! You—all of you—even you," and he looked into his daughter's eyes. "You're only in my imagination, and Eran put you there!"

"No, father. I'm real," Swan sobbed, clinging to him as he started to push her away.

"What are you afraid of the Feds for?" Garrison prodded. "You running from something?"

"Look, you! See, I know how it seems, wartime and everything. But I didn't desert, G-Man! I was brought here, against my will by Eran, and Eran darn well knows it! I'd swear to that before any court martial board the Army could convene."

Alan Garrison just stared.

"Okay. I'll play your nasty little game. Have we beaten 'em yet?"

"What's your name, sir?"

"Eran knows my name. I'm First Lieutenant Peter Goodman, United States Fifth Army, Second Battalion, C Company."

Garrison still stared.

"So, answer me, huh? Did we win the war, fella, or what? If you're who you say you are, maybe you'll convince me this isn't another little fantasy Eran's created so she can— Aw, man!" Goodman turned his face away from his daughter. "Eran's got me believing it! I stopped what I was saying because I wouldn't say that word in front of my daughter!" He grabbed Swan by the shoulders and shook her. "You have no right to rip a man's soul out!"

Garrison was about to intervene, but Goodman let go, his own shoulders slumped. "Eran's good, real good."

"What war, sir?"

"What war! The war!"

"Somehow I don't think you mean Desert Storm?"

"Desert what? General Rommel just bought the farm, they told us. Word was Rommel and some of the other Nazi High Command bigshots were maybe plotting to bump off Schickelgruber himself. You hear scuttlebutt like that, ya know?"

"Holy shit," Garrison rasped.

"Watch your mouth in front of my—"

"You're talking about Erwin Rommel, right? The Desert Fox? And the war you're talking about was against the Axis? Germany and Japan and everybody, right?"

"What the heck war you think I'm talking about, fella? The Spanish Civil War is old news."

"What's the last date that you remember, Lieutenant, before you were brought here?"

"It was the first week in November, 1944. That's gotta be twenty, maybe twenty-three years ago. You know that. Eran knows that. So, did we get our hands on Hitler and the rest of his goosesteppers? Make up a good one, fella. That's what Eran'd want you to do."

"Hitler whacked himself in his bunker in Berlin as the Allies were closing in. Eva Braun was with him. He married her just before they died. Poison and a pistol shot to the head, if I remember it right. A lot of the Nazis got away, but a lot of them were caught after the war."

"I can't see Hitler having the guts to kill himself."

"Nevertheless, Lieutenant Goodman, that's supposedly exactly what Hitler did. According to the history books, anyway. How old were you, sir, in 1944?"

Swan's father seemed to think for a minute. "I was born Thanksgiving Day, 1919. I got outta college about six months before Pearl Harbor. I enlisted nine December 1941. I'd just turned twenty-two. I was going to turn twenty-five in a couple of weeks."

"You look like you've had a tough time of it since

you came here, Lieutenant. And, by your reckoning, then, it's 1964, maybe 1967. Hmm?"

Goodman seemed a little defensive, and a little wary, but in a different way, as he said, "You telling me something different?"

"When I left home, sir," Garrison informed him, "my calendar read September 1998. That's a hair under fifty-four years, not twenty-three years ago. That'd put you looking at your seventy-ninth birthday this November."

"I'm not seventy-nine! You one of them hopheads you read about or something?"

Alan Garrison answered by taking out his wallet. He handed Swan's father his driver's license. "Georgia driver's license. My picture. Not very flattering. License expires in the year 2002. In the middle there on the left? That's my birthday, October 19, 1968. Do I look like I haven't been born yet?"

Goodman's face, which hadn't been rosy cheeked to begin with, turned ashen.

"We've got Eran's people outside, trying to get in. We don't have much time, sir. We've gotta get you out of here, and Swan's magic is about spent out," Garrison informed him.

"I am Eran's brother, Erg'Ran. May I call you Pe'Ter? Or, do you prefer Goo'D'Man?"

"Can't anybody in this darn place say my name right?" And Peter Goodman fell to his knees and wept. Swan knelt beside him and cradled his head against her breast.

# Chapter Fourteen

There was no way of telling how much time was passing. Garrison's wristwatch performed exactly as it had ever since he'd reached Creath. Time was either going by so slowly that the Rolex's sweep second hand seemed barely to move, or the second hand spun wildly rapidly, so fast that Garrison was certain the movement would break. Or the hands of his watch didn't move at all and there was an eternity between the soft ticks as he held the watch to his ear and waited and waited.

Goodman sat on the edge of the bed, and he began to talk. "Eran has spells on me. You could never take me with you. Man, I feel uncomfortable talking like this in front of my daughter." He reached out and took Swan's hands in his hands, kissed them lightly. "When a man and a woman are together like, well, like when your mother and I made you, honey," Goodman said, looking only at his daughter, "well, it should feel good for the man and the woman—gosh, I can't explain this to you! You're a grown woman."

"I think Swan understands the idea behind the birds and the bees, Lieutenant," Garrison volunteered. "You can speak frankly. Honest, it won't offend her, sir."

Goodman looked at Garrison, as if for reassurance, then at Erg'Ran. The older man, who was really younger, said, "Your new friend from Earth is right," and Erg'Ran sounded forced as he squeezed together the two syllables of Goodman's first name and said, "PeTer."

Goodman smiled. He had a decent smile, Garrison thought absently, seemed like a decent guy, too, the kind of guy who'd gone off to make the world safe for children he hadn't had yet, knowing that maybe he never would. And here he was, on the edge of nuts, seeing a daughter he'd been taken away from when she was an infant.

And, in a place where time was some sort of weird, unpredictable thing, there wasn't any time at all to be a father. But Goodman was trying.

There might still be time enough to be a hero, if Garrison read Goodman right and understood the source of Eran's power as he thought that he did.

"You see, your mother and me," Goodman finally went on, "we really loved each other in a kind of strange way. I think that's why she hasn't killed me, that and the other thing. And your mother's afraid, very afraid, afraid of loving anybody. To your mom, love is weakness, and she can't afford to be weak."

"Sir? The key to her power? Is it—?" Erg'Ran fumbled with his pipe as he spoke, didn't look into Goodman's face.

"Yes. I don't know why. I never did. Once, Eran told me that in the real old times here, long before your Mir came along, when things were really bad, one of the most evil of the evil sorceresses discovered a way into the other realm." Goodman glanced over at Garrison. "Our Earth, buddy. She came to our Earth, pal, and she took a human man back with her here and she kept him for—well, I'm not gonna say it."

Garrison nodded his understanding. Under less grim circumstances, Garrison would have asked Goodman if Goodman thought that Judge Crater might have been held prisoner in the next room over. He let it pass.

"It's like she runs down in her magic, ya know? Well, and she uses me—But, when I found out that she was killing people and destroying whole cities and everything, like some kind of Hitler or Tojo or somebody, I told her I wouldn't, well, that I wouldn't. Not again. So, Eran started using—" Goodman looked at his daughter. "I don't like talking about your mom like this, honey."

"I know that she's evil, father. When her magical energy declines, she comes to you and being with you increases her magical energy beyond anything otherwise possible here." Swan's smile, as she looked into her father's eyes, was the sweetest thing Alan Garrison had ever seen in his life.

Goodman spoke again. "She—your mother—she used pain and all sorts of stuff to try to make me do what she wants. When she's really desperate—I don't think she likes reliving how we met—but she casts one of her spells and makes me think I'm back in that little town outside Paris with Dave Spaulding. Dave was my platoon sergeant. Great guy. Aww!"

"What is it, father?" Swan asked at Goodman's sudden exclamation.

"Dave was a couple years older than me. He'd be over eighty now, if he's alive and made it through the war!"

Swan dropped to her knees at her father's feet, gently touching at the shackles on his wrists. There were no chains in them, but he had worn them, Garrison could tell from the marks, for a very long time.

Goodman started talking again. "Anyway, Eran makes me think I'm back there again and I'm this young guy and she's this beautiful, exotic girl hot to climb in the sack—sorry, honey."

"It's all right, father."

"And, that's how she—well, you fellas know what I mean." Goodman paused for a moment, then continued. "And, afterward, she has all the power she needs to do whatever she wants."

"Is it your understanding," Erg'Ran asked quietly, "that this ancient sorceress of whom you speak and Eran are the only two sorceresses who have used a man of your realm thusly?"

Goodman's shoulders shrugged beneath his robe. "I think so. She never mentioned anything else."

"Swan is the only child of your union? Correct?" Erg'Ran pressed.

"Yeah. I'm sure of that. Leastwise, I got a wonderful daughter," Goodman said, touching his daughter's cheek. Swan kissed his fingertips.

"Would you have any way of knowing if the ancient sorceress had issue by her union with the man of your realm?"

"I don't know, but I don't think so. Eran would have mentioned it, probably."

Erg'Ran looked at Garrison, then at Swan. "Do you both understand my meaning?"

Garrison understood it, had started to understand its basic premise—and cooperate with it—as they'd started toward the keep's upper story where Lieutenant Peter Goodman was held prisoner. When Garrison spoke, he looked at Swan. "If Erg'Ran is implying what I'm inferring, then with you being half of Earth and half of Creath, and having magical energy beyond what you'd had, if you and I were to—"

Swan blushed as she lowered her eyes.

"Hey, fella! Wait just a darn minute there!" Goodman snapped. "You can't talk that way in front of—"

"I'm certain, Pe'Ter, that Al'An meant no disrespect at all to your daughter," Erg'Ran declared. "He cares for her deeply. And I mean no disrespect when I say quite truthfully that they would already have been lovers in the most ardent sense of that term had it not been for the prophecy which mandated that your daughter, my niece, remain a virgin until she had found the origin of her seed. And . . . sir, in finding you, she has found that."

Alan Garrison looked at Erg'Ran, wanted to say something. He didn't know what. He could have told Peter Goodman that Creath was just like Earth; if you took advice from your brother-in-law, you could never go wrong. He could turn Goodman on to some great swamp property deals in Florida, too. At last, Garrison thought of what to say and simultaneously said it, without considering the import of his words. "Are Swan and I being used, or about to be?" It came out badly, and especially so since he'd addressed the question to no one in particular.

Swan raised her eyes and looked at him, her glance a dagger in his heart.

"Look," Garrison said, addressing everyone in the room as he began again. "Swan and I love each other. I know that's no different now than it was yesterday. And, tomorrow, we'll still love each other. If we don't get out of here quick, all the magical hailstones in Creath won't keep Eran's people from getting through that doorway. Your wife, Lieutenant Goodman," Garrison announced, looking at him, "evidently came up with some spell that prevents the chemicals which comprise the priming compound in my cartridges from interacting. She had your gun, right?"

"My .45, yeah." Goodman nodded.

"So, my guns are useless. All we've got between us and the bad guys in the black cowboy hats, Lieutenant, is a magical hailstorm outside the door and time that's running out." Garrison looked at Swan. "If

I helped, do you have enough magical energy to get us out of here?"

Swan got up from where she'd knelt at her father's feet. "I don't know, Al'An."

"That's better than a no," Garrison said, smiling at her. He turned his eyes to Peter Goodman. "Sir, are you positive that you can't leave here?"

"Pretty positive, fella."

"Will it hurt to try?"

"I suppose not."

"Then, we'll try, if you're agreeable."

Goodman stood up and took his daughter into his arms, but spoke to all in the room. "If what I think you folks are talking about is what I think it is, maybe my daughter has the potential to unseat Eran, to defeat Eran's power with power of her own. And there's a sure way to help that and help me at the same time."

"How?" Garrison said.

"You guys try getting me out of here. If you can't leave with me and can leave without me, I want a weapon. A dagger'll do. Get my drift, gentlemen? This can't go on, and even indirectly, I'm not going to help Eran to destroy my daughter. If you can't get me out of here and out of Eran's reach, then I'll get myself out of Eran's reach, permanently."

"Father! No." Swan gasped, her hands touching gently at Peter Goodman's face.

"Your father has wisdom and courage," Erg'Ran told her. "It would appear that many of those fine qualities which I and others find so evident in you, Enchantress, at last reveal their source, their origin." Erg'Ran placed his clenched fist over his heart. "You have the courage of Mir, sir, and his wisdom as well."

"I can't believe this!" Swan declared. "We're talking so easily about my father taking his own life! That's insane!"

"Look, honey," Goodman began, his hands gently holding Swan's shoulders. "Sometimes, we've gotta face reality. If I didn't realize how beautiful and fine you are, I'd maybe think that you were kind of figuring that you were the one getting hurt. Finally find your father, right? And you can't spend more than a short while with him. But I realize it's me you're trying to protect. Gosh, honey! Being with you would be the swellest thing. No kiddin'! And, maybe your magic can get me out of here. But being trapped here to be an instrument of your mother's evil isn't a life I've lived more since you walked through that doorway, Swan, than I have since 1944. You gotta believe me, honey. You've just gotta."

Standing perfectly erect, Swan slowly rested her forehead against her father's chest and wept.

Alan Garrison looked away, walked to the doorway, opened the door and peered into the passage. The accumulation of hailstones had reached epic proportions, several feet high at the far end of the passage, and at least a foot high in front of the doorways within which the Sword of Koth and the Handmaidens had taken refuge.

Mitan's hands still orchestrated the flow of ice pellets from within the vortex. Bre'Gaa had his bow partially drawn and an arrow nocked. Gar'Ath, his sword in his right hand, was, at that moment, withdrawing his dagger from the body of the Sword of Koth soldier.

Garrison announced, "It's Swan's father, a man from my realm named Peter Goodman. We'll all be attempting to leave using Swan's magic. Be as ready as you can be when I give the word."

"Aye, Champion. It's a bit cold here, anyway."

Garrison smiled at Gar'Ath's flippancy. Alan Garrison had learned the lesson well that those who laughed in the face of deadly danger were either idiots or those comparative few who were brave enough to stand fast despite the fact that they realized their lives were on the line. Gar'Ath was one of the latter.

Garrison stepped back inside.

He was not shocked, but he was moved. In that very instant in which Garrison looked at Swan and her father, he saw Swan withdraw her dagger from its sheath at her belt and hand it to her father, to use if he must. This was courage and love unlike anything which Alan Garrison had ever witnessed.

"You're the finest woman I've ever known," Peter Goodman declared to his daughter. "I couldn't be a prouder father, Swan. Let's see what happens."

Swan nodded, but did not speak.

Garrison walked toward her. As he passed Goodman, Goodman asked him, "Hey, buddy. You smoke?"

"Yeah. A little."

"Got a cigarette? I haven't had a cigarette since 1944." Alan Garrison smiled, reached into his clothes and pulled out the pack. "Camels, huh?"

"Have the pack."

"One'll do me, fella. If I make it out of here, I can bum another one. If I don't, one'll be all I've got time for." Swan looked away. But, as she did, her father's cigarette lit. "Good trick, honey." Alan Garrison watched Goodman as he brought the cigarette to his lips and inhaled. Never had Alan Garrison witnessed someone enjoying a basic physical pleasure more deeply. Goodman held the smoke in his lungs for a very long time, it seemed, then exhaled slowly through his nostrils. "That tastes great! And I went a lot longer than a mile to get it!"

Garrison clapped Goodman on the shoulder, saying, "I like you, Lieutenant."

"You're not so bad yourself, son."

Alan Garrison nodded.

Goodman inhaled again, exhaling smoke as he said, "I think we should do whatever it is we're going to do, Swan."

Swan reached out and took her father's hand in her right hand, Garrison's hand in her left. Garrison's flesh tingled, and he felt strange. "If the touch of a single man of Earth can increase my magical energy," Swan said, "then the touch of two men of Earth, both of whom I love, should be all the greater."

"Erg'Ran! Get the others!"

"I am doing so already, Champion!" Erg'Ran called back.

"I am still very weak," Swan informed them. "I looked out my father's window. What I plan is a wind summoning spell, and that the wind can carry us down safely into the courtyard. From there, I fear, we'll have to make other plans."

"That should be good enough," Garrison said lamely. He hoped it would be, anyway.

Mitan and Gar'Ath entered the chamber, followed a moment later by Bre'Gaa. "He's a big guy!" Goodman exclaimed, looking at Bre'Gaa. "You're Gle'Ur'whatsit, right?"

"As you say. And you are the father of the Enchantress. I am honored to meet you."

"Pretty well-spoken guy," Goodman said to anyone listening.

Garrison reminded himself that Peter Goodman was a product of another generation, a time in which people were labeled and categorized by their appearance even more than they were in succeeding generations. At any event, this was neither the time nor the place to discuss such philosophical and social concerns.

Swan released Garrison's and her father's hands.

Swan walked to the window. "Al'An. Please hold me."

Garrison snatched up his Golden Shield of IBF and walked over to stand behind Swan, putting his arms around her, the shield on his back.

He felt a gentle tremor through his body as Swan made the window glass disappear. Swan addressed them all. "If I am able to summon the wind, it will envelop us and lift us from here. Do not fight its force, but be one with it." In the next instant, Garrison felt the draining sensation which he had felt before, but this time more intensely. There was a sudden coolness on his right cheek, and a freshness to the air that he had not felt before.

Looking beyond Swan into what appeared to be a post dawn sky of cool, deep blue, Garrison witnessed clouds, stirring oddly, moving progressively more rapidly even as he watched them. Tiny wisps of Swan's hair, which had worked their way loose from her waist-length braid, teased his face.

Goodman said, "Time to lose the cigarette."

Erg'Ran urged, "Stay close together, my friends." The window opening's height suddenly concerned Garrison, and he tried gauging whether or not he'd have to duck his head. Unable to tell, and realizing that so much depended upon the height at which the wind would move them, he abandoned the thought. He'd duck if he had to.

The clouds Garrison had been watching were moving with astonishing rapidity. Garrison felt air circulating rapidly around him, around all of them as they waited, huddled near the open window. He glanced across the chamber and toward the doorway. Ice still lay everywhere beyond the doorway and along the passage, but it would not keep the Sword of Koth and the Handmaidens back much longer.

The wind whistled now, strong but somehow not violent.

Swan's hands stroked the magical energy in the air with a gentle grace, unlike the violence there had been in her hand movements when she conducted the wind which had carried their ships away from the cyclonic wave.

Garrison felt—heard—what, under normal circumstances, he would have attributed as a vagrant wind gust. But, it was something more, something else. He felt his body and Swan's being gently lifted from the chamber's stone floor, the moving air surrounding him imbued with a physical substance unlike anything that he had ever experienced or imagined.

They were moving, closer to the window, rising, higher off the floor. Garrison looked at Goodman. The wind carried Swan's father as well. Garrison almost sighed with relief.

The wind on which they rode rotated ever so slightly, and Erg'Ran was the nearest to the window as the wind lifted them through. Garrison, despite the exhaustion against which he fought, almost laughed. The skirts of Erg'Ran's monkish robe were suddenly thrown up by the wind, exposing the older man's bare white legs beneath. By the wildest stretch of imagination, Erg'Ran's image wasn't even remotely similar to that of Marilyn Monroe standing over a subway air vent.

Mitan was the next through, her greatcape swirling above her, an impish smile on her wide, sensuous mouth. She held Gar'Ath's hand, his hair caught up in the wind, masking his face for an eyeblink. But, as he turned, Garrison saw Gar'Ath's eyes on Mitan, and they too smiled.

Bre'Gaa, the next through the window and into the open air, howled with laughter, shouting, "I am like a mainsail of the *Storm Raider*! The wind fills me! Ha!"

Garrison felt his own body being drawn through the window, and he made the mistake of looking down. "Holy shit!" Nothing was below him, save for the cobblestones of Barad'Il'Koth's courtyard, and those were at least a hundred and fifty feet straight down.

Garrison's arms were still folded around Swan; In the next eyeblink, she was through the opening, her cloak floating around her like a superhero's cape, her braid caught in the wind as well.

Looking back toward the window, Alan Garrison

saw Peter Goodman, his body about to be drawn through the opening, mere millimeters from it.

There was a bright burst of yellow light, the same flashbulb effect there had been when Swan broke her mother's spell at the doorway into the chamber. But the light did not dissipate this time, and Peter Goodman was violently hurtled back from it, broken out of the gentle grasp of the wind.

"No-o-o-o!" Swan shrieked in anguish, the wind falling away from around them.

"Your father wouldn't want you to die!" Garrison shouted to Swan as they began to tumble downwards. Garrison still held her, their bodies turning and twisting, plummeting toward the cobblestones below.

The wind which had abandoned them rushed around them, lifted them higher and higher, higher than they had been before. Garrison saw within the chamber, through the open window, the barrier of light still there. But, beyond the light, Garrison saw Lieutenant Peter Goodman.

And, Garrison saw Moc'Dar, racing into the chamber, a wedge of Sword of Koth and Handmaidens in his wake. One of Moc'Dar's men reached for Peter Goodman; and, there was the flash of dagger steel in Goodman's hands, blood spray as Swan's father severed the Sword of Koth's carotid artery.

Lieutenant Peter Goodman stepped back, looked through the window opening and made that kind of rakish, devil-may-care salute that soldiers always saved for civilians, then blew a kiss with his left hand as his right hand drove his daughter's dagger into his heart.

Swan saw it. Her body went rigid, then limp in Alan Garrison's arms. Again, they began to tumble downward, to their fate all but abandoned by the capricious wind. Garrison heard Erg'Ran's voice shouting, "Mitan! Only you can save us now!"

Swan was either dead or unconscious.

Their bodies spiraled downward. Garrison caught a glimpse of Mitan, her hands flicking outward, her body suddenly upright. Still clutching Swan against him, Garrison tumbled past Mitan, the cobblestone courtyard slamming toward them.

In an eyeblink, the motion of their bodies stopped, Garrison's stomach ceasing its downward motion a nanosecond later, the remnants of the meal which Garrison had consumed before leaving for Barad'Il'Koth fighting upwards into his throat.

Garrison looked at Swan, her body like a rag doll's, but her eyelids fluttered.

Garrison breathed, swallowed.

They hung suspended in the air, the wind erratic, but supporting them. Fifty feet or so below, a handful of Horde of Koth regulars were spilling into the courtyard. Soon, there would be more.

Garrison looked toward Mitan.

Her hands moved erratically; Garrison could feel their motion in the wind which surrounded them.

Garrison looked down again. Below, another two or three Horde of Koth had entered the courtyard, and one of them at least held a bow.

A few seconds later, an arrow vectored toward them.

"Mitan! You've gotta get us down!" Garrison shouted.

"I don't know how!" Mitan cried back, desperation clear in her voice.

Garrison looked down at Swan, her eyelids fluttering again. She was incredibly beautiful, beyond any hope he had ever had of a woman who would be in his arms, his. "Swan. Swan?"

Swan's body moved almost imperceptibly against him. Tears flowed from her eyes as her lids raised. "My father, Al'An!"

"I know," he whispered. Then Garrison looked up. There were Sword of Koth in the open window above them. It wouldn't be long before one of them got the brilliant idea to go find his bow and arrow set and have some fun at target practice.

Another arrow whizzed up from below as Garrison looked toward the courtyard. Like the first, the wind blew it off course and it fell away.

"Swan?"

"I can't, Al'An."

"Your father died for you, not because of you, died so that you could live and wouldn't have to die. You know that. Mitan's keeping us up here, but she can't control the wind to bring us down. You have to, or we'll all die."

Swan turned her face away, but nodded slowly. Her arms, which had hung limply at her sides, rose, and her hands seized the wind. "Release, Mitan!" Swan cried out.

There was a faintly perceptible drop in wind pressure, then it rose, evened out, and—slowly—they started downward.

More Horde of Koth were venturing into the courtyard. There were at least three archers. As if Swan read his mind, she said quickly, "I have very little energy remaining. The wind will repel their arrows, but once we are—"

"But once we're on the ground it's up to us," Garrison finished for her. "I know."

They were nearly to the cobblestoned surface of the courtyard, more Horde of Koth in view. The archers fired repeatedly, but the wind swept their arrows away. Garrison had an idea. "Mitan! When we land—when we are down—can you hold the windspell for a few eyeblinks, then release it?"

"She can," Swan answered for her, Swan's voice terribly enfeebled sounding.

"You can do it, Mitan!" Garrison called out.

"I will!" Mitan answered.

The ground rose to meet them, but the instant before their feet touched the cobblestones, Bre'Gaa twisted his body in the air and lunged, hurtling himself onto three Horde of Koth troopers, bowling them over.

Gar'Ath leaped forward, sword flashing.

Swan, her voice barely audible, whispered, "I release the wind."

"Mitan! Now! Take it!"

The wind nearly died, then rose, Mitan controlling it again.

Alan Garrison swept Swan up into his arms, his sword held uselessly in his right hand. Erg'Ran stumbled, but only to one knee, his peg leg slipping from beneath him.

Mitan's control of the wind was, oddly, better for their purposes, the errant gusts making archery marksmanship even more difficult. As Bre'Gaa and Gar'Ath hacked their way forward, they brought down one archer, then another and another, then the last of those already into the courtyard.

Two Horde of Koth troopers charged Garrison.

The wind evaporated as Mitan shouted, "I release the wind!" In the next instant, her sword drawn, Mitan had interposed herself between Garrison and his two attackers. "Get her out of here, Champion!"

"We'll need horses." Garrison ran as best he could, his own strength all but gone, his legs and arms feeling simultaneously limp, yet stiff and unbending. His eyes flickered right to left as he crossed the cobbled courtyard, cursing himself for not learning the outline of Barad'Il'Koth better before coming here, searching for anything that looked like stable doors.

Near the courtyard's farthest end his search ended.

With the last of his energy, Garrison ran toward the spot, nearly collapsing as he neared the stable doors. When he looked back, Mitan had dispatched the two Horde of Koth she'd fought for him, and Erg'Ran was half the length of the courtyard back, heading for the stables as well.

Garrison sagged to his knees, Swan still in his arms. He heard Erg'Ran's voice shouting something, but couldn't make it out. Blackness washed over him as he fell forward.

"I was draining him of his life, wasn't I? Just by touching him?"

Erg'Ran looked at her and answered, "I'm afraid so, Enchantress."

Swan wanted to reach out to Al'An, but dared not. "How soon will—"

"He should recover rapidly. He must. In eyeblinks, we must be gone."

Swan tried to stand, to go to Erg'Ran and help him as he saddled horses. She could not stand, yet. "I have no magic to give, uncle."

"Your magic is not the reason that we love you, Enchantress. Rest."

She drew her sword, managed to get to her knees. If her mother's soldiers entered the stable, she would die fighting them, fighting for her lover, her uncle, her friends—the memory of her father. "Erg'Ran?"

"Yes, Enchantress," he huffed from behind her.

"You believe that because I am half of the other realm that, if Al'An and I—"

Her uncle mercifully interrupted her. "Speaking bluntly, Enchantress, not as your subject—which I will always be—but as your uncle, it is my belief that if you and your Champion become as one in love, because your seed is of his realm, you will possess magical power greater than your mother possesses, greater than even she can imagine possible."

"I did not want it to be this way. I love Al'An, uncle."

The voice Swan heard from beside her chilled her. "I know that you do. And if you'll have me, I want you forever." So quickly that she felt faint, Swan turned her head toward the voice. Al'An sat up from the stable floor where Erg'Ran had left him after dragging them inside. "I heard what you said, and what Erg'Ran said. I've wanted to be your lover since the moment I set eyes on you." Al'An smiled that wonderful smile Swan so much loved. "It's a rare opportunity, to save a world and have paradise in your arms while you do it."

"Al'An," she sighed, almost touching him.

He edged up to his knees. "Let me catch my strength a little," Al'An implored, smiling again. Shakily, he rose to his feet. "I can help, Erg'Ran."

"Then by all means do so, Champion."

Swan glanced back. Four horses were already saddled. How she so longed for them to need seven mounts instead of six only. Tears filled her eyes again, but at least strength was returning to her. Through the crack between the stable doors, as she looked toward the courtyard again, she saw Mitan, Gar'Ath and Bre'Gaa, more than two score of the Horde at their heels as they ran. "Hurry!"

"This is the last of the mounts, Enchantress!" Erg'Ran advised her.

Al'An asked her, "Can you still light a fire?"

"I think I have the magical energy for that," Swan replied.

"Good! Then once we're mounted, I want you to light my cigarette." She thought that this seemed an odd time to smoke. Al'An told Erg'Ran, "And I want you, as soon as you're mounted, to get ready to shag the rest of these horses out those doors the moment I say so. Right?"

"Aye, Champion! At your command, then."

The doors flew open, Mitan first, Bre'Gaa and Gar'Ath right behind her.

"Mount up, guys! We're getting out of here," Al'An ordered, climbing into the saddle.

Bre'Gaa helped Swan to her feet, lifted her as if she weighed nothing at all, placing her astride one of the six horses. The animal was dark brown with an almost black mane and tail. Swan freed her cloak from the saddle's cantle, drawing the garment around her, cold in her weariness.

Gar'Ath held Mitan's mount's bridle as she stepped up into the saddle, her long legs holding fast to the animal.

"There are gates and a drawbridge," Gar'Ath advised, his own lean frame swinging up into the saddle with perfect ease.

"Good point," Al'An announced. "There's likely a gatekeeper?"

"Aye, Champion, I would imagine so."

"We'll find a way to make him cooperate. Trust me," Al'An told him.

Swan reined back on her mount. It was skittish, likely used to a greater weight than her own in its saddle.

Al'An had a cigarette in his mouth. Without thinking, Swan lit it.

"The rest of these horses—let's shag 'em out of here before they get barbecued!" Al'An ordered.

The concept of barbecue took an eyeblink or so to comprehend, but Swan suddenly realized why Al'An wanted the lit cigarette. Al'An's pockets bulged with straw from the floor, and bales of straw and hay were stacked high along the far rear wall of the stone building and on either side. The structure itself might not burn, but inside it would become a raging inferno.

Mitan swung low from her saddle, tugging the stall ropes open. Gar'Ath used the edge of his sword to sever more of the ropes, then its flat against the rumps of the animals as they started out. Erg'Ran, sword in hand, did the same, urging the animals through the open doors and into the courtyard.

There were more than a hundred horses here, and Swan, barely able to stay astride, smote herself for her weakness, for being unable to help herd them through the stable entrance.

Al'An took a long coil of rope from where it was racked on a peg protruding from a supporting column, then rode along the center of the stable, toward the far rear of the structure. Loosed horses stampeded wildly around him. Swan was barely able to restrain her own mount; its instinct was to follow the others of its kind.

Her eyes turned back to Al'An. He had reached the rear of the stable, but was barely discernible, the stable's darkness and shadow consuming him.

Then, suddenly, there was a bright light.

A burning brand flew from Al'An's right hand, into the center of the tallest stack of baled straw, near its base. Another flew into the stacked hay to Al'An's right, then another into the hay at his left.

There was a long, thin arc of orange light as Al'An's cigarette snapped from his fingers, into the straw near his horse's feet. "Let's get out of here!" Al'An commanded.

Horses streaked past her in a stream which seemed unending, their eyes wild with fear of the flames, nostrils flared against the already foul-smelling air. Erg'Ran, Gar'Ath and Mitan, riding in their midst, urged the creatures onward, shouting at them, waving their swords in the air.

"I will stay beside you, lady," Bre'Gaa told her. "If you should perchance fall from your mount, be assured that I will catch you, Enchantress."

"Noble Captain, I am in your debt," Swan responded.

"Then, let us away, Enchantress!" Bre'Gaa slapped the flat of his sword against her horse's rump and the beast beneath her vaulted forward.

Smoke already wafted along the length of the stable, the fire seeking the greater volume of air at the open doors. Her eyes starting to tear from the smoke, Swan clutched the reins and a knot of her horse's mane in her hand. Bending low over the animal's neck, she struck the flat of her sword as Bre'Gaa had done, her mount picking up speed, racing into the courtyard.

Ahead of her ran almost a hundred horses, the cacophonous din of their hooves against the cobblestones pulsing inside her head, thrumming maddeningly.

Swan looked back. Al'An rode hard, his sword raised high, his ebon mount, galloping toward the doorway, its hooves chucking great clods of debris from the stable floor.

"The gates are this way!" Erg'Ran shouted, wheeling his horse, the animal rearing magnificently. Despite Erg'Ran's peg leg and advancing age, her uncle and mentor sat a horse wonderfully and still cut a marvelous figure in the saddle.

The gates and the drawbridge—it was raised—lay to the far end of the courtyard. More than two score Horde of Koth, phalanx-like, interposed themselves between the stable and the sealed gap in the castle wall. As Al'An's mount cleared the stable doors, Swan noticed for the first time that something was being dragged behind it, at the end of a rope.

Al'An's horse reined back, only half-reared, hind legs deeply bent, its off-front leg fully extended, the other raised, pawing at the air. Al'An shouted to Swan, "Can you light this?" He gestured behind him with his sword.

Swan's eyes scanned along the length of rope to its end. There was a bale of hay knotted there. Swan lit the hay, sagging a little in her saddle as she did so from the use of magical energy. Al'An saluted her with his sword, dug in his heels and the black mare under him sprang forward. The bale of hay spewed burning sparks everywhere in its wake, the already startled horses whinnying with fear and galloping

madly in all directions across the courtyard. Most of
the animals stormed toward the Horde of Koth's line.

Erg'Ran and Gar'Ath were the first to come against
the foemen. With Erg'Ran's and Gar'Ath's swords
hacking and slashing from saddle height, the Horde
of Koth gave way before the onslaught of tempered
steel in determined hands. Their disorganized retreat
quickly transformed into a startled rout. They ran in
obvious panic from the steel-shod hooves of the
terrified horses storming toward them.

Low over his horse's mane, his sword held straight-
armed before him like a lance, Al'An tore through
the melee, toward the raised drawbridge. An officer
in the Horde, brave but foolish, ran toward Al'An,
intercepting him. As the officer slashed with his
sword, Al'An's blade described a long, graceful arc.
Steel met flesh. The Horde officer's hand and the
sword it held flew from his arm in a great spray of
blood. Al'An charged onward.

Al'An reached the gate, reining back, his horse
skidding and nearly falling to the cobblestone. Alan
sprang from the saddle, with a single motion of his
sword severing the rope with which he'd dragged the
burning hay.

Arrows began to rain down from windows and
niches interspersed along the height of the keep.
Captain Bre'Gaa, riding beside Swan, shouted to her,
"We must be gone from here! Soon, there will be no
hope but to stand our ground and fight to the death!"

Far to their right, Mitan, still ahorse, returned fire
with her longbow.

Swan looked from Captain Bre'Gaa to Al'An.
Gar'Ath and Erg'Ran were nearing him at the raised
drawbridge. Al'An's mount began to veer off, but
Gar'Ath intercepted it, catching its reins. Al'An, sword
sheathed, was climbing the wall along the bar studded ladder toward the gatekeeper's niche, the ladder
set into the wall as the watchman's only access to his

nook. Peering down from the stall, Swan saw the man, and as he looked he brought a crossbow to bear. "He will kill Al'An!" Swan virtually screamed to Captain Bre'Gaa.

"Not this day, Enchantress!" Bre'Gaa drew his mount to an abrupt stop, nearly wrestling it into motionlessness. In an eyeblink, his bow was in his hands and he bent it to set the string. In the next eyeblink, he had an arrow nocked and fired.

Swan's eyes tracked the arrow, unconsciously second-sighting in flight, seeing the arrow in infinite detail, the black and grey pattern of its fletching, the grain of its shaft, the keen honing of its broad steel head. Swan blinked and drew in her breath as a scream when the arrow struck the gatekeeper. The arrow penetrated through the bridge of the man's nose and continued into the right cheek below the eye and into the mouth.

When she opened her eyes, she witnessed the gatekeeper tumbling forward from his niche, nearly striking Al'An with his body.

"That is the way the Gle'Ur'Gya are taught to shoot as children, Enchantress! Ha!"

And they were riding again, toward the drawbridge.

Gar'Ath had drawn his bow, in preparation of assisting Al'An, Swan knew, but put it away. He fell to working his body against the great iron studded bar set across the gates, its weight clearly immense.

Swan and her Gle'Ur'Gya shepherd reached the gates, Captain Bre'Gaa handing her the reins of his mount and saying, "If you would, lady."

Captain Bre'Gaa sprang from the saddle and was beside Gar'Ath in the next eyeblink. Effortlessly, it seemed, he set his enormous hands to the bar and shouldered it upward and out of its braces. As if the bar weighed nothing at all, Captain Bre'Gaa flung the bar into the courtyard. When Swan looked back, she saw that he had not wasted his strength.

The bar had struck and bowled over three Horde
of Koth swordsmen who had returned to the fight.

Swan looked up, Al'An clambering from the dowel
rungs and into the compartment lately left by the
gatekeeper. Could Al'An discern the workings of the
mechanism by means of which the drawbridge was
raised and lowered?

As Captain Bre'Gaa and Gar'Ath swung open the
gates, there was an earsplitting crack, and the drawbridge began to fall. Mitan rode up, as the drawbridge
crashed into the open position, the moat beyond the
gates spanned at last.

Gar'Ath snatched back his reins from Erg'Ran who
held both his and Al'An's mount in check, then
vaulted into the saddle.

When Swan looked back into the courtyard once
more, Sword of Koth and Horde of Koth were pouring from within the keep itself and the barracks structures within the walls. Many of the errant horses were
being taken in charge. Small knots of men were being
rallied.

Arrows struck into the gates, ricocheted harmlessly
against the stone of the walls. One buried its head
in Captain Bre'Gaa's saddle. He tore it free as he
remounted, then retook his reins. "We must flee,
Enchantress! Ride now!"

From above them, Al'An's hands clinging to a rope,
she heard Al'An cry out, "Stay near the drawbridge!
I'll need magic once more, Swan!"

Feebly, Swan nodded to him. She knew what he
had in mind.

Captain Bre'Gaa virtually led her horse, coaxing it
onto the drawbridge. Mitan, Gar'Ath and Erg'Ran
positioned themselves in the gate opening, steel ready.

Swan looked up. Where was Al'An? She saw him
again.

"Oh!" Swan exclaimed. "No!" Al'An stood on the
uppermost of the rungs just outside the niche, hands

firmly grasping a rope. In an eyeblink, his body flew
downward through the air, and Swan almost screamed.
Al'An's feet struck the wall, but he pushed himself
away. He came against the wall again, then shinnied
down the rope, jumping from it while still some
distance from the ground. Al'An landed in a crouch,
one hand touching the flagstones. Then he was up
and running in an eyeblink.

The next thing that Swan saw was something unlike
anything she had ever seen before. Al'An angled his
run toward the rear end of his horse and, as he
neared it, he jumped, his hands to the horse's rump.
He sailed over his hands and into the saddle.

Al'An looked at her with a big grin. "Buckaroo
Fishman, the cowboy legend, escaped Geronimo and
a renegade Apache war party down Bisbee, Arizona
way using that mount. I'll tell you the story, sometime. Let's ride!"

Onto the drawbridge, their horses' hooves reverberated against the wooden boards. Al'An shouted to
her, "When we've all gotten across, can you set the
bridge afire?"

"I think I can."

Al'An called out over his shoulder, "Gar'Ath! Mitan!
Erg'Ran! Hurry!"

Captain Bre'Gaa reined in beside her a short distance beyond the end of the drawbridge and Swan
looked back. A score of the Horde were ahorse and
charging across the courtyard, Gar'Ath, Mitan and
Erg'Ran turning their horses onto the drawbridge
and riding, death snapping at their heels.

Hoofbeats thundered across the drawbridge, making
Swan's mount uneasy. Captain Bre'Gaa took its reins,
held them fast.

Erg'Ran was first across, Mitan and Gar'Ath, side
by side, just behind him.

"Not yet!" Al'An cautioned Swan.

Three Horde of Koth horsemen, swords drawn,

were on the drawbridge, three more behind them,
another two behind the three. "Be ready, darling. Lots
of flames, huh? Ready—now!"

Feeling herself completely drain as she made the
magic, Swan set the bridge afire with the very last
of her energy, then collapsed, darkness engulfing her,
the crackle of flames and the screams of men and
animals echoing and re-echoing ceaselessly within
her. . . .

Alan Garrison didn't know about the habits of real
frontier heroes like Buckaroo Fishman, but the movie
and television cowboys always found a grove of cottonwoods where they could make camp. It was invariably
just outside of town, but secluded nonetheless.

If cottonwoods grew on Creath, Garrison hadn't
seen any, nor was he certain ho'd know a cottonwood
tree if he tripped over one. Virtually nothing at all
seemed to grow in Edge Land. But there was a high,
rocky area in the foothills to the north of the plain
of Barad'Il'Koth, and beyond it lay a barren valley.
There were several passes immediately identifiable,
ways in and out of the valley, so there was little
chance they'd be boxed in by enemy troops except
in significant force of numbers.

And Swan very urgently required rest and recu-
peration.

Their expropriated horses grazed poorly in the
almost nonexistent vegetation. Mitan tried making
grain appear magically, but her vortex kept collapsing before anything more than a few specks of dust
materialized.

Mitan did make fire appear, and in the fire Bre'Gaa
and Gar'Ath hardened the tips of wooden shafts they'd
cut with Erg'Ran's axe and whittled to shape with
their daggers, these for use as throwing spears. The
supply of arrows was dangerously low should there
be an assault against them in any force.

Erg'Ran kept vigil beside Swan, who seemed half asleep, half in coma. Alan Garrison kept watch from a rock pinnacle at the edge of the little valley, and was pleased as he saw Mitan striding toward him. "Greetings, Champion!"

"Any change in Swan?"

"Our Enchantress still rests, and Erg'Ran is with her, tending her. Could you use some company, Champion?"

Garrison smiled and nodded. Mitan scampered up along the rocks as nimbly as would a mountain goat. Despite the triteness of the comparison, it was the first thought which crossed his mind as he observed her. On the other hand, he reflected, she was much nicer looking.

When she reached the pinnacle where Garrison was perched—it had taken him three times longer to climb it and he'd been out of breath when he reached the summit—Mitan dropped down to her knees beside him, resting her sword across her thighs. As she drew her cloak over her bare legs, she remarked, "You love her, I know."

"Yes, and very much. More than I could ever weigh, measure or calculate, actually."

"That's good," Mitan volunteered, smiling. She raised her arms, her hands beginning to tinker with her very pretty, well-past-shoulder-length dark brown hair. Garrison found it curious that, despite the considerable length of her hair, her lover's hair was even longer. "Sorry I'm so bad at magic," Mitan said, laughing. "I guess I should have been born male."

"Gar'Ath would have been pretty upset about that."

Mitan laughed again. "Yes, he would have, wouldn't he?" Mitan cleared her throat. She was beginning to braid her hair; after a second or so, the braid started, bringing it over her left shoulder, working the interweaving of her tresses with casual deliberateness, seeming to derive a certain languorous enjoyment from

the task. Her eyes focused on something—likely nothing—far away, Mitan said, "I spoke with Erg'Ran."

"And?"

"It is within your power to restore the Enchantress,
and also to enable her to defeat the Queen Sorceress."

Garrison hunched his shoulders inside his jacket,
happy for the sweater which Swan had magically
knitted for him. There was a stiff, chill breeze. "I
think I can speak for Swan as well as myself when
I say that affairs of the heart can be choreographed
to death. At least where I come from, people don't
really—"Garrison cut himself off.

"Why did you stop saying what you were saying,
Champion?"

"It sounded stupid."

"May I ask you a question, Champion?"

"Sure, Mitan."

"Where you come from, is there virtue in letting
what is good be destroyed needlessly, Champion?"

Garrison just looked at her.

"Well, it seems to me that since you love the
Enchantress and the Enchantress loves you and it was
clear to all who observed the two of you together—
aboard ship and elsewhere—that you could not wait
to be together, well—"

"Well?"

"The Enchantress was to find the origin of her
seed, remaining a virgin until she had done so. That
is the prophecy. Now, it seems to me, that it is time
for the rest of the prophecy to be fulfilled."

Garrison took a cigarette from his pack, looked
away, then looked back. The pack was refilled. He
tried his Zippo lighter, but it had been soaked one
too many times for there to be any viable fuel remaining. Garrison looked at the cigarette and then at
Mitan. "How's about a light?"

Garrison's cigarette lit.

"My one big magical ability! The simplest thing!"

"Just because you're no magical whiz," Garrison reminded her, "doesn't mean you're any less of a woman, Mitan; you're manipulating me quite well, indeed."

"Manipulating?" Mitan asked with a coy smile.

"Yes," Garrison replied. "Manipulating. When we went to Bre'Gaa's ship, the *Storm Raider*, for the first time, you didn't have to dress as though you were going to Cinderella's ball. You were already driving Gar'Ath crazy looking at you when you were dressed as you are now in your fantasy woman warrior outfit. So, the beautiful princess look was just enough to push him over the edge. You did him a favor, compelled him to overcome his inherent shyness so that the result which you both desired would be attained. Manipulating. Perfectly normal. Men want to be manipulated by women, at least smart men. Men are frequently more direct, whereas women will more often approach a problem from the side. Whereas brute force or intimidation might achieve a certain result, that same result or an even better one might be achieved with guile. Trust to your femininity, Mitan, regardless of your magic; your womanliness hasn't failed you."

Garrison stood up.

"Where are you going, Champion?"

Alan Garrison smiled down at Mitan. "Where am I going! Really! Ha!"

"Yes! Where are you going?"

Alan Garrison merely shook his head. He started the long—for him—climb down from the pinnacle; paradoxically, Garrison realized that he was ascending to a new stage in his life rather than descending at all, committing himself to the love which had forever and would forever change his life. . . .

The courtyard was filled with men and horses. On a balcony far above in the highest tower of the keep,

the Queen Sorceress stood, watching. Moc'Dar feared
that, at any moment, his Mistress General might
choose to transmute him once again into the cursed
creature he had been before. On lower balconies, the
Handmaidens, in groups of six, waited, ready to
perform their Queen Sorceress's bidding.

The odor of the incinerated remains of the drawbridge and the even worse smells from the gutted
stable somehow still permeated the courtyard, despite
a bitterly cold wind which swept over the walls. Had
Eran summoned it? Moc'Dar shivered.

To his knowledge, the Queen Sorceress, Mistress
General had used no magic yet. Even the drawbridge
was being rebuilt by hand. Within a very little time,
it would be completed enough that it was half its
original width, and his forces could storm across it
in pursuit.

Moc'Dar stood in his stirrups and called out to
the Sword of Koth and Horde troopers, most of
them already ahorse. "There is a limited distance
which the traitorous Swan and her vile accomplices
could have traveled. It was clear that she had little
magical energy remaining to her. We must find her
before her magical energy is restored or can be
enhanced. Any man who fails to give me his all will
answer to me with his life. My personal future
depends on the outcome of our endeavors. Should
I fail, death would be welcome. Remember this as
you ride the pursuit, as you hunt the quarry. And,
remember, too, that we are to return the Virgin
Enchantress and her Champion from the other realm
to our Mistress General unless such proves impossible. The old Erg'Ran, as well. Should we be unable
to bring them back alive, we shall lay their rotting
corpses at the feet of the Queen Sorceress and beg
her forgiveness!"

Moc'Dar looked toward the high balcony. Eran
would have heard. Did she approve?

Moc'Dar looked once more to his black-clad warriors, then to the drawbridge. It was completed enough, he decided. To a lieutenant at his side, he ordered, "Take six Horde of Koth, and order them to ride at full gallop by twos across the drawbridge. If it does not fail beneath their weight, we take the field in the next eyeblink."

"Yes, Captain Moc'Dar!" The lieutenant raised his clenched fist over his chest. "You! And you and you and you! And you two, also! By twos, at full gallop, cross the drawbridge now!"

The six men, already ahorse, wheeled their mounts toward the drawbridge, the horses around them whinnying loudly, pawing the courtyard surface. Twenty-four hooves thundered across the cobblestones.

The first two were across, the second two, then the final pair of riders.

The partially completed drawbridge held.

Moc'Dar stood in his stirrups again, shouting, "Woe beyond pain, suffering greater than death to the foes of the Queen Sorceress! We ride to victory!"

Moc'Dar glanced up to the highest balcony again. Had Eran nodded her approval? Or was it merely the wind toying with her hair?

Moc'Dar wrestled his animal toward the drawbridge and dug in his spurs, crossing the courtyard onto the drawbridge, across it, onto the trail, the full might of the Sword of Koth and two companies of the Horde in his wake. . . .

Eran stepped from the balcony, listening as the click of her boot heels replaced the hammering of hooves, letting her cloak fall from her otherwise naked body beneath.

Pe'Ter was dead of his own hand. In the eyeblink as she learned this, her heart was filled with two emotions: loss, and disgust. That she felt a genuine

sense of loss at the death of the only male whom she
could truly have considered a husband, the father of
the only child she had ever borne, consumed her with
self-loathing.

That Moc'Dar had failed to prevent Pe'Ter's death
and Swan's escape filled her with disgust for his
blithering incompetence. Moc'Dar came within an
eyeblink of feeling the full force of her wrath, but
she stayed her impulse.

Perhaps such newfound restraint accompanied the
realization that her magical energy needed to be used
very wisely now that Pe'Ter would be forever unavail-
able; and, that Moc'Dar's very incompetence might
serve her best purpose, affording her a new source
of that special energy which she so craved.

In preparation for such contingency and in order
to minimize the frivolous use of her magical energy,
Eran strode across her apartment to the bell pull
beside one of the tapestries and tugged it. The bell
would summon those six Handmaidens of Koth who
sometimes attended her personal needs.

Now, Eran would cause herself to be dressed in
perfect finery, to look her most alluring, most sen-
sual and beautiful.

There might, after all, soon be a new other realm
man to plunder her willing body. . . .

"Some little of the Enchantress's magical energy
returns to her, Champion, but so slowly. When one
has drained oneself as my niece has done, it is to be
expected. There are tales told from the days before
the coming of Mir of sorceresses who died in battle
with one another, not at the other's hand, but by so
depleting their magical energy that there was no
longer the sufficient strength to live. There is magical energy within us all, you see, even those who do
not know that they possess it. When this final reserve
is exhausted, there can be nothing left but death,

because the magical energy and the energy of life are one and the same. We are all the better for the Enchantress's being young and strong."

Alan Garrison sat on a rock beside Erg'Ran, a cold wind blowing from the north. "How much longer before we can travel?"

"Within a day we could risk it, Champion. What are you thinking?"

Garrison stared down at his hands. He'd bloodied them here, and would bloody them again if he lived. The battle with Swan's mother was just beginning. "I'm thinking that since Swan's father is dead, and her mother is someone none of us could just sit down and chat with, you're the logical one."

"For what, Champion?" Erg'Ran was packing the bowl of his pipe.

Garrison rubbed his hand over the stubble of his beard. "Well, I kind of feel I should, uh—I want your blessing to ask your niece to marry me. However you do things like that here."

Erg'Ran struck flint to steel, smiling over the bowl of his pipe as he did so. "Blessing?"

"You know, that it's okay by you."

"And what if I said no? Would you not entreat for her hand? Would you love Swan any the less, or she love you the less?"

"That's not it. Of course, we'd still love each other, and I'd still ask her to marry me."

"Then," Erg'Ran persisted, "this request which you make of me is merely formality?"

"Yes. But, still, I'd like you to give us your blessing."

"Whatever that means to you, Champion, you have it."

Garrison nodded. Staring down at his hands, he said, "One other thing."

Erg'Ran looked back at him quizzically through the smoke curling up from his pipe.

"Could you stop calling me Champion and start calling me Alan? Or, even Al'An?"

Erg'Ran smiled. "I will consider that, Champion."

Garrison nodded his head, stood up, and started up into the rocks where Swan had been resting. He cleared his throat, threw his shoulders back. Alan Garrison was a little nervous. He had, after all, never proposed marriage to anyone before, nor had he ever dreamt that, assuming that the girl in question accepted, his next question would be about making love together immediately so that they could save a world. It sounded like a desperation play pickup line, really, the kind of thing a guy said after "Wanna boogie, mama?" failed miserably. . . .

Al'An was walking up the slope toward her, and it required no magical ability to know why.

Swan had never imagined that what she knew was about to transpire would come about in such a way. She had always pictured it that she would give herself to the man of her dreams only after a wedding in some flower-dotted grove where Ka'B'Oo trees grew and beautiful white horses awaited to bear them to some happy place. And she would never be dressed as she was now, in a man's cloak, jerkin and stockings. For her wedding, she would wear a dress of magnificent white lace; for the moment when she surrendered her most special physical intimacy, she would wear some soft, wondrous linen gown that he, in turn, would take gently from her body, replacing its texture against her with a feeling she had never felt before.

Tears filled Swan's eyes, happiness that the moment she so longed for with Al'An was about to arrive and that she still lived to share it with him, and sadness that this terrible conflict with her mother, the Queen Sorceress, had dashed the last of her hopes.

"Swan."

She was able to sit up a little, propping herself on one elbow. "Al'An."

"Will you be my wife and take me as your lover?" As he spoke the words which quickened her heart, Al'An dropped to one knee before her. She put her hand in his. "I love you more than I ever thought it would be possible to love anyone. From the moment I saw you, it was— I don't know how to say it, Swan."

"Yes."

"I mean, you're so incredible. The magic and all, that's just fine, but it's you I love. I wouldn't care if—"

"Yes," Swan said again. "Yes, I will marry you, Al'An, but only if you still feel that I should after you bring the magic into me and I possess greater magic than my mother. And, yes, I will take you as my lover in this very moment, and you will be the only lover that I shall ever take. This I swear by the courage of Mir."

Al'An took her into his arms and crushed her lips beneath his own, his mouth devouring hers, their tongues touching. Swan felt her body go rigid in that very eyeblink, then soften beyond any softness she had known.

Al'An's hands swept over her, and his strength filled her with delicious weakness. Her head fell back and his hands loosened her hair, his lips caressing her throat, her cheek, his hands moving over her again.

Swan raised her hands to Al'An's face, her arms embracing his head, drawing it close against her. His hands were at her waist, moving upward along her body. A chill went through her and her body was closer to his than before, molded to every contour of his body, the strength of his arms wonderfully crushing her, his mouth smothering her.

The black jerkin unlaced beneath his hands, as did the neck of her white blouse. His hands touched her where no hands but her own had touched her since infancy, his fingers exploring gently within the linen of her camisole.

In the eyeblink that his hand brushed against her left breast and her nipple hardened to his touch, Swan cried softly and touched her lips to Al'An's cheek.

Above her waist, her clothes were all pushed away and her skin felt cold and hot simultaneously, the sleeves of her blouse binding her arms ever so slightly. Al'An leaned back, shrugging out of his jacket, his baldric and his firespitter sheaths, standing to pull the sweater she'd made for him off over his head. He tugged off the shirt beneath it—he called it a T-shirt—and his upper body was naked before her.

Swan knelt before him, touched her mouth to his abdomen and to his chest as he dropped to his knees before her. The soft hair which grew from a man's flesh was odd feeling to her lips, wonderful feeling. Without knowing why, but wanting to, Swan kissed first one, then the other of his nipples.

Al'An took her into his arms, their flesh nearly one, her breasts on fire with desire for him. Al'An guided her onto her back and his hands were at her waist, fumbling with the stockings. Swan laughed softly, bringing her own hands to help his.

"I have to," Al'An whispered, apologized, in desperation tearing the second skin of stockings from her own.

Al'An's hand brushed against her hip, his fingers trailing along her thigh, down to her knee.

Swan's breath left her so rapidly that she almost screamed. Al'An's fingers moved slowly up the inside of her thigh, then touched where she knew that he would touch her, had wanted and feared that he would touch her. A shiver pulled her into herself, all of the breath gone from her and, in an eyeblink, her lungs filling with the chill air. Swan tossed her head back and Al'An kissed her throat, his fingers knotting in her hair.

Her hands, without conscious will, tugged at the belt girding Al'An's waist, discovered how to open it. There were these things Al'An called buttons, coin shaped and of metal, and her fingers struggled with them.

At last, she had them open.

Al'An laughed softly as she struggled to lower the garment which restricted her from touching the flesh below his waist.

Al'An let go of her, leaned back. Swan knelt at his feet and pulled first one, then the other of his boots from his feet. His stockings made her laugh because they were so short, not even to his knee.

"Pull on the pants legs," Al'An advised her.

She did that and Al'An sprawled back, laughing. And Swan flung the garment aside, but there was still more covering him. Al'An smiled, started taking off the little pants, but Swan would not let him, put her hands on the waist of the garment and pulled it down.

Swan gasped.

"What's wrong?" Al'An asked her.

"I had never imagined that it looked like that!"

"It doesn't always, only on special occasions."

"Is this a special occasion, Al'An?"

"The most special," Al'An informed her, then pulled her body down over his.

Al'An rolled her over onto his clothes. "Ouch!"

"Sword got in the way," he smiled, shoving his baldric aside.

"And your other sword? What will you do to me with it, Al'An?"

"Many things," Al'An told her, looking her square in the eye.

"Then, prithee, run me through and through again, my lover," Swan begged.

Al'An's left hand came to her back, arched her upward as his hips slipped between her thighs. Swan screamed.

"I don't want to hurt you," Al'An whispered, the fingers of his right hand caressing her breast.

Swan exhaled into his ear and Al'An shook his head and her teeth found the shell of his ear and her fingertips and then her nails gripped his flesh.

Swan screamed again.

Al'An was inside her.

A flash of thought, of a flower-dotted grove where Ka'B'Ou trees grew and beautiful white horses awaited to bear her and Al'An to some happy place. And Swan opened her eyes and the flowers and the trees and the horses were real and there. On the ground beside them lay a dress of magnificent white lace, and her arms were no longer entangled in the blouse she'd worn with her mannish jerkin and stockings, but in a gown of pale linen trimmed with fine lace and ribbons blue as the sky.

"Al'An," Swan murmured.

The air around them was warm and full of magical energy and, flowing into her, coursing through her blood was the magical energy of the universe.

"I love you, Al'An, and I am yours throughout life and beyond death for all eternity," Swan whispered, Swan vowed.

# Chapter Fifteen

Snow, borne from the icy sea Woroc'Il'Lod, carried inland over the mountains on winds of unrelenting force, showered round Moc'Dar's force, spicules of ice assailing whatever bare flesh might be unwisely exposed.

Even Moc'Dar's black leather mask of the Sword of Koth afforded him little protection, and he found himself squinting his eyes against the unremitting, bone-chilling onslaught. The heavy, wet snow flakes and needlelike shards of ice, driven diagonally, worked mercilessly against them, infiltrating to the innermost reaches of their clothes; and when the wind gusted and howled in higher register than the steady shriek Moc'Dar's numbing ears were becoming used to, the weary horses visibly shuddered and stumbled, riders huddled deeper in their snow-splotched black cloaks, swayed wearily in their saddles.

Some magic had been used, either that of the old man Erg'Ran or the warrior woman's, covering the tracks of the Enchantress and her comrades before the snow had begun to fall. Where there had been snow, there was only virgin white, and the rock

surfaces, now totally obscured, had shown no scuff-
ing or scratching from steel-shod hooves. Because
time was of the essence—the Queen Sorceress was
not noted for infinite patience and each eyeblink's
delay might allow the Enchantress to renew or
enhance her magic—Moc'Dar had improvised a plan.

There were only so many directions in which the
daughter of the Queen Sorceress and her band of
rebels might go. Traveling further inland would gain
them nothing, the overland route away from Edge
Land the only possible goal and one that would be
counterproductive to their ends, at least so far as
Moc'Dar understood them.

The rebellious daughter and her co-conspirators
would head for Woroc'Il'Lod, where the remainder
of their pitiful force vainly attempted to distract the
Queen Sorceress with naval maneuvers, threatening
a landing of some sort in modest force, an attack
which could easily be repelled.

Bearing in mind all of these well-reasoned assumptions, Moc'Dar had split his sizeable force into eight
different elements, all of which would converge at the
most logical place for a landing. Each element had
with it one Ra'U'Ba, in the event that reinforcements
would be needed, or field intelligence needed to be
shared by way of the Ra'U'Ba.

Despite his Captaincy, Moc'Dar had been given
field command over the entire operation, placing him
in the oddly satisfying position of having superior
officers in the Horde and the Sword of Koth ordered
to take his orders.

If he failed in his charge, Moc'Dar had already
decided that he would take his own life rather than
remain alive to be punished by the Queen Sorceress
again.

Leading a unit of four score Horde of Koth and
a score of Sword of Koth, Moc'Dar took the route
along which his best judgment dictated that the Virgin

Enchantress was most likely to travel. It snaked through the foothills which paralleled the mountains forming the most rugged and treacherous portion of the coastline with Woroc'Il'Lod. There were numerous places along the way in which a small band might take shelter, hide from the second sight.

Although there was still no evidence of any horses crossing through the area, blaming the magic, cursing the cold, fearing his future, Moc'Dar rode on along the bleak far edge of the plain of Barad'Il'Koth. . . .

Although he had not eaten, Alan Garrison's stomach felt pleasantly full. Although he had not touched a razor to his face, his skin felt the slight tightness which only the closest, cleanest shave imparted. Although he had not bathed, his hair and body were immaculately clean, as were the clothes he had lived in for far too long. His sword was freshly honed and, like his firespitters, lightly oiled. Alan Garrison wondered if, somehow, Swan had counteracted her mother's spell and his pistols would actually shoot?

There would likely be the chance to find out about that.

All around him there was beauty, but it frightened him. Pleasantly warm sunshine from a robin's egg blue sky bathed this little valley, but visible in all directions was a sky so darkly overcast in grey as to be nearly black. When he listened very carefully, he could hear the faint howl of vicious winds. Flowers grew in abundance as did grass, upon which their own stolen horses and the two white horses (which had magically appeared) eagerly grazed.

Most disconcerting of all was Erg'Ran's appearance. The lines of age in his face had somehow grown softer, less noticeable. His eyes seemed brighter, keener. And his peg leg was gone, in its place (although Garrison hadn't asked Erg'Ran to remove his left boot) presumably a normal, healthy foot. His monkish robe was clean and new looking.

Mitan's leathers gleamed, and her hair shone with the luster of fresh washing and brushing. Her body, always eye-catching, was all the more so.

Gar'Ath's wild mane of hair was nearly as perfect as that of his lover, Mitan, and the few dueling scars Garrison had only subconsciously taken note of before—one on his neck, two on his right hand—were gone.

Captain Bre'Gaa's mail glistened as if it were made from the finest silver, painstakingly polished. And the hair which covered the visible portions of his body, his facial hair and mane, all seemed to almost glow with cleanliness and good health. The Gle'Ur'Gya Captain's great kilt was spotless, without wrinkle, its fabric somehow richer looking.

Alan Garrison watched Swan, his heart compelling him. She knelt in the luxuriant grass, her skirts billowed round her like the petals of some shimmering blossom. She was a bloom more magnificent than the profusion of flowers surrounding her.

Erg'Ran attended her.

Swan wore a long-sleeved, satiny gown of her own making, the texture and color of which mirrored the muted reds of the upthrusting buds all about her, its square neckline at once modest yet revealing.

Alan Garrison followed Swan's gaze as she stared into the distance. Was she thinking about the storms which raged around them, one literally, the other figuratively? Or did she consider the scope of her magical powers? Swan could, it seemed, bring into reality that which she desired merely by imagining its existence. Was this, he wondered, the true essence of magic?

Garrison shuddered, dismissing the thought as quickly as it came that he, too, might only be a thought in her mind, existing only at Swan's will.

If a tear should fall from Swan's perfect eye, would it be as equally capable of magically transforming into a diamond of dew dotting the petal of a rose as a white-flecked torrent raging over the bodies of drowned enemies? If such a tear ran down her velvet cheek, would it be one of sadness for the terrible deeds still to come or of happiness for the bliss they had shared together and might share again?

At this moment, true happiness still eluded her, he knew, as it might forever elude them both. Garrison desperately wanted to picture Swan running into his arms, embracing him with all her might, every day for the rest of their lives, never letting him go. Had he magic, he would make it so. But, he wondered, had destiny intertwined their fates only briefly, deceived them with the promise of a fate they would forever be denied?

Alan Garrison could not take his eyes from Swan. . . .

"You cannot do this, Enchantress," Erg'Ran informed her. "It was I alone who made the decision to lop off my foot—it had to be done—and I did not ask you to give me a new foot."

The Enchantress smiled gently. "It was not my intention to be arrogant, uncle, but merely to do something, well—nice! If you do not wish to have a left foot, I will change it back for you."

"No, no," Erg'Ran explained, shaking his head. "This, all of this, is a waste of magical energy! I did not need a new robe; the old one was perfectly fine. Your heart is in the right place, but do you truly realize how much magical energy you are using in order to maintain the conditions you brought about in this valley, while all around us a storm rages? You may need every last iota of that energy to combat your mother, Enchantress."

"I have more power than she ever had," the

Enchantress answered matter-of-factly. "I just know, somehow, that I do."

"And you have the resource with which to renew that power, whereas Eran—at the moment—does not. I know that, Enchantress."

"What do you mean when you say 'at the moment,' Erg'Ran?"

"Your mother, my sister, has two options, dear one. The third option—to surrender—she would never consider. If I understand her thinking, as I feel that I do, this is her strategy. She will conserve her magical energy at all costs, as she did at the keep, while causing you to expend as much magical energy as possible, in the hopes that when a confrontation comes you will find yourself lacking. Unless, of course, her minions, by some fluke, are able to kill or capture you. You see, even if she wins against you, the source of the greatly magnified power to which Eran has become accustomed is now denied to her. Hence, her two options."

"Which are?"

Erg'Ran fumbled his pipe, Swan packing and lighting it for him in an eyeblink. "That is exactly the sort of wasteful use of magical ability to which I refer, Enchantress. Thank you, at any event. The two options are, I'm afraid, rather obvious. Would you care to suggest them?"

Swan's eyes widened, and Erg'Ran knew that she'd realized at least one of the options. "Al'An?"

"Oh, yes! Definitely, the Champion! If Eran can somehow overpower or destroy you, that is. As discussed before, he would have to take his own life. Eran's magic would be such that she could convince him that she was, in fact, you, and he would happily be her lover."

"Erg'Ran! No!"

"Understand," Erg'Ran told her, "that your Al'An would think, all the while, that he was in your arms, not hers, never realizing until she'd finished with him that she had taken advantage of him, created a fantasy in which he was merely her toy."

"And the other alternative? My mother's second option?" Swan asked.

"Failing that she could possess the Champion for her purposes, she would have to transport herself to the other realm and bring back another other realm male. While she was gone, of course, if you lived, you would be able to seize control of Creath. If the Champion lived, although, indeed, your powers would be greater than hers because you are half K'Ur'Mir and half of the other realm, there would be sufficient parity that the warfare could go on indefinitely." Erg'Ran glanced skyward. It was not yet dark, but he made the allusion at any event. "You would be like the sorceresses of the two moons. All of Creath would suffer."

Swan seemed to consider his words for some time. "Could she not," Swan inquired at last, "have left already for the other realm, Erg'Ran?"

Despite the balmy air and warm sunshine, Erg'Ran was suddenly chilled to the marrow. . . .

Time was now their worst enemy, Swan realized. And Erg'Ran had been right. She must use her magical energy more wisely than ever because of its enhancement. Otherwise, all of that for which the Company of Mir had fought would be forever lost.

Surrounded by Gar'Ath, Mitan, Erg'Ran and Captain Bre'Gaa, Al'An at her side, Swan stood at the center of the meadow she had formed within the magically protected valley.

"We must, I fear, act quickly, my friends. All may already be lost. Each eyeblink's delay could precipitate a disaster from which Creath might never recover. I could use considerable magical energy to transport to Barad'Il'Koth the companies of our ships, but we would still be hopelessly outnumbered by the Horde of Koth and those other foemen whom my mother can send against us.

"For that reason," Swan went on, "I have decided on a course of action, in counsel with Erg'Ran, which my mother, the Queen Sorceress, would never consider."

Erg'Ran spoke. "The problem, simply put, is that, even as we speak, Eran might already have transported herself to the other realm, have found an other realm male, mated with him and be fully prepared to continue warfare on Creath of infinite scale and duration. In all of my planning for the events which I had hoped would bring victory for the Enchantress and freedom for Creath, I failed miserably to consider that one possibility. It might prove our undoing, and the fault will be mine alone should such circumstances come to pass."

"Enough of that," Swan told him, meaning it. "We began as friends and shall end as friends, and the responsibility for whatever transpires, for good or ill, is mine alone, and I am the most fortunate of womankind that we endure whatever it is that we must endure together."

"What is your plan, Enchantress?" Gar'Ath asked.

Swan looked at the young swordsman and smiled. "We need an army, and there is only one army in the history of Creath which stood strong enough to combat the forces which my mother will assemble against us, and which can resist the force of my mother's magic."

Al'An just looked at her, understanding not at all, while Mitan and Gar'Ath were visibly shaken.

Captain Bre'Gaa said, "There is only one army of which I know which was ever that numerous, that strong. It is the army which was raised and led by Mir against the sorceresses, ending the dark times."

"It is that army of which I speak," Swan answered

softly. Mitan sucked in her breath in what could have been a gasp. . . .

The storm through which they'd interminably ridden was dissipating almost as quickly as it had fallen upon them. Moc'Dar's horse, nearly spent, heaved with each breath. He raised his right hand and signaled that his column should halt.

With great weariness, Moc'Dar dismounted, the fallen snow rising half the height of his knee boots.

"Dismount!" Moc'Dar ordered, his command echoed and re-echoed along the column's length.

The Ra'U'Ba near him asked, "Why do you order this? We can go on. The sky is clearing, Captain. See!"

"I know that the storm passes, as any fool knows." Shaking his head, he humored the Ra'U'Ba and glanced skyward. "Look!" Moc'Dar shouted. "Look there!" Gathering the folds of his cloak close about him, Moc'Dar began to clamber up the ridgeline. The clouds were breaking, what sky was visible a dully gleaming grey. But, in the distance, there was incredibly bright blue. "Send the Yeoman Spellbreaker!"

Halfway up to the ridgeline, Moc'Dar looked back. Trundling gracelessly through the snow and into the drifts at the ridge's base came his Yeoman Spellbreaker. Moc'Dar called back. "Ra'U'Ba! You will join us at once!" The blue had to be magic, had to be the work of the Virgin Enchantress.

Moc'Dar dropped to his knees, then to a prone position at the very height of the ridgeline, the snow wet and cold and working its way through his cloak and the leathers beneath. After what seemed an eternity had passed, but only a few eyeblinks really, the Yeoman Spellbreaker knelt beside him. "They may have guards second-sighting. Down flat, boy!"

"Yes, Captain Moc'Dar!"

The Ra'U'Ba reached the ridgeline and Moc'Dar ordered him down also. Ra'U'Ba looked oddly comical

under normal circumstances when getting up or
getting down, their characteristically heavy tails awkward seeming at best. But, attired as this one was—
legs heavily wrapped under his skirt, the tail wrapped
as well, upper body swathed in cloak upon cloak—
the spectacle was beyond bizarre.

At last, the Ra'U'Ba as flat as he could get in the
snow, Moc'Dar ordered the Yeoman Spellbreaker,
"Second-sight me what is on the ground beneath that
clear patch of sky, boy. Be quick and accurate."

"Yes, Captain!"

Moc'Dar didn't even look at him, until he heard
him. "Specters!" The Yeoman Spellbreaker screamed
the word like a tortured woman. . . .

Swan, exquisite, her arms upraised, palms open,
fingers outstretched, a fierce wind from nowhere
tousling the wild mass of her auburn hair, ceaselessly
assailing her skirts, commanded the magic.

Since he had come to Creath and learned to
believe in the reality of magic, Alan Garrison had
never been witness to a vortex like the one he now
beheld. He doubted that anyone had. Its texture was
velvet black, its substance darker than the deepest
shadow, all light—save for tiny pinpoints, like stars
in the night—absorbed within it. And, as he watched,
Alan Garrison realized that he was peering into death
itself.

From within the vortex, moving independently of
touching anything, their horses' hooves trodding thin
air as though it were hardest ground, rode an army
of the dead, girded for battle.

In a column of twos they rode. Pennants, mounted
atop gleaming lances, stiffened before a wind which
had not blown for a thousand years. Leather and steel,
long since decayed in rot and rust, were solid matter once more. Polished and burnished, it creaked and
clanged. Sinews and muscles—human and equine

alike—surged with movement long foreign to them
and voices spoke, echoing forgotten words from out
of the grave.

Their armor was a mixture of articulated full-
plate—so often wrongly associated with Arthurian
Britain, but actually coming to flower in the late-
fourteenth century—and mail with leather. Some were
surcoated, heraldic symbols emblazoned to the chest
as both a badge of identity and a challenge to foemen.
Spurs tinkled, hooves clopped and horses of power
and majesty whinnied, the exanimate army splitting
into two files as it exited the vortex onto solid ground,
fanning out to either side of the valley, riding onward.

Soon, riding alone in the wake of a dozen dozen
knights, was a single man. His countenance, beneath
a full head of closely cropped auburn hair, was heroic,
an aquiline nose below a high forehead and deepset penetrating blue eyes, a wide mouth rigid with
determination within a jawline appearing to have been
chiseled from granite or cast from steel. The tendons
of his neck were tensed, disappearing beneath a coat
of burnished mail. Over his armor, he wore a surcoat
emblazoned simply with the hilt of a great sword
penetrating a round shield, but the shield was a
vortex.

His shoulders were broad, his upper body erect,
exuding strength and purpose. He rode a great white
steed, the carriage of its head and the powerfulness
of its neck reminiscent of purebred Arabian, its height
and musculature more like that of a Percheron. The
animal's trappings were magnificent; a great high-
cantled battle saddle, silver mounts matching the
adornments of its bridle and chest plate, an equine
counterpart to its rider's white emblazoned blood red
surcoat draping its body.

First handing off the great helm carried under his
arm to the knight at his right hand, the rider dismounted. He was tall, long-legged and arrow straight.

He approached Swan and dropped to one knee before her, deliberately drawing his sword, raising it to her in salute—his lips kissed its hilt—then lowering it, point to the ground. The bowed forehead touched its bronze cruciform hilt. "You are the Enchantress of whom I prophesied, but no longer virginal, or else you would not have had the power to summon me and my knights to your service. I pay homage to you for the great honor with which you charge me, that I might fight for you and for Creath."

As he spoke, the knights under his command continued to ride from within the black vortex, a double rank forming, completely circumferencing the valley. The man stood, smiled, took Swan's offered hand in his, bowed over it and kissed it.

"Had I fought throughout all eternity for this one shared touch, Enchantress, such efforts would have stood as an insignificant price to pay."

"I knew of your wisdom and courage, sir, but had only guessed at your gallantry," Swan informed him, her smile beaming.

He smiled again, saying, "Your gentle speech unduly flatters an old soldier, Enchantress. I entreat you cease." And he turned from Swan and looked Garrison straight in the eye, assessing him. Extending his hand, he said, "Hail Champion! I am Mir and would that I might bear sword beside you in the great fight."

Garrison clasped Mir's hand, expecting that his own hand might pass through it, that this man before him was ectoplasm rather than substance. But the hand was even warm.

"I do not understand any of this, sir," Alan Garrison declared, the words coming very slowly, deliberately.

Mir's eyes twinkled as he smiled and responded, "The magic! Yes! I once was like you, Champion. More than you might suspect. Know this, that before I ride back through that vortex into the repose of death, I will with you share a secret known by none living in these days."

Mir turned away, addressed Swan, "With your permission, Enchantress. I take it that we ride against Barad'Il'Koth, for nowhere else on Creath would there be the seat of evil power."

"Indeed, great sir."

"May I then speak to all present?"

"You do us wondrous honor that we should be privileged to hear your words, sir."

Mir nodded, called to the knight to whom he'd passed his helm, "Have it that my knights dismount, Tre'El."

"It shall be so, Mir." The knight ordered, "Prepare to dismount!" Along the entire length of the valley, the command was echoed and re-echoed. At last, Tre'El gave the word, "Dismount!" As one, the knights stepped down from their saddles, the creak of leather and the clang of steel rising in a crescendo, then gone. There was, indeed, not a sound but the crunch of ground beneath Mir's feet as he paced a few steps forward.

Once again Mir drew his sword. Placing its point to the ground, Mir rested his hands upon its quillons. "The day foretold has come," Mir began, his voice not a shout, but clear, reverberating along the length of the valley and to all sides. "And she who was foretold is among us!"

A hurrah rose up spontaneously.

As the cheer subsided, Mir continued. "We have been honored beyond measure that, in Creath's time of greatest need and greatest opportunity, we once more can fight against tyranny, fight for freedom!"

Again, voices raised in approbation.

"As we serve our Enchantress, we serve Creath. I cannot tell you what fate might await any who fall in battle. Would we return to our deaths, or would our spirits forever be denied that ease? But as we once

gambled life for death, shall we now, in the cause of
good and right, gamble death for the unknown?"

It began as a single voice, then a dozen, then a
hundred, until all of the knights who thronged the
valley chorused, "For the Enchantress! For Creath!"

"Then we shall take horse anon and, under the
banner of freedom, in company of the Enchantress
and her fierce Champion, we shall smite the enemies
of goodness and justice and honor. To all of this shall
we swear our destinies and our swords?"

As if one voice, the single word, "Yes!" thundered
from the army of the dead.

Then all was still. Mir raised his sword, its steel
gleaming white gold beneath the sunlight. At the top
of his lungs, he shouted, "Enchantress! Prithee close
the vortex from death! All in this valley now to horse!
To Barad'Il'Koth! To victory!"

If he hadn't already signed on to this war, Alan
Garrison realized that he would have enlisted on the
spot. Swan clapped her hands closed and the vortex
disappeared into itself. She turned and looked at him,
smiled, then kissed his cheek. "I love you, Al'An."

Alan Garrison told her honestly, "Always," then
started to look for Swan's horse. As he turned his
head, he saw Erg'Ran. The old man wept. . . .

Eran sat in her throne chair. The six Handmaidens
who most closely attended her made themselves
prostrate on the treads at her feet, she and they the
only living things in the great hall. Torches flared
smokelessly in sconces everywhere along the side walls
and great braziers filled with magical fire which
consumed no fuel and gave no heat burned on either
side of her.

"Which one of you will dare speak?" Eran inquired,
knowing full well that it would be Belan, the most
gifted and most beautiful of them, as it always was.
"She may rise to her knees before me."

Belan rose. Head bowed beneath her veil, she began, "O mighty Queen Sorceress at whose feet we fawn, I would beg to speak."

"So be it."

"There is communication from the field, Great One, passed by the minds of the Ra'U'Ba."

"Speak to me of it, Belan." Eran lifted her heavy velvet skirts, rearranging them as she leaned forward, perching on the edge of her throne, her chin resting in her hands.

"It would appear, Mighty Queen, predicated upon the magical power which was reportedly witnessed, that the union between the Daughter Royal and the other realm man has—"

"No!" Eran rose so violently to her feet that the wine cup beside her tumbled, spilling its blood-red contents across the stone. Belan shrank back in fear, reassuming the fully supplicant posture of the other witches.

"What sort of manifestation?" Eran reseated herself.

Belan's voice trembled, was muffled by the stone step against which her face was pressed. "Mighty Queen, it is reported that there was a vortex, unlike any ever witnessed, enormous and black. From within the vortex, Great One, rode an army of armor-clad warriors."

"And?" Eran realized that her own voice trembled and she clasped her hands tightly in her lap because, like the rest of her body, they shook.

"The leader of this army, Great Queen Sorceress, a knight of heroic bearing, wore emblazoned on his red surcoat the sword penetrating the vortex shield, the symbol of—"

"I know whose accursed symbol it is!" Eran shrieked as she sprang to her feet. The Handmaidens shrank from her in terror. Eran began to descend the steps leading from her throne, the Handmaidens grasping at her dress, eagerly pressing their lips to its hem. Eran had no strength to pull clear of them, was barely able to walk.

Her life was falling into ruin and she silently cursed the day she brought Swan's life from her womb.

In the history of Creath, there was no other army of knights like that which Belan had described. Nor, in all of history, was there anyone who wore the symbol spied on the knight's surcoat, save for one: Mir.

Swan had summoned the dead to be her army, and they would be invincible foemen.

Three choices remained to her, capitulation unthinkable.

Eran could utilize virtually all of her magical energy to summon once again the Mist of Oblivion, to devour her enemies. But, if Swan had indeed mated with the other realm male—which she obviously had—Swan might be able to seize control of the Mist and turn it against her. If Swan drastically depleted her own magical energy in doing so, she could easily replenish it by using the other realm male to her purpose.

Eran knew that she could flee, flee to the other realm and find an other realm male with whom to mate, replacing Pe'Ter. By the time that she could return, Swan would have seized Barad'Il'Koth, banished the Horde to the four winds, and—if she had the stomach for it—seen to the execution of the Sword of Koth and the Handmaidens of Koth.

Because Swan's blood was half of Creath and half of the other realm, her magic might even now be greater than had ever been known in Creath, materially stronger than Eran's own. Giving Swan time to learn to use it could prove to be a strategic error from which Eran might never recover.

There was one final option, and Eran would require the assistance of her Handmaidens in order to attempt it. If she succeeded, she could destroy her daughter and the army of the dead. "Handmaidens! Attend me quickly!" Eran screamed. She drew up her skirts and ran from the great hall, laughing uncontrollably. . . .

Through the Ra'U'Ba, Moc'Dar received the order from the Queen Sorceress, Mistress General, "Fight my Daughter Royal and her army of the dead until your own death, Moc'Dar, or suffer in unimaginable horror and degradation throughout eternity as the despised object of my unremitting wrath."

Head bowed low, Moc'Dar sat on a rock surrounded by drifted snow. Tears streamed from his eyes beneath his mask. In his hands, he held a dagger. With it, he could end his life, obviate the consequences of failure in battle and the continuance of life. Moc'Dar could still see himself, feel himself as the contemptuous, despicable beast into which Eran had once before transformed him. Failure in service to the Queen Sorceress this time promised a fate incomprehensibly wretched, remorselessly certain.

Moc'Dar raised his head, sniffed back his tears, stood. Clearing his throat, he called out to the Ra'U'Ba who stood some distance away, eating something nearly as disgusting looking as the Ra'U'Ba himself. "You! Feed your face if we are victorious! Contact the others of your kind with my force. Tell them where we are and that we will execute a strategic withdrawal toward the keep, then stand and fight. I need all with me who can be with me. Any man who fails me will wish that he were dead. Make this known, and do it now!"

Moc'Dar had decided that he would fight to the death and welcome death when it came to free him. . . .

"Tell me more about this person Bu'Cka'Roo Fi'Sh'Man, Champion," Gar'Ath requested.

Alan Garrison, Gar'Ath and a dozen of Mir's knights,

Mir's Knight Commander Tre'El among them, had been riding point ahead of Mir's main column for some time, seeing nothing but rocks and snow instead of enemy troops. Swan would be second-sighting periodically, of course, but it was still prudent to have a scouting party. "Well, you see, where I come from, and not very long ago really, there were wild and untamed places and they attracted men who were the same. There were some of these men who fought for good, and some who were very evil. Buckaroo Fishman, although little known, was one of the good guys. He was a fast hand with a Colt Single Action—a firespitter—and wickedly effective with a Bowie knife. A Bowie knife is a kind of dagger, Gar'Ath, named after Jim Bowie."

"I see, Champion. This Bu'Cka'Roo fought bravely then against many adversaries, as did this Bo'Wie?"

"Oh, yeah. Wouldn't mind having Buckaroo Fishman or Jim Bowie along with us right now, I'll tell you, Gar'Ath. And, we could throw in Wyatt Earp and Doc Holliday, too, for good measure. And, since we're fantasizing, I wouldn't mind Robin Hood and his Merry Men of Sherwood Forest helping us. Bruce Lee might come in handy, too."

"Who are these other heroes of whom you speak, Champion?"

Garrison patted the neck of his mount, looked at Gar'Ath and started to answer. But, past Gar'Ath's shoulder, about a hundred yards distant, he saw the glint of what might have been steel reflecting under the feeble sun.

A hundred yards was a doable but less than ideal shot for an average longbowman, Garrison surmised, at least against a man-sized target. It was less likely still to be made with a crossbow. So, whoever watched them—if, indeed, someone did—had to be scouting for intelligence concerning their movements. "Be ready for trouble. Don't look, but there may be somebody out there around a lancethrow away."

"Aye, Champion. I noticed it as well, but it's a bit further off than a lancethrow, I'd wager."

Without turning around, Garrison called out to the Knight Commander, "Tre'El?"

"Yes, Champion?"

"We may be under observation from that direction." And, Garrison inclined his head to indicate the spot toward which he referred.

"I will alert the knights, Champion."

Garrison nodded.

Gar'Ath, his voice low, presumably so that his utterances would not be overheard by Tre'El, asked, "Did you ever think that dead men could be returned to flesh and blood such as these? It is, I think, quite vexing to consider."

"Vexing? You're putting it mildly, Gar'Ath!"

"'Tis true. But, verily, the magic of the Enchantress surpasses all understanding, Champion."

"You're putting it mildly again," Garrison agreed. His horse was starting to act oddly skittish. He was no expert horseman, nor certainly able to read the equine mind, but the animal might have smelled something, sensed something, that he could not. "I've got a funny feeling," Garrison remarked, as inconspicuously as possible loosening the lashings which held his shield to his saddle so that he could access it more quickly. Gar'Ath had given him a few quick pointers in the use of the shield—for practical reasons and to kill time—before Swan had summoned Mir and his knights through the vortex. The brief instruction had convinced Garrison that, under the circumstances which he might be about to encounter, the Golden shield of IBF could be a decided asset, however inexperienced he was in its use.

Their small column approached a rise, ridges extending toward them from either side of it, not truly significant geological features but of sufficient height that a clever enemy could keep itself hidden until the very last moment before a trap was sprung.

"I've got a funny feeling," Garrison announced again.

Gar'Ath only nodded, his eyes focused on the horizon.

"I saw this in a Western movie, once," Garrison remarked. "The Apaches—or maybe it was the Sioux or Cheyenne—they had their ponies lying down on the ground and kept them there by lying down over the horses' necks. When the Cavalry or wagon train or whatever rode past, every man in the war party sprang onto his mount and they rode up over the ridges they'd been hiding behind, just like they'd popped up out of the ground."

"Of what do you speak, Champion? When did these events transpire?" Gar'Ath pressed, sounding perplexed.

"Tell you later," Garrison promised. His eyes flickered from side to side, ridge to ridge. "You think Mitan knows that deal with the second sight where she can use a spell and see around obstacles?"

"I don't know, Champion. Why do you ask?"

"I was just kind of sorry Mitan stayed behind with the main column. Wishful thinking, that's all."

Garrison stood a little in his stirrups, as if stretching. Still, he could see nothing. The glint of steel he'd spied before was long gone. It couldn't have been a carelessly discarded aluminum pop can, not on Creath. Garrison made a decision. "Tre'El! Split the column. Have eight of your knights fall off with their weapons ready, and wait until we're at the top of that rise before they join us."

"What is it, Champion?" Tre'El asked.

"If it's a trap, no sense letting the enemy spring it the way they'd planned, is there?" Garrison drew his sword; he hadn't checked his firespitters to see if Eran's spell against them still held. He'd thought to ask Swan if she could do something about that, but then the vortex appeared and Mir and his knights rode out and everything happened very rapidly after that.

Gar'Ath unsheathed his blade as well.

Tre'El rode up even with them, settling his sugar-loaf-style helmet over his mail-coifed head. Garrison could barely discern that there was a living being— so to speak—beneath the helmet. Its long, narrow eyeslits were the only true openings. There were, additionally, numerous tiny holes—like the openings in a colander—corresponding to the positions of the wearer's cheeks, presumably for air intake and ventilation. From within the helmet, Tre'El's voice sounded oddly muffled as he said, "You have a talent for tactics, Champion."

"Tell me that again if we get out of this alive," Garrison said.

Tre'El only laughed. "Death isn't really what you might think."

"Honestly, it would be fascinating to discuss it with you, Tre'El, and I hope I live through this in order to have that opportunity, among other things."

Gar'Ath announced, "The moment approaches, my friends."

"Let's really surprise the crap out of them," Garrison said. Extending his sword before him and drawing up his shield to protect the left front side of his body, he shouted, "Charge!"

Garrison dug his heels into his horse's flanks, Gar'Ath's and Tre'El's mounts coming to a gallop on either side of him. A quick glance over his left shoulder confirmed that the other three knights with Tre'El were right behind them and the eight who'd been ordered to stay back were couching lances, drawing swords, readying flails. . . .

"They are madmen," Moc'Dar growled from within his mask, and he felt himself smile. The Roc'Ar'Kar, lying flat on its right side beneath him, stirred, its powerful hooves pawing the ground. "Yes!"

Moc'Dar sprang from the horse's neck to his feet, giving a tug to the reins, the mighty animal leaped upright. Moc'Dar wrestled the Roc'Ar'Kar into obedience and grasped the animal's high-cantled war saddle, mounting quickly as he ordered the five score soldiers with him, "We attack!" To the animal's flaring ear, Moc'Dar cooed, "We shall both die as we have lived, in the flame of battle!"

Moc'Dar drew his firesword, the Roc'Ar'Kar jumping the low ridge of rock, bounding down into the defile, toward the Champion and the others. "I defy you!" Moc'Dar screamed at them.

The Sword of Koth immediately flanked him, men scrambling to their frantic mounts, running beside their animals, flinging themselves into the saddles. Looking behind him, he saw the scores of the Horde taking to their animals. As he'd withdrawn, buying time, five of the remaining seven elements of his original force had rejoined him.

Surprised, as he turned his head, Moc'Dar saw the Ra'U'Ba. Moc'Dar not only held the Ra'U'Ba in contempt as a race, but had come to dislike this one on a personal basis. The Ra'U'Ba called out to him, saying, "You are not the only one who can die bravely in battle, Captain! I will die with you!"

Moc'Dar nodded, and with his sword gave the Ra'U'Ba a salute, then flicked the sword's flat against the rump of his Roc'Ar'Kar and leaned into its neck. The animal's mane lashed at Moc'Dar's leather masked face, his eyes stinging from the occasional random impact and the cold wind around them. He spurred his animal faster, faster.

The Champion and the five men with him—four of them were knights of the old days from the time of Mir—reined in their mounts. Would they stand and die or flee, Moc Dar wondered?

Eight more knights, several lancethrows back, formed themselves into a skirmish line.

The Champion's horse reared, the other realm male keeping to the saddle with little grace but noticeable strength of will. "I would have your blood on my sword, Champion!" Moc'Dar called out.

The Champion and his five companions readied their weapons. No firespitter would save this other realmer now, and Moc'Dar acknowledged within himself that the Daughter Royal's Champion showed courage, refusing to give ground in the face of certain death.

Less than a lancethrow away, Moc'Dar's troops thundering in his wake, Moc'Dar's heart sank. The Champion and his cohorts wheeled their horses, spurred their animals away. "Cowardly bastard!" Moc'Dar shouted after him, enraged.

Moc'Dar reined in, his men doing likewise. At the top of his voice, Moc'Dar commanded, "Sword of Koth! Form skirmish line!" His men rode forward, falling into a rank on either side of him, stretching from horizon to horizon, as far as the eye could see. One of the Sword Generals used his horse to shove the Ra'U'Ba aside, and Moc'Dar ordered his titularly superior officer, "Give place to the Ra'U'Ba!"

"Yes, Captain."

Moc'Dar's eyes and the eyes of the Ra'U'Ba met, and then the moment was passed.

Moc'Dar raised his voice again. "Horde of Koth! Form three skirmish lines behind the Sword of Koth!" The clopping of hooves, the rattle of equipment, the creaking of leather, all formed a wondrously reassuring cacophony surrounding him.

Moc'Dar stood in his stirrups. One hundred score of men, all of them ready to fight and die, were ahorse and ready. Moc'Dar edged his Roc'Ar'Kar forward, inclining his head toward the Ra'U'Ba to join him. "Can your mount keep up?"

"If it falls, I'll run beside you, and then ask if your mount can sustain the pace."

Moc'Dar truly laughed, and felt a freedom he could barely recall having ever felt before.

"Good man!" Moc'Dar raised his voice one more time, shouting more loudly than he had before. "On my signal! Ready! At a canter! Forward!"

The Sword of Koth a stride behind him and the Horde behind them, all gradually picked up speed.

The Champion, his five companions and the eight knights who had stayed back were all mere silhouettes in the distance, and Moc'Dar knew where they were heading. He would follow, as they wanted him to.

They would lead him to the army of the dead.

Nearly out of sight, the Champion and his cohorts stopped.

This would be it.

As if materializing out of the ground behind them, there was a line, what little sunlight remained reflecting from swords and helms and armor, knights so numerous that the rank they formed not only stretched from horizon to horizon, it seemed, but beyond, as if, somehow, their numbers girded Creath, a barrier which could not be circumvented.

The Champion and his cohorts were lost among the knights who composed the army of the dead. Every other man in their rank rode a few strides forward, the knights in the now anterior rank raising their lances.

Running out ahead of this rank were archers, countless in number. After they formed, every other of them moved two paces forward and dropped to one knee, the rank behind them closing together. As one, the two ranks of archers drew taut their bows, fired a volley, their arrows landing in the ground. Another volley was fired, the arrows landing closer to the archers. They were setting distance for their longbows, marking the range. The archers remained formed, but slackened their bow strings.

Moc'Dar wanted to feel the wind on his face one last time.

The reins to the Roc'Ar'Kar in his teeth, with his left hand Moc'Dar reached up, slipping the knot at the nape of his neck which bound closed his head-cloth. He flung the black fabric aside. His fingers untied the lashing which bound his mask over his face. He spit the reins away, then tore the black leather from his skin. Moc'Dar cast the mask of the Sword of Koth to the ground beneath his horse's hooves.

Gathering the Roc'Ar'Kar's reins, Moc'Dar leaned well back in the saddle, brandished his sword at arm's length above his head and screamed, "Follow me to death!" And to freedom. . . .

Erg'Ran, ahorse, zigzagged his way among the ranks of mounted knights, nearing Mir, calling to him, "I must know before you enter battle! I must know!"

Eyeblinks remained, Swan knew, before the battle would be joined, the first arrows shot. Mir had requested that she remain behind with a rear guard, and she would honor that request, Mitan with her.

Beside Swan, Mir had already donned arming cap and mail coif and was about to lower his helmet into place. But he stopped, turning his face toward the sound of Erg'Ran's voice. "And what is it that you must know, uncle and mentor to the Enchantress? I am honored that you do think so well of me."

Erg'Ran, despite the fact that he was on horseback, was out of breath. Sniffing once, he looked Mir in the eye and asked, "Whence cometh your gift of prophecy, sir? Who are you?"

Mir crossed his right leg over the neck of his great steed, his right elbow coming to rest on his knee, and

his chin settling into his leather-gauntleted hand. "You
have studied my teachings, I am flattered to know,
for it is you who led the Enchantress so wisely to this
time and place." He smiled, almost laughing, but not
derisively. "Were I to reveal to you the answer to
either of these two questions which you set before
me, Erg'Ran, would you believe it? Or, as well used
to the enigmas in which I have wrapped many of what
you have spoken of as prophecies, would you see my
answer merely as a riddle?

"You, Erg'Ran, of all who breathe the magic of life,
are most well-suited to understand what answer I
might give. You risk your life for the benefit of all.
Within your brain is a repository of great wisdom, yet
you constantly seek more knowledge. You have magic
well beyond the ken of any male ever of Creath, yet
you foreswear its use for your own ends. When lately
I inquired of you from the Enchantress, she regaled
me with such facts as these, and most happily enliv-
ened our discourse."

"I—I do not understand, sir."

"Ah, but you do! I am a man, and never was I
more, nor do I hope ever to be less. I asked questions and sought answers. I was not content in darkness, and struggled for the light of wisdom. A fate
was lain before me, and I could not deviate from its
design. Like you, I realized that I trod an unforgiv-
ing path."

A voice called out from the foremost rank of
knights. "The enemy is near to range for the longbows, Mir!"

"Anon! Anon!" Mir retorted. He looked again at
Erg'Ran. "My destiny awaits me once again, as will
yours. Only in that hour shall you truly know the
answers which you seek. But here are my answers.
The gift of prophecy which you credit to me is not
prophecy at all, but logic. If one sets out a plan
for future history, a time when evil shall be

crushed by good, there will always be persons of good heart who see such prophecies as hope and shall endeavor, beyond their ordinary abilities, to bring such happier times to pass. They will find wellsprings of strength which they never knew that they possessed, and courage in greater measure than a thousand thousand armies such as mine." Mir's right hand gestured around him, to his knights and archers. "Specificity is the ruination of prophecy.

"And your second interrogative I have already answered, but will vouchsafe to say again: I am a man." Mir donned his helmet and charged Erg'Ran, "Care for your Enchantress as you do always. Remember, Erg'Ran, that the sweet scented flower and the rankest shrub sprout from the same ground; while quiet diligence nurtures the blossom, unreasoning zeal can foster the weed."

Mir swung his leg back over his saddle and drew his sword. Quietly, he rode forward, immersing himself in the sea of armored warriors beneath wind stiffened pennants.

Had she been a man, Swan realized, she could have ridden between Mir and her Champion, fought beside them; but, were she a man, there would not be stirring deep within her those feelings for Al'An which so quickened the woman's heart which beat within her breast.

"Uncle?"

"Yes, Enchantress?" Erg'Ran responded, his gaze at last turning from Mir.

"Al'An will survive the ordeal which is before us?"

Erg'Ran smiled, reached across the gulf between their mounts and closed his hand over hers. "A man fights for many reasons. Al'An genuinely feels for the cause which brought us to this place, to this time. And, of all men, because he loves you, he has great reason to return from the field of battle, to once again be at your side. If passion, then, can armor a man against his enemies, your Champion is well-shielded from hurt."

Swan nodded.

One thing had been missing from Mir's words of explanation to Erg'Ran. Had there been nothing more to Mir's great prophecies than logically based conjecture concerning the course of future history—as Mir purported—then how had he known that the Virgin Enchantress was to seek the origin of her seed? How had he known that she would find a Champion in the other realm? By Mir's own words, "Specificity is the ruination of prophecy," Mir had contradicted his very contention.

Swan asked Erg'Ran, "Did you notice something odd in Mir's words, uncle?"

"Riddles within riddles, Enchantress. Mir draws one into logical befuddlement, concealing his true nature within the very enigma which he leads one to believe that he is about to unravel. There is mystery to Mir, and well he knows it and well he keeps it."

Perhaps Erg'Ran had so diligently studied the teachings of Mir that he had begun to think like Mir. At times, he certainly talked like him. Swan shook her head and looked away, the fighting about to start. She would second-sight the battlefield, perhaps seeing more than she would wish to see. But before she did that, there was one thing more important than anything. She urged her mount forward, into the knot of men gathering around Mir. Her eyes moving to right and left, at last she saw that for which she searched, the face of Al'An. He conversed with Gar'Ath and one of Mir's knights.

Swan turned her horse toward him, patted its neck with her hand, the animal moving forward. "Al'An! Al'An!"

Al'An turned his head, saw her, said something to Gar'Ath, then spurred his mount toward her. In an

eyeblink that seemed like an eternity, their horses had
stopped and they sat facing one another.

"I wanted to tell you that I love you, Al'An," Swan
said.

"And I love you."

"Then, kiss me only once and I shall keep your
touch on my lips until once again we kiss when the
battle is done."

Al'An leaned forward, his horse closer to hers now,
his right arm encircling her waist, drawing her close
to him. And his mouth came against hers and her
limbs were weak and she pressed her body against
his. "I won't die, Swan," Al'An whispered. "I promise, darling."

"I shall hold you to your promise, my love."

Al'An touched his hand to her cheek, turned his
horse with a tug to its reins, rode off. A tear fell upon
Swan's cheek and she made no attempt to brush it
away. . . .

A gap formed within the first rank of knights, Mir
leading them into it. Alan Garrison, shield up, sword
drawn, rode beside the once again living legend, and
with Garrison were Captain Bre'Gaa, Gar'Ath and,
hastening to join them, Erg'Ran. Tre'El, Mir's Knight
Commander, sat on horseback between the rearmost
rank of archers and the leading rank of knights,
awaiting Mir's signal that the battle should begin.

Riding along the broad defile, their numbers
stretching from horizon to horizon, their horses at a
steady gallop, were the forces of the Queen Sorceress.

"The Enchantress second-sighted on them, just an
eyeblink ago. Moc'Dar, only a Captain, leads them,
Generals among them. Most peculiar," Erg'Ran
announced. "The Enchantress tallies their number at
one hundred score foemen."

Mir said, "Numerically, we are then evenly matched.

They cannot win over us, they know that. Lightly armored foot soldiers, ahorse on animals which will be more than half-spent before engagement, pitted against heavily armored knights and ranks of archers! For whatever reason they take the fool's gambit, blood-sworn foemen though they may be and however evil their cause, we do not cross steel with cowards this day."

Mir leaned across his saddle and told the knight beside him, "Let the word be passed that each of the enemy who fights with honor is rightwise due an honorable death."

"Yes, Mir!"

Mir looked forward. "Tre'El! The archers shall stand down and retire to take up a defensive position in support of the Enchantress. We shall take no unfair advantage in the field."

"Yes, Mir!" And, Tre'El ordered, "Archers! Stand down!"

Garrison looked at Mir. Alan Garrison had met brave men and foolish ones, but never before a great man.

As the archers threaded their way past the mounted knights, Mir stood in his stirrups, his visor lowered. "At a gallop! For the Enchantress!" Mir charged his knights. "For Creath! For freedom!" Brandishing his sword high above his head, Mir shouted, "We ride to victory!" The magnificent white horse on which Mir was mounted moved forward at its rider's urgings, Garrison knocking his heels against his own animal's flanks.

As if the front rank were one organism, it moved forward, at first snakelike, but after a few strides the horses and their riders formed into a remarkably straight line, lances still raised. The second rank, as Garrison glanced over his shoulder, began its advance, about a dozen yards behind the first.

Garrison strained to look along the line. He saw Tre'El, he thought. He caught possible glimpses of the other knights who had accompanied them for the reconnoitering. One man was distinguishable from another solely by the color combinations of surcoat, helmet plume, and lance as all helmet visors were lowered, all faces obscured.

The army of the dead advanced.

Coming down the defile toward them, still at least a mile or better away, rode the armies of Barad'Il'Koth.

Mir sat rapier-straight in the saddle, his sword low at his side, his body moving in perfect rhythm with the white charger which he rode.

Garrison looked at Erg'Ran. His drawn sword, once his father's, hung easily in his right hand, the cowl of his robe thrown back, his lips drawn apart against the wind giving him the appearance of a smile, and perhaps it was.

Bre'Gaa rode with both hands on reins and cantle, the horse—of normal height and girth—looking almost too small for him, rather like the image of a Mongol warrior on a tiny Asian horse.

Gar'Ath's long hair seemed to float on the wind, almost arrow-shaft straight behind him. His right hand held his sword, his fist flexing round its hilt, as if constantly testing the weapon's balance.

All three of Garrison's compatriots looked well at ease as they rode into battle. Garrison, on the other hand, felt a mixture of fear and exhilaration, certain that the fear would grow until there was no time for it, the heat of the moment consuming it.

The horizon-to-horizon skirmish line in which they rode was quickening, almost imperceptibly. Mir raised his sword over his head, held it there for a long moment, then lowered it so that its hilt rested along his right side. As Garrison looked from right to left, the lances of Mir's knights arced downward, couching preparatory to impact, almost mirroring the precision of a Busbee Berkley choreography from a 1930s movie.

The army of the dead and the armies of Barad'Il'Koth were now only a little more than a thousand yards apart.

Garrison looked up, noticing at once two things which seemed very odd, but which he almost instantaneously dismissed. A great, black bird, the size of an eagle, but its wingspan wider, soared over what was to become the battlefield. And, in the distance, from the direction of Barad'Il'Koth, there was a peculiar black dot in the sky. He thought that it might be another bird. . . .

Swan grasped Mitan's arm.

"What is it?" Mitan asked, shrugging off her hooded cloak and starting to draw her sword. A stiff wind, cold and bitter, had arisen in an eyeblink, clouds of silver and black racing across the sky. That wind tore at Mitan's hair, lashed her bare flesh with its icy force.

At the sound of steel against leather, the archers notched their bows and the leader of the two score of knights ordered, "Draw swords!"

The second sight, as Swan had feared it might, revealed to her more than she wished to see. "My mother is second-sighting us, I think, through means of the great bird which circles above. But there is terrible danger afoot."

"What is it, Enchantress?"

"My mother— Mitan, the Queen Sorceress has summoned the Mist of Oblivion."

Mitan touched her fist, still clenched round her sword hilt, to her forehead. Her voice little more than a whisper, she invoked the courage of "Mir!"

Swan raised her voice, calling out to the knights and archers, "I shall need that all of you step away from me, leaving a clear space. You will take your instructions in certain tasks from the woman warrior Mitan. Do not be afraid of what you may see or hear or think!"

Swan glanced at Mitan, Mitan asking her, "What is it that you wish me to do, Enchantress?"

"There is only one thing which *I can do*," Swan told Mitan, realizing in that eyeblink that Mitan was the only female friend whom she had ever had. "If I were to place shift and somehow destroy my mother while she is weakened with controlling the Mist of Oblivion, that would only mean that the Mist would run its course, out of control, and might devour all of Creath. And the Queen Sorceress knows that I know this. She can have only one plan, and if I fail to counter it, all is lost forever. My mother is willing to risk the total obliteration of all of Creath, all life, in pursuit of her ends.

"I tell you this, Mitan, so that you will know that all that which I require of you must be accomplished with great diligence."

"Your will is mistress of my fate, Enchantress."

Swan embraced Mitan, kissing her cheek. "Dear friend, you must go out onto the battlefield, find Al'An and bring him to me. Have these knights of Mir, from whatever materials they can, construct an enclosure, around me, but not over me. Al'An alone must enter the enclosure. I will be like I have never been and hope never to be again. There will be grave danger. Al'An must know this and choose, of his own free will, to aid me. And you must tell Al'An that, if he does, whatever he sees, he must again become my lover, as soon as he has entered the enclosure. My life, his, yours and Gar'Ath's, Erg'Ran's, and all life on Creath will depend upon this."

"I fear for you, Enchantress and friend."

Swan embraced Mitan once again. "Hurry that what needs be might be accomplished before the Mist o'ertakes us all."

Mitan dropped to one knee, touched her forehead to Swan's hand, stood, then began issuing orders to Mir's knights and archers.

Swan's fingertips pinched the fabric of her skirts and lifted them slightly as she walked to the center of the ring of knights and archers. Already, the knights were stripping away their surcoats, taking their swords to their lances.

Swan had known since her girlhood that her mother, who had once shown genuine tenderness toward her, displayed unspeakable evil in her interactions with others. As Swan's body grew into womanhood, so did the depth and breadth of her understanding, her grasp of her mother's other self. When her mother realized that the Daughter Royal would not become chief among the Handmaidens of Koth, aiding her mother's evil magic, all loving kindness left their relationship. It was replaced by that same evil with which Eran systematically strangled the life from Creath, destroyed the K'Ur'Mir and all who opposed her. Swan fled with Erg'Ran to the summer palace, where evil magic could not hold sway. Only a long time afterward, her education well under way, was a truce effected between her and her mother. It allowed that she should dwell alone in her own castle, unmolested on condition that she take no active part in combating her mother's designs.

She should have realized then, as she finally did now, that there was magical power within her which her mother gravely feared, yet simultaneously wanted to employ.

That power was about to be put to its ultimate test.

Despite the magical energy which Swan had expended in the opening of the vortex into death and the summoning of Mir and his knights, she told herself that she still possessed adequate power to do what needed to be done.

Found within the scrolls destroyed when her castle was consumed by the Mist of Oblivion were many writings from before the coming of Mir, among these many of those same forbidden writings by means of which her mother's evil had grown to know no bounds.

The reading of them could sometimes evoke evil. As Erg'Ran had labored to translate them, he had wisely begun at their ending and worked toward their beginning, thus obviating the chance that the spell or summoning would become unintended magical reality.

As with everything which she read, these, too, were committed to memory.

Swan raised her voice, her arms outstretching to the sky, her fingers splayed, palms open to the magical energy surrounding her, drawing it into her. Its current surged throughout her body. She spoke, reciting one of these proscribed writings, saying the text in its natural order, the reverse of how she had learned the incantation.

Swan pressed her palms together between her breasts, becoming one with the energy around her. Light, dazzlingly bright filled her, exploded from her. Fear consumed her as the utterances left her lips. . . .

A sudden rising of wind, bitter cold, swept over the defile, and dark, luminescent clouds rushed to fill the dome of sky above the opposing armies. Mir thrust his sword toward the enemy forces, his blade at the full extension of his right arm, ordering in a voice which no howling wind, no thrumming hoofbeats could obscure, "At a gallop, charge!"

The ground beneath them shook and Garrison's ears pounded from the drumming of steel shod hooves, nearly two thousand fully armored knights, countless tons of heavily geared battle horses, men and animals in harmony, riding in almost perfect synchronization, a symphony of thunder.

The armies of Barad'Il'Koth quickened to a gallop, Garrison realizing full-well that this was all battle strategy. Two hundred yards separated them, would be gone in an instant, but not before the last hundred yards the enemy army crossed finished their horses to exhaustion. Those mounts which Mir's men rode would be fresher, stronger.

From the direction of Barad'Il'Koth, Alan Garrison saw a gathering darkness, blacker than any cloud could be, fog the color of the bottom of an inkwell devouring the sky.

"It is the Mist of Oblivion!" Erg'Ran was screaming.

Garrison could not have shouted back over the cacophony which surrounded them, only nodded that he had heard, understood. But, he did not, really. How could nothing consume something? And, he realized, the Mist would not only devour Mir's knights, but all who rode this defile. Eran was fully willing to kill virtually her entire army.

"Mir! It's the Mist of Oblivion!" Garrison tried to shout the warning. If Mir heard him, the legend did not acknowledge doing so. As if Garrison were not sufficiently terrorized, when he looked at Mir's white charger, Alan Garrison felt his heart skip a beat. The animal's gait seemed unaffected, but below the knee its off hind leg was becoming transparent.

Twenty-five yards.

The rising wind and the slipstream surrounding horse and rider blew froth and sweat from Garrison's mount back across Garrison's face, into his eyes. Garrison wiped it away with the sleeve of his bomber jacket.

A dozen yards. The leader of the armies of Barad'Il'Koth, although otherwise uniformed as Sword of Koth, was bareheaded and wore no black leather battle mask. Moc'Dar. Garrison looked along the length of Moc'Dar's red hot glowing firesword. There was fire, too, in his eyes, an expression akin to laughter etched across his face, his lips drawn back, teeth bared.

Alan Garrison thrust his sword out at full length

and leaned into his horse, its lather-soddened mane lashing at his face.

The sound, as the two armies met, was not the heroic oaths and villainous epithets of human voices, nor the shrieking of frightened animals, but instead like the impact of one heavy object slamming suddenly against another. And then, there was the clash of steel. Four thousand warriors fought to the death.

From the north, from Barad'Il'Koth, the Mist of Oblivion drew ever nearer.

Garrison had one last look at it, his horse bowled from under him by the thrust of a sword through its chest. He fell from the saddle, impacting the ground over his Golden Shield of IBF, scrambling away from the killing weight of the dead horse and the murderous hooves of the animals around him. A Sword of Koth, his firesword sizzling blood, bore down toward Garrison, Garrison throwing up his shield, deflecting the blow. Mir's white steed—its entire off-hind leg was now ghostly transparent—muscled between Garrison and the Sword of Koth. Mir's mighty sword arm swung, his blade cleaving through his enemy's skull from crown to jaw bone. "The magic, Champion! The Enchantress's magic is fading. Fight rapidly!" And Mir rode off.

For what seemed an eternity, Garrison stood in the middle of the battle, unhorsed, easy prey to his enemies, but his heart and mind obsessed with worry over Swan.

Two riders from the Horde closed toward Garrison. Garrison slammed the Golden Shield of IBF against the forelegs of the horse to his left, sidestepping the rider to his right. The horse which Garrison had impacted with his shield stumbled, fell to its knees. During the instant in which its Horde rider fought for balance, Alan Garrison stepped closer, slamming his shield against the rider now, his sword skating along the right edge of his shield, thrusting into the rider's chest.

As the horse staggered upright, Garrison flung himself onto its saddle, shouldering the dead Horde trooper to the ground. Garrison couldn't find the reins, instead grabbed a hank of mane and jerked it left, turning the frightened animal toward the second of his two attackers, the man bearing down on him with a sword. The horse began to stumble, for a fleeting instant Garrison wondering if it had broken a leg. Without thinking, Garrison looked down. The dead Horde of Koth's right foot was tangled in the right stirrup, half under the horse. Garrison swore at his own barbarism, hacking downward with his sword and severing the dead man's foot from the ankle. The horse half reared, gave a whinny more like a scream of fear, then vaulted forward.

Garrison's second attacker swung his sword, Garrison oriented in the opposite direction to be able to respond in kind, instead taking the full force of his opponent's blade on the Golden Shield of IBF. Garrison's body vibrated with it, his left arm numbing.

Guiding the horse with nothing but his knees, even his grasp on its mane lost, Garrison hacked downward with his sword as the horse wheeled round. Garrison's cut opened a wound in his attacker's right thigh and across the right side of the chest of his attacker's mount. The horse veered away. Garrison lunged, overextending himself to the point of nearly falling from the saddle. But the very tip of his blade punctured the right shoulder of his opponent, doing no serious damage.

Feeling was coming back into Garrison's left arm, and pain with it. He grabbed a handful of mane again, wheeling his horse a full ninety degrees. A Sword of Koth, blade gleaming bright red, charged toward him.

As Garrison tried to vector his own mount out of his enemy's way, he caught a fleeting glimpse of

Gar'Ath and Moc'Dar, both men still on horseback, locked in combat. A freeze-frame which would forever be emblazoned in his memory, had Garrison blinked he would not have seen it. Moc'Dar's firesword arced downward. Gar'Ath, his horse rearing under him, held to his saddle by his clenched left fist, his left arm at full extension, his left leg, bent at the knee, braced against the cantle.

Gar'Ath's body swung outward, right arm pistoning forward, the sword in his right hand impaling Moc'Dar through the heart.

The hint of laughter which Alan Garrison had seen etched in Moc'Dar's expression was still there as his head flung back and his body went rigid in death.

Garrison looked around. His Sword of Koth attacker was nearly upon him. There was nothing for it but to fight. Garrison dug in his heels, and the horse beneath him leaped forward. Garrison's mount and that of his enemy slammed against one another. The Sword of Koth's blade hacked downward, past his animal's head. Garrison deflected the blow with his shield, the sound of metal striking metal like the clanging of a bell. This time, Garrison had deflected the blow, not taken its full impact. He punched forward with his shield, hammering it against the head of his enemy's horse.

The horse lunged away, the Sword of Koth who rode it slashing with his blade. Garrison's horse took a deep cut along the left side of its neck. Rather than using his sword crossbody, Garrison slammed his shield against his opponent's left arm and shoulder.

Garrison's horse wheeled ninety degrees. Before his Sword of Koth attacker could respond, Garrison hacked downward with the K'Ur'Mir sword, missing his opponent's left shoulder, but opening a long cut along the Sword of Koth's upper arm.

Garrison dug in his heels, his attacker riding off, Garrison after him, sword raised, cleaving downward, this time finding its target, drawcutting from the right shoulder toward the spine, the tip of his blade snagging for a split second against the ribcage.

Garrison pulled back on his horse's mane, looked to right and left. At the far left edge of his peripheral vision, he saw Mitan. She fought her way toward him, her bare arms bloodied, more blood splotching her left cheek.

Garrison glanced skyward. Again, he felt his heart skip a beat.

The empty blackness which was the Mist of Oblivion was nearly over the battlefield, but from behind him, where he had left Swan in supposed safety, rose a gleaming golden vortex of incalculable size. Swan, ghostly transparent, floated in the air within the vortex, white hot energy emanating from her body. Swan and the vortex were one, energy flowing from it, into it, as if from the core of Swan's being there had formed a star and she was its fiery heart.

"What's happening!?" Garrison screamed, but knew that Mitan could not possibly hear him.

Two Horde of Koth troopers rode at him. "Not now!" Garrison threatened, begged. But they could not hear him, because he could barely hear himself, nor would it have mattered to them if they could hear him. Garrison saw Mitan's lips moving, but he could hear nothing over the din of battle.

Garrison grabbed a greater hank of mane and dug in his heels, spurring the animal toward the two Horde troopers. As he did so, he spied Mitan again, breaking clear of the knot of enemy personnel around her, riding toward him.

The two Horde of Koth vectored their mounts so that Garrison would ride between them, and Garrison did just as he realized they wanted him to do, but hoping to deny them the result that they desired. He tried what he'd tried before, using his shield as a weapon against the mount of the enemy to his left, if nothing else fending off one attacker while he dealt with the second.

The man to Garrison's right hacked his sword through a wide arc, Garrison barely halting the blade's travel in time, catching the enemy sword's edge against the flat of his own, his left arm—aching—hammering the Golden Shield of IBF first against the head and neck of the other Horde trooper's horse, then against the man himself.

Garrison's horse took a draw cut along the front of its neck and began to falter. Garrison started slipping from the saddle, the blade of the attacker on his right hacking toward him again. Garrison did the only thing that he could do. He wheeled his horse as it fell. Letting the Golden Shield fall from his left arm, Garrison jumped from his saddle, hurtling the full force of his body against the man to his right. With the hilt of his sword, Garrison hammered at the man's face, pounding and pounding until movement of the sword arm beneath him ceased and the man's body began sagging from the saddle.

Garrison couldn't clamber onto the horse, slipped, fell to the ground. His second attacker came at him in a rush, the man's sword swinging toward Garrison's head. Garrison still had his own sword, but tried something Gar'Ath had shown him. Inverting the sword in his hands, holding the blood-slicked steel by the blade, Garrison swung. One of his sword's drooping quillons caught the enemy's sword, the hilt of Garrison's sword skating along the other sword's spine. Garrison's sword locked with the other sword's hilt. Garrison was still in the swing, remembering his brief and less-than-promising Little League experience as a kid. "Follow through with the swing, son! Follow through is where it's at!"

As Garrison felt that he was about to auger himself into the ground, his arm muscles felt an incredible tug. Garrison lost his balance, looked up. His sword's hilt was still locked with that of his enemy, and his enemy was tumbling from the saddle.

Garrison let go of his sword, grabbing one of the automatic knives from his pockets, push-buttoning it open as he half-dove, half-fell onto his opponent. Garrison's knife missed its target, burying itself half the length of the blade into the ground. Garrison's left fist crossed the man's jaw. A knee smashed up into Garrison's abdomen, knocking the breath from him. Garrison fell back, but hadn't lost hold of his knife. The man drew a dagger, clambered to his feet and jumped. Garrison rolled to his right, the Horde of Koth soldier impacting the ground. Garrison rolled left, and as the enemy soldier started to move, Garrison's knife punched downward between the man's shoulder blades.

Garrison sagged back.

He looked up.

A Sword of Koth, firesword glowing red hot, charged him from horseback. Garrison wrestled his knife from the body of the man beside him, managed to get to his feet, no time even for the second knife.

Garrison knew what he had to do, his only chance and a poor one at best. As he was about to throw a body block against the knees of the Sword of Koth's mount, there was a flash of movement, the glint of steel.

The Sword of Koth soldier tumbled from his saddle. As Garrison looked past his fallen enemy, he saw Mitan, her sword freshly blood-slicked.

Garrison spotted his sword on the ground, picked it up, with his other hand closing and pocketing his knife, then grabbing for the reins of the dead man's mount.

Garrison grasped the saddle and half-jumped, half-collapsed into it.

Raising his head, he saw Mitan again, gesturing that he follow her. Garrison nodded, the reins tight in his left hand, his heels kicking hard against the animal's flanks.

The edge of the battlefield seemed much nearer than it should have been, and Alan Garrison realized that, if he were right, it meant that the armies of Barad'Il'Koth were being beaten back, Mir's knights winning.

Garrison felt a moment's alarm, Mitan swinging low out of her saddle, reaching for something on the ground. In the next instant, he realized what she'd reached for. She had recovered his shield.

A dozen yards or so away from the fray, Mitan reined in, next to Alan. "You fought well, Champion! The Enchantress needs you, and quickly!"

Garrison couldn't have answered if he'd tried, his breath coming only in gasps.

Mitan was already galloping off, toward the brilliantly glowing vortex, toward Swan. Garrison thwacked the flat of his sword against the dead man's horse that he rode, and followed.

A glance stolen over his left shoulder as he bent low over the horse's neck revealed things at once heartening and frightening. Indeed, Mir's knights were defeating the armies of the Queen Sorceress. But many of those knights, whom Garrison could see, and their mounts as well, were fading into transparency. He remembered Mir's words to him: "The magic, Champion! The Enchantress's magic is fading!"

And the Mist of Oblivion had grown to where it all but consumed the sky over the battlefield. Its fingers of deadly blackness were beginning to reach toward the ground.

Garrison dug in his heels, and rode toward the light of the vortex and Swan. . . .

For some stupid reason, Alan Garrison held his K'Ur'Mir sword clenched tightly in his right fist as he ducked to enter the enclosure made from the knight's surcoats, its framework from their splintered lances.

The sword fell from his hand. Involuntarily, Garrison turned his face away, shielding his head with his arms.

"Don't be afraid, Al'An. You must aid me, my love."

Squinting against the light, Garrison tentatively lowered his arms. What he had seen emanating skyward from within the enclosure had not prepared him for what he witnessed having entered.

Swan's body lay seemingly lifeless at the enclosure's exact center, as unmoving as if she were dead. The cone of magical light, which shown above the enclosure, out of which the vortex took its energy, emanated from within her hands, these clutched together between her breasts. But Swan's voice came again, not from her body but from above. "Lie beside me, my love, and be unafraid."

Garrison didn't move.

"Swan? What's going on?"

"I will die if you do not lie beside me Al'An, and share with me what only we can share."

"What, uh, what are you doing with the vortex?"

"Lie beside me, Al'An."

Alan Garrison looked upward, into the light. Involuntarily, he raised his arms once again in order to shield his face. There was no heat from the light, and despite its brilliance, as he gradually opened his eyes more fully, he could see, as if the light weren't really there.

"What do I do?" Garrison stared through the light, at Swan's ghostly image above him and the glowing vortex surrounding her. "What do I do?"

"Lie beside me," her voice spoke again. He saw no movement in her image, and he felt his skin goosefleshing as he realized that he wasn't hearing at all, that her voice was inside his head.

"I'm afraid, sweetheart. I'm afraid!" Garrison looked away, felt his hands tremble.

His eyes turned to her lifeless seeming body. She would die, Swan had said, if he did not lie beside her. If she died, what was there to be afraid of? Death would be welcome. "All right! So, just, uh, just lie down and—and then what?"

"Lie beside me, Al'An."

Garrison walked to the center of the enclosure, dropping to his knees beside Swan's body. He bent over her, touched his lips to her forehead. Her flesh was neither hot nor cold, and she was neither alive nor dead.

Garrison looked up once more, told himself that he wasn't seeing her ghost hovering above him within the glowing vortex, but her spirit or something, and that this was magic and, when she didn't need it anymore, it would all go away.

Garrison kissed her lips. There was no response, of course. He laid down beside her, his eyes staring up into the brilliance of the vortex and Swan's exquisite spectral image. A million thoughts raced through his mind. He'd really died when the bomb went off back in Atlanta and he was finally going into the light that everyone talked about in near-death experiences.

He was a tactless teenager again, and one of his buddies said that maybe, if he strained his eyes, he could see under Swan's dress. He awoke from a scary dream and his mom and dad were beside his bed, his mom holding him, asking if he'd had too much ice cream and cotton candy, his dad wanting to hold him or say something, but trying to look as though he didn't. He went into a dark house with two other agents, guns drawn, and then there was shooting everywhere and one of the agents was down and Garrison was dragging the guy's body behind some boxes and there was more shooting and a too calm voice said, "We got him, fellas. Somebody get an ambulance. A couple ambulances." He held a girl in his arms, a Ricky Nelson song playing on an oldies station; he was dancing with her, his palms very sweaty, and he was self-conscious because he had to be getting the back of her dress all wet from his hands. The SAT test. His number two pencil broke. It was the third pencil he'd broken. Gunfire from behind the packing crates on the other side of the warehouse, the gun-shot agent bleeding all over them both. He returned shots, too rapidly, his magazine empty. Where were his spare magazines? Had he brought a fourth number two pencil? Would the girl he danced with ever dance with him again? Did dad think he was a baby because he woke up crying from a bad dream? He wouldn't look under a girl's dress like the guys wanted him to, because she'd see him and she'd be embarrassed and maybe she'd cry.

Garrison blinked. Below him, he saw his body. He was floating upward, his body getting smaller and smaller as he rose into the light.

Within him, he felt Swan's voice. "Al'An."

"Yes, Swan."

"The energy that is life which flows into us and from us and within us will be one, and all of the magical energy of the universe will be mine to command, my love."

"Are we dead?"

"The answer would have no meaning, Al'An."

Swan's apparition hovered before him, and he could see his physical body far below them, beside hers, and he saw through the hands and legs and torso of the apparition which he had become.

Garrison was aware of moving, moving ever nearer to Swan's specter. And, as if that which was not physical could touch, they touched, and something passed through him, filling him, electrifying him, this body which was not a body was within Swan and she was within him and he tried to say something, but was inundated by Swan's being, lost within her.

The Mist of Oblivion approached. The magical energy flowed from them into the vortex and the vortex seemed to explode, enlarging exponentially, its light brighter than a thousand suns, more serene than the freshest breeze, cool and soft, enveloping them and they were one with it.

They advanced against the Mist as its inky tendrils dipped to touch and devour the warring armies on the battlefield.

Within the Mist, there dwelt an entity as well. A part of them thought the word, "Mother!" The vortex touched the Mist, light touching darkness. Cold and fear gripped them and the vortex trembled and an infinity of images and feelings flowed through them. Specters, like that which they had become, but filled with terror and longing, passed through them, gripped them, shrieked out their horror, fled.

Weakness, draining, fear.

Light and dark fully commingled, the darkness drawn into them. Garrison was separated from Swan for an instant, an eternity. He could not tell which. The light of the vortex began to fail and the darkness enshrouded them. He was with her again, self-awareness ceasing, melting into oneness with Swan.

The vortex shuddered and its light grew and the darkness filled the light and the cold and the fear and the images of terror dissipated.

Alan Garrison's flesh tingled. He coughed, opened his eyes. "I've got eyes!" He coughed, rolling over onto his side, his head on Swan's chest. Garrison raised his eyes to her face, touched his hands to her flesh and felt something passing from him and into him simultaneously.

Swan's eyes opened. "Al'An."

"I'm here."

"There is one more deed, my Champion, one more deed which must be accomplished."

Garrison helped Swan to her feet, for the first time

realizing that the sound of battle had ceased. "What happened?"

"The Mist has entered a vortex which shall never be opened again, Al'An."

"And your mother?"

"I know what she is doing, and where she does it. We must go there."

"The magic way?"

Swan raised up on her toes and kissed his cheek. "Yes. Hold me in your arms, my love," Swan whispered.

Garrison took her into his arms, and she turned around, her back to him. Swan outstretched her arms, her hands grasping for the magic in the air around her, Garrison feeling it, too, feeling its current surging through her body, strengthening her, strengthening him. She uttered the words of the place shifting spell which Garrison had heard her use before. Swan pressed her palms together between her breasts, becoming one with the energy around her, and Garrison one with her as well.

Light, dazzlingly bright, burst around them, filled her, filled him, exploded from her, magical energy enveloping them. There was a sound, soft, like the rumble of thunder heard at a great distance.

A darkness, glowing like light, neither light nor dark, cocooned them. The glowing darkness slowly faded. And there was light which was not magical at all, but the light of bonfires burning, flames flaring high on a bitterly cold wind, groping toward blue-black clouds in the steel grey sky above.

All was barren here.

Garrison knew the place.

They had ridden past it, across it in their escape from Barad'Il'Koth.

And now, he knew its purpose.

There were six fires in all, formed in a great circle. Surrounding the circle were the Handmaidens of Koth, their dresses, their head-to-toe translucent black veils flung to and fro at the wind's caprice. The Handmaidens were formed into six circles, the six circles interlocked, thirty-six of the women in all. A great black horse, its leather trappings silver mounted, pawed the ground anxiously just beyond the circle's perimeter.

A thirty-seventh woman stood within the circle of bonfires.

Alan Garrison felt suddenly stupid. He carried three "firespitters" which probably still didn't work. His sword was miles away in the enclosure where he'd found Swan and dropped it. Two knives were his only weapons.

"You won't need weapons, Al'An."

"You don't read my mind, do you?"

"No, but I know you, Al'An."

They stood within the six-by-six circle formed by the thirty-six Handmaidens. The women chanted, perhaps in a trance, perhaps ignoring the intruders. "Can they see us?" Garrison asked.

"They could, but don't. It would break their concentration, break the summoning spell in which their magic aids that of my mother."

"Summoning spell?"

"Yes," Swan answered, the single word she spoke revealing everything as Garrison looked within the circle of bonfires. Not only was there a thirty-seventh woman there, but there was something else, a body lying on a bier before her.

"Your father," Garrison almost whispered.

"My mother has spent her magic, and unwisely so. Once I realized that she had chosen to use the Mist of Oblivion against us all, I knew what would transpire here. It must be stopped."

Swan raised the skirts of her dark grey dress and began walking toward the ring of bonfires. The wind, growing in force, tugged at her dress, molded the fabric against her legs, began, inexorably, to dismantle the arrangement of her hair. Swan touched her hair, freeing it, the wind whipping it round her.

"You told me once," Garrison insisted, "that you can't raise the dead, that once the spirit has left the body, death is final. But what about Mir and his knights and his archers? And what about your father? And what about what happened to us? Back there, I mean."

Swan's answer was astonishingly quick. "I did not raise the dead, nor can my mother. Such power is beyond any magic in the universe. I summoned the spirits of Mir and his army and, with my magic, gave them form and substance. When my magical energy was draining away as I wove the vortex of light, you might have—"

"Mir told me that your magic was fading. I saw them, some of them, their bodies and the bodies of their horses becoming transparent, like they were just fading away." Garrison smiled, shaking his head.

"What is it?" Swan asked him. They were nearly to the ring of bonfires.

"Something I read years ago, about old soldiers never dying. I'll tell you later. If your mother can't—"

"Then, what is she doing? Do you remember, Al'An, when I took your life force from you before it left you, there on Arba'Il'Tac? I placed it within the bird so that when your body would be fatally damaged the life force would not escape it? My father's life force escaped his body with no where to go but into death. When you and I were one within the vortex and our life forces left our bodies, they went into the vortex, did not just escape our bodies. I could summon my father's spirit from death, as I did with the spirit of Mir and those of his knights and archers, but their bodies are long since gone to dust, as will the body of my father. With his life force gone, the body remaining is only a deteriorating husk. The witches can only reanimate his body, not return the life force energy to it. "

"What's she want with—"

Alan Garrison didn't get to finish the question— what would the Queen Sorceress want with a dead body? Swan stopped walking, only a few feet away from the crackling bonfires. "Mother?"

The woman inside the circle did not turn around, but called out, "I laud your abilities, child. But you have not won. You could win, but will not, because you will not kill me, nor will you harm your father. You are good, and that is your problem."

Eran turned away from the body before her and faced them. Garrison was stunned. Eran wore a dress of deepest red, accentuating a figure that a Hollywood actress would have killed for. The dress's neckline was low, showing a cleavage that glistened in the firelight. A magnificently carved black baldric was suspended from her right shoulder to her left hip, its engraved silver buckle further drawing the eye to her breasts. Sheathed to her left hip was a sword, its hilt ornate.

The only odd thing were the riding boots, visible beneath the hem of the red dress and the hint of white linen under it. Strapped to the black leather boots were glinting silver spurs.

Her complexion was flawless, her black hair falling to her shoulders and beyond in heavy, undulating waves. The liquid green of her eyes was impossibly beautiful. Garrison blinked. The eyes were just like Swan's eyes as he looked more closely, a little grey in them, making them prettier still. He blinked again, and the face was Swan's face.

Garrison took a step back. It was Swan, not her mother! This was Swan. Her hands touched at her throat and her fingers trailed lazily down across her bare skin to her breasts and her lips formed a kiss as Garrison started to step between the bonfires and reach for— "Mother! You do not have the power to make Al'An think that you are me!"

"I just did, child."

Garrison staggered, blinked. His hands were inches away from Eran's body, and now they shook. Eran stepped back, deeper within the circle of bonfires, laughing at him. He felt Swan's hand tug at his arm. He shook his head, took a step back.

Looking into Eran's eyes, his voice low, Alan Garrison snarled, "You lousy—"

Eran cut him off. "And this is your Champion! You picked a handsome fellow. Al'An, is it? I hope he performs to your satisfaction, daughter. There are ways to enhance that, if you wish."

Garrison felt oddly awkward, like a rock on the ground or a piece of furniture—or a sex object. He was being talked about as if he were just a decoration or something. And Eran's eyes were undressing him.

"Mother?"

Eran's eyes left Garrison, flickered to her daughter. "Yes?"

"You made a mistake. Don't make another mistake."

"You mean with your father?"

"You cannot bring him back to life. You don't have sufficient magical energy to leave Creath and find another other realm male. I can command all of the magical energy of the universe. You cannot prevent my removing you from power. You can, however, live out your life in what peace and happiness you can find."

"You would do that for me? You are good. And, remember, child, that good shall be your undoing. I won't step down. You won't kill me. You are wrong. I do not make a mistake, an error, whatever you choose to call it. My Handmaidens even now summon your father to life. Do you want to watch us while I take my energy from him, see your mother and father—"

A glance at Swan's face told Garrison that he had to shut up her mother—quick. He said, "Hey, come on now, Mrs. Goodman!"

The pretty eyes weren't pretty as they bored into him. "I am not Mrs. Goo'D'Man! I am the Queen Sorceress!"

"Yeah, and you're also g'urg outta luck; but, on the other hand, a good-looking widow like you—"

"Silence! Or I will—"

Alan Garrison gave her his best smile. "You're beautiful beyond description, on the outside. But, inside, I don't think so."

"Mother, you cannot do what you intend."

"Watch me. Watch us."

"Al'An, we are going!" Swan announced matter-of-factly.

Alan Garrison just looked at Swan. "You can't be serious! I mean, this isn't like we're some married couple at a dinner party and the hostess just brought out a tray of drugs or something. We can't just—"

"I really think we should go."

"You're going to let her grab some more magical energy and start another damn war? I don't think so, sweetheart!"

"Please, Al'An?"

Eran laughed. "Please? Turn him into something like Mul'Din over there," and she gestured toward the solitary horse outside the circle of witches. "Even just for a while, and teach him some manners. Remember who you are. Even though I will, someday, destroy you, you are my daughter! Remember that!"

"Yo! I love your daughter and she's not turning me into something, or anything like that! She loves me." He almost choked with laughter as he thought of it, Eran as his mother-in-law. "And I'm gonna marry her. And you can butt out!" He looked at Swan. "It's really okay to go? She's not going to—"

"We should go now, Al'An."

Garrison took Swan's hand. They started walking away from the circle of bonfires.

"Don't leave! Watch us! Don't you want to see your father one more time, child? Watch us!"

"Squeeze my hand. Tight!" Swan hissed through her teeth.

"Take it easy. She really can't—" As Garrison looked at her, he saw that Swan was crying. The chanting of the witches grew louder, faster. Garrison looked behind them. The bonfires were rising in intensity. Eran's arms were outstretched toward the sky, her fingers splayed. "She's trying to take magical energy—"

"I have it all at my command. She can take nothing."

"This deal with your father's—"

Swan stopped in her tracks, looked at him, anger, disgust, sadness, all visible in her eyes by the firelight.

"You mad at me?"

"No. Never at you. If you must be certain, then watch. But I have warned you."

Alan Garrison started to ask Swan what she meant, but before he could speak the fires flared more brightly still and the wind gusted so strongly that he clung to Swan lest she'd be knocked down.

The Handmaidens of Koth, witches all, caught fire, living torches lighting one after the other, their bodies remaining unconsumed within the fires, motionless.

"What's—"

"It is too late, Al'An!" Swan shouted over the howling wind. "It's too late! It's happening."

The witches' circles within circles were all ablaze. Garrison looked at Swan again, followed her eyes. She stared into the inner circle, at her mother, at the body lying on the bier.

Garrison thought that he saw it move, knew in the next instant that his eyes hadn't deceived him, when

Swan's own body tensed in his arms. "I'll get you out of here," Garrison shouted over the roar of wind and fire.

"No."

"Then you get us out of here with your magic!"

"You were right, Al'An." Swan's voice was almost a scream. "I can't run from this, because it will be ugly. I cannot leave it unfinished." Swan turned in Garrison's arms, looked straight at her mother and the reanimating corpse of her father.

The body sat up, stiff legged.

Eran. Garrison realized that Eran had lost her mind. Her hands raised the baldric from her shoulder, and she let the sword belt and the weapon it carried fall to the ground at her feet. Her hands moved behind her neck, under her hair. In a moment, Garrison realized that she was unfastening her dress. Eran's arms twisted behind her and her hands busily worked her dress open the rest of the way.

Eran slipped her arms from the dress and was naked from the waist up. Eran moved almost imperceptibly and the dress fell to her feet. She wore a white petticoat, trimmed in lace. Her fingers did something at its waist and the petticoat fell away. Eran was entirely naked now, except for the boots. Her body was magnificently erotic as she stepped out of her clothes and approached the bier.

Swan shivered. Garrison held Swan more tightly.

Eran climbed onto the bier, her hands touching the chest of the reanimated corpse, her mouth about to touch its mouth.

Garrison started to raise his hand to cover Swan's eyes, but Swan pushed it away. "It is almost finished," Swan told him, her voice barely audible even though she clearly was shouting to be heard over the wind and the crackling of the fires.

There was a tightness in Garrison's throat. Swan's body was rigid in his arms.

Eran fully embraced the corpse of Swan's father,

leaning the body back, simultaneously straddling it and touching her lips to its mouth.

In the instant that their bodies joined together, the howling wind ended and the witches' fiery circles within circles ceased to blaze and the bonfires died.

The Handmaidens' bodies dissolved to dust.

Eran lifted her body from the corpse, flung out her arms from her sides, threw back her head and uttered a piercing scream.

As Garrison watched, Eran's body began to collapse into itself, implode. Her arms, still outstretched, were disintegrating to dust. Her head sagged into a torso which could no longer support it, her legs shriveling. A breeze, but not the wind which had lashed the barren ground, rustled Swan's skirts, tugged gently at Swan's hair, at Garrison's hair.

The breeze must also have touched what remained of Eran's body.

Garrison blinked.

A dust devil rose from the bier and what had remained of the Queen Sorceress's body was gone.

The ashes from the bonfires were caught up in the breeze, vanished as well.

Garrison looked around them. The breeze swept clean the ashes of the Handmaidens of Koth, as if they had never been.

Garrison looked skyward. The darkly luminous clouds scudded away, the newly revealed sky a rich blue.

He and Swan stood alone beneath it. The body of Swan's father, Peter Goodman, lay alone, once more, unmolested on the bier.

Garrison heard the sound of hooves on hard ground. The black horse, saddle empty, reins swaying free, galloped off toward the horizon.

Alan Garrison touched his lips to Swan's forehead, to her cheek, turned her in his arms so that she faced him. Tears streamed from her eyes.

Alan Garrison held Swan close.

# Chapter Sixteen

Alan Garrison looked up from the book. The size of the crowd had surprised him. He was even more surprised that since he'd begun the reading, instead of his audience surreptitiously fleeing, more people had entered the room, standing at the back and on the sides. He cleared his throat and continued reading. "Swan told me what I had feared that she would, what Erg'Ran had hinted at, that there was danger beyond understanding in the magical power which she now possessed. And, if I, a man from the other realm, were to stay in Creath and take her as my wife, Swan would be at risk of falling into the well of depravity within which her mother at last had drowned. Eventually, Swan and I might end as Eran and Peter Goodman had ended.

"The worst part of it, although I could not imagine Swan's ever turning to evil, was that I loved her too much to risk it.

"And so, I witnessed Swan's magic as only a bystander for one more time, knowing that her next use of magical energy would be to return me to where she had found me.

"We'd burned Peter Goodman's remains. The magical energy Swan had used to summon the vortex of light with which she destroyed the Mist of Oblivion had robbed the summer palace of its magical aura. When she returned to it, restored it to as it had been, she would take her father's ashes with her and scatter them in the gardens which never ceased to bloom.

"So it was even stranger to see Peter Goodman standing there with us, having form and substance once again, however briefly.

"Swan had summoned his spirit, as she had done with the spirit of Mir and the spirits of his knights and archers. Peter Goodman stood with us as Mir approached. Mir dropped to one knee and touched his lips to Swan's outreaching hand.

"'Hail to you Enchantress!'" Mir stood, resting his hands on the hilt of his great sword. "'You have done well. Rule Creath wisely and with honor, lady. And, should it ever be that I may have the honor to serve you again, lady, you have but to summon me.'

"'I would ask a boon of you, Mir.'

"'Name it, Enchantress, and I will grant it if such is within my power.'

"'My father, too, was a soldier, Mir. And, like you, he was a hero. The boon which I crave is that his spirit may accompany you, that he may ride at your side in death.'

"Mir looked at Peter Goodman, then extended his hand. Goodman clasped it.

"'You honor me with your request, Enchantress, and I shall be forever honored that he who is the origin of your seed will be with me.'

"Mir said his farewells, to Gar'Ath and Mitan—on whom Mir seemed to very much enjoy gazing—and to Captain Bre'Gaa and to me. 'Champion! The name suits you, lad. I made a promise that I would share with you a secret known by none living in these days. I do that now. I am like you.'

"'What?' I asked, dumbfounded. 'Like me?'

"'I, too, came from the other realm. It is much changed there now, I would think, albeit that time here and time there have little correlation. Still, many ages must have passed since I rode out on my quest and never returned.'

"'You were a knight,' I whispered.

"'Of course I was a knight, Champion! Would you think me an imposter? I would not have taken unto myself the weapons and habiliment of a knight were I not one! But, unlike many who wore the spurs, I was also a scholar. Those two moons in Creath's sky?' And Mir actually winked. 'One of those lovely moons was the sorceress who brought me here and whose bed I shared at her command and from whose clutches I escaped. Her charms were most appealing, lad, but as a knight I was sworn to defend against evil, not to fuel it. The loveliness of her body could not make me forgive the vileness of her heart.'

"Swan had begun to form the black vortex out of which Mir and his army had ridden, and into which they would return, her father with them. I was almost afraid to ask Mir what was on my mind, but I asked him anyway, 'Under what King did you serve, Mir? And, on what quest did you ride out that day when you were taken from the other realm?'

"Mir smiled at me. 'There was but one quest, Champion, and is still. And you well know it, I suspect. Men are men, and the quest itself becomes the goal rather than the pursuit of which the quest was first begun. The King whom I pledged to serve I serve still.' Mir clasped my hand and started to turn away, then looked at me, smiling once more as he said, 'And you well know it, I suspect.'

"Tre'El held his horse, Mir taking the reins from his Knight Commander and mounting his great white charger.

"For one last time, Swan embraced her father.

"As Mir was about to lead his army into the vortex, to return to death, he turned his horse aside and rode straight over to Erg'Ran, dismounted and clasped both hands to Erg'Ran's shoulders. Mir embraced him, then remounted his steed.

"Swan stood beside me, her hand in mine, and we waited there until the last of Mir's army had passed through the vortex and there was only darkness. A tear in her eye—for Mir and his brave knights, or for her lost father?—Swan at last took her hand from mine and clapped both hands together, closing the vortex.

"We looked at each other, Swan and I, and I knew that the time which I so dreaded was upon me."

Abruptly, Alan Garrison closed the book, his throat suddenly tight and his voice about to crack. He had never before—aloud—read the final chapter of *The Virgin Enchantress*. He'd done readings from elsewhere in the book, of course, but not from this last part. He could not read the ending pages without totally losing control of himself, the memory of his parting with Swan too intense, still. And it always would be.

Hurriedly, so that his mind could shift focus to something else, Garrison forced a laugh. "Sorry about that, guys! But you're going to have to buy the book. My voice is starting to go, anyway," Garrison added lamely.

"May I ask a question, Mr. Garrison?" a blond-haired woman in her thirties called out from the back of the room. He'd seen her around a few previous DragonCons, but didn't know her name.

Garrison cleared his throat, his voice sounding strained to him as he said, "It's Alan, please. Yes, what's your question?" He took a sip of water from the tumbler on the table.

"When I read the book, I wondered why you chose a kind of downer ending. I mean, don't get me wrong!

I really loved the book. And I have a second question?"

There was some laughter in the room, other hands already raised for questions.

"What's your second question?" Garrison inquired.

"Well, the main character was an FBI Agent and you were an FBI Agent up until—"

"I resigned from the Bureau, lived off my savings, crapshot on the book and here I am. What's your question?"

"Did you fantasize yourself in the character of the hero?"

Garrison forced another laugh, saying, "He's better looking and a hell of a lot more courageous." There was good-natured laughter. Garrison raised his voice and added, truthfully, "I never fantasized myself as the guy in the book." It hadn't been a fantasy, but he had never said that to anyone and wasn't about to say it now.

He'd returned from Creath to his own "realm" in the instant after the grenade had made a little noise and a lot of smoke and never actually detonated, had his cuffs on the fanatical terrorist bomber William Culberton Brownwood before Wisnewski and his agents even got through the doors into the registration area.

Jim Sutton, his BATF friend, had run up to him, asking him, "You okay, Alan? You look weird."

Alan Garrison hadn't said anything. Glancing around, he'd seen Brenda in her cat outfit, Alicia and Gardner with her. Walking slowly, trying to keep himself under control, Garrison approached Brenda and asked, "Do you remember the girl I was with? Real pretty? You guys hung out with her earlier. She asked one of you guys about me?"

"Swan? Yeah. Where'd she go?"

Alan Garrison remembered falling to the floor because he had to sit down. Putting his hand into his pocket, he felt his shield, no longer of heroic proportions, or its lettering reversed. Intentionally, city ordinances notwithstanding, he took a cigarette from the full pack in his pocket, found his lighter—it worked—and lit up. When he looked at the pack— one cigarette gone—his heart sank.

Garrison's mind came back to the present. "Your first question, about the downer ending. Maybe it wasn't a downer," Garrison told the blond-haired woman. "I mean, they still love each other—the two characters in the book, I mean—and, if you believe in fate or destiny, you can always tell yourself that somehow they got back together, sometime, somewhere." He told himself to shut up about it before he lost it.

There was brief applause.

One of the programming coordinators for the con held up his hand, fingers splayed, signaling five minutes before the room had to be emptied. Garrison said, "I'll take one more question."

A dozen hands went up and Garrison pointed at the man in the wheelchair in the front row. "Yes, sir?"

"Alan. What's your next book? Another fantasy novel?"

Garrison grinned at him. "It'll be out next year. I think you're just going to have to wait and see. And I hope you like it. Thank you all!"

Garrison stood up, grabbed his sportcoat from the empty chair beside him and signed his way through a sea of copies of *The Virgin Enchantress* as he made his way to the door. A few people followed him into the corridor, asked a few questions, asked him to sign a few more books.

After several minutes, the last question asked, the last book signed, Alan Garrison reached the stairs and started down. He still smoked as little as he always had, but all someone had to do was post a sign announcing that smoking was prohibited and he wanted a cigarette.

He had checked convention records and a one-day membership had, in fact, been sold to a woman named "Swan Creath" and there was always Brenda, and Alicia and Gardner, too. They remembered her.

There was no Swan Creath living in the entire United States. Before leaving the Bureau, he'd run the name with the best people finder program to be had.

What he remembered as happening had to have been real.

He had the nonscars to prove it. Before he'd met Swan and been magically whisked off to Creath, he'd had the usual unremarkable collection of dings people got from daily life—a mark on a finger where a wart had been burned off, a tiny chicken pox scar at the corner of his left eye, a reminder on his right leg of a serious collision with a formica tabletop when he'd been a kid. All of those scars were gone.

Wisnewski had recommended Garrison for a commendation in the arrest of William Brownwood. Garrison resigned before it was approved, but they sent him the commendation anyway.

Brownwood had been in a state of mental collapse when he was arrested. If Brownwood ever got well enough, Garrison assumed that he'd be called to testify in the man's trial.

Garrison reached the ground floor and looked for an exit, the closest one at registration; or, as Swan would have put it, ". . . the great hall through which all who come here must pass."

It sucked, Garrison told himself. Swan existed in her "realm" and he in his. He couldn't call her, send her flowers, anything. All he could do was love her. And, the way that time passed so oddly there, a hundred years or only a hundred minutes might have gone by. "Sucked" was too mild a word.

Garrison almost punched open the door leading outside. Despite the time of year for Atlanta, the weather wasn't that terribly hot. He took off his sportcoat, anyway. Even though he'd left law enforcement, he still carried a gun, but just the little .32 Seecamp in the Pocket Natural holster in the side pocket of his trousers.

He started digging around in his jacket pockets for his cigarettes. "G'urg," Garrison snarled.

There were a bunch of people hanging around outside the entrance, some in hall costumes, most not, some older than he, most of them younger. Nearly all of them stood and smoked, while a few sat on the sidewalk and smoked.

Garrison pulled a cigarette out of his half-empty pack, started to flip the cowling back on his lighter.

His cigarette lit.

Garrison's jaw dropped and he almost lost the cigarette from his lips.

He didn't look right or left, in front or in back.

Instead, Alan Garrison stared at his pack of cigarettes. It was full.

He raised his eyes, glanced around. There were people everywhere. "Swan?" Garrison whispered. He saw her. "I'm crazy." She was crossing the street on the green light, and he almost didn't recognize her. Her auburn hair was cut to just past shoulder length. Instead of a medieval-style dress, she wore a cream-colored sleeveless knit top and an ankle-length brown skirt with a cream-colored floral print. She was wearing sandals. He could see her toes! He'd never seen her toes, the one time he'd had the chance his eyes were too busy elsewhere.

Garrison glanced down at the cigarette, ran into the street, but stopped dead.

He asked himself aloud, "Am I crazy?"

She stopped in the middle of the street.

Garrison stood maybe a foot away from her. "Swan?"

"Al'An."

Garrison took the solitary step that brought him right in front of her. "Swan."

"I decided that magic stifled technology, and that while the people of Creath depended on magic, there would be no reason for them to depend upon themselves. I appointed Mitan and Gar'Ath to rule Creath so that someday the people of Creath will learn to rule themselves. Erg'Ran will advise them, of course. Captain Bre'Gaa has convinced the Gle'Ur'Gya that his people and the people of the Land should try to live in peace. I think it will work."

"So, uh—you're here on vacation?"

"No. I'm not."

The light had changed, Garrison noticed absently, from green to red. He could hear a lot of horns honking.

"You here to stay?"

"If you want me to, Al'An."

"What about the, uh— Well, I mean, will it be dangerous to you when we—?"

"If you will help me, I think I'll be okay."

Alan Garrison drew Swan into his arms, looked into Swan's grey-green eyes. "I'll help you—every chance I get," he promised her.

Alan Garrison let his cigarette drop into the street and kissed Swan so hard that his lips hurt. Cars kept honking at them and honking and honking and honking.

# Miles Had a Cunning Plan . . .

# *A*
# CIVIL
# CAMPAIGN

## by Lois McMaster Bujold

*The following is an excerpt from the new novel in the
Hugo-winning Vorkosigan series, available in
hardcover from Baen in September 1999*

0-671-57827-8
$24.00

# CHAPTER ONE

The big groundcar jerked to a stop centimeters from
the vehicle ahead of it, and Armsman Pym, driving,
swore under his breath. Miles settled back again in his
seat beside him, wincing at a vision of the acrimoni-
ous street scene from which Pym's reflexes had
delivered them. Miles wondered if he could have
persuaded the feckless prole in front of them that
being rear-ended by an Imperial Auditor was a privi-
lege to be treasured. Likely not. The Vorbarr Sultana
University student darting across the boulevard on foot,
who had been the cause of the quick stop, scampered
off through the jam without a backward glance. The
line of groundcars started up once more.

"Have you heard if the municipal traffic control
system will be coming on line soon?" Pym asked,
apropos of what Miles counted as their third near-miss
this week.

"Nope. Delayed in development again, Lord Vor-
bohn the Younger reports. Due to the increase in fatal
lightflyer incidents, they're concentrating on getting
the automated air system up first."

Pym nodded, and returned his attention to the
crowded road. The Armsman was a habitually fit man,

his graying temples seeming merely an accent to his brown-and-silver uniform. He'd served the Vorkosigans as a liege-sworn guard since Miles had been an Academy cadet, and would doubtless go on doing so till either he died of old age, or they were all killed in traffic.

So much for short cuts. Next time they'd go around the campus. Miles watched through the canopy as the taller new buildings of the University fell behind, and they passed through its spiked iron gates into the pleasant old residential streets favored by the families of senior professors and staff. The distinctive architecture dated from the last un-electrified decade before the end of the Time of Isolation. This area had been reclaimed from decay in the past generation, and now featured shady green Earth trees, and bright flower boxes under the tall narrow windows of the tall narrow houses. Miles rebalanced the flower arrangement between his feet. Would it be seen as redundant by its intended recipient?

Pym glanced aside at his slight movement, following his eye to the foliage on the floor. "The lady you met on Komarr seems to have made a strong impression on you, m'lord . . ." He trailed off invitingly.

"Yes," said Miles, uninvitingly.

"Your lady mother had high hopes of that very attractive Miss Captain Quinn you brought home those times." Was that a wistful note in Pym's voice?

"Miss Admiral Quinn, now," Miles corrected with a sigh. "So had I. But she made the right choice for her." He grimaced out the canopy. "I've sworn off falling in love with galactic women and then trying to persuade them to immigrate to Barrayar. I've concluded my only hope is to find a woman who can already stand Barrayar, and persuade her to like me."

"And does Madame Vorsoisson like Barrayar?"

"About as well as I do." He smiled grimly.

"And, ah . . . the second part?"

"We'll see, Pym." *Or not, as the case may be.* At least the spectacle of a man of thirty-plus, going courting seriously for the first time in his life—the first time in the Barrayaran style, anyway—promised to provide hours of entertainment for his interested staff.

Miles let his breath and his nervous irritation trickle out through his nostrils as Pym found a place to park near Lord Auditor Vorthys's doorstep, and expertly wedged the polished old armored groundcar into the inadequate space. Pym popped the canopy; Miles climbed out, and stared up at the three-story patterned tile front of his colleague's home.

Georg Vorthys had been a professor of engineering failure analysis at the Imperial University for thirty years. He and his wife had lived in this house for most of their married life, raising three children and two academic careers, before Emperor Gregor had appointed Vorthys as one of his hand-picked Imperial Auditors. Neither of the Professors Vorthys had seen any reason to change their comfortable lifestyle merely because the awesome powers of an Emperor's Voice had been conferred upon the retired engineer; Madame Dr. Vorthys still walked every day to her classes. *Dear no, Miles!* the Professora had said to him, when he'd once wondered aloud at their passing up this opportunity for social display. *Can you imagine moving all those books?* Not to mention the laboratory and workshop jamming the entire basement.

Their cheery inertia proved a happy chance, when they invited their recently-widowed niece and her young son to live with them while she completed her own education. Plenty of room, the Professor had boomed jovially, the top floor is so empty since the children left. So close to classes, the Professora had pointed out practically. *Less than six kilometers from Vorkosigan House!* Miles had exulted in his mind, adding a polite murmur of encouragement aloud. And so Ekaterin Nile Vorvayne Vorsoisson had arrived. *She's here, she's here!* Might she be looking down at him from the shadows of some upstairs window even now?

Miles glanced anxiously down the all-too-short length of his body. If his dwarfish stature bothered her, she'd shown no signs of it so far. Well and good. Going on to the aspects of his appearance he could control: no food stains spattered his plain gray tunic, no unfortunate street detritus clung to the soles of his polished half-boots. He checked his distorted reflection in the groundcar's rear canopy. Its convex mirroring widened his lean, if slightly hunched, body to something resembling his obese clone-brother Mark, a comparison he primly ignored. Mark was, thank God, not here. He essayed a smile, for practice; in the canopy, it came out twisted and repellent. No dark hair sticking out in odd directions, anyway.

"You look just fine, my lord," Pym said in a bracing tone from the front compartment. Miles's face heated, and he flinched away from his reflection. He recovered himself enough to take the flower arrangement and rolled-up flimsy Pym handed out to him with, he hoped, a tolerably bland expression. He balanced the load in his arms, turned to face the front steps, and took a deep breath.

After about a minute, Pym inquired helpfully from behind him, "Would you like me to carry anything?"

"No. Thank you." Miles trod up the steps and wiggled a finger free to press the chime-pad. Pym pulled out a reader, and settled comfortably in the groundcar to await his lord's pleasure.

Footsteps sounded from within, and the door swung open on the smiling pink face of the Professora. Her gray hair was wound up on her head in her usual style. She wore a dark rose dress with a light rose bolero, embroidered with green vines in the manner of her home District. This somewhat formal Vor mode, which suggested she was just on her way either in or out, was belied by the soft buskins on her feet. "Hello, Miles. Goodness, you're prompt."

"Professora." Miles ducked a nod to her, and smiled in turn. "Is she here? Is she in? Is she well? You said this would be a good time. I'm not too early, am I? I thought I'd be late. The traffic was miserable. You're going to be around, aren't you? I brought these. Do you think she'll like them?" The sticking-up red flowers tickled his nose as he displayed his gift while still clutching the rolled-up flimsy, which had a tendency to try to unroll and escape whenever his grip loosened.

"Come in, yes, all's well. She's here, she's fine, and the flowers are very nice—" The Professora rescued the bouquet and ushered him into her tiled hallway, closing the door firmly behind them with her foot. The house was dim and cool after the spring sunshine outside, and had a fine aroma of wood wax, old books, and a touch of academic dust.

"She looked pretty pale and fatigued at Tien's funeral. Surrounded by all those relatives. We really didn't get a chance to say more than two words each." *I'm sorry* and *Thank you*, to be precise. Not that he'd wanted to talk much to the late Tien Vorsoisson's family.

"It was an immense strain for her, I think," said the Professora judiciously. "She'd been through so much horror, and except for Georg and myself—and you—there wasn't a soul there to whom she could talk truth about it. Of course, her first concern was getting Nikki through it all. But she held together without a crack from first to last. I was very proud of her."

"Indeed. And she is . . . ?" Miles craned his neck, glancing into the rooms off the entry hall: a cluttered study lined with bookshelves, and a cluttered parlor lined with bookshelves. No young widows.

"Right this way." The Professora conducted him down the hall and out through her kitchen to the little urban back garden. A couple of tall trees and a brick wall made a private nook of it. Beyond a tiny circle of green grass, at a table in the shade, a woman sat with flimsies and a reader spread before her. She was chewing gently on the end of a stylus, and her dark brows were drawn down in her absorption. She wore a calf-length dress in much the same style as the Professora's, but solid black, with the high collar buttoned up to her neck. Her bolero was gray, trimmed with simple black braid running around its edge. Her dark hair was drawn back to a thick braided knot at the nape of her neck. She looked up at the sound of the door opening; her brows flew up and her lips parted in a flashing smile that made Miles blink. *Ekaterin.*

"Mil—my Lord Auditor!" She rose in a flare of skirt; he bowed over her hand.

"Madame Vorsoisson. You look well." She looked wonderful, if still much too pale. Part of that might be the effect of all that severe black, which also made her eyes show a brilliant blue-gray. "Welcome to Vorbarr Sultana. I brought these . . ." He gestured, and the Professora set the flower arrangement down on the table. "Though they hardly seem needed, out here."

"They're lovely," Ekaterin assured him, sniffing them in approval. "I'll take them up to my room later, where they will be very welcome. Since the weather has brightened up, I find I spend as much time as possible out here, under the real sky."

She'd spent nearly a year sealed in a Komarran dome. "I can understand that," Miles said. The conversation hiccuped to a brief stop, while they smiled at each other.

Ekaterin recovered first. "Thank you for coming to Tien's funeral. It meant so much to me."

"It was the least I could do, under the circumstances. I'm only sorry I couldn't do more."

"But you've already done so much for me and Nikki—" She broke off at his gesture of embarrassed denial and instead said, "But won't you sit down? Aunt Vorthys—?" She drew back one of the spindly garden chairs.

The Professora shook her head. "I have a few things to attend to inside. Carry on." She added a little cryptically, "You'll do fine."

She went back into her house, and Miles sat across from Ekaterin, placing his flimsy on the table to await its strategic moment. It half-unrolled, eagerly.

"Is your case all wound up?" she asked.

"That case will have ramifications for years to come, but I'm done with it for now," Miles replied. "I just turned in my last reports yesterday, or I would have been here to welcome you earlier." Well, that and a vestigial sense that he'd ought to let the poor woman at least get her bags unpacked, before descending in force.

"Will you be sent out on another assignment now?"

"I don't think Gregor will let me risk getting tied up elsewhere till after his marriage. For the next couple of months, I'm afraid all my duties will be social ones."

"I'm sure you'll do them with your usual flair."

*God, I hope not.* "I don't think flair is exactly what my Aunt Vorpatril—she's in charge of all the Emperor's wedding arrangements—would wish from me. More like, shut up and do what you're told, Miles. But speaking of paperwork, how's your own? Is Tien's estate settled? Did you manage to recapture Nikki's guardianship from that cousin of his?"

"Vassily Vorsoisson? Yes, thank heavens, there was no problem with that part."

"So, ah, what's all this, then?" Miles nodded at the cluttered table.

"I'm planning my course work for the next session at university. I was too late to start this summer, so I'll begin in the fall. There's so much to choose from. I feel so ignorant."

"Educated is what you aim to be coming out, not going in."

"I suppose so."

"And what will you choose?"

"Oh, I'll start with basics—biology, chemistry . . ." She brightened. "One real horticulture course." She gestured at her flimsies. "For the rest of the season, I'm trying to find some sort of paying work. I'd like to feel I'm not totally dependent on the charity of my relatives, even if it's only my pocket money."

That seemed almost the opening he was looking for, but Miles's eye caught sight of a red ceramic basin, sitting on the wooden planks forming a seat bordering a raised garden bed. In the middle of the pot a red-brown blob, with a fuzzy fringe like a rooster's crest growing out of it, pushed up through the dirt. If it was what he thought . . . He pointed to the basin. "Is that by chance your old bonsai'd skellytum? Is it going to live?"

She smiled. "Well, at least it's the start of a new

skellytum. Most of the fragments of the old one died
on the way home from Komarr, but that one took."

"You have a—for native Barrayaran plants, I don't
suppose you can call it a green thumb, can you?"

"Not unless they're suffering from some pretty
serious plant diseases, no."

"Speaking of gardens." Now, how to do this without jamming his foot in his mouth too deeply. "I don't
think, in all the other uproar, I ever had a chance to
tell you how impressed I was with your garden designs
that I saw on your comconsole."

"Oh." Her smile fled, and she shrugged. "They were
no great thing. Just twiddling."

Right. Let them not bring up any more of the
recent past than absolutely necessary, till time had a
chance to blunt memory's razor edges. "It was your
Barrayaran garden, the one with all the native species, which caught my eye. I'd never seen anything
like it."

"There are a dozen of them around. Several of the
District universities keep them, as living libraries for
their biology students. It's not really an original idea."

"Well," he persevered, feeling like a fish swimming
upstream against this current of self-deprecation, "*I*
thought it was very fine, and deserved better than just
being a ghost garden on the holovid. I have this spare
lot, you see . . ."

He flattened out his flimsy, which was a ground plot
of the block occupied by Vorkosigan House. He tapped
his finger on the bare square at the end. "There used
to be another great house, next to ours, which was torn
down during the Regency. ImpSec wouldn't let us build
anything else—they wanted it as a security zone. There's
nothing there but some scraggly grass, and a couple
of trees that somehow survived ImpSec's enthusiasm
for clear lines of fire. And a criss-cross of walks, where
people made mud paths by taking short cuts, and they
finally gave up and put some gravel down. It's an
extremely boring piece of ground." So boring he had
completely ignored it, till now.

She tilted her head, to follow his hand as it blocked

out the space on the ground plan. Her own long finger made to trace a delicate curve, but then shyly withdrew. He wondered what possibility her mind's eye had just seen, there.

"Now, *I* think," he went on valiantly, "that it would be a splendid thing to install a Barrayaran garden—all native species—open to the public, in this space. A sort of gift from the Vorkosigan family to the city of Vorbarr Sultana. With running water, like in your design, and walks and benches and all those civilized things. And those discreet little name tags on all the plants, so more people could learn about the old ecology and all that." There: art, public service, education—was there any bait he'd left off his hook? Oh yes, money. "It's a happy chance that you're looking for a summer job," *chance, hah, watch and see if I leave anything to chance,* "because I think you'd be the ideal person to take this on. Design and oversee the installation of the thing. I could give you an unlimited, um, generous budget, and a salary, of course. You could hire workmen, bring in whatever you needed."

And she would have to visit Vorkosigan House practically *every day*, and consult *frequently* with its resident lord. And by the time the shock of her husband's death had worn away, and she was ready to put off her forbidding formal mourning garb, and every unattached Vor bachelor in the capital showed up on her doorstep, Miles could have a lock on her affections that would permit him to fend off the most glittering competition. It was too soon, wildly too soon, to suggest courtship to her crippled heart; he had that clear in his head, even if his own heart howled in frustration. But a straightforward business friendship just might get past her guard. . . .

Her eyebrows had flown up; she touched an uncertain finger to those exquisite, pale unpainted lips. "This is exactly the sort of thing I wish to train to do. I don't know how to do it *yet*."

"On-the-job training," Miles responded instantly. "Apprenticeship. Learning by doing. You have to start sometime. You can't start sooner than now."

"But what if I make some dreadful mistake?"

"I do intend this be an *ongoing* project. People who are enthusiasts about this sort of thing always seem to be changing their gardens around. They get bored with the same view all the time, I guess. If you come up with better ideas later, you can always revise the plan. It will provide variety."

"I don't want to waste your money."

If she ever became Lady Vorkosigan, she would have to get over that quirk, Miles decided firmly.

"You don't have to decide here on the spot," he purred, and cleared his throat. *Watch that tone, boy. Business.* "Why don't you come to Vorkosigan House tomorrow, and walk over the site in person, and see what ideas it stirs up in your mind. You really can't tell anything by looking at a flimsy. We can have lunch, afterward, and talk about what you see as the problems and possibilities then. Logical?"

She blinked. "Yes, very." Her hand crept back curiously toward the flimsy.

"What time may I pick you up?"

"Whatever is convenient for you, Lord Vorkosigan. Oh, I take that back. If it's after twelve hundred, my aunt will be back from her morning class, and Nikki can stay with her."

"Excellent!" Yes, much as he liked Ekaterin's son, Miles thought he could do without the assistance of an active nine-year-old in this delicate dance. "Twelve hundred it will be. Consider it a deal." Only a little belatedly, he added, "And how does Nikki like Vorbarr Sultana, so far?"

"He seems to like his room, and this house. I think he's going to get a little bored, if he has to wait until his school starts to locate boys his own age."

It would not do to leave Nikolai Vorsoisson out of his calculations. "I gather then that the retro-genes took, and he's in no more danger of developing the symptoms of Vorzohn's Dystrophy?"

A smile of deep maternal satisfaction softened her face. "That's right. I'm so pleased. The doctors in the clinic here in Vorbarr Sultana report he had a very clean and complete cellular uptake. Developmentally, it should be just as if he'd never inherited the mutation at all." She glanced across at him. "It's as if I'd had a five-hundred-kilo weight lifted from me. I could fly, I think."

*So you should.*

Nikki himself emerged from the house at this moment, carrying a plate of cookies with an air of consequence, followed by the Professora with a tea tray and cups. Miles and Ekaterin hastened to clear a place on the table.

"Hello, Nikki," said Miles.

"Hi, Lord Vorkosigan. Is that your groundcar out front?"

"Yes."

"It's a barge." This observation was delivered without scorn, as a point of interest.

"I know. It's a relic of my father's time as Regent. It's armored, in fact—has a massive momentum."

"Oh yeah?" Nikki's interest soared. "Did it ever get shot at?"

"I don't believe that particular car ever did, no."

"Huh."

When Miles had last seen Nikki, the boy had been wooden-faced and pale with concentration, carrying the taper to light his father's funeral offering, obviously anxious to get his part of the ceremony right. He looked much better now, his brown eyes quick and his face mobile again. The Professora settled and poured tea, and the conversation became general for a time.

It became clear shortly that Nikki's interest was more in the food than in his mother's visitor; he declined a flatteringly grownup offer of tea, and with his great-aunt's permission snagged several cookies and dodged back indoors to whatever he'd been occupying himself with before. Miles tried to remember what age he'd been when his own parents' friends had stopped seeming part of the furniture. Well, except for the military men in his father's train, of course, who'd always riveted his attention. But then, Miles had been military-mad from the time he could walk. Nikki was jump-ship mad, and would probably light up for a jump pilot. Perhaps Miles could provide one sometime, for Nikki's delectation. A happily married one, he corrected this thought.

He'd laid his bait on the table, Ekaterin had taken it; it was time to quit while he was winning. But he knew for a fact that she'd already turned down one premature offer of remarriage from a completely unexpected quarter. *Had* any of Vorbarr Sultana's excess Vor males found her yet? The capital was crawling with young officers, rising bureaucrats, aggressive entrepreneurs, men of ambition and wealth and rank drawn to the empire's heart. But not, by a ratio of almost five to three, with their sisters. The parents of the preceding generation had taken galactic sex-selection technologies much too far in their foolish passion for male heirs, and the very sons they'd so cherished— Miles's contemporaries—had inherited the resulting mating mess. Go to any formal party in Vorbarr Sultana these days, and you could practically taste the damned testosterone in the air, volatilized by the alcohol no doubt.

"So, ah . . . have you had any other callers yet, Ekaterin?"

"I only arrived a week ago."

That was neither yes nor no. "I'd think you'd have the bachelors out in force in no time." Wait, he hadn't meant to point that out . . .

"Surely," she gestured down her black dress, "this will keep them away. If they have any manners at all."

"Mm, I'm not so sure. The social scene is pretty intense just now."

She shook her head and smiled bleakly. "It makes no difference to me. I had a decade of . . . of marriage. I don't need to repeat the experience. The other women are welcome to the bachelors; they can have my share, in fact." The conviction in her face was backed by an uncharacteristic hint of steel in her voice. "That's one mistake I don't have to make twice. I'll never remarry."

Miles controlled his flinch, and managed a sympathetic, interested smile at this confidence. *We're just*

*friends. I'm not hustling you, no, no. No need to fling up
your defenses, milady, not for me.*

He couldn't make this go faster by pushing harder;
all he could do was screw it up worse. Forced to be
satisfied with his one day's progress, Miles finished his
tea, exchanged a few more pleasantries with the two
women, and took his leave.

Pym hurried to open the groundcar door as Miles
skipped down the last three steps in one jump. He
flung himself into the passenger seat, and as Pym
slipped back into the driver's side and closed the
canopy, waved grandly. "Home, Pym."

Pym eased the groundcar into the street, and
inquired mildly, "Go well, did it, m'lord?"

"Just exactly as I had planned. She's coming to
Vorkosigan House tomorrow for lunch. As soon as we
get home, I want you to call that gardening service—
get them to get a crew out tonight and give the
grounds an extra going-over. And talk to—no, *I'll* talk
to Ma Kosti. Lunch must be . . . exquisite, yes. Ivan
always says women like food. But not too heavy. Wine—
does she drink wine in the daytime, I wonder? I'll offer
it, anyway. Something from the estate. And tea if she
doesn't choose the wine, I know she drinks tea. Scratch
the wine. And get the house cleaning crew in, get all
those covers off the first floor furniture—off all the
furniture. I want to give her a tour of the house while
she still doesn't realize . . . No, wait. I wonder . . . if the
place was a dreadful bachelor mess, perhaps it would
stir up her pity. Maybe instead I ought to clutter it up
some more, used glasses strategically piled up, the odd
fruit peel under the sofa—a silent appeal, *Help us! Move
in and straighten this poor fellow out*—or would that be
more likely to frighten her off? What do you think,
Pym?"

Pym pursed his lips judiciously, as if considering
whether it was within his Armsman's duties to spike
his lord's taste for street theater. He finally said in a
cautious tone, "If I may presume to speak for the
household, I *think* we should prefer to put our best
foot forward. Under the circumstances."

"Oh. All right."

Miles fell silent for a few moments, staring out the canopy as they threaded through the crowded city streets, out of the University district and across a mazelike corner of the Old Town, angling back toward Vorkosigan House. When he spoke again, the manic humor had drained from his voice, leaving it cooler and bleaker.

"We'll be picking her up tomorrow at twelve hundred. You'll drive. You will always drive, when Madame Vorsoisson or her son are aboard. Figure it in to your duty schedule from now on."

"Yes, m'lord." Pym added a carefully laconic, "My pleasure."

The seizure disorder was the last souvenir that ImpSec Captain Miles Vorkosigan had brought home from his decade of military missions. He'd been lucky to get out of the cryo-chamber alive and with his mind intact; Miles was fully aware that many did not fare nearly so well. Lucky to be merely medically discharged from the Emperor's Service, not buried with honors, the last of his glorious line, or reduced to some animal or vegetative existence. The seizure-stimulator the military doctors had issued him to bleed off his convulsions was very far from being a cure, though it was supposed to keep them from happening at random times. Miles drove, and flew his lightflyer—but only alone. He never took passengers anymore. Pym's batman's duties had been expanded to include medical assistance; he had by now witnessed enough of Miles's disturbing seizures to be grateful for this unusual burst of level-headedness.

One corner of Miles's mouth crooked up. After a moment, he asked, "And how did you ever capture Ma Pym, back in the old days, Pym? Did you put your best foot forward?"

"It's been almost eighteen years ago. The details have gone a bit fuzzy." Pym smiled a little. "I was a senior sergeant at the time. I'd taken the ImpSec advanced course, and was assigned to security duty at Vorhartung Castle. She had a clerk's job in the archives there. I thought, I wasn't some boy anymore, it was time I got serious . . . though I'm not just sure that wasn't an idea she put into my head, because she claims she spotted me first."

"Ah, a handsome fellow in uniform, I see. Does it every time. So why'd you decide to quit the Imperial Service and apply to the Count-my-father?"

"Eh, it seemed the right progression. Our little daughter'd come along by then, I was just finishing my twenty-years hitch, and I was facing whether or not to continue my enlistment. My wife's family was here, and her roots, and she didn't particularly fancy following the flag with children in tow. Captain Illyan, who knew I was District-born, was kind enough to give me a tip, that your father had a place open in his Armsmen's score. And a recommendation, when I nerved up to apply. I figured a Count's Armsman would be a more settled job, for a family man."

The groundcar arrived at Vorkosigan House; the ImpSec corporal on duty opened the gates for them, and Pym pulled around to the porte cochère and popped the canopy.

"Thank you, Pym," Miles said, and hesitated. "A word in your ear. Two words."

Pym made to look attentive.

"When you chance to socialize with the Armsmen of other Houses . . . I'd appreciate it if you wouldn't mention Madame Vorsoisson. I wouldn't want her to be the subject of invasive gossip, and, um . . . she's no business of everyone and his younger brother anyway, eh?"

"A loyal Armsman does not gossip, m'lord," said Pym stiffly.

"No, of course not. Sorry, I didn't mean to imply . . . um, sorry. Anyway. The other thing. I'm maybe guilty of saying a little too much myself, you see. I'm not actually courting Madame Vorsoisson."

Pym tried to look properly blank, but a confused expression leaked into his face. Miles added hastily, "I mean, not *formally*. Not *yet*. She's . . . she's had a difficult time, recently, and she's a touch . . . skittish. Any premature declaration on my part is likely to be disastrous, I'm afraid. It's a timing problem. Discreet is the watchword, if you see what I mean?"

Pym attempted a discreet but supportive-looking smile.

"We're just good friends," Miles reiterated. "Anyway, we're going to be."

"Yes, m'lord. I understand."

"Ah. Good. Thank you." Miles climbed out of the groundcar, and added over his shoulder as he headed into the house, "Find me in the kitchen when you've put the car away."

*(the above was an excerpt from* A Civil Campaign, *by Lois McMaster Bujold, available September 1999 from Baen Books. ISBN 0-671-57827-8, $24.00 hardcover)*